LOVE
AND
Warner

FOLLOW ME

To keep up to date with her writing and more, visit S.L. Scott's website: **www.slscottauthor.com**

To receive the newsletter about all of her publishing adventures, free books, giveaways, steals and more:

https://geni.us/SLScottNL

Follow on IG: https://geni.us/IGSLS
Follow me on TikTok: https://geni.us/SLTikTok
Follow on Bookbub: https://geni.us/SLScottBB

ALSO BY S.L. SCOTT

Called **"The Most Romantic Book Ever,"** We Were Once, is available and FREE in Kindle Unlimited.

We Were Once

The international sensation, **Best I Ever Had**, has won readers over and is available in ebook, audio, and paperback, and Free in Kindle Unlimited.

Best I Ever Had

Audiobooks on Audible - CLICK HERE

Peachtree Pass Series (Stand-alones)

Long Time Coming /Lead Me Knot /Small Town Frenzy

The Westcott Series (Stand-alones)

Swear on My Life / Never Saw You Coming

Forgot to Say Goodbye / When I Had You

Never Have I Ever / Speak of the Devil - Faris Family

Hard to Resist Series (Stand-Alones)

The Resistance / The Reckoning

The Redemption / The Revolution / The Rebellion

The Crow Brothers (Stand-Alones)

Spark / Tulsa / Rivers / Ridge

The Crow Brothers Box Set

DARE - A Rock Star Hero (Stand-Alone)

New York Love Stories (Stand-Alones)

Never Got Over You / The One I Want / Crazy in Love

Head Over Feels / It Started with a Kiss

The Everest Brothers (Stand-Alones)

Everest / Bad Reputation / Force of Nature

The Everest Brothers Box Set

The Kingwood Series

SAVAGE / SAVIOR / SACRED / FINDING SOLACE

The Kingwood Series Box Set

Playboy in Paradise Series

Falling for the Playboy / Redeeming the Playboy

Loving the Playboy

Playboy in Paradise Box Set

Stand-Alone Books

Best I Ever Had

We Were Once

Love and Warner

Along Came Charlie

Missing Grace

Finding Solace

Until I Met You

Lessons on Love

Lost in Translation

Sleeping with Mr. Sexy

Morning Glory

PLAYLIST

If you enjoy music as much as I do, check out the companion playlist that inspired me while I wrote this book. Here's a sample of what can be found on Spotify: SPOTIFY - CLICK HERE

1. So Easy - Olivia Dean
2. Take It Slow - Louis Metric
3. How High - Midnight Beverage
4. The Last Time - Taylor Swift, Gary Lightbody
5. 12 to 12 - Sombr
6. Two Sides of a Coin - Hidanny!!
7. It's Almost Like You're Here - Yndling
8. You Noticed - Lola Young
9. Stuck - LANY
10. I Told You Things - Gracie Abrams

LOVE AND WARNER

S.L. SCOTT

CHAPTER 1

Warner Landers

"Are you going to close this deal, or do I need to handle it, Carl?"

The sky has darkened, causing my office to dim with it. The lamp on my desk can't fight the gray cloud cover sheathing the city outside the floor-to-ceiling office windows. Rain is imminent. I welcome the downpour. It suits my mood.

"I won't let you down," he says. "I'll get it done. Promise."

"I don't want your promises. I want the preliminary paperwork on my desk by five on Friday for review. Do you understand?"

"All parties have been notified of the final deadline, sir. I'll get the paperwork to you for approval and send it out right after," he replies, though I know he tacks on the sir more in sarcasm than respect. I'm not bothered. I don't need his respect. He was hired because he closes deals. That's what I need him to do this time as well. "You'll have the contract on your desk in two days."

"See you then." I hang up and walk the length of my office as if I'll see something new from a view I've stared at for the past four years. The blanket of clouds seeps into the avenues and wraps around the New York skyline in desperation to shield the buildings from me. *Nothing is safe in this city. Not if I have a say.* Those were the last words my father imparted before his death came too soon, leaving me in charge of his empire.

I'll do anything to make him proud. Closing the last three deals he couldn't, will be carried out in his name. The celebration is already planned for Friday night with my mother in attendance. I won't let anything stop me from honoring his legacy.

The phone on my desk rings, causing me to return to my desk. I hit the speakerphone button to answer my assistant, and ask, "Yes?"

"Ms. Bayetti is on line one for you, Mr. Landers," Jocelyn replies.

"I don't know who that is. Please take a message."

Just as I'm about to disconnect, she adds, "She said it was urgent."

"Urgent?" I've never heard of the woman, and now she has business that requires my immediate attention? Chuckling, though I find no entertainment in the failed attempt to call me out of the blue and discuss matters that surely don't involve me, I reply, "If I took every call that stated that, I wouldn't have time to breathe. Take a message, Jocelyn. Thank you."

"Yes, sir."

Resting back in the leather chair, I stare at the monitor taking up most of the real estate on my desk and scan the unopened emails. If I scrolled the page, they would keep me here past midnight every night of the week to deal with them. This is the list after Jocelyn cleaned it up. Dropping my head, I rub my index finger and thumb across my brow in an effort to ease some of the tension that's set up permanent residency there.

When the time came, I was ready to be CEO. I still am, but I thought it would include big ideas, managing projects, and guidance on buyouts to grow the company. I used to sit in on meetings and participate in the growth. But now, menial tasks of reassuring investors in emails and on calls seemed to be my only purpose.

The door opens. "It's going to rain," my best friend says as he walks in. He kicks the door closed behind him and goes straight to the couch, where he flops down and props his feet up on my coffee table.

"I appreciate the personalized forecast." Watching as he settles in like he's at home, I ask, "What brings you by, Jimmy?" I've known the guy since we were in kindergarten. We both grew up in the city, but I was driven home to Park Avenue after school while he took the subway to StuyTown. However, the distance didn't stop us from meeting up and treating this city like our own playground.

"Got out of a meeting early a block over and thought I'd stop by to visit my best man. What's going on today?"

"Have some deals closing and too much taskwork. Nothing worth discussing."

With his arms spread wide across the back of the couch, he says, "The work of a CEO is never done." His eyes pivot to the windows again. "I was going to see if you wanted to grab a beer, but that cloud cover looks downright vengeful up here."

At thirty-four, and on the brink of his wedding, it's not

only his life that's changing but ours. From two of us to three . . . *the two of them*. Am I losing my best friend? Am I now a third wheel? I don't genuinely believe that, but deep down, it's time to accept that change is on the horizon. Feeling nostalgic for the good party days of our college years, I ask, "Since when did we let a little rain stop us?"

Chuckling, he brings his feet to the floor and leans forward, resting his forearms on his legs. "It never did. But your work has gotten in the way plenty of times."

He's not wrong. I glance at the emails. I'm in no mood to deal with the mundane for another hour. With a smirk, I say, "Let's remedy it." I stand and come around, grabbing my phone from the desk and tucking it into my back pocket. "I'm buying the first round to celebrate."

"You're buying all the rounds, moneybags."

He stands and follows me to the door. I laugh as I march toward the door like we'll get busted if we don't get out quickly. I leave my suit jacket hanging in the closet and start to roll up my sleeves to loosen my mood.

When I open the door, Jocelyn looks up. Her eyebrows rise, and then the slightest smile taunts the corners of her mouth upward. "Looks like you're off to an important meeting."

"Yes," I reply, shoving my hands in my pockets. Nodding, I grin. "Very important. Take messages unless it's an emergency. I have my phone on me."

"Will do. Have fun."

I turn on my heel before others notice me escaping before five o'clock on a Wednesday. "Have a good night."

Jimmy and I walk down the corridor of the office toward the exit. When I open the door to our waiting room, the receptionist stands, seemingly startled just as a woman on the other side of the tall counter shifts to stare at us. There's a chill in the air between them despite interrupting what feels like a heated conversation.

I've never seen this receptionist before, so it's safe to assume she doesn't know who I am either. Heading out the door is not the time for introductions. Eyeing me and then Jimmy, she says, "Hello." There's an impatience to her voice, and her eyes appear frantic from the angular dip at the corners and the way they search between us for help.

"Hello," I reply, sweeping my hand over my hair. "Everything okay?"

"Fine. Fine. I was just letting our visitor know," she says, referencing the other woman, "that she can't just show up expecting to see someone. She needs to make an appointment."

I glance at the other woman. Her lighter blue eyes are set on mine as if I'll give her a different answer. She moves closer, the skirt of her dress not moving under the small step. "It's *very* important," she says much quieter as if I'm the only one here. The plea has me weakening, but my employees are trusted to do their jobs.

I don't need to step in to handle it, but guilt coats my gut. I'm shirking responsibility. My father would be disappointed. I take a breath. Knowing the right thing to do is stay and deal with her inquiry, I open my mouth. "How can—"

"Elevator is almost here," Jimmy says with a not-so-subtle hint.

Stay strong and leave. *That's all you have to do, Landers.* Walk to the elevator and leave with Jimmy, the friend I've been blowing off for months to work more than I should. "I'm sure . . ." I glance at the receptionist again. Since I don't know her name, I say, "She'll make sure the message is delivered." When I glance at her again, she nods. I'm intrigued by what could be so pressing, but I refrain from asking. "Have a good day."

Jimmy grins when he sees me coming. "Almost lost you." Stopping beside him, I glance back at her and overhear her tell the receptionist, "Please. You don't understand—"

"There's nothing I can do," she snaps. "I've already left a message with Mr. Landers' assistant."

My shoulders fall. Fuck. There's no familiarity when I look at her, but the attractive woman has piqued more than my curiosity. I debate again if I should get involved, introduce myself, and ease the tension between the two women. She is desperate to see me for some reason. "Surely we can spare a minute or two."

"Or thirty to an hour like usual," Jimmy replies under his breath. The elevator dings, making the decision for us. When the doors slide open, I'm bumped as Jimmy steps around me. "Leave it at the office, man."

He's right. I don't need to involve myself. More importantly, a drink with him takes priority. Maybe that's a careless decision, but I'm willing to take the heat later for it. I get in the elevator after him, settling into the corner and leaning against the wood-paneled wall. Just as the doors begin to close, a hand—no rings, specifically not on a certain finger—waves between the doors, causing them to part again. The woman steps on with a hand stuck to her hip and a smile plastered on her face.

"Thanks for holding it, guys," she says, the sarcasm hitting like a Mack truck, making me realize her smile isn't so genuine.

As we're met with her back, she double taps the lobby button that's already lit up and then crosses her arms over her chest under heavy exasperation.

The doors close as if she made a difference, which causes me to grin to myself.

Not sure why this is entertaining. Too many late nights working and exhaustion finally kicking in, I've officially lost my sense of humor? Not enough fun in my life so something basic is a highlight? Maybe entertaining is the wrong word. Mildly amusing works better, but I still chuckle, even knowing it would be wiser if I kept my mouth shut.

I study the shape of her body and the way her shoulders meet her neck in a graceful curve, the small straps loop over them as if that could possibly drag my attention away from that face. Even her profile is sharp at the chin, giving it a heart-shaped tip. Does she want a job? She's not dressed for it, though I appreciate how her dress cinches in at the waist and then blossoms to the span of her hips. She's quite beautiful. Tempting fate, I ask, "Bad day?"

She glances over her shoulder, not making eye contact. Her gaze still takes full advantage of the opportunity and slides down my body, even lingering below my waistband. "You could say that." I'm struck by her acidic tone and sharp glare. It doesn't suit her or the fine features of her face, the gentle slope of her nose that I'd bet money crinkles when she laughs, or the way her beauty isn't overshadowed under the bad lighting.

It's the fire that flickers in her blue eyes, carrying the weight of her anger that is most prevalent, making her even more fucking gorgeous.

Unbothered by the icy demeanor, just as she turns away from me, I reply, "I did say that." The demand in my own tone causes Jimmy to glance over and glare at me like I need to shut the fuck up. I could listen to the silent warning, but where's the fun in that?

Her head whips sideways on her neck so fast I wonder if

she needs a doctor. "Excuse me?" Her eyes narrow under arched brows as the flames grow bigger inside the blue. There's no dousing them now. The woman can't hide her rage. *Why is that so sexy?*

I'm surrounded by yes people in my professional and personal life. It's boring and predictable. Doesn't matter how pretty a date might be, disappointment always sets in when I'm being used for connections, money, even sex. I'm not so bothered by the latter, but the former has me tired of dating altogether.

Under her fiery attitude, I know the only way this woman would say yes is if she meant it.

She huffs, not letting the chance pass her by to show off her irritation, and tightens her crossed arms. "What is your problem?"

Jimmy sighs, drifting back until he's leaning against the side of the elevator farthest from us. Unfortunately for him, we still have fifteen floors to go.

Pushing off the wall, I stand upright before her. The short little thing full of ire and defiance can't be more than five-two, five-three on a good day. Apparently, it's a bad day, though, or so she alludes, so I'll hold off on granting the extra inch. "I don't have a problem, but it seems you do. Back in the office, you were demanding to barge into someone's office despite being told he's not in—"

"I wasn't demanding. I was begging. There's a difference." Her arms return to her sides, but her hands ball like kitten fists just past her hips.

"Why would you beg?"

The question strikes her pretty features with offense and causes her head to jut back. "I..." She glances at Jimmy, who has smartly busied himself on his phone. "If you must know," she says, tilting her chin up while lowering her voice,

"I need to talk to the asshole owner of that company, or my family will lose their restaurant."

And that is why I shouldn't have opened my damn mouth. There's no getting out of it now, so I bite. "And what does the owner of that company have to do with your family losing their restaurant?"

"The asshole, you mean?" Her eyes are wide as her lashes flutter innocence in direct contradiction to the swear words escaping her mouth.

"Yes, the asshole," I reply, chuckling. "What's the story?"

When the elevator suddenly jolts to an abrupt stop, I grab her arms reflexively to steady her. But playing with fire will get any man burned when she's the one lighting the torch. I drop my hands back and tuck them in my pockets. As expected, no thank-you for saving her life comes, but the dirty look that follows could make most men shrivel. I'm not most men.

Jimmy darts out and then stops to look back. "Are you coming, Warner?"

Irritation vanishes under recognition, and she steps to the side to block my exit. "You're Warner?" Her arms cross over her chest again as that fury returns to her eyes. "Warner Landers of Landers Ventures?"

Would it be so wrong to lie to get out of this situation so I can head to a barstool to drink bourbon with Jimmy instead?

Probably.

Under a heavy sigh, I glance at Jimmy. "I'll meet you there, Jimmy."

Confusion wrinkles his brow as he looks at me like I might need the backup. "Are you sure?"

She stabs him with a stare when she steps off the elevator, and snipes, "He's sure, Jimmy."

Jimmy shakes his head with a laugh. "Good luck with this one. I'll have a drink waiting for you."

"Make it a double." I get off the elevator just after someone hops on. When the doors close behind me, and my friend is exiting the building, I turn back to her. "You've got two minutes."

CHAPTER 2

Delaney Bayetti

TWO MINUTES...

Two minutes to plead my case.

Two minutes to save my family's business.

Two minutes to convince this jerk that destroying the average Joe living in the shadow of his fancy New York City penthouse is not just a business transaction.

Warner Landers starts walking through the large lobby toward the exit. I double step to catch up. "I appreciate you listening, but I need more than your ears."

He stops and eyes me, his blue eyes piercing me like a piece of tissue paper that never stood a chance against his sharp edges. "What do you need?"

"Your heart."

Balking, he tilts his head back as a humorless grin splits his cheeks. "You're not getting that."

"Why?" I cross my arms over my chest, indignant to the insult of his laughter. "Because it doesn't exist?"

"Funny."

I shrug, cracking my own grin with a little pride bubbling inside. "I thought so."

"One minute," he says, the warning as incisive as the turn away from me when he starts walking toward the exit. "Good night, Jerry." He gives the slightest acknowledgment to the guard standing behind a tall desk in the center of the lobby.

His quick stride resounds through the barren room minus the one seating area on the other side of it. His broad shoulders are straight with the confidence of a nepo-baby, which I discovered he is through my research. He's cocky and rude; utter assholery all wrapped up in one annoyingly attractive shell of a man who is clearly vacuous otherwise.

The rubber heels of my favorite flats are quiet in comparison as I chase him down. "Listen, Warner—"

"Mr. Landers to you."

Jerk.

I rush behind him just as he reaches the door and pushes through. The sounds of the city—car horns, chatter, even the wind whipping down the street—hits me just before the door does. Wow . . .

I shove it open and hightail after him down the sidewalk, and shout against the noise. "You promised me two minutes, Mr. Landers, and you've given me nothing but a hard time."

He stops with his back to me, causing me to come to such a quick halt that I tip forward over the toes of my shoes. I catch myself and lower to my heels again, raising my chin and crossing my arms over my chest. I'm enraged more than I was in the elevator when I found out who he was. Glaring at me, he doesn't say anything. He just stares into my soul as if he's slowly picking the meat from the bones to leave me for dead, like all his other capitalist ventures.

"You don't intimidate me," I say, keeping my eyes set on his and trying to steady my voice. Though, I feel anything but that in this standoff. "Despite your best efforts."

"I'm out of practice, I suppose."

I can't tell if that's an effort at humor or a confession. I start closer, the gap shrinking between us until there's only enough room for groveling, which is what I'm thinking he's hoping for. I'm not above it if it benefits my cause. When he checks the time on his watch, I roll my eyes. "You're behind the deal that will put my family's restaurant out of business, or worse, work it for pennies on the dollar as you scrape everything good about it out and leave the scraps of what was once a thriving restaurant."

"Writer?"

The question throws me off-kilter. Why would he ask that? "No."

"Hmm. What do you do, Ms. . . .?"

"Bayetti."

"Italian?"

"Mr. Landers, you've given me limited minutes of your time. I really don't want to waste them talking about things irrelevant to my purpose of being here."

"And that purpose is to have me wave some magic wand and stop the sale of your family's restaurant like a Hollywood romcom where the hero does the right thing and spares the heroine's business?"

"Well," I reply, shifting my weight to the other foot. The hard concrete of the sidewalk causes my feet to ache. "Basically . . . though it's more complicated than that."

"I don't have a magic wand, and I don't deal with family restaurants, but if it's fallen under a larger deal that's been made, there's no going back now. It's done." He turns and starts walking away again.

"It's not done. No paperwork has been signed," I explain, sliding up next to him. "And there's an out clause. A fee that can be paid, but the price is too high. We could never come up with that kind of money." My situation nor myself, apparently, doesn't even warrant a glance from this man. "Please listen—"

His eyes strike mine like a thief in the night, stealing the bravery I had been so desperately trying to hold on to since I talked myself into this fool's mission. The cold in his eyes doesn't match the warmth of the spring day. It's impressive he can produce such hatred in an instant. Guess I bring it out in him.

"Ms. Bayetti, don't tell me to listen. I have been listening. I've been listening to a girl tell me nothing more than 'save my family's restaurant.' I have no idea about your family's circumstances or how they ended up under a roster of my company's deals. I can promise you that if they are, they lost the restaurant long before we came along. Rent is due, and I'm here to collect."

I could be insulted that I've been relegated to a girl and not even a woman, but he's not entirely wrong. I don't know what I'm doing. I felt compelled to act, even if it meant risking personal insult. If that's the worst that happens, it's better than losing everything else. Our eyes stay locked as I tilt my head. "At the cost of destroying a family?"

"If your family is destroyed, it wasn't meant to survive." He starts for the corner of the street, but stops to add, "Sorry, sweetheart. That's the cost of business."

"Why are you so hateful?" Glancing up at the skyscraper next to us, I say, "You have the whole world at your feet, and it's not enough, is it? What will be? When will you be satisfied? Is it even possible anymore, or are you so far gone that there's no concern for the 'little people' any longer?" I've been accused of speaking before I think, but I wouldn't take back one word of what I've said to him.

The shake of his shoulders and a chuckle that bridges the distance between us are all I'm given in response to where he left me standing on the sidewalk. But then he stops. No laughter. His posture unrelenting in its severity. My breath catches from fear I might have just made matters worse. I brace myself, but I'm not given anything but a harsh glare.

I finally take a breath and move closer again. This time, I keep my voice lower, only for his ears to hear, and say, "You could have given me the courtesy of treating me like a human."

"The treatment you received was from the incitement of the situation." He moves, his head almost above mine, stopping just shy of the intrusion, probably so he can look down on me like he prefers. I gulp under the intensity of his glare, but I don't blink. I stare into his lifeless eyes that hold nothing beyond the empty windows I can only hope used to expose someone with a heart. I doubt it. People don't change overnight. "You need to be careful, little girl, or you might get hurt."

"Is that a threat?" I lick my lips and take the slightest breath under the pressure cooker of this encounter before biting my tongue, so I don't explode. That won't serve either of us any good. *Especially him.*

"I don't threaten people, Ms. Bayetti. I'm a CEO, not a mob boss. But you're pushing luck that you don't have." His words coat my face followed by his breath fragranced with mint. My lids bat closed to soak—I mean gather my strength for the battle ahead.

I may be an elementary school teacher, but I'm not intimidated by him because he carries a bigger title. When I reopen them, my chest rises with anger and then releases with intent. "I'm here," I start, keeping my voice calm, even after the earlier "little girl" insult. "Asking you to reconsider—"

"I don't know what deal involves your family, and as you can clearly see from your stalking, I'm not at work. So there's nothing that can be done tonight."

Taking a step back to make sure he sees the depth of my conviction, I ask, "Tomorrow then?"

"No."

"No?" I throw my arms out wide. "That's it? Just no, like we don't even matter?"

He sighs, irritation sending his gaze to stare in the distance over my head. He takes a beat before finally looking me in the eyes again. "This is not personal. It's business. Any deal that's left to be closed is being closed for a reason. It's about making money."

"To line your pockets," I snap, too annoyed to even look at him. I shake my head, feeling defeated. "I knew it would be pointless to try to reason with you." Returning my gaze to him, I take another breath. "Nothing matters to you but money."

"Everything revolves around money. You're a fool if you believe otherwise." He checks his watch once more.

"I'd rather be a fool than someone like you."

A smile slides onto half his face. Amusement finally reaches his eyes. "And who is someone like me?"

"Heartless."

The smile falls, though it's slow to fade. He looks me over once more before he shoves his hands in his pockets again. "Good day, Ms. Bayetti."

The sun shines on him like he's a Greek god, bathing him in golden rays of light. And then I'm met with the wide expanse of his back and shoulders as he walks away. It's fitting since walking away from me seems to be a running theme with him.

Did I actually expect a different outcome? Not really, but that doesn't take away the sting of rejection. Warner Landers is crueler than anticipated. How did I ever think I could reason with someone as cold as ice? There was no soft side to appeal to, no kind heart to reach. No, there's just a man who has everything yet walks around soulless.

I have forty-eight hours before that paperwork is signed, and my parents are served an eviction notice. The restaurant has been around longer than I have. It means the world to them. I can't let them lose everything.

Watching him reach the corner, he looks back at me over his shoulder. He probably loves that I'm still standing here while he's celebrating his victory. I can feel the waves of arrogance rolling off his back from here. What a jerk! If Warner Landers won't help me, I'll find another way. Whatever it takes, I'll save the restaurant.

It doesn't change the fact that I'm not only out of ideas but options.

When he turns around on the corner to give a little wave with a cocky-ass grin on his face, my temper flares into a full-on blaze. I've never met a more infuriating, narcissistic, self-righteous, frustrating man in my life. And I've encountered a few over the years.

I should go home to start working on the next plan, but he's triggered me, and I realize I still have nothing to lose. *Literally.* I march my way back into his orbit. I don't need to reach the corner, just close enough for him to hear me when I shout, "Hey!"

Passersby stare at me, but I don't care. They'll keep

moving like they never saw anything, like a proper New Yorker would.

"You called?" I hate him. I hate that smug smirk on his jerkish face and the way every woman who passes smiles at him. They don't know him, the real him.

I've already gotten to see too much of who he is and called his number from the moment I laid eyes on him. But it's the grin he's still sporting that makes me want to slap it off his face, that gets me the most. Fisting my hands at my sides, I say, "You're an asshole, you know that?"

He's nodding before I finish speaking, as if he already knew what I was going to say. Then a good laugh takes hold of him like salt to my wounds. The crowd around him has crossed without him, leaving his ego as his only ally. He shrugs as he walks backward like he knows these streets by heart. Which we know is impossible, since that's the one organ he seems to be lacking. "Don't be mad, Ms. Bayetti. It's only business."

"Screw—"

The impact is instant, the car coming out of nowhere and propelling his body unnaturally to the concrete. A gasp consumes my throat, leaving my lungs vacant of air. As I stagger through breathing, I cover my mouth with shaky hands. Paralyzed to the spot, I stand in utter shock from seeing him hit so violently, as if I had somehow willed it. He might be the worst human being I've ever met, but I didn't want him dead.

Oh God, please don't be dead.

CHAPTER 3

Delaney

Was that real or a figment of my imagination?

I blink a few times, trying to determine what I just witnessed before stumbling away from the assembling crowd around him. Calls for 911 grow louder as tears form in my eyes and panic overwhelms me.

I was just talking to him. Just arguing, yelling, begging for mercy on my parents' behalf, and now . . . now he could be lying on the ground dead in front of me. Did I cause that? Distract him from watching where he was going? I'll never forgive myself.

Oh God. I called him an asshole so many times. It's one of the last things he heard before . . . Remorse ravages my gut as my heart starts beating out of my chest. I suck in a harsh breath as a thought occurs. I'm pure evil, but it's too late to save my soul. I can't believe it would even cross my mind. I stare ahead at the scene playing out before me, and at the center of it is the man who signs the final deed to close the deal. The only thing that would keep that jerk from signing is if he's—*Delaney!*

Oh God, this is not who I am.

With no sound of sirens on the horizon, I can't just leave him there to die all alone, or worse, surrounded by strangers. I'm no friend to him, but now I'm obligated to make sure he gets help in some twist of fate that has tied our lives together.

Without a thought, my feet move slowly at first, but I'm driven faster by desperate fear. My heart is still racing as concern takes over. I push around a guy holding a box fan in his hands and past a lady sipping her coffee over the body. I kneel beside my newfound enemy and run the tips of my fingers gently over a scrape on his face. "Warner? Warner, can you hear me?"

When he doesn't react, I look up through watery eyes and see that the woman with her coffee is now filming as if she wants to memorialize the moment. Anger courses through my veins, and I shout, "Have you called 911?"

"They're on their way," replies a woman next to her, holding a grocery bag in one hand and her phone in the other. You'd think it was a planned exhibition and not a man's life on the line by how many phones are out and filming.

I return my attention to the man who showed me no kindness or understanding toward my plight, and I offer it to him. Touching his shoulder, I look him over only for my chest to tighten when I discover blood in his hair. "He needs help." I look up to scan the crowd. "Anyone? Please."

As if I willed it, the crowd parts as two emergency techs cut through and kneel beside him. "What happened?" asks a paramedic in a blue uniform. He drops a medical bag beside him, looking at me as he lowers his ear to Warner's mouth to listen for him breathing. *Oh God, is he breathing?*

He checks for a pulse while I scramble for an answer. "He was hit by a car, one of those driverless cars. It stopped and then drove off." My words are rushed like my heartbeat that's threatening to leap from my chest. "Is he alive?"

"He has a pulse." *Thank God.* Another paramedic maneuvers to secure his neck in a brace. "Name?" the first paramedic asks me.

"Warner." I pause, his last name at the top of my shitlist for the past week as I tried to end this nightmare deal he's doing to destroy my parents' restaurant, but my mind momentarily blanks under pressure. "Um. . ." I glance up at the building towering over us. I can't see any names on the side of the building, but the metal letters before the receptionist flash like gold in my mind. "Landers Ventures. Landers. Warner Landers."

Another medic comes through carrying a stretcher and places it on the ground beside him. "On the count of three," he says to the others.

As soon as he's safely on it, they stand together, lifting the stretcher into the air and cutting back through the crowd. I rush through before the opening closes, sticking close to their heels. I'm unsure what to do in this situation, so I'm following as if I have the right. It's self-serving, and he'd hate it, but that thought only inspires me to stay closer.

Warner is loaded into the ambulance, and then the paramedic who asked his name turns back to see me aimlessly standing there. Holding the door in his hand, he asks, "Are you going with him?"

"Yes," I answer with no other excuse than I replied without thinking. I don't owe Warner a thing, and in fact, he owes me, but I'm climbing in like a besotted fangirl. I sit where I'm told as the door is slammed shut.

What am I doing?

I glance toward the tiny back windows as if they're an option to escape when I'm found out.

What if he wakes up?

That would be great. Ideal. I can disappear as soon as we arrive at the hospital knowing I didn't cause his death. *Oh God.* I close my eyes and drop my head into my hands, wishing the events of this afternoon had played out differently.

How will I explain who I am?

I'm the girl who practically assaulted—verbally, of course—this . . . this . . . this jerk of a CEO, causing him to look back when I yelled "Hey" like a psychopath on the street to get his attention. I couldn't bear the thought of him getting the last word in, so I was going to outdo him. That sounds awful, even to me, and I know the reasoning behind it. I'm a horrible person. They might as well call the cops on me now. Holding out my wrists, I'm mentally letting them lock me and throw away the key.

"Ma'am."

I look at the EMT on the other side of Warner . . . *Do I really have a right to call him by his first name?* I'm acting like we actually know each other. We don't. He's the asshole who's—"Miss?"

I bring my gaze from Mr. Landers (that's better) to the EMT again. "Yes?"

"His birthday?"

The gasp of shock strikes my vocal cords and dries my throat. I glance at Warner again, feeling worse than I did before, and that was already pretty awful. "It's his birthday?"

"I'm asking the date of his birth. When is it?"

"Oh." I sit straight again, my mind fumbling through the question like I might stumble upon the answer. "I'm not sure," I reply quieter. How is it possible for me to feel embarrassed that I don't know this stranger's birthday? I have no idea, but I do. "Maybe he has his wallet with him. We can check." I feel his pant pocket on the side closest to me, hitting something hard . . . "I think it's here."

The EMT stares at me with a brow so furrowed it might be a pinched nerve. "Do you know this man?"

"Do I know this man?" I laugh nervously. "Do I know this man?"

"Do you?" he asks again, his gaze unrelenting in its severity.

I pause. This is my stop, a chance to hop off this lie before it's too late. "Of course, I know him." I signal with my hand to his lifeless body. "It's Warner Landers of Landers Ventures."

The medic blinks at me, then narrows his eyes. "Okay, but you don't know his birthday?"

"We had a business relationship, so we hadn't gotten to birthdays." I glance down at his wedding ring finger. No ring. No tan lines. No marks left behind by someone who was sneaking around without one. "He's not married."

"No one is accusing you of anything. We're trying to get as much information on him as we can for the file."

He looks at his e-pad and starts jotting down some notes. It's the way he peeks up at me like he's now concerned for Warner's safety, *from me*, that has me shifting in my seat, and looking toward the light, a.k.a. the two windows at the back, and ask, "Are we almost there?"

"Yes," he replies. "What's your name?"

I'm not falling into that trap. No way can I give my real name. If Warner finds out I was here, that deal is as good as signed. But my brain is blank of names except for some unknown reason "Delaney Landers" rolls off the tip of my tongue and onto the body of the man passed out between us. Or was he knocked unconscious? *What am I doing?* Holy hell, I need to get out of here.

"You have the same last name as Mr. Landers but don't know his birthday?"

"Coincidence."

"I should say so," he mutters under his breath just as the ambulance comes to a hard stop. He's out of his seat and helping to push the doors open. The chaos of the moment leaves me there to climb out last and follow them inside.

A nurse comes up beside me and says, "We're taking him back to be examined. A doctor will come out to discuss if surgery is needed and the next steps." She guides me into a glass box full of chairs, old TVs mounted on the walls, and a few others scattered about. "You can wait here for more information regarding your husband."

"Okay—*wait, what?* He's not my . . ." The nurse has already disappeared down the hall. I stand there, unsure of what to do. Leaving would be best. I have no business being here in the first place. But now he's all alone with his friend waiting at a bar for him to arrive somewhere in the financial district.

I flop into a chair, knowing I can't leave him like this. Warner Landers is a jerk, but he's mine to deal with until his family or friend comes to claim him. I drop my head into my hands. The image of him getting hit plays over in my head, causing me to open my eyes and sit upright. Is this karma getting her dues?

What a mess.

But more so, I feel awful that I'm the one who is here for him when someone who matters could be instead. I should try to contact someone in his life. But how?

An idea comes to mind, giving me an inkling of hope. I pull my phone out of the purse situated on my hip and call his office. "Landers Ventures."

Looking around, I keep my voice low so no one else in the waiting room can hear, "Hi, Mr. Landers's office, please."

"He's not available. Would you like to leave a message?"

"Is there anyone I can speak to?" I hate the panic in my voice. Taking a quick breath, I then whisper, "Please."

"Unfortunately, they're not available. I can send you to his assistant's voicemail. She'll forward your message to him."

I really don't think telling the receptionist I got her boss killed is a good idea. "I'll call back. Thank you." I hang up and search for his name online. Maybe I'll find his parents or a sibling, or a girlfriend. I don't care who, as long as I get someone who cares about him here to the hospital.

"Mrs. Landers?"

I scroll the screen, hoping to find one person. That's all I need. Come on. There must be someone he's close to, but perhaps he's only close to his friend on the elevator. I can't say I'd be surprised. He's intolerable.

And then I land on — "Mrs. Landers." My shoulder is touched, startling me and causing me to look up. A nurse smiles at me, but it's full of sympathy and not reassurance. "We're still checking for injuries to his head, but your husband will need his arm reset and to stay overnight for observation. We're going to run a few more tests to make sure we didn't miss any internal injuries and reexamine his head around the cut he sustained. It may not sound like it, but overall, he's very lucky."

I stand, setting my phone on the chair I abandoned. "What is the surgery for?"

"His right arm is broken. We'll discharge him with instructions on how to care for it. No broken ribs, surprisingly. Though I suspect he'll be sore for the next few days, possibly up to a week. But again, we'll send him home with instructions when he leaves."

I sit there blinking at her as I absorb the information like I'll need it later. This is the out I've needed. I'm not his wife. I'm not his girlfriend or friend, or family or anyone familiar with him in life. I'm just a girl who came to beg him not to do a dirty deed to my family. But for some reason, those words stay glued to the roof of my mouth and not a word is uttered.

She says, "Do you have any questions?"

"No."

There's that smile that makes me feel like I have a stake in his life. She feels sorry for me. I hate when people feel that way, but I also can't walk away and leave him. Even if he is an asshole in real life.

She steps back and rubs her upper arms as if she's cold. It is cold in here. I hadn't had a chance to notice until now. She says, "We'll let you know when he's settled in his room after surgery and recovery, but you have time to go home if you need to. It will be at least six hours or more before you'll be able to see him."

When she walks out of the room, I pick up my phone and sit down again. Why am I waiting? I know why. I feel bad for him. Other than his friend, who was probably only a colleague, knowing Warner, or someone being paid to hang out with him, I might be the only person who cares about what happens to him.

Does he deserve my kindness? *Not really.* But will I make

sure everything with his surgery and recovery goes well? *Sure will.*

I can despise him all I want, but he's still a person who needs someone in his corner. And I'm the one still standing here like I belong.

CHAPTER 4

Warner

"I APPRECIATE you repeating yourself for *my* benefit, Nurse," I say, struggling to keep the sarcasm out of my voice and my eyes fully open. A fog of grogginess clouds my clearer thoughts, but my pride still wants to argue with a nurse who dropped the bombshell of the car accident and subsequent coma, a.k.a. "catching up on sleep," as she called it. I call it being blindsided twice—first by the car, and now by my own nurse who won't tell me the truth. "I comprehend the words. It's how I ended up here in the hospital with a broken arm and in a coma that evades me."

Nurse Edi eyes me over the top of her red-framed readers and then laughs. "I've told you twice now. You weren't in a coma. You have a concussion from the—"

"Car accident. I know. I know. But—"

"No buts, Mr. Landers," she finally snaps. "That's all I can tell you."

"Can or will?" I steady my temper in the face of a lack of

information, refraining from shifting and putting any weight on my right side.

She huffs, having lost her patience with me the first time she came in to check on me. This round, she's not putting up with any shit or questions I might have, it seems. Well, she can get in line. I'm not an idiot, and when she couldn't or wouldn't answer the question, I asked for the doctor. Always go to the top.

Now I'm enemy number one in her book and she's punishing me by swiping the pudding from my tray and then shoving it back down ten seconds later like I just won a damn prize. I don't give a shit about pudding. I want to know what the fuck happened to me yesterday. *Why is it such a secret?*

I try a different approach. "I apologize if I offended you—"

Her laughter tears through the room and my apology. "You didn't offend me. I was assigned to you for a reason."

Offense takes hold of me, causing me to shift in this bed that really needs to be replaced. "What reason is that?"

"I've worked with the orneriest patients in this wing of the hospital for the past forty-three years. I was assigned to you for a reason, Mr. Landers." As if that puts my questions to bed, she turns her gaze to the e-pad and starts writing with a stylus. I'm hit with a hard glare before she adds something else on the pad. "I work with all the difficult patients."

Difficult? She keeps scribbling like she's penning her autobiography in my chart. "What are you noting?"

"I'm noting that there is no helping you, as a warning to others." She cackles under her breath, then sets the e-pad by the monitor in the corner. *I really don't like her.* Who treats patients like this? Apparently, Nurse Edi. With another laugh, she pulls her glasses from her face and drops them to dangle from a beaded chain around her neck. "I wrote that you're paranoid and might need to be moved to an evaluation room."

"You did not."

She laughs again, really impressed with herself. "No, but don't push your luck, Mr. Landers. Enjoy the pudding." Walking toward the door, she pulls it open and then turns back. "I think it's safe to say that you're alert enough for visitors."

"I have visitors?"

"Your wife is an angel. She's been here since you arrived."

"My wife?" My gaze darts to my left hand. The door closes, and I'm still speculating what the hell happened to me. As I tick through the memories I can recall, I remember being in my office.

The door opens, the light from the hallway silhouetting a woman's frame. Another nurse, a doctor, or . . . my *wife*? I'm not married, so I'm not sure if Nurse Edi was just goading me or what, but nothing was funny about that joke.

I'm a terrible patient, especially when I have very few answers as to why I'm here. Even more so with strangers invading my space at any given moment. But my heart monitor alerts the visitor to my anxiety. So much for trying to play it cool.

"Hello?" The lilt of a soft voice is as tentative as this woman's entry. When she finally steps over the threshold, the door slams closed behind her. The low light from the afternoon sun struggles to filter through the cheap metal blinds, accentuating her entry like lines on a piece of paper. They're also bent in four spots, but I've tried not to dwell on the imperfections so as not to raise my blood pressure. Plus, one of the bent pieces highlights the shape of her jaw and those pouty lips.

"Hi," I reply. "Are you a nurse?"

Stepping into the light, she says, "I'm sorry for intruding." A wave of apprehension rolls off her, altering the air between us.

Intruding? What is going on here? I try my best to remember her features, but nothing is registering while my heart monitor beeps loudly again and pain shoots through my head. "Who are you?"

"It's me," she replies like I should know who she is. "Delaney."

Shit. I thought Nurse Edi was joking about the married thing. I glance at her left hand this time. No ring on that particular finger, but a thin gold band wraps around her middle one. "Delaney . . ." I say, leaving it to hang in the air between us and praying to God that she fills in the blanks of my memories so I don't look like an idiot.

"I was with you during the accident. Well," she says, coming closer, "just before the accident." The diffused sunlight still manages to shine in her blue eyes like stars that would make the night jealous. A mouth that doesn't shine with gloss but from licking her lips, somehow managing the perfect shade to complement her gently tanned skin and the freckles scattered across her nose and the apples of her cheeks.

She's pretty. *Remarkably so.*

Should that matter? Probably not, but I'm suddenly not as upset by the intrusion. And if I were to have a wife, she'd be a good fit, even though I'm not one to typically go for brunettes. I could devour the innocence locked in her eyes without a second thought, but I'll restrain myself. I'm in a hospital gown for fuck's sake. I'm not quite in the position I typically am when I talk to a woman I'm attracted to.

"What do you mean you were with me?" *Please don't let her tell me I'm married.*

"Oh, you're eye." The tips of her fingers press above her mouth. I reach up to touch under my left eye. She says, "It's the other eye. It's bruised. Does it hurt?"

I didn't know since the nurse didn't say anything, and the doctor has been scarce except for the five minutes he spared me at seven this morning. "The meds must be working. Is it bad?"

"Nothing you can't heal from." She leans in like we're people who inspect each other's wounds. "The scratch isn't too bad either."

"Scratch?" I look around the room, but there's nothing for me to see what the hell I look like. Here, I was worried about a concussion and a broken arm. Now, I need to be concerned about being bruised and cut up. Looking back at her, I ask, "Why were you at the scene of the accident again?"

"We were talking."

Nothing about her seems familiar, so I hope our conversation will stir some memories. "About?"

When she slides her hand along the rail of the bed, she angles her body, allowing light to settle over her. She's younger than I would have guessed even a minute prior. The veil of age eludes her smooth skin, drawing my eyes to travel down her neck to her chest. A strap has fallen over her shoulder, tempting me to lift it back into place. I don't, though the desire pits deep in my stomach.

It's the blotted spots discoloring her sunny yellow dress that has me wondering if she was also in the accident. Is that blood? Not the conversation I want to have despite my curiosity.

My gaze drifts higher, and I notice the slightest of shadows under her eyes as if her makeup has smudged to stain her skin. Water pools in the corners of her eyes like they're waiting for the command to fall. When she takes a breath, my eyes are pulled to shamelessly watch the rise and fall of her chest. So much emotion is ready to spill out of her that my guard goes up. Emotional women and I don't mix. At least, not usually. I try my damnedest to avoid those situations if I have a choice. I'm not sure I do since I'm trapped in this hospital bed waiting on who knows what before I return to my life again. I say, "You seem upset."

"It's just been a long night." As if cued, she sniffles and then tips her head back, encouraging the tears to withdraw.

Tidbits of information start linking together, leaving me more confused than before. "You waited here all night for me?"

"Yes. Of course, Warner."

Of course?

Warner?

She's sounding suspiciously like someone who knows me, or worse . . . *a wife*. My throat tightens like my chest, a band stretched to its limits and about to burst as breathing becomes harder. The sound of my heart beating faster alerts both of us to the fact.

Looking back at me, she asks, "Are you okay?" She touches the top of my hand, the tips of her frigid fingers sending shocks of electricity up my arm. "Should I call a nurse?" Panic streams through her voice as her fingers press against me.

"No," I reply, staring at the connection. "No. It's fine." I'm good not being on Nurse Edi's radar the rest of the night.

Who knew a woman who I'd be surprised tops out at five feet could be so intimidating?

"You went pale, so I thought—"

"I'm fine." I readjust again, moving my hand from the mattress to my lap. "What happened yesterday?" This whole event sounds ridiculous to my ears. How is it possible that I was hit by a car? I'm not a careless man by nature. Every move I make is calculated. Every plan plotted. Nothing is done on a whim. So when an emotion I haven't felt in longer than I can remember sets in, I almost don't recognize it. And when I do, embarrassment settles in as I confess, "I've lost the better part of the past twenty-four hours." She's a stranger to me but acts as if we're familiar. "Can you fill in some details for me?"

"If I can." She nods and then shifts farther down the bed, her hands moving to her sides before slipping into hidden pockets. "What do you want to know?"

"You've been freed, Mr. Landers." The door is barely open before Nurse Edi announces like she's won the lottery. Maybe she has if I'm being released. She looks at the woman standing at the end of my bed. "I'm glad you're here, Mrs. Landers. You'll be able to sign the paperwork and then he's all yours again." I catch the scowl before she plasters a smile back on her face for Del—*oh shit*. I'm married.

I glance at my hand again, rubbing the tip of my thumb under the finger that should have some form of representation of such a union. There is none. Did I lose more than a day? Did I lose the memory of my wife, of getting married, the honeymoon, and our life together? I eye this Delaney lady. I would have thought sex with her would be more memorable.

My skin itches under this chalky cast smothering my arm. *What else can't I remember?*

Nurse Edi leads her out of the room, leaving me lying here staring out the window at the surrounding buildings. Their shadow finally reaches my window, slowly shoving me into darkness, which matches the holes in my mind.

Reaching over, I flick on a small bedside lamp. I scan the nightstand for a phone, my wallet, anything that gives me access to the outside world. I'm not sure if I should escape while Delaney's gone or invite her to my place when she returns. *Our place?*

What the fuck is happening?

None of this sits well with me. *Something is definitely off.*

The moment the door opens, I ask, "Do you have my phone?"

Delaney enters, shaking her head. "No. The hospital said it wasn't on you when you arrived." She comes bedside and hands me my wallet and watch. My dad's watch. The face is cracked, one of the lugs sports a deep indent, and the bezel is scratched on the top. The second hand is miraculously ticking as if time never stopped for me. I'll take it as a good sign since I'm somehow here after being hit by a car.

"Thanks." I start putting the watch on my left wrist. Reaching down, she helps secure the clasp. Handy since I can't use my right for shit now that my arm is broken and fingers a bit stiff.

"You're free to go home, but they want to wheel you out the door." Walking to the closet, she pulls the clothes out. "Do you need help getting dressed?"

"No."

"I have brothers, if you're worried." I stare at her, curious how that matters in this predicament, especially if she's my supposed wife.

What the fuck is happening? If I find out Jimmy set up

this elaborate prank, he's a dead man. "Did Jimmy put you up to this? Did he set up this whole thing?"

"A car accident? No, he didn't set this up." Placing my clothes on the bed, she says, "I can leave the room. I don't have a car, but I can call a cab or a rideshare if you prefer and have it waiting outside."

I stare at her. "Is this for real?"

"Is what for real?"

"You. Me. This whole thing?"

Her shoulders fall as if I've hurt her feelings. When I see her expression sink, I'm quick to add, "It's a lot to take in."

I'm given a defeated nod before she says, "I understand. It has been a lot." She walks out, and as soon as the door closes, I'm not sure if she's just getting a car or leaving altogether. I'm also unsure what I want to happen next, other than showering and sleeping in my own bed.

I get up and slowly step onto the cold linoleum. With my working arm, I start to lay out my shirt to help me put it on, but then I realize it's never going to fit over this cast. It's ripped and covered in blood anyway, so it's not worth the effort. I toss it in the trash bin and manage to get my pants on, though my belt is not cooperating. I let the hospital gown fall over my waist. I'm too tired to give a shit about how I look.

I slip on my shoes, skipping the hassle of putting on socks and then walk out of the room. I wasn't expecting a ticker-tape parade, but a greeting or goodbye would have been nice. Heading toward the door, I'm greeted by Nurse Edi and a wheelchair. "Get in, Mr. Bossy Pants."

"Is that why you're mad at me? Was I bossy?"

"We've never had bossier." She starts pushing me down the corridor. "You were ordering stocks like they were items on a menu, and you told one of our newer nurses that you could do a better job than she could."

My lips part, the apology owed to most of the staff, from what it sounds like, on the tip of my tongue. "Can we blame it on the anesthesia?"

"We already did. And then I was assigned to deal with you. It's not been so bad, though, right, Mr. Landers?"

"No." I grin just a little. "Not so bad."

I search the waiting room for Delaney as we pass by. When I don't see her, I focus forward. Nurse Edi rolls me outside and then stops on the sidewalk. "Time to say goodbye."

Standing, I look at her. Maybe I judged her wrong. "Goodbye, Nurse."

"Take care, Mr. Landers. Put some frozen peas on that black eye tonight and watch where you're going."

"Good advice. I'll make sure to heed it next time I cross the street."

Her boisterous laughter echoes under the hospital awning. "You do that." She starts back with the wheelchair but stops. "She probably won't tell you, but Mrs. Landers never left the hospital, not even when you were in surgery recovery. She was here all night, worried about you. Thought you should know. Not everyone has someone who cares about them like she does you."

She stays all night, but then leaves when I'm released? I'm really fucking confused. Nurse Edi has already retreated inside when I turn to figure out my next step.

The streets of New York are unforgiving—windy and dusty, with people annoyed when I dare step outside and in their path. The sun has set, though the warmth of spring still holds on past daylight hours.

If I knew Jimmy's number, I'd call him, but my bad for

not memorizing phone numbers when I have them programmed instead.

"Warner?"

My gaze follows the sound of my name to see Delaney standing with a door open in front of her. Her skirt wraps around the corner while she holds her hair back from blowing in her face. I can't say she's not a welcome sight, even despite wondering what game she's playing with my head. I start walking toward her. No use fighting this. Home is where I need to be recovering with my phone and in my bed. When I reach her, I say, "Homeward bound, dear?"

The smile I would expect from my wife doesn't appear. She's quick to duck into the car and slide across the seat to wait for me. With lingering grogginess, my brain isn't fully functioning. I have a headache coming on, and my body is lethargic. I get into the car, but don't say anything, choosing to lie back to conserve what little energy I have.

The car pulls away from the curb like he already knows where he's going. Suspicious indeed. One way or another, I guess I'm about to find out if she's for real or not.

CHAPTER 5

Delaney

WARNER LANDERS HAS A LIFE. A prestigious CEO job and thriving career, from what I dug up online. He has too many friends to consider them all close, and his family is always present at the events he attends. All according to Page Six in the *New York Times*. He's surrounded by people who appear to care about him, yet not a single person showed up at the hospital.

No one worried about him.

No one missed him in his absence.

Even the friend he was with before the accident wasn't there to check on him.

After talking to the nurses, no one even called for Warner.

I shouldn't care, but I might be the only one. Unfortunately, that doesn't help with my predicament. I can't afford to walk through the prime real estate of Tribeca, much less dream of ever standing in the "foyer," as he called it, of his penthouse apartment.

He stops at the end of the short hall ahead and looks back at me. "Is everything okay?"

"Fine." Nodding, I force my feet forward to continue playing this charade until I come up with another plan. I slipped into being his wife a little too seamlessly at the hospital. Without even really trying, which should worry me. But the pieces fell into place so easily. When I was given his wallet, his home address was on his driver's license, so I entered it into the app before I returned it.

I expected more questions, but he didn't ask one. The silence on the drive over became anxiety-inducing. I thought for sure he was going to call me out, but he never did. Is he playing with me, or does he really not remember if I'm his wife?

I shouldn't feel insulted that I'm so easily forgotten, though ounces of injury to my pride seep through my veins. Pride is the last thing worth saving. So I used the ride to figure out my next move but came up empty. Except for one idea, an absolutely terrible one at that. No. *I can't.* I shouldn't.

Could I?

As I reach the end of the hall, perfect lighting greets me, highlighting the best features in this large room. Before I can stop it, my jaw drops. "My entire apartment could fit inside this one sp—" I stop, clamping my mouth closed, realizing I'm exposing myself as the fraud I am.

With a glass of water in his hand, he lowers it to the stone counter, where soft beige and creams swirl together, with flecks that gently sparkle when the light hits it just right. And I thought white countertops were fancy. Now I know this stunner exists.

Standing in a hospital gown hanging over his pants, he should look more foolish than he does. Instead, the lines of his biceps peek out from under the teal fabric, and the shape of his ass pushes through the slit in the back where he didn't bother tying up the loose strings. *Don't, Delaney.* This is nothing more than a job I need to get done, like a thief in a heist movie. "This *is* your apartment, dear wife," he says, interrupting my wandering thoughts.

There's a spit to the end of his comment that echoes the hiss of a snake. It's a good reminder that I'm in enemy territory. "I meant my first apartment. I've moved on up." I tried for cheerful, but I'm not sure I'm selling it, judging by how he's staring at me like he can see the lies oozing from my pores.

Shit.

"You sure have." Lifting the glass again, he takes a sip, but his gaze stays firmly on me.

The large open space is modern yet filled with warmth, encompassing his kitchen and living room, as well as an expansive dining table perfect for large dinner parties. The area aligns with a balcony, divided by glass doors that I bet open wide, seamlessly bringing the outside in or vice versa. Those dinner parties must be pretty spectacular.

I'm afraid to move or speak until I know what I should say. Do I fess up and get the heck out of here? *I should.* Then I remember the legal paperwork I signed to get him discharged and the ramifications of my gut reactions. My gaze swings to the tired expression on my *husband's* face, and my resolve crumbles. It's an omission. He wouldn't have been hit by that car if I hadn't tried to get in the last word, and I could have been scot-free if his friends or family had shown up for him. *But they didn't.*

Not to mention my family's restaurant. *God, I'm so screwed if he catches on. I can do this.* How hard can it be to play the role of the doting wife until the deadline passes next month? Convincing myself is the easy part. Convincing him is a whole other story. I'm a terrible liar, but if he hasn't figured it out yet, this ludicrous plan is still possible.

There are only two ways to find out—try to pull this off or run now.

I walk toward the back doors, needing out from under the interrogation of his gaze to think more clearly. Spotting the lock, I move across the room like I do this every day. I pull the latch, turn the bolt, and then slide the door just enough to fit through. The sounds of the city are alive, and even at this height, it's loud with horns and sirens blaring in the distance. Peace is also found in the air up here. Night has fallen like a blanket around me, wrapping me in connection to the city that raised me. Though it was nowhere near this fancy neighborhood, I feel calmer breathing the same air as my stomping grounds. Under the cover of darkness, I find hope that this plan might work.

"Do you have instructions for me?"

His voice is deceptively calm, almost candid in tone like the lie of marriage to me might not be so far-fetched. I can't let my guard down. From what little I know of him, he's never to be trusted.

Leaning my back against the concrete railing, I throw out a question I heard almost every day of my life from my mom to my dad to test if this is even possible. Seems like a good generic thing to ask. "The dishwasher probably needs emptying."

His brows tug together as his stare hardens. "What does that have to do with anything?"

I stand straight, abandoning the rail to stand up to him. "You asked for instructions, so I gave you some."

Annoyance sends his eyes shooting into the air to the side of my head. He takes a deep breath, then looks at me again. "Doctor's instructions. In case you've forgotten, I have a concussion and broken arm." Pointing to his eye, he adds, "A black eye."

"Oh." I slide my eyes over his injuries. "Right." I unzip my purse that I'm still carrying around like someone who doesn't live here and pull out a folded piece of paper. "It didn't seem complicated, except for showering." I walk toward him with the paper held out in front of me.

"Okay, what does it say other than don't get the cast wet and ice the eye?" He takes it, but then frustration pinches his lips together, whitening them. Glancing back at me, he asks, "Do you mind unfolding it for me?"

Although I have a feeling those words pained him to say, I help him without piling on more to make him feel worse. As soon as I hand it back, he turns away from me to go inside. "I'm going to shower." My hand is still in the air like the fool he takes me for. Lowering it, I look once more into the distance of the street lined with buildings on either side, soak in the sounds of the city, and then return inside.

I'm not surprised by the treatment. I have no doubt he would treat his wife like a bother. He's such an asshole. I bite my tongue as I move to the kitchen to wash my hands.

Staring down at the paper on the counter before him, he doesn't give me the courtesy of acknowledging my presence. He simply asks, "What are you doing?"

I pause my hands under the stream of water and then pump the soap and start rubbing them together. "What does it look like I'm doing? I'm washing my hands."

Maybe his love language is bitterness because my tone captures his attention. I'm positive he thought he'd get away with that once-over. *He didn't.* "You should shower." I don't let his assessment bother me. I am a mess and feel gross.

"A shower would feel amazing." The moment I finish

speaking, I realize I just fell into the trap he set. "I know you really want to take one. You go first." I rinse my hands and search for a towel or paper towels to dry my hands.

"Middle drawer to your left." He moves around me like I'm a hurdle he has to jump and gets an ice pack from the freezer. After wrapping it in a dish towel, he holds it to his eye.

I should really know that as his wife, but I'm failing miserably at this charade. I pull out a towel and dry my hands before angling to face him while he stands at the end of the island. He says, "I can wait a few more minutes to take a shower. I'll ice my eye while you wash up. I'm sure you'd like to get out of that dress and into something clean."

How do I answer this without giving away the truth? I have no clothes, no toiletries, nothing of me in this entire place. I'm such a fool. This is impossible to pull off when all he has to do is look around to see I'm lying about our relationship. "I . . ." My gaze drops to the wood floor.

Lowering the ice pack, he asks, "Why do I get the feeling you're not telling me something, Delaney?"

What could I say that would excuse my nonexistence from this apartment? One absurd plan deserves another off-the-wall idea layered on top of it. At this point, there's nothing to lose but everything. "We're separated, Warner." I hold disinterest in my expression, though my heart is ready to pound out of my chest.

"We're separated?" Disbelief shadows his eyes as he processes the admission.

"Yes. I left yesterday."

"Yesterday? The same day I got hit by a car?" The inkling of a grin lifts the left side of his face. "That's a huge fucking coincidence. I mean, one might think that the two were related."

"One *could,* but they'd be wrong." I pull my shoulders down from their defensive positioning near my ears. "I was leaving you."

Laughter erupts from his chest. "*You* were leaving *me*?" Then his grin falls, as does his expression, including the chuckle that dared crinkle the corners of his eyes.

"That attitude is one of the reasons I was leaving. You're a real arrogant ass, you know that?"

"You must have found it attractive at one point since you said yes."

I shrug. "Actually, it's always been a problematic trait of yours." I think that's safe to assume. Only luck is carrying me. I need a few minutes to myself to figure this all out. "Listen, you take a shower. You were the one who was hit. I'll be fine waiting."

Resorting to his typical brand of intensity, he stares at me with the mastered indifference of a professional. He's certainly good at locking his emotions away. It's a skill I've never honed, but maybe it's because I'm not a closed book like he is. I'm rather open and usually kind, but Warner Landers brings out the worst in me.

He comes closer, causing me to nervously lick my lips in preparation for the verbal standoff brewing between us. He stops toe-to-toe, not leaving so much as room to breathe in the remaining space between us, so I hold mine as our eyes latch together. Kneeling, he opens a cabinet, his hand bumping into my leg. He grabs something and then rises to his full height to tower over me again. "I shouldn't be long, but I need a trash bag to cover my cast." He puts the ice pack back in place and curves around me.

The potency of the interaction doesn't lessen until he disappears down another hallway to the left side of the living space. I take a breath like I wasn't allowed one in his presence. But it's not him who made me hold it. It's the house of cards built on lies. If I say one wrong thing, make one wrong move, he'll know I'm being dishonest. *Then what happens?*

He could remove the buyout option for my parents altogether if I'm not careful. I wouldn't be surprised, considering he thinks someone can actually pay that ungodly amount with only a month's notice. The deal he's offering is criminal.

My parents won't be able to come up with the money. There's no way. I'm going to stick to the plan because it's our only and last resort. What's the worst that could happen? He'll have me arrested for impersonating someone who cares.

What's the best that could happen? I'll sweet-talk him out of the deal and save the restaurant.

First things first, I sneak down the hall to where he disappeared, passing two closed doors and then one more on the far left that's cracked open. Opposite it, the door is wide open. The soft glow of a lamp welcomes me into the space, and the sound of the shower behind another door helps soothe my racing heart.

The bed is enormous—the biggest I've ever seen—with fluffy covers and large pillows, likely filled with pricey down or memory foam, which disrupts the sterile image I envisioned for his bedroom. Clean lines of the shades at half-mast carry the modern vibe into the room. But it's the chair and ottoman situated in front of a fireplace that have me wishing to curl up with a good book and waste some hours.

There's no time for daydreams. I open a door, hoping it's the closet. Bingo! I start grabbing hangers full of pressed shirts, pants that hang full length under suit jackets, and shove them into one section of the closet. Grabbing folded shirts and shorts from two shelves, I stacked them into a small cubby that only housed two pairs of shoes. I put those on the floor and then stand back. I snap my fingers. Drawers.

After tugging the top drawer open, I scoop up his neatly tucked and folded underwear—shockingly all black, though I shouldn't be so surprised—into my arms and then use the toe of my shoe to pull open the bottom drawer. Dropping all the underwear in there. A pair of black boxer briefs falls to the pristine beige carpet, so I grab and stuff it inside with the others before forcing the drawer to close as much as it can.

After one quick scan again, I dash out and close the door behind me. When I hear the bathroom door opening, I jump into the chair and grab the throw pillow to wrap my arms around it like I wasn't just destroying this man's closet.

My unexpected presence causes Warner's forward motion to halt abruptly. "What are you doing in here?"

Looking at him shirtless, some bruising covers his right shoulder, and he has scratches on his chest as well as one on his temple. The bruising hasn't set in, but the red patches will look nasty by tomorrow. I rub my sweating palms along the soft fabric arms of the chair. "Sitting."

"I can see that." His lips twist, giving me the slightest glimpse into seeing his foundation shaken. "Do you mind helping me with this?"

My eyes pivot to the trash bag wrapped around his arm and a tie he was attempting to use to hold it up. "Sure, but the shower will ruin the tie. Do you have a rubber band?"

"Not that I know of. *Do we*?" Why does he make it sound like he knows I'm lying? There is no reason this man would put up with shenanigans, so I really don't think he's playing along. What would he have to gain from doing so? Nothing but a good time, I suppose.

I get up and come around the back of the chair toward him. "I'm sure they're hidden in the junk drawer somewhere."

"What's a junk drawer?"

I stop and shake my head. Everyone has a junk drawer. This guy doesn't? He probably thinks he's too good for one. "Never mind. I have one." I dig around inside my purse and find a hair elastic. Holding it up, I say, "This will work."

I toss the tie on the bed. His eyes follow it as it slides off the side to the floor. That's how I discover a certain someone has a case of perfectionism. *Noted.* I'm starting to find joy in the little irritations I cause him.

"Why are you still wearing your purse like you're a guest in your own apartment?"

Sliding the elastic into place, I pop it against the bag wrapped around his bicep. "There you go. All set." Nothing like causing a distraction from questions I really have no answer to. When he winces, I grab for his chest, resting my hands gently on top. "Oh my God. I'm so sorry. I totally forgot."

"You forgot I'm injured? I'm only asking for your help because I'm injured. You're only standing in this apartment because I'm injured. I—" He tosses his head back and takes a deep breath before sliding his bag-free hand over his face. When he looks back at me, he says, "I'm going to shower now."

"Okay." I sound weak like a mouse in the wake of the anger he's holding back. When the bathroom door closes, I stand there until I hear the disruption in the sound of the water as he moves under the spray.

"What are you doing, Delaney?" I've asked myself this a

million times since I met this man yesterday. One rash decision has led to a series of irrational ideas. I'm probably only making things worse.

I gaze down at my ruined dress, aware that the right thing to do would be to leave. Get out now before I dig this grave any deeper.

Starting back down the hall, I enter the living space and soak in a much-needed breath. I have about five minutes to make a final decision on what's best to do in this situation. I'm realizing that I'm not going to be able to trick him into thinking we're married. I can tell he doesn't even believe it now. How will I drag this out for another month?

The answer is right in front of me. It has been all along. The decision was already made. *By him.*

I look around once more, glad I got to see how the others live. He can keep his beautiful palace in the sky and rule over his company like a king. That doesn't make my life worth less than his, although it does make me wish the good guys could win. But not all fairy tales have happy endings.

CHAPTER 6

Warner

I BLINK TWICE, adding a third slow blink for good measure.

Surely, this can't be real. I have a concussion, so I must be seeing things. I back out of the closet, close the door, and count to five before opening it again. It's still the same—a fucking mess. But it makes no sense. How would it get like this?

I open the top drawer to find it empty. Am I losing my mind? Looking lower, I see the bottom drawer sticking out, so I open it to find everything from the top drawer shoved inside it without care. Nothing is folded. Nothing is organized. There's just a mess of black cotton crowding the drawer. Irritation spirals through me, causing my head to ache more than it already did. I work on a pair of boxer briefs, cursing myself for choosing underwear that's difficult to get into, and then start searching for my other clothes.

I grab a T-shirt that's fallen on the floor on the opposite side of where it normally lives and try to pull it over my head. I'm only half successful. This broken arm business is really going to fuck with my day-to-day. I spot a pair of sweatpants and tug those on. I don't bother trying to tighten the drawstring, since the cast hinders my maneuverability.

Looking around once more, I scratch the back of my head. Delaney tries to come off innocent, but there's more to this story than she's sharing. I still don't fucking know what it is, and it's doing my head in. Well, the concussion is probably more to blame, but she's clearly someone with a hatred for orderly closets.

Wife, my ass. There's no way I would marry someone who lives in such disarray. No fucking way. It would drive me to the edge of sanity looking at that mess every day. I scoff, leaving the closet, cutting through the bedroom, and ready to return to my normal life. As normal as someone who was just in a car accident can be.

My home office silently calls to me when I pass by, just as it did earlier. Staring at the monitor while ordering what I need was enough to take a break from the blinding light. It's probably wise to let the healing process take its course and leave business for tomorrow. Hey, look, I'm turning over a new leaf. Guess that's what nearly dying does to a man.

I stop when I spot her in the kitchen. Boppy music infiltrates the area around her, and she's mouthing along, her singing here and there. I take a breath to keep calm. I won't heal if my blood pressure keeps going through the roof.

Starting toward her, I say, "I didn't expect you to still be here."

Her gaze hits me, but then a smile works its way to the corners of her mouth. I can't deny it looks like she's struggling to hide her dislike of me. Maybe we were married. Still are . . . separated. *Fuck.* This is wild.

She comes around to stand so close to me that I can feel the heat of her body. Without me asking, she takes the cotton shirt and stretches to the side, carefully looping my broken arm through the short sleeve. I whisper, "Thank you."

She drags the hem down over my abs, and without looking up, she whispers, "You're welcome." A glimmer of a smile appears when her eyes find mine again. "I couldn't leave you all alone." She leaves too quickly to appreciate the proximity.

"Well, you could have, but you chose to stay." Stationed on the other side of the island from her, I eye the stovetop and the small stack of pancakes on a plate next to it. "I thought you'd be long gone by now. Not making pancakes for a man you supposedly hate."

With an apron I didn't know I owned, wrapped around the front of her, and a spatula held tight in her hand, she rests her hands on the counter between us. "Let's get two things straight, Warner." I settle onto a barstool, thinking this might take a while. "One. I don't hate you."

"Then why are we separating?"

"Because I find you intolerable. That's not hatred. That's a lack of patience for your BS." Eyeing the shirt wrapped around half my body, she adds, "Anymore."

It's impressive how she talks like she actually knows me. "I have my memory," I say, testing to see her reaction.

Aside from her righting herself, the reaction is minimal. A few rapid blinks are followed by panic widening the darker pupils of her blue eyes. She licks her lips and then tugs the bottom one under her teeth to gnaw before releasing. "Everything?" Shit, I was only teasing, but her reaction has me wondering if she *is* responsible for my accident.

"Everything."

Turning around, she hides her face, cutting me off from

studying and seeing her emotions playing out. When she drops her head down, she whispers, "I'm sorry."

The song changes, and the flitting tune doesn't fit the mood. I get up and reach over the counter to stop it on the screen of her phone. Leaning my left hand on the counter, I ask, "Why are you sorry, Delaney?"

"For lying to you." I knew we weren't married. My gut told me what my mind can't seem to remember. She spins back and says, "I still want to be with you, Warner." Planting her hands next to mine, she leans over the counter so close that I can smell that she's already dipped into the maple syrup. I start to wonder if her lips would taste as sweet as her breath. "I should have never moved out."

I'm snapped out of that urge and back into this mess. "What do you mean?"

Her hands cover mine, and she replies, "I should have stayed and fought harder for us."

Shit...

Is this real? *Are we?*

The doorbell chimes with our eyes still connected. "Expecting company?" she asks, returning her attention to the pancakes, and only briefly glancing back at me. "I can make more."

I push off the counter, but before I leave, I ask, "What was number two?"

She laughs. "Who said these pancakes were for you?"

It's best if I walk away before saying something I regret, like letting her still be here. While walking to answer the door, the chime goes off once more, but I ask, "Do you happen to know why my closet looks like it does? I swear it was in perfect order the last time I used it."

I stop to wait for her response before rounding the corner toward the door. She looks at me square in the eyes without so much as blinking, and replies, "I was in a hurry to get my clothes when I left yesterday."

She's good, really fucking good.

Picking up my pace, I reach the door and look through the peephole. I open the door once I see the doorman standing on the other side. "Hi Baker, how are you?"

"Good, Mr. Landers." Eyeing me, he asks, "You okay?" He's older, closer to my dad's age when he died, and has worked here longer than I've been a resident. He's the happiest guy in Manhattan. Never has a bad word to say about anyone or the day. It's always a good day when I see Keith Baker in the lobby. He keeps things light when the rest of the world is heavy.

"I was hit by a car, so I can honestly say that I've been better."

"Sorry to hear that. A broken arm isn't too bad if you've been run over." Always looking on the sunny side, he adds, "You're here. So you must have more work to do here on earth."

"Work is the last thing I want more of."

He chuckles, moving off to the side of the door, angling toward the elevator. "It's probably not your job that needs the attention. He hands me a box. "Lose your phone?"

"Yeah, never made it with me to the hospital."

"Glad you got a replacement." As he starts down the hall, he says, "Let me know if you need anything, Mr. Landers. Happy to help however I can and get you healed quicker."

"I appreciate it, Baker. Have a good night."

"You, too, sir."

I close the door and look at the box. All it will take is for me to call anyone in my life to ask about the woman making herself at home in my kitchen, and I'll know the truth. Or sound like I got hit harder than I initially thought. At least, I'll get answers.

Answers!

I swing the door open to ask Baker about "my wife," but he's already disappeared in the elevator. I shut the door and lock it. I only take a few steps before Delaney appears at the other end of the hallway. "Who was it?"

Holding up the box, I say, "Baker delivering my new phone." It almost feels natural to respond to such mundane things with her. I wish it didn't.

"That was fast." She smiles. "You're such a workaholic. Are you hungry? I was only kidding about the pancakes. Of course, I was making them for both of us. I was starving. I'm sure you are as well."

"I could eat. Are they safe?"

Her laughter fills the short hall and lingers after she walks away. "Don't be silly. You think I'm going to spend all night at a hospital worrying about you if I had plans to poison your pancakes and force-feed them to you the moment you get home?"

"That's a little too on the nose for my liking," I note, following her back to the kitchen. "And I can't say that sells me on eating your pancakes." I open the box on the counter and start to set it up.

She laughs, a hint of a snicker in the resonant notes. She might be pretty, but she might also be evil. "Eating my pancakes." She laughs again. "That's so naughty."

Naughty? I'm close to asking if she's been drinking, but the more I look at her, I think it's delirium setting in. "When's the last time you slept?"

She sets a plate of pancakes in front of me and hands me a fork. "Not last night since I was stuck in that waiting room all night." She places the syrup within my reach. "Eat up, Buttercup."

I shake my head when I hear that nickname. It better not stick.

It's hard to forget I have a concussion, but it's been a feat to consider the possibility that she might be telling the truth. Hearing her now, the honesty in her admission—that she waited all night to make sure I was okay— I begin to trust her. Why else would she have stayed at the hospital all night?

No way, no how, am I trusting these pancakes, though.

She reaches over with her fork, cuts off a bite of the sweet stack, and shoves it in her mouth. "Happy?" She finishes chewing and swallows. "They're safe to eat, Warner."

As if on cue, my stomach growls, so I dig in. I take a bite and add syrup while I chew. They're good. Fluffy. She knows how to cook, I'll give her that. I kind of feel bad now. She was there for me. She made sure I got home safely and cooked food for me. I don't even know if that stove has ever been used before. It hasn't been by me. I'm glad she broke it in.

"Delaney?" She looks up at me with surprise shaping her expression, her eyebrows arching higher, and her pretty mouth rounding when she opens it. Was it hearing me say her name that caught her off guard? "Thank you for all you've done for me."

When her smile rises at the corners of her mouth, it appears genuine. "You're welcome, Warner."

The gray smudged under her eyes is still there, her hair is not as controlled as it was earlier, and that dress . . . she really needs to get rid of that dress. Even the apron does a poor job of hiding the disaster it's been through. "Hey, you should shower. I think you'll feel a lot better."

"I'm not feeling so bad, but I really would like to get clean." She sets her fork down. "But I don't have anything to change into."

"You can wear something of mine." I grin like we're in on a secret together. "I think you know your way around my closet."

"Our closet, and I do." She laughs, but it's softer this time like her voice. "Famous last words."

"For us anyway."

Her smile falls as she looks away from me. "I think I'll take you up on your offer, and shower."

She walks around the counter, passing me and heading down the hall, but stops to retrieve the purse she left on the counter, then her phone. It's almost like she doesn't trust me. I don't say what's on the tip of my tongue because I'm invested in how this night will end. Either she'll sleep over or leave me again. I'm starting to root for the former.

Knowing I won't be able to retire for the night with the kitchen a mess like she left it, I start by cleaning up the dishes, then load the dishwasher before running it. I fill my glass with water from a pitcher and take a pill for my head and to help with the throbbing in my arm under this cast. It was too late to pick up the prescription. That's what I get for choosing the local pharmacy instead of a chain, so this will have to do. I got hit by a car, so I can survive one night on Ibuprofen.

I lock the balcony door and double-check the front bolts. Working my way around the apartment, I shut off the lights as drowsiness sets in. I check the spare room to find the bed made up and ready for guests. She can sleep in here for the night. Come tomorrow, she's out of here—my bed, my apartment, and my life.

I walk into my bedroom to see her curled up on the bed under the covers. Her hair is damp, and her face has been cleaned of old makeup. She's more beautiful like this, sleeping like an angel in my bed. When I see the shirt that she chose to wear, I grin. Of all the T-shirts in the closet, she chose one that represents me more than most—my alma mater.

Letting her rest, I brush my teeth and get ready for bed. Although it was a struggle to get on, I have no trouble pulling the shirt off over my head. I leave my sweatpants in a pile on the floor, which isn't like me at all. I'm too tired to care.

I return to the bedroom to see her still lying in the same position. She might be more tired than I am. I can't move her to the other room. That means I'm getting z's next door. But I stop before I leave the room and look back. "Fuck it," I mutter, then turn off the lamp and climb in next to her.

The bed is large enough for us to sprawl out and still never touch. It feels so good to be lying here again, and way better than that hospital bed. I look to my side again since enough moonlight has determined it's also spending the night with us.

I reach over and run the back of my fingers over the soft skin of her exposed neck. She doesn't stir as if this comes naturally between us. She's not my wife. I know it deep down. If she were, I'd feel it in my bones. I just know it. But she's been nice company to have around, and she makes a great pancake.

We have a lot to discuss tomorrow, but here in this bed tonight, I'm glad she stayed.

CHAPTER 7

Delaney

THE LIGHT of early morning pours through the window, causing my lids to flutter open. My head spins like I got wasted at a bachelorette party instead of experiencing the mayhem of bad decisions. I had hoped rest would balance my overwrought brain, but the dizziness of the situation says otherwise.

The reprieve while I rested is only temporary as the unfamiliarity of everything surrounding me causes panic to rise in my throat. The air smells of some exotic location—musky with a warmth of sweetness, homey, the soft sheets against my bare legs, the coziest bed I've ever slept in, the weight of a warm hand on my inner thigh—*Hand?*

My eyes fly open as I suck in a harsh breath. Fear races through my veins, but I still my breathing, harboring the next breath in my chest. Turning my head slowly, I'm careful not to disturb the person next to me.

Just enough light streams into the room to see Warner lying on his back next to me. My heart is quick to find a rhythm with the sound of his steady breathing, calming my initial concerns. He's handsome when he sleeps, like he is when he's awake, but more so when he's not speaking. He sure has a knack for pushing buttons, especially mine. In the peace of his sleep, I can pretend he's not an awful human being trying to destroy my family's lives.

I can even find comfort in the warmth of his hand between my legs. *Wait, what?* I should shift, but I stay still instead, enjoying the heat his touch radiates to the rest of my body, even reaching my toes.

Lying here, I drape my arm across my forehead and stare up at the ceiling. With Warner's hand on my thigh and the scent of his soap floating in the air, my thoughts scroll through snapshots of the past twenty-four hours. *I let this man believe he's my husband.*

Squeezing my eyes shut, I inhale a deep breath and look at him again. The bridge of his nose has the slightest of bumps, and his full lips appear soft in the morning light juxtaposed against the hard cut of his jawline. The hills and valleys of his muscular shoulders lead my gaze across his chest, but a heaviness weighs on mine, causing me to look away. I take a deep breath, refusing to get caught up in him.

Everything I learned from the old con-job movies I used to watch with my dad taught me that Warner is a target. *My target.* That's it. Stay focused on the job at hand.

On the edge of delirium last night, I had to make a choice. Whether it was a wise decision or not remains to be seen. But today, I'm fully committed. It's not like I have another option at this point.

Warner Landers has made himself clear.

It's time Delaney Bayetti does the same. I'm not here to play. I'm here to win him over and talk some sense into him.

The lies are already embedding themselves under my

skin just enough to slide off my tongue when necessary. He was testing me last night. He'll do it again today. I have to be ready for him, or I'll give myself away.

I only wish I didn't love the feel of his hand spanning the inside of my thigh like I do. And how bold he was to slide it between my thighs like I'm his girlfriend, or worse, his wife. Did he really think I wouldn't notice? Technically, I didn't, but that's neither here nor there in this situation. I have a scroll length of excuses lined up and ready to toss out on a moment's notice.

One. I went almost forty-eight hours without sleep. No one is any good without solid rest. I got that here last night. *Finally.*

Two. The amount of mental gymnastics I've had to perform for this man to convince him we're the real deal has been an expenditure of energy I didn't know I possessed. We might not be a couple, but it's been fun living like a queen in his castle.

Enough of the mush, Delaney. I'd be wise to remember the man is a monster with no heart. I'm not interested in spending my time trying to redeem him so he's tolerable. He's not, so there's no use hoping for the best in this mess. I've come to accept he is who he is. I know exactly what I'm working with and will act accordingly.

Plus, I can't stay like this all day.

Moving ever so slowly, I roll to the side of the bed to get up. When his hand falls to the mattress, I still and look back over my shoulder. He shifts, but there's no reason to believe he's awake. I slink out of bed and tiptoe to the bathroom, pushing the door shut quietly until my back rests against it. A much-needed breath brings clarity rather than the usual rush of panic. *I'm doing the right thing.*

He might be the one with the concussion, but I'm the

one acting like I was in the accident. Logic has gone out the window. I know what I'm doing is wrong. I feel it in my gut. But at what point will morals outweigh purpose? I shake the guilt from my shoulders and look in the mirror. My gaze dips to my chest with a university's name emblazoned across the front. If I'd gone to Harvard, I'd be blasting it out there, too. Warner Landers might have expensive suits and this incredible apartment. He even has a fancy pedigree in legacy and degree, but it doesn't seem like he actually enjoys his life. He's wound up tighter than a bobbin. It's the lack of fun, I just know it is.

Happiness might also be a culprit. Why else would someone find joy in ruining other people's lives? And that is what tells me all I need to know about him. *Focus on the job, Delaney.* Get in, sweet-talk him into tossing this deal away, and get out.

"Take no prisoners," I whisper. It would be a lot easier if he didn't have that stupidly handsome face of his. It's not fair for him to win all the awards from wealth to good looks. He does have his flaws, but even his personality is becoming easier to overlook.

I grin, glancing at the shirt again, even half-heartedly to give him credit where it's due. It's an impressive achievement. And though I'm not surprised he went to Harvard, I am by how soft this T-shirt is. Wonder how many washes it took to achieve this cotton perfection.

After snooping around the bathroom, I find a clear container of brand-new toothbrushes. Of course, he has them neatly organized and a supply to last twenty years. I roll my eyes. Does this man *ever* have any fun? I'd have to see it to believe it.

I brush my teeth and then use the face wash he keeps in the shower. It felt so luxurious when I used it last night that

I didn't even need moisturizer afterward. After patting my face dry, I put on my strapless bra and then ball up my dress in the corner. Sneaking through the bedroom, I quietly grab the first pair of shorts I find, slipping them on but holding them up at the waist as I tiptoe back out toward the door. I glance over at him sleeping so soundly and smile before I get frustrated for giving him the courtesy of thinking he looks cute all snug as a bug in that bed.

I close the door behind me and pad down the hall to the main living area to have a look around in the daylight. The sun hasn't risen above the buildings, so the place is still cast in shadow, but it is no less impressive.

Pulling the drawstring as tight as it will go at the waistband, I knot it and hope it keeps the shorts from falling. That would be embarrassing. I get my purse out from behind the large plant pot in the corner. Hiding it seemed like a good idea last night. I didn't want him rummaging through it for evidence that I'm not who I say I am.

Strangely, in the light of a new day and looking back, I'm not so sure he would have cared. He's wily but still not operating at one hundred percent.

Today might be a different story.

I would never wish harm on someone, but if he could keep that memory loss front and center for a while, I wouldn't be upset. I slide onto a barstool and pull out my phone. Seeing the time makes me feel less rushed. It's not even seven, though I'd bet money that Warner probably typically gets up before the sun and works out or something. He's got the body to show for it.

Hard abs.

Defined biceps.

The man has the perfect balance of athleticism—not overly bulky, yet he can hold his own. Those shoulders made me want to cling to him like a monkey to see, but I have no doubt he could hold me if he wanted to. Why he'd want to is a whole other issue.

This con would be easier if he were less . . . less at everything. Looks, finances, apartments. Not easier to take advantage of, but I wouldn't get so distracted around him. I would sound less like a bumbling fool every time I open my mouth. He would get the real, confident, and independent version of me.

Looking down at my phone again, I realize that with less than 5 percent battery, I won't get far in this city, so I unplug his new phone to charge mine for a few minutes. I turn to look out the window, assuming I won't have a lot of time before he wakes up. What happens next?

I need clothes. I need my toiletries. And makeup. I need to see my family. Turning back to the kitchen, I make note of things I need to get. After scrounging through the fridge and cabinets, pancakes were all I could think to make. The fridge looks new, given how few things are in it. There's no old cheese or rotting vegetables in the drawers. There's no cheese or vegetables at all. Talk about bare bones living. I'm not sure how he survives off probiotic active yogurt, bottles of Evian water, and French butter, so I'm certain he must have restaurants programmed on his speed dial.

His phone . . . *Shoot*. That will be an issue. One call will ruin it all.

I take it, tucking it into my purse because if I've gone this far, I might as well leave more destruction in my wake. Then I snatch the cord out of mine. I need to make a good and big impression, and I know just how. I have to get a move on, though. I slip on my shoes and head for the door.

The elevator comes quickly at this hour and spits me out into the lobby just as a lady and her dog stroll on as I exit.

She stares at me, with no smile in sight. When her face pinches, I worry she's swallowed something sour until I realize it's me who's left a bad taste in her mouth. *Wow.* Tough crowd. "I know I look odd, but I'm doing the best I can here, so cut me some slack, lady."

She snoots and tosses her nose in the air after picking up her poofy little dog like I threatened its life. I didn't, for the record. When the elevator closes, I glance down at the baggy basketball shorts I've knotted at the waist, which are barely clinging to my hips, his tee, and my flats. Wiggling my toes, I choke down the mortification and head toward the exit.

Seeing the doorman ahead, I realize that people in Warner's life, even the folks who are only acquaintances, will know that I'm not his wife. What would it take to make him play along?

I'm too broke to give a reasonable bribe like I've seen in the movies. So he's stuck with my awful effort at charm. "Hello," I say, resting my arms on the top of the high counter. "I'm Delaney."

"Good morning, miss. My residents call me Baker. How may I help you?" His smile is kind, and his thick accent is from one of the boroughs. I already like him.

"Baker . . ." I start by sweetening my tone. "Do you happen to know Warner Landers by chance?"

"In the penthouse? Sure, I know Mr. Landers. Good guy."

"Hrm." I smile, though I can't relate to the comment. "Yes, well, that remains to be seen. Anywho, I'll be staying with him for a while—"

"Ah!" He stands. "This must be for you." He sets a shopping bag on the counter. "The bag was delivered around six, but we don't disturb our tenants before eight unless prior authorization is given. That's why it's still here."

I peek inside the bag. And now I'm grinning. *Damn him.* Why'd he go and do something nice for me? It's so uncharacteristic of Warner.

Holding a pair of leggings up, I ask, "Do you have somewhere I can change down here?"

"A bathroom on the other side of the elevator."

"Thanks." I change into the spandex pants that hold everything in like I didn't have pancakes for dinner last night, then check out my butt in the mirror. "Warner did good."

The socks are thick, and the sneakers fit like a dream. He's making it hard to hate him. I know it will only be a matter of time before the emotion returns in full force again. Probably as soon as I see him, he'll say something out of touch, like the city should let landlords charge whatever they like. Okay, maybe that's too harsh. I don't know how he feels about Manhattan pricing, but I do know that he's part of the problem for me and my family.

My sweet family. My heart clenches thinking of all the Thanksgivings we had at the restaurant, my mom always leaving the door open for strangers with no other plans or no home to go to. A hot meal and laughs. The joy of cooking together and feeding the staff, who have become like family.

So many birthdays have been celebrated around the table upstairs in the apartment, Christmas trees shining in the front bay window, and neighbors who looked out for us kids like we were their own.

I wipe under my eyes and raise my chin. *I can do this.*

I walk back out and set the bag on the counter. "Would it be any trouble to hold this bag until I return? And I want to get Mr. Landers a coffee and a bagel. Do you have any suggestions?"

"No trouble at all." After setting the bag down, he comes from behind the counter and walks toward the door. "And there's a great local place at the corner. Their everything bagel is one of the best in the city, and I would know. It's my favorite."

I grin even wider. "I trust you. Thanks. I appreciate it." He opens the door and holds it, then joins me outside. I'm about to walk off, but I turn back coyly, swallow my nerves, and say, "I have a favor to ask, Baker."

"Happy to help. What is it?"

I lean in conspiratorially, which makes sense because I'm literally conspiring. "Mr. Landers was in an accident."

"I saw. How's he doing?"

Bobbling my head, I reply, "He's been better. The thing is, he's lost part of his memory."

"Oh wow. That sucks."

"It does suck. What sucks even more is that the part he lost is his life with me." His silence, shock, or both leave me an opening. "We were married, and now he doesn't remember at all. It's quite the issue."

When his expression contorts, he shoves his hands in his pockets. "I can see how that can be an issue."

"We got married on a whim." The lies flow like wine as I gesture in the air to help my explanation. "I kept my place. He has his. We love each other, but we got into a big fight, and I never quite moved in. I thought I had more time, but this accident has shown me I don't. We must make the most of every day we have together."

He scratches his head. "And Mr. Landers feels the same?"

I laugh, though I don't hear the humor I'm trying so

hard to inject. "He's had a bad concussion. I can't speak for him, but our feelings for each other are mutual."

With a nod, his eyes soften along with the lines around his mouth. "You mentioned a favor?"

"Oh yes, I almost forgot." I didn't forget, but I did get caught up in my own story. That was a doozy. "He may be questioning things. You know, since he has a concussion. The doctor advised treating him as usual, but not to stress him out. If he asks about me, it's probably best to gently remind him I exist, but let me know so I can report any progress or slips to the doctor." I hate myself for being so good at this. And here I thought I was a bad liar. I could win Oscars for this performance.

"Alright. I can do that."

"I appreciate it, Baker. Thank you." I start to walk away, but then I turn and keep going backward. "Can I get you anything? How about one of those everything bagels?"

"I won't say no to that offer."

And just like that, I have one base covered.

Pulling his phone from my purse, I need to take care of that base next.

CHAPTER 8

Warner

"Fuck me." I fall back on the bed, holding my hand over my heart. "You scared the shit out of me, Delaney."

She's sitting up next to me, smiling like a solid handful of golden rules aren't being broken. The audacity of this woman. "I'm just sitting here eating a bagel, not making a sound at all."

"Yeah, that's the problem." I glare at her. I sit back up and slide my body until my back settles against the head-board. "Why are you eating a bagel in my bed?"

"Our bed."

I take a deep breath before I lose my patience altogether. "Are those poppy seeds?"

"It's an everything bagel. They're Baker's favorite. Since I was getting one for him, I figured I'd make it a round. Who doesn't like everything on their bagel?" She laughs at her own joke as she holds the bagel smothered in cream cheese up to her mouth, while I'm left wondering how she knows my doorman. Before she takes a bite, she shoves it in front of my face. "Hungry?"

Shaking my head, I push her arm away. "I'm good. Anyway, eating in bed is against the rules."

"Whose rules?"

"My rules," I snap. "It's like a cardinal sin. Everyone knows that."

"Guess I missed that day at Sunday school. I'm surprised you were allowed in church. I thought the holy cross was meant to keep the demons out?"

"I—" Fuck, I don't even know what to say to that. My brain is lagging while hers is running at full speed. It's still damn ballsy to eat food in someone's bed like they won't care.

Wearing my T-shirt like it's hers, a smear of cream cheese adorns the shoulder. Don't react, Landers. It will come out in the wash. Don't sweat the small stuff. "I got you coffee," she says, distracting me. Pointing at the nightstand beside me, she grins. "No sweetness added, like your soul."

"Real funny."

Shrugging, she says, "I thought so."

Unaffected by my fake laughter, she takes another bite that is too big for her mouth. She's going to end up choking. Am I really the one chosen to supervise this criminal activity? "No one is going to steal that from you, you know? You don't have to finish it in four bites. You *are* allowed to enjoy your food."

"Not at my house." She tosses her head against the headboard and laughs. "If you don't clean your plate in eight seconds flat, my brothers will clean it for you."

"Why?"

Surprise widens her eyes. "Do you not have siblings?"

"Do I really need to answer that?"

"You just did." She sets the bagel on the bare wood of the nightstand. No napkin. No plate. She just sets it down like it won't leave a permanent mark.

I turn, setting my feet on the floor. With my head beginning to pound and my arm already aching and itchy from the cast, I start to wonder what I did to deserve this. Not the accident. *Delaney.*

"I need to pick up my prescription."

"Already did. It's next to the coffee getting cold."

I look up to see the paper coffee cup on the nightstand with no coaster in sight. Not how I would do things, but this isn't a battle I have the energy for. Next to it is a prescription bottle.

Crawling across the bed, she drapes her legs over the side next to me, but her feet don't touch the floor. I don't know why that makes me want to smile. I kill that thought to make sure I don't. "It's for pain and says to take up to twice a day when necessary. They said they expect that to last if you're having any. So moderation is key, and make sure to have food on your stomach." She swirls her hand in presentation in front of me, looking pleased as punch. "Hence, the bagel."

My blood pressure lowers under the gesture. She's a total stranger to the part of my brain that's working, but she's caring for me like she's more. A lot more. It's not something she has to do. She's here in the trenches with me, helping me recover. "Thanks. You didn't have to go out of your way."

"I was going out anyway. I'm just returning the favor. Coffee and a bagel are the least I can do." Dropping to her feet, she plucks the fabric at her thigh. "Thanks for the clothes. This was thoughtful of you, Warner."

"It was nothing." I try to harden my jaw, but it's no use.

"It was just a quick email last night before my shower. It's not like I worked miracles."

"I don't know. It might be. All you had to do was snap your fingers, and clothes arrived at your door before seven in the morning. Sounds like a miracle to me." She rubs her hands down the sides of her legs, sending poppy, sesame, and whatever else kind of seeds on that bagel spiraling to the floor.

I must have died in the accident. That's the only thing that explains the hell I'm living in.

She says, "Small confession. I've never had sneakers that cost that much in my life. It's like walking in heaven."

"Of course it's heaven for you. As for me . . ." I sigh. "Never mind. Taking another shower would be too much of a hassle even if it would lessen the tension she causes in my muscles. I get up and head to the closet, but then I stop and detour out of the bedroom. I'm in no mood to see the catastrophe of what used to bring me peace.

I can hear her quickened footsteps behind me. "What can I do to make you feel better?"

"Nothing. I need to work to take my mind off . . ." I hit her with a glare when she enters my periphery. "Off you."

The words cause her to physically jerk away from me. I'm instantly struck with regret. "Delaney—"

"No," she says, raising her hands in front of her. "I think you need some time alone." Grabbing her purse from the island, she picks up the sneakers and walks around the corner to the hall in her sock-covered feet.

"Delaney, wait." I rush to the hall and stand there as she slips on the sneakers, leaving the laces untied. "I didn't mean—"

"It's okay." Keeping her eyes on the task, she replies, "Couples fight. It doesn't mean anything."

"We're not a couple." Her eyes find mine as she stands back up. Wrapping the strap of her bag over her head, she sighs, letting the disappointment penetrate her eyes. Seeing the pain that would only be revealed if we meant something to each other has me believing we were real or are. *Fuck.* I drag my hands over my head and rest them on top. "I'm sorry."

She nods once, her eyes leaving mine as she turns away from me and opens the door. There's no snarky comeback or detail of our life I can't remember thrown out like it happened yesterday. There's nothing, not her blue eyes or sharp tongue. Not even a goodbye when she leaves, closing the door behind her.

This is best. If we're a couple, we were separated for good reason, and I feel privy to what that might be now. If we aren't together, it's good that she's gone.

I stare at the door longer than I should for someone who's certain in his stance. Aren't all fools? I leave the bolts unlocked and return to the island. But I can't stop myself from stealing one more glance as if she'll walk through that door like she never left. When she doesn't, I double down on regret. She didn't deserve my reaction or my anger. I fucked up.

What am I doing? I wanted her gone, and now she is. Why do I feel like shit, then?

I look back once more, as if the situation has taken a new turn. It hasn't, and rationally, I recognize that's for the best. That I even doubted that for a second sends me reeling. Get your head out of her ass, Landers. *Work.* That's what I need. I should lower my head and get the job done. I can only imagine how many emails have piled up. Strange that Jocelyn hasn't tried to contact me.

I look for the new phone so I can set it up with my

contacts, add the email apps, make some calls, and get back on track, but there's nothing here except the cable used to charge it. I bend to look at the end as if I'll find it on the floor. When I stand, I search the countertop and scan the living room. "Okay, this makes no sense."

Returning to the bedroom, I peek in to see if it's on the nightstand, but all that's there is the coffee that apparently matches my soul and a bagel ruining the surface. I turn back, then go inside and grab the bagel. How can anyone live in these conditions? Messy everywhere, a graveyard of seeds sticking to my feet, and I can't even look in the direction of the closet without getting angry when the images of clothes piled on the floor return.

I should be elated that she's gone. Instead, I'm wondering how I'm going to take a shower without her assistance. A woman helped me once, and now I can't manage my own life. This is asinine. I'm a grown man. I can take a shower without anyone's help. I've done it most of my life. When did I become helpless? I'm not.

Just to prove a point, I struggle for twenty minutes to wrap this cast in a trash bag so I can take a shower, letting the water pummel the top of my head. With my eyes closed, my hair flattens to my forehead as the water runs down my face and body.

Shuffling through an extensive list of things to do, Delaney interjects herself right between follow-up emails and getting some suits altered to accommodate this cast. Why does it feel like she's pulling the wool over my eyes and loving every minute? How can I remember so much of my life, basically all of it except hours involving the accident, but have no recollection of my wife? *Staggeringly impossible.*

I finish up, slip on some clothes, and then remember to take my meds. I lift the lid off the coffee just to see if she did match it to my soul. I shouldn't grin, but I do. I even chuckle. Whether she's my wife or someone putting in a lot of effort, Delaney really is something else.

The apartment is too quiet, which is the opposite of what I typically prefer. I'll blame the concussion for turning on background music, and I move down the hall to my office. I don't have a phone, but I have my computer.

Sitting down at the desk, the monitor lights up for me. I scroll through the messages, some popping out more than others. Jocelyn and Jimmy specifically. I click one to read a panicked message from my assistant. "Unlike you." Scanning further, I mumble, "Are you okay?"

I reply that I appreciate her concern. I was in an accident, but I'll be in the office on Monday and can explain in more detail then. I click on Jimmy's next. I reply the same, and that I'll contact him from the office tomorrow.

Glad to hear someone was concerned about my absence.

The other emails compete with images of Delaney popping into my head to fight for my attention. She's winning, which I'm positive would thrill her. Me? Not so much.

I probably should have read the directions on the pill containers. It's too late now as drowsiness takes hold of me. My eyelids grow heavy, so I stumble into the bedroom and crash onto the bed.

As I lie there, sleep is about to drag me under, and all I can think about is I bet she knew this would happen. She'd be thrilled to knock me out. But more importantly, is she coming back?

CHAPTER 9

Delaney

I SCREWED UP.

As his wife, I should know he has siblings. Though I don't think he caught my flub, he can't be trusted. The wrong slipup could cost me everything. He's intelligent and quick, even with a concussion, but hoo-daddy, he really needs to work on his patience. He has absolutely none. And I'm trying hard not to dwell on his anger issues. I think I've discovered limits he didn't know he had.

I need to try harder to stay on his good side.

"I love it," I reply, holding my hand up in front of me and looking at the cubic zirconia shine like a diamond on my ring finger. "I'll take it."

"Would you like me to put it in a bag for you, Delaney?" Darla has been more than helpful, and the best part is she'll keep my secret. Just one of the benefits of growing up in Clinton Hill. New York is a big place, but our little neighborhood is still cozy and welcoming, especially for the locals.

"I'm going to wear it."

She rings me up and gives me a discount because we do the same when she comes into the restaurant. It's just what neighbors do for each other.

I throw away the receipt as soon as I see a trash can on the street. No evidence. I check out the ring again, finding myself smiling too big, considering it's fake and all part of this charade. But still, I like it. It's dainty with the thin gold-ish band and the sweet little diamond. Would this be the ring Mr. Tribeca would buy me? If we were dating for real, I think he'd get the ring I wanted, not just one that shows off his wealth. That's probably why we'd never work out. Money wafts, like he was born to emit the scent of wealth. Although I do really love that soap he uses. Pure money, baby.

The smell of fresh garlic bread reaches my nose before the restaurant comes into view. Before crossing the street, I tuck the ring into a pocket inside my purse, then look both ways before taking another step. I have no intention of ending up like Warner did.

Bayetti's Italian Eatery has been a neighborhood staple for three generations. Plenty of celebrities have visited over the years. We've also attracted our fair share of tourists since being named on a "Best of" list ten years ago, but it's the locals' support that keeps us here. Unfortunately, the restaurant has really started to show its age. The green script above the door has faded with time. The gold script painted on the large front window is flaked. The thick wood trim around the windows could use a new coat of red paint. The brick could even benefit from a power washing along with the sidewalk out front, but it's never felt so good to come home.

I walk in the front door and greet the new hostess. I pass customers who have stopped in for an early lunch, through the heavy wooden four-top tables, and weave along the red vinyl booths that line each wall. I duck under a large tray of food, but stop to ask, "Need any help, Luca?"

"All good, Delaney."

As I push into the kitchen, the staff is hustling, so I don't want to distract them. I turn into a narrow corridor, pass the bathrooms, and enter the last door on the right. My dad looks up at me over the top of his glasses. He smiles and then rocks back in his office chair. "My sweet Delaney." He holds his hand out to signal the chair that's crammed in the minuscule space beside the door.

The room really only holds his desk and a small one in the corner, two beige filing cabinets shoved in the opposite corner, and this chair. I'm used to the cramped quarters, so I sit. "Hi, Dad."

"How's my little cannoli?"

I still smile every time I hear the well-earned nickname. "Yeah. It's all good. How about you?"

Taking his glasses off, he sets them on the desk and pinches the bridge of his nose like he's staving off a headache. "I'm good. Though I can't say the same for these books. I'm surprised we haven't been audited with such bad bookkeeping."

"I thought Joe was doing the books on the side of his day job?"

"Your brother is, but it's a full-time job, and he can only work on it at night." He smiles, showing off the lines that dig deep into his cheeks. "Did he tell you he has a new girlfriend?"

Why is Warner suddenly on my mind? I glance down at my naked finger and shake my head. "No, I hadn't heard."

His hair is graying, but I don't remember him without even a few here and there. It's so easy to see against the dark color. "She's a buyer at Macy's in the men's shoe department. That's how they met."

"Oh yeah?" Imagining my brother trying on shoes and flirting with someone isn't so far-fetched. "I'll have to get the details when I see him next."

"Your mother said you've been staying with friends from school."

It was one thing to fib in a text to my mom, but telling a bold-faced lie to my dad's face is a new low for me. "It's been fun." *Not a lie.* It's been a ball torturing Warner.

"It's good to get out of the house sometimes, to live your life like the young woman you are instead of being stuck with your folks in an apartment above a restaurant." He shuffles some papers, but then his smile fades as he looks at me. "How are you really doing, kiddo?"

His calming voice has always been a comfort to me. He just has a way of making me feel safe to be me and say anything I need to get off my chest, to confess secrets and crushes. This isn't something I can share with him. Anthony Bayetti would send me to an early grave if he knew what I was up to. That's why he can't and won't know. He's too proud to ask for help even when he needs it most.

Good thing for him, I have no pride to worry about. There is no low too low for me to go, apparently. I should feel more shame . . . or any at all, but as I look at the lines weighing the corners of my father's eyes, my resolve solidifies. This is all for him. He'll understand when I save the family business.

I stand and shimmy along the wall to get to the other side of the desk. He stands to wrap me in those big dad arms of his and kisses the side of my head. I whisper, "I'm doing good, Dad. No need to worry about me."

"It's my job to worry about you."

When we part, I tap the desk. "It's your job to cook these books." I laugh. "Legally, of course." As I maneuver out of the tight space, I add, "Don't want our family fighting tax evasion charges."

He chuckles as he settles back in his chair. "Bayettis are always on the right side of the law. And if we're not, we'll blame your brother." His chuckle is hearty, though I know he'd never let anything happen to us. When the laughter softens, he asks, "How's the job search going?"

"Crickets." I shrug. "You might be stuck with me at the restaurant forever at this point."

"I can think of worse things. Seeing you every day would be a dream, honey." He's a big guy, old school about stifling his emotions, but sometimes they get the best of him. Inhaling a deep breath through his nose, he appears to suck back whatever he was feeling. "I know you'll get something soon. Hopefully, it will be in the city so we can still see you."

Standing behind the chair, I grip the back of it. "I hope so, too but teaching positions seem to be hard to come by in Manhattan. I've been applying in the boroughs, but I might have to expand my search out to Jersey."

"What's meant to be yours will be."

Silently, I manifest with him, but mine involves a contract being ripped up, and Mr. Landers learning a hard lesson. Not sure if that is possible, but I'll do whatever it takes to make it happen. I laugh while opening the door. "You have such faith in me, Dad."

"Always. I'd bet everything I had on you, Delaney." I know he would. He would for any of his kids.

"Love you."

"Love you, cannoli."

Giggling, I close the door. My smile travels with me as I work my way back to the front of the restaurant and out the door. In the sunshine of the block, I walk to the next door and punch in the code to release it. I don't bother checking the mail, hurrying past and dashing up the stairs. I unlock the door located on the first landing and shoulder check it open. Sometimes it sticks. This time, it didn't, so I stumble inside. I catch myself before landing on my face. "Jesus."

"Language, Delaney." I want to roll my eyes, but if I did that every time she warned us about our choice of words, my eyes would be stuck at the back of my head. "Lorenzo oiled it the other day," my mom says from the kitchen. "But you wouldn't know since you haven't been home in days. How are your adventures away from your family?"

I exhale the exasperation that will be heard in my voice if I don't release it and walk to the other side of the peninsula where she's making cookies. *Uh-oh.* It's almost like she knew I'd stop by and was preparing for her guilt trip. "You make it sound like I'm purposely avoiding you guys." She might not be entirely wrong.

"You're not?"

"No, I'm not." I can't resist her double chocolate cookies, and she knows it. She must really be upset that I've been gone. I reach for a cookie, but a plastic spatula swats my hand. I angle my head. "I can't have one?"

"No. Not until you tell me what's going on with you."

"Nothing is going on with me," I reply, keeping my tone even so I don't raise suspicion, though I think it's safe to say it's already raised as high as it can go. Nothing gets past my mom. "I've just been hanging out with a friend."

A smile and her eyes gleaming in delight are the first warning. She's about to come in for the kill. "Is this a male friend by chance?"

I'm twenty-four. It wouldn't be so out of the ordinary if I had male "friends" as she likes to call them—guys I might be dating versus actual friends who are males. I'm not sure Warner would classify as a male friend or a male "*friend*" of mine. He's just a male. The enemy. "Might be." Might not be, but I really don't want to go into this. "I'm not ready to talk about it just yet, but I promise not to keep you out of the loop forever."

"Forever?" The ends of her bobbed brown hair sweep over her shoulders in reaction. So many of my features came from her—my blue eyes, hair color, even my shorter stature. Growing up in Connecticut, she has her quieter, deep-in-thought moments. Pleasant small talk comes naturally for her and rubbed off on me, though I'm certain Warner would argue otherwise. Sometimes she leans into my dad's Italian side with gestures of love, kisses, and hugs. We're not shy about making our feelings known, and I adore the warmth I feel in this home.

I grin, already cruising to my bedroom. "Not forever. For now. I love you, Mom."

"I love you, Delly."

When I open my bedroom door, particles of dust float in the ray of sunshine streaming in through the window. You would have thought I hadn't been here in months. Two days have already changed things. I even feel different standing here, like the little girl no longer exists.

I'm not really married.

I'm not playing house.

I'm not dating him, and I sure as heck am not in love.

This is ridiculous. It may not be a fully thought-out plan, but it has enough legs to get me going. It's up to me to stay on track. No emotions needed. No feelings should be involved. *Other than detest.* That one I'll allow when it comes to Warner.

I grab a suitcase from under my bed and lay it open on

the mattress. A few things from different drawers get tucked, a couple pairs of flats, and then I stand at my closet, blanking on what I should pack. I shouldn't overthink it. It's a heist of his heart so that I can inject some humanity back into it. "Black, it is." I pull a black sweater, a blue satin tank top that always looks good on a night out, and some fitted pants from the shelf. I tug a red dress from the hanger and neatly fold it on top. After adding a pair of jeans, I give the case a once-over before slipping over to my dresser to grab a body spray. I set it back down when I remember how divine his soaps smell. My spray smells cheap in comparison. I return it, but spot a framed photo of me shoved against the windowsill by books I had to read for class. I grab it and a few other knickknacks and place them on the dress so they don't break.

Dabbing a little makeup on, I don't overdo it, but I do add some color back into my face. Exhaustion has zapped more than my energy and installed dark circles. Nothing a good concealer can't cover. After adding gloss to my lips, I toss it all in with my clothes.

Last order of business—tuck the newly broken phone into the base of the suitcase. Once that's done, I seal her up.

Trying to exit without a scene will be an interesting task. I know as soon as my mom sees the suitcase, I'm going to be given a hard time again. But as luck would have it, she's standing at the bay window on a call. I hug her from behind and kiss her shoulder. "I'll be back in a few days. Text if you need me."

Whispering, she says, "Take a cookie." She nods, but I can tell she's pulled back into the phone conversation. "Mom, I said I'll come out next Friday . . ."

I grab a cookie and the case on my way out. As soon as the door closes, I breathe easier. I don't know why. I'm leaving the safety of my home to re-enter the lion's den. Shoving the cookie in my mouth, I think, *Lord help me.*

It's a quick subway ride down to Tribeca. Not enough time to talk myself out of following through with this plan. *Fully commit*, I remind myself as I walk down two blocks to his building. Just before I reach the door, I stop and slip the ring on again. I wiggle my finger, admiring it before looking up to see Baker already holding the door open for me. "Showtime," I whisper under my breath.

"Need help with the case, *Msss . . .?*"

"Landers. And I got it. Thank you."

I don't hang around to spot his reaction. It will make me too nervous, so I keep walking like I live here and enter the elevator. Punching the button for the penthouse isn't something I ever thought I'd be doing. If I'm busted, this might be the only time, so I savor the thrill it brings.

When I reach his door, I check the time. I've been gone for hours. What am I walking into? His anger again? His frustration? Irritation with me? Only one way to find out.

I steel my nerves and knock loudly. *Annoyingly loud.*

CHAPTER 10

Warner

RELIEF WASHES through me the moment I lay eyes on Delaney again. Another emotion takes over when my gaze dips to the suitcase set at her side. Annoyance? Exasperation? Irritation? A combination of all three, I believe. "Moving in?"

She walks past me, leaving the suitcase behind. I assume for me to retrieve. "Back in."

"Moving back in?" I laugh like she made a joke when I know damn well she didn't. She's as serious as the concussion I have.

"Yes," she calls from the other end of the hall before rounding the corner to the bedrooms.

I grab the suitcase with my good hand because that's what I now have—one good hand and one bad—and lock the door. Trailing in her path, I remark, "Back in because you supposedly moved out two days ago," I say it more for myself like I might believe the words if said out loud.

I didn't even know if she was coming back. She's back

alright. Back to spin me into her tangled web again. I would say of lies, but there's still that minutest chance that she's telling the truth. If she is, I'll be the fool for not knowing my own wife from a stranger on the street. But if my gut instincts are proven correct, there will be hell to pay.

When I reach the spare bedroom, I flick on the light, wondering why she's standing in the dark. "Delaney?"

"In here," she calls from *my* bedroom. Her tone is way too comfortable for someone who's knowingly invading my space. Again.

I set the suitcase down before marching down the hall to my bedroom. "You're not staying in here," I say as soon as I see her curled up on the bed.

Flopping her arms wide, she rolls onto her back. "I must stay in here. I've missed this bed so much." The bed, not me. *Noted.*

"You're not staying here." Thumbing over my shoulder, I glare at her. "The bed in the other room is already made up *for* guests."

She props herself up onto her elbows, those blue eyes shining with the devil inside. "I'm not a guest, dear husband. I'm your wife. If you'd be more comfortable with us sleeping in separate rooms, then the guest room bed is all made up for you to enjoy."

"Listen, Delaney—"

"Oh geez," she huffs, falling flat on her back again. Only her eyes pivot toward me. "Do we have to do this? It's not like sleeping together killed you."

"It almost did when I saw that bagel in the bed."

Her laughter comes easy as if there's no strife between us at all. Rolling to her side, she rests her head on her hand with her elbow punctuating the bed. "That was delicious. Did you eat yours?"

"I saved it for you." I come to the edge of the mattress to grab her by an ankle and pull her closer. Not closer *to me*, but to the edge of my bed. Pulling her off it onto the floor seems a little harsh, even for me. A squeal and a trilling giggle leave her smiling like . . . *like*. . . like she might not hate me. "Do you know how long I spent getting poppy seeds out of the carpet?"

"No, but I'm willing to wager your entire life savings that you're going to tell me."

Wonder if she got credit for snark as a second language. She's damn good at it. "I'm not wagering anything other than you'll be in that bed one way or the other." Fed up, I decide to remove myself from the situation before I burst a blood vessel in my head.

But before I reach the door, she says, "If you're trying to seduce me, Mr. Landers . . ." Her dramatic pause draws me back, connecting our gazes once again. "It's working."

Although she frustrates me like no other woman ever has, she's also fucking gorgeous. The afternoon sunlight filters through the surrounding buildings, kissing the shine on her lips and making me wish I could do the same.

I turn away. With my back to her and my eyes set forward, I refrain from saying something that could be used against me in court. Or that she'll use as ammo for the rest of the night. I leave.

I'm heated, and my head starts pounding. I'm about to be out of the "watch zone" as the instructions they gave Delaney stated. She has repeatedly claimed to be the one there for me, from the hospital to being here in my apartment. So it's not out of the realm to have her here during that time period. But after, she'll have no reason to stay. And since she's not here for the sparkling conversation, my guess is she'll leave.

Hunting again for my phone, I keep thinking I'm missing a piece of the puzzle, the one that tells me what's in it for her. Money? Feels too basic for this woman. Look at her. She could marry some old guy and inherit his net worth without trying so hard.

I'm young, only thirty-four. Healthy. I take care of myself. She'd be in it for the long haul with me. Since she doesn't seem to like me too much, I'm thinking it's not money.

Sex?

Nah. She could get any guy she wants. That is if she can stay hinged long enough to round the bases. After that, she's home free.

I'm checking under the couch cushions when I hear her come into the room behind me. "Can't we both just share the marital bed like we did last night?"

Standing up, I turn to look at her. She's still wearing the leggings like they're pants and not made exclusively to work out in or lounge around the apartment. My Harvard shirt looks incredible on her, but it doesn't change the fact that I have a feeling it'll go missing from my closet for good if I turn away from her for a second.

A flood of pink deepens her cheeks under my gaze. The tip of her tongue dips out to lick her lips, and she shifts, putting more weight on her right than left. Is it possible she really does belong here? If I ignore my own instincts like they don't scream the opposite, I'd say yes. She appears to be at home here and with me.

Holy shit. I'm married.

A quick spell of dizziness has my brain spinning. I sit down on the couch that I didn't have time to put the cushions back in place before I needed a place to land. The realization leaves me lying flat on the couch, eyes closed.

"Are you okay, Warner?"

"I've been better." The sound of her socks sliding against the wood has me peeking my eyes back open. Kneeling beside me, she stares at me like I'm a science experiment gone wrong. She has a real talent for making me feel worse. I close my eyes, needing some space, and since I can't get it in my own apartment, I'll escape mentally.

It's been a long time since I've been on vacation. Digging deeper, I'm not sure I've gone on one since my dad died four years ago. I wince from the feel of her ice-cold fingertips gliding across my forehead. "You're burning up."

I open my eyes to see her just inches away from me. Pushing myself up, I reposition to sitting and then feel my head with the back of my hand. "I don't feel hot. Anything would feel hot to those cold digits. You need some gloves to bundle up in this tested-for-exact-comfort-during-the-day seventy-two degrees?"

Resting back on her heels, she says, "You mock, but I think you should get a professional opinion. Do you have a thermometer?"

"You're my wife, supposedly, and now you're my nurse?" I slip out over the arm of the couch, avoiding her perimeter to retrieve the first-aid kit. She's making me feel like I have no sense of myself anymore. If I have to prove her wrong, I will. *Happily.*

"It actually hurts my feelings when you say things like that, Warner."

It's not her words. Sure, there's a lot of nonsense to weed through the things she says, but there's meaning in some of it, like now. My bullshit detector tilts, throwing off the balance I live my life by—that I'm always right. What if I'm wrong this one time?

I glance over my shoulder to see her still sitting on the floor waiting for me to return like she has nothing better to do. It's that there that fucks with my head. The soft corners of her eyes, the gentle smile that doesn't take over but provides reassurance, and the slope of her shoulders in comfort that she's found here. She looks like she genuinely cares. And belongs.

That's more than I can say for anyone else in my life. Where are they? My mother. Jimmy. I thought for sure my office would have filed a missing person's report by now. Well, even with me emailing, it's still out of the ordinary for me to miss work.

Do I give them the grace of my not having my phone?

Jimmy and I don't talk every day. Would I have noticed if he'd been out of action for a couple of days? Probably not. Should I? Yeah. He's my best friend.

I only see my mother once in a blue moon and at events and the occasional meal if she can squeeze me into her busy schedule. I could be gone for months, and she wouldn't know any better.

But Jocelyn would. I didn't even receive a reply other than "Take care of yourself." Which is nice—I'll give her that—but the lack of emails and contact from her is strange.

Shit . . . unless they all know my wife is taking care of me.

No fucking way. *Is there really no way?*

Turning away, I walk down the hall, scraping my fingers through my hair. In the bathroom, I search the medicine cabinet for antacids to help with the budding distress in my stomach. But I grab the thermometer because I know there's no medicine to help with this affliction. It's time to face Delaney head-on, standing my ground, and with honesty.

I can't live in these conditions any longer. The stress she's causing is worse than the concussion. *Integrity, Landers.* There's no need to hurt her more than she claims she already is.

Walk in there. Tell her the truth. And call a car so she can return to living her own life instead of continuing to flip my world upside down.

Standing on the far side of the room, she doesn't hear me when I enter. Her arms are crossed over her chest, her gaze staring through the window somewhere in the distance, but her mouth is twisted as she gnaws on the inside of her cheek. On second notice, I don't see the light in her eyes like she's high on life when she's looking at me. Concern is more prevalent in her furrowed brow.

This feels invasive, like something she wouldn't want me to see. Real. Raw. Honest. Having seen this side of her reflects on me in guilt. Am I being too harsh? "I'm sorry I hurt your feelings." She angles toward me, a morphing of her body language as if she had momentarily lowered her armor and was caught with her guard down. She's quick to rectify the situation, her shoulders straighter and head held higher. She doesn't say anything, which is surprising, but I do. "I've not been myself the past few days."

"We've not been ourselves in so long." The wistfulness of her tone, the longing in her eyes, and the lowering of her arms, hanging without tension, leave little room for doubt. The release of a deep breath provides some relief, but entertaining the possibility of a past life shared with her lowers my guard around her.

What concerns me more is the fact that I had many opportunities to find the truth, but I chose to ignore those options. Do I need to hear it from her? Why would anything she says hold more weight than the internet, my friends, or even my assistant, Jocelyn? They would know. Granted, I would sound like a fool for asking them.

Hopefully, it won't come to that.

Her usual energy has calmed as she approaches me.

New angle? "Front or back," she asks, taking the thermometer from me.

"What do you mean?"

"Do you want me to take your temp orally or . . ." She
taps her head to the side twice like I'm supposed to understand. "Jesus, Warner." She rolls her eyes as if I'm the one
who took it too far.

"What the fuck? No, I don't want it—" I snatch the thermometer back. "Just give it to me." After shoving it under
my tongue, I cross my arms over my chest and stand my
ground, staring at her. There's so much I want to say that
she's damn lucky I'm currently not allowed to speak.

In challenge, she crosses her arms over her chest again
and stares back at me. Her blue eyes have a fire that blazes
hot, and her lips are pouty and pink, so ripe and ready to be
kissed. The rise and fall of her deepening breaths cause my
eyes to travel lower to see nipples peaking under the
maroon shirt.

My pulse quickens, desire for this pest of a woman a
complete betrayal in my search for truth. But the swanlike
curve of her neck is very tempting to suck enough to leave a
mark on her like she's already left on me.

I shift, letting her win this round of the stare off, so I can
readjust in the sweatpants. When I turn back, she plucks the
thermometer from my mouth and turns to walk away. "Let's
see what's going on with you, Mr. Landers."

Why is hearing her call me that such a fucking turn-on?

I don't have a fever, so why did I even humor her?
"What's the verdict?"

"No fever," she says, smiling. I'm almost convinced that
she is happy for me. *Almost.*

She moves into the kitchen to set the glass stick down.
Guess I'll be washing that since she appears to have no

intention of doing it. I will never understand how someone lives in chaos, much less by choice. Tugging at the hem of my shirt when I move around her, she doesn't release it. "I'm hungry, Warner. Can we go out?"

A change of scenery, that's what I need. Access to other people who know me well enough to know if I'm married. Time to put this matter to bed. "Great idea. I know just the place." I head for the bedroom to change clothes with her hot on my heels. When I suddenly stop, she runs into my back. I turn to catch her rubbing her nose.

"Give a girl some warning next time."

Inhale. *Exhale.* Inhale. *Exhale.*

"I meant to ask you."

"What?" she asks, hanging on my every erratic breath. "What did you want to ask me?"

"Have you seen my phone?"

CHAPTER 11

Warner

"YOU COULD ENTER FOOD-EATING COMPETITIONS." I'm still in awe after watching Delaney devour that cheeseburger. I've never seen a woman eat a burger that fast. Must be the brother-stealing issue again. It's unnerving and making me feel rushed. "Unless it's fuel, food really should be enjoyed."

She laughs, her gaze returning from outside the window to me sitting across from her at a dive bar around the corner from my office that always serves a good burger and cold beer. "This is fuel. Other than the bagel early this morning, I've only had a cookie. I was starving, and it was a really good burger." I'm not drinking while on meds, but she's washing her food down with a lager. When she sets the pint glass down on the table, she rubs her stomach. "I wish I had stayed in the leggings, though. These jeans have no give. Ugh."

"Where did you get the cookie?"

Despite the complaints about tight denim that I did

notice look damn good on her, she picks up a wedge fry and taps her bottom lip with it. "A baker I know."

I was never told where she went during the hours she was gone, and I didn't feel it was my place to ask, especially after how we left things. When she returned, she never seemed mad, though I had been brusque with her during the earlier conversation. She came back and acted like it never happened. So I'm curious where she went to pick up her suitcase and which bakery she got this cookie from. I'd like any information I can get about her, since I've not been given much, and I'm not sure I can trust what I've been told. "I like cookies. What kind?"

"Double chocolate, but I took you more for a brownie man."

"Why is that?"

She shrugs, glancing at a couple who passes by the window. "They're soft. Doughy. Cakey. You know what I mean." Dropping that bomb of an insult must have made her hungry because she's suddenly super focused on her fries and shoving as many as she can in her mouth while laughing to herself.

Doughy? Soft? Fuck me, she's brutal. I need to breathe through the anger, but every time I do, she lobs something else my way. "You should come with a trigger warning."

"Oh yeah?" Why does she look genuinely intrigued by my comment? She chews her food and downs more beer like she's at a kegger. "Why is that?"

"You have an innate sense for how to find my buttons and jab them repeatedly until you set me off."

"This may be hard to believe, Warner, but I'm not trying to set you off. I'm trying to—"

"Another beer?" Our server has great timing.

I'm not amused. I wanted to hear her response. I reply, "No," just as Delaney says, "Yes, please."

The server's eyes volley between us, and I can tell by the worry in her expression that she is silently begging one of us to put her out of her misery. Delaney reaches across the table to rest her hand on mine. Giving it a little squeeze, she angles her head toward the server and grins. "My husband says I can't have another."

She plays dirty.

"I didn't say you can't have one."

The server replies, "You did say no."

"I'm not her boss." *Fuck.* Guess I'll never be able to show my face around here again.

"Or CEO," Delaney adds with a shrug and waggles her ring finger. "Just my dearly beloved."

When my eyes lock on the diamond sparkling on her hand, she conveniently keeps her focus on the young server. "She'll take another," I say. "I'll take the check. Thank you." My gut twists, my world once again flipped like a pancake carelessly in the air. I don't say a word until we're alone and Delaney's eyes meet mine again. "That's new."

"Not really." If I didn't know her wicked ways, I would mistake it as a symbol of our love by how she admires it on her finger.

"What made you start wearing it again?"

"I only stopped two days ago."

Okay, I'll bite . . . Looking at my hand, I ask, "Do you know where my ring is?"

Annoyance conspires her eyes to narrow on my bare finger. When her glare hits me, she asks, "Where *is* your ring? Couldn't wait to be the most eligible bachelor around town again?"

"Again, that would imply I was doing it prior. I've never

participated in those rankings. As my wife, you'd know that."

"I know you were asked. Should I pull up the evidence?"

"Why does this sound eerily like we're picking up where we left off in an unfinished argument?"

The beer arrives. The girl's sadness, or sympathy, or whatever she and Delaney are silently exchanging through a shared look of understanding, makes me want to get up and leave. I take my wallet out of my pocket, and though it takes longer than I'd like to wrangle it open with the hand of my broken arm while my other pulls the bills out, I finally manage. Placing three large bills down on the tray, I've lost inspiration to be out of the penthouse. "Drink up, sweetheart. I'm not hanging around to fend off dirty looks from the staff."

"What's wrong?" Delaney's eyebrow is arched as she brings the glass to her lips.

Leaning in, I glance around to make sure no one is listening. "You made me sound like a controlling monster."

"If you don't want to be perceived as controlling, then you shouldn't try to control everything in your life and mine." I push back from the table. "Warner?" she calls as I walk away.

I don't know where the day has gone, but evening has already begun to set in, with the sun being blocked by buildings when I push out through the exit. I look both ways before heading west.

"Warner? Wait." The distance grows between her voice and my footsteps.

My pace stays as controlled as I apparently am. And steady but she probably considers that a bad trait, so I'll keep that to myself. I stop at the corner because, call me paranoid, but I hesitate now before crossing the street. Being hit by a car will do that to a person.

"Warner? Come on."

I wait with others for the signal to go, and long enough for my personal nut-ball to catch up with me. I must have been a really bad person in a past life to pay for it like I am in this life. Karma has a name. I just didn't know it until I met Delaney.

"I'm sorry," she says, pressing against my side.

I finally look at her. "Why are you doing this, Delaney?"

"Doing what?" She comes around to stand in front of me while everyone else is crossing. "Trying to care for you? You always made it so difficult." Throwing her arms out wide, she says, "You act like it's a crime." Turning on her heel, she storms forward.

I hear the car before I have time to look.

Grabbing Delaney, I wrap my left arm around her as I use my casted arm to pull her against me in a rush and ending in a thud. Her scream was silent but ripped the air from her lungs. My breath is ragged, but I hold her tightly to me and maneuver out of the crosswalk.

Against the busy path of the sidewalk, I lean my shoulder against a brick wall. Closing my eyes, I drop my head to the top of hers as the reality of what almost happened sets in. "Are you okay?" I whisper while the scent of my shampoo, *of me*, fragrances her hair.

With her body melding to mine, she turns in my arms, keeping her head tucked to my chest. "No." Only the one word is said, but as her shoulders rattle with a quiet sniffle, I realize her emotions are laid bare.

The carefree spirit of this woman I hardly know has been shaken. That's how fast our security can be ripped away. One step too late and our lives are forever changed.

Like now. I've become desperate to console her, so I slow my breath to assuage my racing pulse because I'm no good to her if I can't calm her fears. "It's okay. You're okay."

She nods her head and then looks up at me. "You saved me, Warner."

The praise feels unearned somehow. "I wouldn't go that far."

Taking a step, she slips from my arms to lean her back against the brick wall. Her breathing is still unregulated, but her emotions have quelled. When she looks over at me, her smile seems to come naturally. "Seems I'm in your debt."

"Don't worry," I say, chuckling. "I won't hold it over you." This, whatever *this* is we're doing, feels too good to be real. No tension. No distrust. No questioning what we are or aren't. We're just two people sharing a laugh.

I know that's not all it is, but at this moment, it feels too good to mess it up with wild accusations. I'm tired of the back-and-forth. The woman's wearing a ring on her finger, for Pete's sake. What kind of lunatic would go to those lengths to trick me into believing I'm married? No one. Nobody would do that. What would there be to gain? I would never marry without a prenup in place.

Oh shit. A prenup.

That's it!

I need to call my attorney.

I reach for my pocket, but I still don't have a phone. She helped me look for it, but neither of us found it. *Still.* So fucking annoying. Since we're only a block from my office, I nod to signal to go. She joins my side as we walk down the sidewalk away from the crosswalk. In the shadows of the buildings, it's cooler with some wind gusting past us. She wraps her arms around herself and then says, "Thank you."

"For what?"

With a laugh and a shoulder nudge to my arm, she says, "You know what. For saving me back there."

"We don't have to put that much weight on it. Anyone would have done the same."

"Not true." Her smile falls as her gaze redirects ahead. "Some would stand there and debate for a good solid minute if I were worth saving and then worry that they made things worse by waiting too long to help."

I stop on the sidewalk, watching her walk ahead. "What?"

She glances back and then stops. It appears to take all her effort to reorganize her expression to make a smile reappear. She blinks twice and then replies, "Just saying what could have happened, not that it did. You grabbed me before I made a fatal mistake. My point is that not everyone would have helped." Raising her arm out of upset, she continues, "Most people would rather stand around and film someone than help." Her stance relaxes as her grin returns. "But not you. You jumped in to save me without thinking." Walking back to me, she gets so close to me that I must look down to see her eyes. With her hands placed on my chest with care, she swallows. Even on the loud streets of Manhattan, it's heard, but I don't point it out, refusing to embarrass her. "I didn't think there was any hope that you were inherently good beneath that asshole exterior. I'm so glad to be wrong."

Not sure what to say to that, I reply, "Thank you. I guess."

We start to stroll again. This time, our pace is a little slower, the company not as maddening as usual. We round the corner and walk to the middle of the block, stop in front of the doors, and then look at each other. She asks, "Why did you bring me to your office?"

A subtle ribbon of offense passes through her words. "I need to check on something."

"What?"

She's starting to sound like a wife. My father told me to never marry. Not to keep me from a broken heart but to save me from being nagged. My mother barely spoke to him, so I always wondered if he was referring to a girlfriend he had on the side. I spent years studying couples I was around to understand what marriage is supposed to be like, versus the version I was shown. What I found was the same wherever I would go.

Happiness isn't found in a piece of legal paperwork.

I don't know where it's found, actually, but her questioning me like I owe her an answer strikes a familiar nerve, making me hear my dad in my head again. Walls I didn't know I had lowered start to rise as I level my eyes on her. "It's none of your business, Delaney."

Stepping away from her, I open the door and enter the lobby. The guard behind the counter isn't someone I've seen before. I walk up to the desk already pulling out my wallet. "I'm Warner Landers."

He swivels in his chair back and forth, then crosses his arms over his chest. "And?"

Okay. "See that lettering on the marble behind you. The one that says Landers Ventures? I'm the Landers in that title."

"Oh." Standing like I ordered him to, he scrambles to grab his hat from the desk and put it on his head. "Sorry, sir. How can I help you?"

"I need a key card to my office. I left home without mine." I hold out my ID for him to inspect. I don't do it because he asked, which he should have. I do it because it's protocol, and I always follow the rules.

I balance my wallet against my cast on the counter and shove the ID back into it with my left hand. Once it's securely back in my pocket, I take the key card he set down on the counter and say, "Thanks."

I expect to see Delaney waiting nearby, but when I turn back, she's nowhere to be seen, not even outside where I left her. She probably wants me to chase her, but I'm finally in a place where I can get answers. I take a step toward the door, but I stop myself from going any farther.

She's kept me from finding out the truth at every turn. I'm not even convinced that my phone walked off by itself, like she claims. She seems to thrive when I'm embarrassed and is always orbiting me like she's the rings to my Saturn.

The elevator dinging on arrival is a stronger pull, and I jog to catch it just before the doors close again. As soon as I punch the button and the doors close, I feel bad, worse for leaving her behind, and not looking for her at all.

I'm not her sitter, just like she's not my handler. This strange relationship needs to be defined. The truth be told, we need to work from a factual starting point. And there's only one way for that to happen.

The doors slide open, and I step out into the waiting room of Landers Ventures. I tap the universal key card to open the next door and work my way through a mostly empty office to mine on the far side of the open concept room. It is worth noting that a few workers are still scattered around; a bonus will be given in the near future. I can be a hard-ass in business, but staying after hours and putting in the extra effort is the way to my heart.

If she were here, I'm sure Delaney would be more than happy to point out that my chest is hollow of any major organ or emotions. A few days ago, I would have quickly agreed. Now, I'm not as certain. I sure have been feeling a lot of everything when I'm with her.

I look back as if I'll suddenly see her coming through the door when I know that's impossible. She'd never be given a key. She already made her choice earlier. She did what was best for her. I'm going to do the same.

Opening my office door, I flip on the light and rush to my desk to pull up the contacts on my computer. As soon as I find the number, I pick up the interoffice intercom phone on my desk and call my attorney.

"Warner, to what do I owe the pleasure?" he asks, his jovial nature, which I've always found strange for a lawyer to have, booming through the speakerphone.

I sit in my chair and lean back to avoid the blasting of his voice. "Thanks for answering."

"Anytime. I'm always here for you." He chuckles. "That's why you paid that big retainer fee."

Not finding the same humor in his so-called joke, I say, "I didn't forget. Hey, Richard, I have a question for you." All I'm doing is seeking the truth. So why do I feel like I'm betraying Delaney?

The pause extends as I debate whether to hang up or push forward.

"Warner? You still there?"

"I'm still here, yeah," I start again. "I know this sounds unlike me or anyone since this is something a person would know. Ignore that. I'm not going into details at this juncture."

"Intriguing."

"I called because I need to know if I have a prenup in place."

This time, the pause is on his end. My heart rate picks up as I wait silently, impatient for his reply.

He says, "As in active?"

I sit forward. "Yes."

"Did you get married and not tell me?"

I stare at the phone as if I were staring at Delaney. Confused. Deceived. Conned. Stupid. I swallow down the last speck of pride I was holding on to and say, "Thank you, Richard. That's all I needed to know."

"Okay. Anytime. Have a good one."

"You, too," I mumble, standing and walking to the window. I used to love this view, but I'd grown tired of it more recently, tired of everything in my life. It's been gray buildings and little sunshine since I moved into my father's office.

It's gone dark outside, but I finally see the light.

I don't know who this Delaney Landers is or why she's pretending to be my wife, but it's time to flip the script and find out the truth.

I turn off the light and head back out. There are so many ways to handle this, but one thing keeps playing on repeat in my head. *Let the games begin . . .*

CHAPTER 12

Delaney

WARNER LYING ON THE STREET.

A crowd gathering and blocking my view.

The shock of watching a car hit him like he wasn't a human.

The guilt. The debate. The disappointment. The race to save him.

The memory plays out like a movie in my head, causing my hands to shake. The panic I felt, the concern, the weight of prayers I laid on that man in hopes of his survival wash through me like a tidal wave.

As memories spiral, a shiver runs down my spine. Cool air hits my neck moments before I come back to the present. *Someone is touching me.* My hair is stroked to the side just as lips find my neck, and I shriek.

"Hey—Argh!" My elbow is still attached to his gut when I realize it's Warner. "I think I'm going to puke." He's bent over heaving with his broken arm held against his stomach.

"Fuck, Delaney. You punched the air out of my lungs. I can't breathe."

"Sounds like you're doing just fine by all the yapping." I pat him on the back and leave my hand there. "Anyway, I don't know what world you live in, but don't sneak up behind a woman on the streets of New York and accost her."

He straightens up as much as he can, which still leaves him slightly hunched forward. "I wasn't sneaking up."

Moving in front of him, I look him over just in case I really did some damage. Other than him being red in the face, whether from the blow or his anger, I think he's good. "Well, whatever you thought was a good idea wasn't. Good news, though, you're going to live, Warner. As long as you don't try that again."

"I was kissing my wife," he groans. "Trust me, I won't make that mistake again."

The words run through my veins like the smoothest of wines in the Italian countryside, warm like a cozy fire after coming home from a wintry day, or the softest sheets wrapped around me while sleeping in Warner's bed.

"Delaney, hello?" He waves his big paw in front of my face. "Delaney? You still with us?"

"No, I slipped away," I snark, and turn from him, too afraid to meet his eyes and have the bubble burst, leaving me back in a reality of lies. I much prefer this version. Under this guise, it's more idyllic and less venomous. I turn back to see if the world has come to an end or if we're still in the middle of a sham. The warmth of his eyes holds less ire and more . . . *consideration*? "Humanity looks good on you, Landers."

Damn it. I even find the line between his furrowed brows attractive. I must be coming down with something. All this just because he called me his wife?

I knew this plan was ridiculous and most likely wouldn't work, but I didn't think I'd react as ludicrously to him. He's a man. A guy. *That's it.* Who cares if the soulful blue of his eyes lures me in every time he stares at me like he wants to either kiss me or kill me? It might be both. Either way, he looks good.

And I'm not going to even mention those hands of his as I stare at them now. Big, ready to hold more than a handful of my smallish frame. I could perch like a parrot from that palm of his and be perfectly content.

"What are we talking about?" His voice throws a wrench in the cog of my thoughts. "Delaney?" He snaps his fingers in front of him, the sound pulling my attention back to him. "Disappeared again? Am I going to have to tie you down?"

"Shh. Let's not ruin it." I flip my hair over my shoulders, wishing I hadn't lent him my only hair elastic. I never got it back. My mom always says nothing is ever a loan. Just gift it and be done with it. I never understood what she meant until now. "What . . . what do you mean by tie me down?"

"So you don't float away from me again."

First, I'm his wife that he wanted to kiss. Now, he wants to tie me to him? Though the image of him tying me down to his heaven of a bed isn't his worst idea. Or was that my idea? Either way, there's tying between us.

What the heck is going on?

He went up to his office, where I knew for sure I'd be busted as some woman with a vendetta impersonating a wife he never had. But that's not how it played out. Whatever happened in that building is working in my favor. Thank the Patron Saint of Suggestio Falsi for saving my behind and keeping the plan on track.

Warner Landers's charming ways would typically have me eating up the sweet nothings. It's Warner, though, so my guard goes up instantly. Am I losing control of the situation? Falling prey to a hot guy? Again? It's not the first time I've made the mistake of crossing lines with someone who didn't deserve my time.

This is a stark reminder that he's the man who is callously stripping away not only my family's livelihood but also our home. That makes my stomach twist into knots. It's almost easier to put the emphasis on the restaurant than the home my family has lived in well before I was born. Tears will come if I give it even a minute of my time. *Don't think about it, Delaney.*

I exhale and fix my disposition. A new Warner means fresh opportunities to make his life hell before he drags down mine and my family's. I smile at him, but can tell it's too big, and probably too telling of my intentions, judging by how he takes a step back. I'm tired of being on, so I release that energy and try to relax. "Hey?"

He comes closer and we start strolling. I'm glad to leave that situation behind and to be moving forward. Literally and figuratively. "Hey." He bumps his arm against mine. If I'm not mistaken, he's almost playful. Oh, he's good. "Are you thinking what I'm thinking?"

"Let's find out." I stop again to use my hands. Holding three fingers out, I say, "Spill it on the count of three. Three. Two. One—"

"Gelato."

"Ice cream." My mouth falls open. "Wow, we *were* thinking about the same thing."

"Almost," he replies, walking down the sidewalk from me.

I jog to catch up. "Almost is accurate. Ice cream is far superior to gelato."

"No."

Stopping at the corner, I glare at him. "What do you mean, no?"

He shrugs, but his gaze narrows. It's subtle, but I think his breathing has quickened when I see his chest moving. The flex of his fingers and the lick of his lips don't deter him from staring at the crosswalk signal like his life depends on it.

Oh.

Swiping the back of his hand across his forehead, he opens his mouth to take in air as if he wasn't getting enough. I'm no expert, but I think he's close to having a panic attack. That would make sense. Here we are in the vicinity of where it happened. No doubt he's lucky to be alive with only minor injuries, considering what could have been horrific on another level.

I'll probably hate myself for doing this, but right now, I don't matter. *He does.* Looking between us, I slip my hand in his and tighten my hold on him. His gaze stays forward, but his fingers curl around mine as if this is something we regularly do. When the signal changes and the others around us take off, I move close to him, and whisper, "We can cross together."

There's no response, not verbally anyway, but he holds my hand across the two lanes. Although I expect him to drop my hand like a hot potato at any moment, he doesn't. Warner's grip tightens with no intention of letting go, as if I'm his to hold. My mouth goes dry as I attempt to swallow and fail. I clear my throat, hoping it helps my mind. It's not my mind I'm most worried about. It's another stupid organ in my chest.

And when his breathing evens out again and color returns to his face, he says, "Ice cream is not superior." Picking up as if there was never a lapse in conversation. The transition was abrupt, but for his ego, I won't bring up what just happened. Seems he prefers it that way. "I can appreciate the creaminess. It's heavy, though. Gelato is lighter but packed with flavor. You don't need syrup or cherries—"

"No whipped cream or bananas?" My head is still stuck on the fact that he's holding my hand. Willingly. I glance down just to see the connection firsthand again.

Chuckling, he connects his gaze with mine for the first time since we crossed. Life has returned to his eyes, a playful mischievousness, but only for the quickest moment in time before he returns his focus ahead of us. "Not needed."

"Speak for yourself. Don't you just love popping that cherry?" His feet stop suddenly, causing my body to yank in protest because I foolishly kept walking without noticing the change in pace. I steady my footing, angling to look up at him. "What?"

"You can't say things like that and expect me not to react."

"Say what?" Rewinding through the immediate conversation, I laugh. "The cherry thing? I didn't even think of it that way, ya dirty bird."

"I'm the dirty bird?" He manages his broken arm against his chest as if my insinuation inspired the move. But it's not that side effect that has my chest feeling tight. It's that he forfeited using his "good" hand in lieu of holding my hand. He's chuckling. "I'm not the one going around talking about popping cherries. You are with your wide blue eyes and those lips that look dipped in juice."

"Juice?"

"Cherry juice."

"Oh." And although I have so many follow-up questions to that statement, we're not those people. We're enemies who have laid down our weapons for a little while, and this hand-holding business has muddled my emotions. "It's a new lip stain I bought at the drugstore earlier this week. Glad it's working."

"It's working alright."

I hold tight to the thoughts busying my mind, the ones that are sending my heart to beat into overdrive. I swallow them down to protect myself. Maybe it's the conversation or the warmth of his hand or the good time this has turned into, but if I'm not careful, I might fall for this man. Even if he is getting easier on the eyes as time passes, I can't let it happen. Not when I know the real circumstances of our relationship.

Keeping my head on straight, my heart in check, and him in the dark is best. I slip my hand out of his as easily as I had placed it there. He carries on like it makes no difference at all to him, rambling on about something to do with density in creams and how gelato is made in some special way. It's dumb that I've put myself in a position of being vulnerable to him. I'm probably just tired and out of sorts from the chaotic few days we've lived.

"Where did you say this place was?"

With a glance over at me, he grins. "I didn't. I know a place nearby, though."

I desperately need this distraction. My head is doing me in when he's not already affecting me. To get out of my brain altogether, I hold my fingers to my mouth and send a chef's kiss. "I need a little something for my sweet tooth."

"You have a sweet tooth?"

"Kind of. It's more for desserts at night than candy during the day."

I hear his hum before he mutters under his breath, "Fascinating."

Not worrying about his views on anything to do with

me, and more focused back on why he's suddenly treating me like his wife, I should move this along. "Why does it feel so late?"

Checking his watch, he replies, "Eight fifteen."

"Would you be mad if we skipped this trip and headed back to the apartment?"

"Why would I be mad?"

I shrug. "I don't know. You wanted gelato?"

"I can have gelato waiting for us before we get back home." *Home* rolls off his tongue so effortlessly that goosebumps cover my arms in response. "I'll need to borrow your phone, though. Mine is still mysteriously missing."

Pulling my phone from my purse, I hand it to him. He only has it long enough to make a quick call and hand it back to me. But it's enough time for my heart to squeeze from this turn in the relationship, the way I feel safe in his company while still quietly reveling in the use of the word home like it represents both of us.

When he's finished, he steps to the curb, looking both ways. When his arm goes into the air, I realize it's a getaway. But not from me. *With me.* To go "home" together.

I had already planned to stay the night, and after the way goose bumps covered my skin from just a brush of his lips against my neck, I can't say I'm opposed to more. But Warner is making me think that gelato is code for a trap, especially when a cab pulls to the curb and he's quick to open the door for me. It was one thing when I was leading this charge, but under his command, what situation am I getting myself into?

CHAPTER 13

Warner

THE CAB next to ours lays on its horn. It's the first sound in six blocks, and I'm coming out of my skin. It isn't like Delaney to sit quietly. At least not the version of her I know so far. But it doesn't take a genius to know when she's quiet that she's either devising her next step to torture me more or something else has briefly stolen her attention.

Maybe I'm finally getting to her, closer to cracking her chaotic outer shell or throwing in the towel and ending this ridiculousness she's caught us in. I'm surprised the silent treatment is working. I've never fallen for it before. Never been worried enough to entertain such a petulant act. Refusing to indulge her anymore, I ask, "What's on your mind?"

Do I think she'll tell me the truth? She might. I don't think every word out of her mouth is a lie. I just don't know how to decipher between her lies and the truth. *Yet.* She's harder to read than most, which I suppose is on purpose since, so far, I've not seen the real Delaney.

With a great outer package, a clever mind, and whip-smart mouth, I'm curious if there's a side of her that isn't *on* all the time. She replies, "You really want to know, Warner?"

"I really want to know, Delaney." I crack a grin and dare to slide my hand over and loop my little finger over hers.

She glances down at the connection but doesn't move away. "A lot happened today." I want to fill the void when she pauses, but I don't because I want to know what she thinks about, what upsets her, and makes her happy.

Shit, I care?

My chest tightens, so I reach up before remembering my arm is broken. I use my exposed fingers to massage the knot that's forming inside me, hoping to make it disappear.

Caring is an impossibility. It's only been two days. That would be illogical. I always keep my feelings in check. That's not going to change just because her bottom lip shines, drawing my gaze every time I look at her, or the way she wears a pair of jeans. I like how the denim hugs her hips. I can admire her appearance without letting my feelings loose to roam. That's how caring happens. Did I just mentally travel a loop to end up where I started? Damn, she's rubbing off on me.

She says, "You saved me and then. . ." Her gaze moves through the windshield and distances. "You were." A shake of her head casts her eyes down to her lap. "It was a lot today. My emotions are sort of tattered at the moment. I'll be fine, but slowing down has given my mind too much time to process what happened."

"Seems we're even."

I catch the start of a smile despite a lackluster effort to restrain it. When she looks over at me in the back of the cab, she laughs. It's light but feels freeing, the sound even working on me. "Seems we are." Pointing at me, she adds, "Just this one time, though."

"I agree. I can't wait to have you owing me."

Laughter trickles off as her eyebrow arches. "What would I possibly owe you for?"

"I don't know, but I'm sure I can find something to hold over your head. I mean . . . it wouldn't be hard. You're not much bigger than a kitten."

"Wow, not even a full-grown cat, huh?"

My lips tighten while shaking my head. "I'm afraid not, but that's for you to take up with your parents." New ammunition is locked and loaded, ready to fire. *And go!* "How are they by the way? It's been too long since we've met them for dinner."

Horror steals the lightheartedness of the conversation as she briefly looks away from me. When she turns back, the way her bottom lip quivers causes my stomach to drop. "That's not funny. Don't joke about my dead dad. He's off-limits."

"Oh shit, I'm sorry, Delaney. I don't know what I was thinking." *Fuck me.*

Her forehead is furrowed, but she says, "We'll blame it on the concussion since you have a touch of amnesia. Though I'd say more than a touch, considering you gave the eulogy."

What do I say to that? I'm lying out my ass, but this is taking it too far. "Hey," I say, my voice lower to match the somberness overtaking the car. "Are you okay? I'm sorry. I really am."

"You should be." She bursts out laughing. Reaching over, her hand lands on my leg, and she pats me, "My dad is alive and well. You really do have amnesia. I wasn't sure, but dang, you fell right into that trap."

Now I'm really left speechless. She's no amateur. I need to up my game.

"I haven't forgotten everything."

If sweating bullets were a real thing, she'd be a prime example. "Have you started to remember?"

"Yes." Inserting a pregnant pause gives me time to study her reaction. If I didn't know she was fucking around with me, I would consider this a major asshole move. She wipes across her forehead with the back of her hand. Fine. I'll put her out of her misery. "Only flashes here or there. For some reason, your friend popped into my head. The blonde." Or I'll drag this out a little longer. "What's her name again?"

"Juniper?" A gulp practically swallows the end of the name. She tucks her hair behind her ear and glances past me through the window as if tracking her place in the city for her escape.

I have no fucking idea what her friend's name is, but I snap my fingers. "That's it." It's the look we exchange in the lowlight of the back seat that puts us on a level playing field. This is the first time she's been backed into a corner. Hope she recognizes the sound of triumph. Because it's coming. "Anyway, I didn't get much else."

"That's too bad. Oh look," she says just as the car pulls to the curb, "we're home." I glance out the window, giving her the distraction she desperately needs.

"Time flew by."

"Yep. Here we are." I pop the door open and step out. She slips her hand in mine when I hold it out for her. The relief on her face has me grinning. I don't think I've smiled this much in a long time. Even if it is with malicious intent, it feels like winning, and that's my favorite thing to do. That and closing deals. When she's steady on the sidewalk, we're face to well, my chest, but I tilt my head to the side to get a good look into those pretty eyes of hers.

The building tension inside the taxi has disappeared. "Here we are, home again," she says with a spark of light shining in her eyes like she got away with something. It's quite the accomplishment to gain the upper hand after we were tied just minutes before. I'll take the credit and do a victory lap, mentally patting myself on the back.

A doorman rushes from the other side to open the door for us. "Good evening."

"Good evening," I reply. "Was a package delivered for the penthouse? Landers."

Grinning like he's happy to have company, he says, "Yes, sir. Not five minutes ago." He jogs around the counter and sets a small cooler on it.

Delaney shoots me a look, though her widened eyes give away that she might be impressed. "Having a party, Landers?"

"Party for two." I tap her on the nose, leaving her speechless, and turn back to the doorman. "We haven't met. I'm Warner Landers." I hold out my hand, which he shakes with vigor.

Grinning ear to ear, he replies, "Robert, but you can call me Rob."

"It's nice to meet you." Angling to my side, I add, "This is my wife, Delaney." I grin as soon as she starts choking on her saliva. Rubbing her back, I lean in and whisper, "Are you okay, honey?"

Her breathing is as rapid as her blinks. "Fine." She clears her throat. "All good." Redirecting her eyes to Robert, she says, "It's nice to meet you." She's not much louder than a mouse, but her smile could knock any man on his ass.

Fortunately, she's not dealing with any guy. She's dealing with me, and since she came to play, I'll play.

"You, too." Rob says, "Let me know if you ever need anything."

"We will," I say, taking the cooler by the small handle. It's disconcerting how easy it is to fall into the pattern of marriage with Delaney. At least to the outside world. Holding out my broken arm, she latches onto it, and we walk onto a waiting elevator.

As soon as the door closes, she flies across the small space, gripping the railing behind her as if she's holding on for dear life. Releasing one hand, she gestures to my face with two fingers aimed like darting her eyes on the targets of mine. "What are you doing, Warner?"

"What do you mean?" I ask, tossing gullibility into my tone for kicks since that's what she considers me. I'm surprised the elevator can hold such an epic eye roll. I don't bother to contain my laughter.

Annoyance narrows her eyes before she glances up at the floor indicator. "This is my wife," she mocks, her voice transformed into a silly version of her own. "I'm Mr. CEO who can have anything I want at any hour."

"Not *any*thing," I correct.

"What can't you have? Name one thing that you can't afford to have delivered to your door at any hour."

"You." There's no teasing in my tone and no smugness in my expression. I start to question if I just answered honestly.

She parts her lips, and her chest rises in response. Glancing down at her shoes, she twists her ankles to the side and then stands upright again. There's a softness to the outer corners of her eyes, easing the tension she was gripping in her shoulders. "You had me."

"And lost you." My breathing deepens without permission, the lie digging into my chest and wrapping around that knot again. "You're here. You've been with me since the hospital, barely leaving my side. Are you staying?"

The elevator dings, alerting us to our floor and breaking the spell I was falling under. Method acting is intense. When the doors slide open, she gets off quietly. Our bubble has been invaded by the outside world. We walk, but neither of us breaks the silence.

When she reaches the door, she waits for me without so much as a glance back. I stand behind her, staring at the top of her head. She asks, "Are you going to unlock it?"

"I thought you had a key?"

"I . . . um," she stammers, keeping her eyes locked on the door. Avoiding me, I suspect. "Just use yours. It's handier."

Not really since my right hand can't fit into my pocket these days. "The key is in that pocket. Do you mind getting it?"

She shoots a look over her shoulder, slowly turning around as her eyes travel down my body. After blinking a few times and what appears to be debating with herself, which includes a little mumbling under her breath, she reaches forward and dips her hand into my pocket.

The tips of her nails scrape through the thin fabric of the pocket against my leg. I shouldn't have tempted fate. I resituate so she doesn't have an encounter that she didn't expect, but shifting doesn't get the job done. The moment she touches my dick, her gaze jets to mine as she rips her hand from the pocket.

I could apologize, but I consider it a hazard of the job. The woman is sometimes unhinged, but she's still hot as fuck. More so since spending time with her today and getting to know her a little better. Who knows, it could have all been fake. She's a good actress, if it is. If it wasn't, I bet we wouldn't be at odds if I knew the truth of what she's up to.

She says, "I think you should get the key." I set the cooler down and dig into my left pocket. "Hey! You said it was on your right side!"

"Did I? I guess I mixed them up." Pulling out the key, I say, "Voilà." I unlock the door and open it for her. Holding it with my foot, she marches in, shaking her head, which tells me I'm winning this battle. I grab the cooler and follow her inside.

Detouring toward the bedroom, she says, "Good night."

"Wait, where are you going? We have gelato, like lots of gelato."

She stops and turns, her head dropping to the side as her energy depletes through her shoulders. "As tempting as that is, I'm so tired."

"It's barely nine."

"Early to bed. Early to rise." She starts walking down the hall again, her steps echoing through the penthouse.

I set the cooler on the counter. "You won't even stay up to keep me company?"

"I really am tired, Warner. Maybe tomorrow night."

I decide to push a button to see what happens. "What if you're not here? We should make the most of the night we have."

Her feet stop, but I'm still only given her back to stare at. When she turns back this time, she asks, "Why wouldn't I be here tomorrow?"

Casually throwing my arm out to the side, I reply, "You left me, Delaney. I'm on the mend. I don't even need meds tonight. I appreciate that you stayed, but I'm out of the zone they were concerned about regarding the concussion tomorrow. So why would you stick around?"

If I had blinked, I would have missed her mask slipping. It's back in place before I have time to process if I saw something real. She smiles and I instantly know it's in opposition of the person accidentally revealed, even if it only lasted a split second. The smile is pretty and could pass for most, but I know it's not real, not compared to what I just saw. She says, "What if I made a mistake?"

"Mistake in leaving me? I can't answer that, Delaney. Only you can."

With a nod, an unexplainable understanding passes between us before she enters the bedroom. The air left in her wake isn't heavy. It's light as if hope has entered the conversation.

What the fuck are you talking about, Landers?

She's a con artist. This elaborate scheme leaves me no choice but to play along. What's the con, though? "Do you want me to keep you company in bed?" I call out as I unpack the containers of gelato and put them in the freezer.

Poking her head out, she says, "I can't keep you out of our bed."

I rest my left hand on the counter, staring at her with my mind going to places it probably shouldn't. "Is that an invitation?" Too late.

I win a smile out of her. "You wish."

"I actually do wish."

Rolling her eyes, she disappears with a laugh back into the bedroom.

I pause for a moment too long, watching the empty doorway as if she'll reappear. Shaking my head, I turn and pull a glass from the cabinet, ready to fill it with water. It occurs to me that I could drink something stronger since I'm not taking any more pain medication. The occasion certainly calls for it. *The occasion referring to Delaney.*

Pulling a bottle of bourbon from the bar set up in the dining area, I fill the glass halfway before taking a sip and then topping what's missing back up.

Delaney?

Delaney...

Is that even her real name?

With no other sound to disrupt, irritation rushes through me. I'm sure as fuck that Landers isn't her last name despite her claim to it. Like the bed she's about to tuck herself into. How is she so fucking good at this?

I need to get invested. 100 percent. The situation, a.k.a. Delaney, should be monitored at all times. But first, I take a gulp of the amber liquid. The bourbon goes down smooth, tempting me to take another drink. I don't need liquid courage to handle her, but one more gulp won't hurt.

With the glass in hand, I head down the hall.

It's not been ten minutes, but I walk into a scene of seduction. A candle flickers on the nightstand, and something exotic fragrances the air. The lights are dim, but she's tucked in a book like she can read in the dark. Or at least giving it her best effort.

I reach the doorway a moment before she knows I'm here. My Harvard shirt has been replaced by a thin top with spaghetti-like straps, and her nipples are pertly at attention. Delaney is downright sexy, sitting in my bed and looking like she belongs. When she looks at me, she asks, "What are you doing?"

"What does it look like I'm doing?" I stand there as if I need permission to enter my own bedroom. I walk in and cross the room toward her. "I'm coming to bed." A small frame sits beside the candle, the crystals sparking with each flick of the flame. Interesting . . . "I like what you've done in here. You're really making it your own, almost like you intend to stay."

Her eyes don't leave the book in her hands, but I know deep inside she's dying to peek. "It feels homey again like before I left." She turns a page, and then I'm struck with a devious look in her eyes. She gets such pleasure from triggering me.

Take a breath. I struggle to maintain a face of indifference as I stand next to the bed, but I manage to get by. *Barely.* Setting my glass on the nightstand, no coaster, just barebacking that wood like it won't be ruined from condensation, I strip off my shirt and rub my hand over my abs. "That was a good burger. Too bad I'll never be allowed back in the joint after the spectacle you put on."

Is that drool?

Her tongue dips out and runs over the corner of her mouth before she bites her lower lip. I think I just found her Achilles' heel. It's more predictable than I would have expected of her. With her eyes glued to the six-pack of muscles I work hard for, she huffs through her nose. "You, um, I . . . It is so good. I mean, was. The burger. Ugh. You know what I mean." She closes her book without the impact I think she was hoping for since it's a paperback. Licking her lips, she asks, "What's gotten into you?" I start on the button of my pants. "Warner." A cautionary tone from her lips doesn't stop her eyes from drinking in the view.

I keep teasing her by stroking my abs. "What?"

Finding the will to pull her attention away, she glances at the glass on the nightstand before darting to me. "Are you drunk?"

"I'm not drunk, sweetheart, but I feel our connection." Bumping against her to settle in the little space on the edge of the bed, I manage to make some room. When she refuses to move, I shove my hip against hers, causing her to tumble sideways to the mattress. "Tell me, do you feel it, too?"

"What are you feeling exactly?" Propping herself up, she scoots to the middle to give me room. I quickly hog more space than I need to make myself at home next to her. "The only thing I'm feeling is that I'm being tested."

"Why would I be testing you?"

"Oh, I don't know," she replies sarcastically, rolling her head around on her neck. "Maybe to get under my skin."

Remembering the mission, I'm not above making her feel paranoid. Come on strong. Get a confession. *See ya later, lady.* Taking the book from her hand, I toss it off the end of the bed. "Is it working?"

"It's not. You'll need to try harder and hope you didn't damage my book. I hate bends in the covers."

"Challenge accepted, and don't worry about the book. I can buy you a new one." Leaning in, I close the gap between her ear and my lips. I'm pretty sure she's not breathing. I whisper, "I want to make up for lost time."

I don't think she's blinked in the past thirty seconds either. A gasp leads to her sucking in air. On the end of a gentle and torturously slow release, she says, "You may not be drunk, but something has gotten into you. I'm thinking booze is to blame. Exactly how much have you had to drink?"

"Not enough to be unaware of exactly what I'm doing."

CHAPTER 14

DELANEY

I'M NOT sure how much Warner had to drink before he entered the bedroom, but the glass next to him doesn't seem empty enough to justify the sudden reversal in his behavior. Unfortunately for me, it's been a while since I've been kissed, much less anything else. Between the push for finals and then graduation, the job search, and working full-time at the restaurant, dating was the last thing I had time for.

I figured he was a workaholic, but maybe he's in his office doing sit-ups all day. How else is that man built like that? His flashing those unreal abs of his while that large and strong hand rubbed over them was cruel. How am I supposed to be on top of my game when he's distracting me like that? He has me temporarily losing my better judgment. I could say that about this whole scheme I'm buried three days deep into as well. But there is no point in quibbling about the small things I can't change.

Tit for his tat, I say, "Should have brought me a glass."

He hands me the glass. "We can share. Since we're married, swapping saliva doesn't bother me."

With a roll of my eyes, I laugh. "Swapping saliva? You sure do make it hard to resist with that description." I take the glass because the straight liquor will surely kill any cooties Warner Landers might have. Holding the crystal-cut glass to my mouth, I only tip it back enough to let the liquid coat the rim, then press it to my lips for a taste. The heat is instant, my throat warm from the introduction. I take a small sip, then hand the glass back to him.

His eyes stay set on mine as he drinks from the glass. Watching the tip of his tongue dip to catch any remains on his lips has me wanting to tackle this man. Then I remember it's him . . . the man wanting to destroy my family's livelihood and home. He probably gets off on crushing the little guy. That he's attractive, ungodly so, doesn't deter me from reaching my goals. Admittedly, it makes it easier. I mean, it's not hard to look at him or those abs.

God, I sound so shallow.

He could have any woman he wants, so sue me for wanting to be on the receiving end. He doesn't seem to be in a relationship since no women have knocked down his door, and somehow, his personality switching today has been a nice change.

Don't let up, Delaney.

The moment I detour to give him grace, I'm sure he'll do whatever he can to make things worse for me. Just like when he brought a "friend" out of nowhere. He forced me into a corner, digging my grave even deeper than it already was by lying some more. What else was I supposed to do? I felt trapped.

His demeanor has changed, so mine needs to adapt. The man is suddenly turned on. I think it started when I was digging into his pocket. What will I do if he wants to have sex? I inwardly grin. I'm thinking there could be worse positions to be in than flat on my back under him.

Ugh. Get your mind out of the gutter. I need to figure out how to bring up the deal about the restaurant without appearing suspicious. I reach forward, taking the glass from him again, and take a bigger sip this time. The other stuff will work itself out when the timing is right. I need to relax and figure out a way out of the direction we're currently headed. Or do I take the reins and lead him to water?

Tempting . . .

Our backs pressed to the headboard, our eyes ahead in the candlelit room. It's hard to make out anything personal in the unfamiliar room, but there's not much other than furniture. It's not only a clean home, it's barely lived in. There's no life built in. The halls are barren of laughter. Forget about anyone else. Warner barely exists in the space other than his physical presence, which is currently taking up a lot more space as he spreads his legs a little wider. At this rate, I'll only have a foot of space to exist.

I could always straddle him. He talks a big game, but can he walk it? "So . . ." I say, letting it hang in the air to see what he wants to add.

"I've been thinking . . ." He drops his own lingering start, but I'm much more curious how he'd finish it. He doesn't.

Taking the glass, I ask, "About?" I sip and then sip again. The liquor burns, but the smoky, sweet aftertaste is quite nice.

"I've never had sex with a broken arm before."

"Have you had sex with a concussion? Is that even safe? I can't imagine the doctor would advise such an activity."

"Do doctors ever advise having sex?"

"Sure." I glance over at him. "I had one tell me it will

help alleviate migraines." I take a sip, remembering what happened next. That calls for another drink before handing it back. "And then he volunteered."

"What the fuck?" He angles toward me, and says, "Delaney, please tell me he's no longer your doctor."

"He's no longer my doctor." I bounce my shoulders up and down once. "I discovered I was getting migraines from the incense my friend was always burning in her room when we would study there. So we stopped burning incense."

"Juniper?"

A burst of laughter leaves my chest. "Yes. Juniper. My friend. The blonde you supposedly remember so well." Good Lord, have mercy on me. This guy is exasperating. "Speaking of, it's interesting you remember her . . ." *Especially since she doesn't exist.* "But not me. Your wife."

His gaze travels my legs that are tucked under the covers before he reaches over to slide his knuckles against my thigh. Even the blanket and sheet between us doesn't stop my heart from quickening. "I'm sure there's something we can do to trigger the memories to return. Don't you think?"

"I think you're coming on to me."

Shifting to set the glass back down, he's slower because of his broken arm, but the shared moment between us is flaming-red hot when he returns. Damn those incredible abs, those eyes that peer into my soul, and that husky seducing voice of his. The reprieve wasn't long enough for me to recover before he smirks just enough for his confidence to shine through. "Would it be so wrong for a husband to be attracted to his wife?"

I take a breath, hoping it's steady and doesn't give away the filthy thoughts I'm having of him. Laying it on as sweet as honey, I bat my lashes. "Even after all that's happened?"

"That's the beauty of amnesia, baby. I'm a blank slate. A fresh start. There's nothing to hold us back from creating new memories together." He leans closer, his hand sliding behind my lower back. In one swift move, I'm pulled onto his lap so fast that I don't have time to squeal. I wouldn't have protested anyway.

The covers slide off my thighs, leaving only the thinnest of satin covering my lower half. My loose top with a lacy hemmed bottom brushes against my belly, exposing the space the fabric doesn't cover. His pants are still on, the flap of the open button rubbing against my ass. While I notice the little things like that, there's a much larger problem growing between us.

My swallow is too loud, and my cheeks feel hot from being so obviously nervous. "Warner," I whisper, looking into his eyes. I touch his cheek. The rough scruff of growth from the past few days is little spikes against my hand. The scene is set. The outcome is in our hands. The warmth and slightest scent of his skin wrap around me like a wool scarf. His large hand slides from my hip to my waist, making my body respond to him. There's no hiding my hardening nipples or the way my hips press harder against him, the pressure becoming mandatory for my survival.

It's all too much. His size compared to mine and the way the devil looks at me like I'm a prize worth fighting for do me in. I lean in, brushing my lips against the fullness of his, but catch myself before I give in and pull back again.

His breath has deepened like mine, his eyelids heavier, and his lips are parted, ready to kiss me if I'd let him. I don't because I'd lose all control if I did, sliding off his lap, I keep moving until I'm standing on the other side of the bed. I glance through the windows at the city that's lit like stars and then to this palatial room fit for a king and queen. But

I'm not his queen. I'm not even part of his court. I'm just a peasant compared to this life.

I've asked myself a million times what I'm doing, ignoring the fact that I was going against my own moral compass. Why am I trying to play in the Major League when I can't make the minors? Dropping my head with the shame overcoming me, I run the tips of my fingers over my forehead.

"Delaney?" he whispers, not making a move. I appreciate the space, but I have to admit I miss our connection. He gets off the bed and stands on the other side of it. "Do you want to talk about what's going on?"

"No." I can't find the lies to hide my truth and the emotions I'm battling. I turn my head away from him, keeping my mouth shut and staring out the window instead. The sound of the crystal glass being lifted has me looking back. Warner swipes his hand across the wood to discourage the puddle of condensation from pooling. It would be a safe bet to know it's really about not staining the nightstand.

When he grabs his discarded shirt from the floor and wipes the surface, a grin wiggles onto the left side of my mouth. He grabs the sparkly frame with his fingers sticking out the end of the cast. "Is this you?"

I start to come around, keeping my steps light like I might disrupt something I'm not supposed to be a part of. I stand just to his side and look at the photo. I smile, the hope and happiness I felt that day rushing back. "Big sunglasses, red lips, my hair was slick and shiny with the most perfect wave from pin curls." I tap the photo as if he doesn't know what I'm referring to.

"Coney Island?"

"It's how I celebrated graduating from college. I got that top and skirt for twenty bucks at the Dumbo clothes exchange they hold each spring. It was a steal. New, it would have been over a hundred and fifty." Staring at the photo, I study the whole look, still loving the outfit. But maybe it wasn't just my appearance. It was the hard-earned achievement. "I wore it tucked in for the ceremony since my family was there, but tied the front of the shirt in a knot to bare my midriff at the carnival." I laugh, wanting to roll my eyes at myself. I don't know why I feel a little embarrassed. I shouldn't. Leaning my head against his arm, I add, "I felt rebellious for doing it. But I also felt pretty. I remember asking some random guy to take my picture, hoping he wouldn't run off with my phone. Spoiler alert: he didn't."

Warner sets the glass back down and brings his arm around my lower back to hold me close to him. His skin is warm against mine, the connection zapping every particle in my body from the electricity. Peeking down at me, he asks, "Why couldn't someone in your family take the photo?"

I'm not mad is something I've prefaced this topic in my head a million times. Their reason is acceptable. Unjustifiably, I'm still hurt. "They had to get back to the restaurant to prepare for dinner service."

"You went alone?"

"It beat sitting in my room or working at the hostess stand. I had the night off, so I took myself to Coney Island. I hadn't been since I was little, and it just seemed like a good place to get lost for a few hours."

He sits on the bed, takes my hand, and pulls me to him. Our knees touch, my outer to his inner, the union feeling as intimate as when I was on his lap. I gulp, hating to disturb the silence with such nonsense. "Can I ask you something?" he whispers, looking into my eyes.

"Of course."

"How long ago was that photo taken?"

It's such a roundabout way of asking my age, but I like that he wants more information about me, and he cares enough to find out. "Two years ago."

"So you're twenty-four?" I nod, worried about this new territory he's leading me into. "How long have we been married?"

I was getting too comfortable with my armor set aside on the floor. I could almost feel his heart beating like it was my own when I touched his face earlier. My stomach sinks as the lies rise like bile in my throat. "Not quite a year."

"I must have been quite the asshole to lose you before our first anniversary."

"You're telling me," I try to joke, but I'm not even feeling it, so I know he doesn't hear it. I still push forth. "I had to live with you."

My hand falls to my side when he releases me. Standing with our knees still bumped against each other, his gaze falls between us. He rubs the bridge of his nose and then looks back up at me. "I'm thirty-four." There doesn't seem to be a destination for his admission.

I didn't realize that he was ten years older. From his looks to his personality, he has some age range he could fall into. So it's not shocking news. I trail the tips of my nails under his chin and put my hand at my side again. "It's so cliché to be in an age-gap romance."

"Is that what we are? An age-gap romance?" He chuckles. "I've never felt so old in my life."

"Come on." I smile, feeling the tiniest bit of empathy for him. "It's alright to be an old man with a hot younger wife." I give a little shake of my hips.

A smile finds its rightful place on his face, but there's no smugness or arrogance attached. "That's not why I feel old."

"Oh yeah, then why do you feel that way?"

"You may be my wife—"

"I *am* your wife," I correct with a set-in grin.

"You're my wife, but the things I've thought about doing to you make me feel like I could be arrested."

Leaning down, which isn't far for me to go despite him sitting on the edge of the bed, I run my fingers through the hair over his ear, and lock eyes with him. "Good thing I'm well above the legal age to fulfill such desires." I move even closer, our mouths only a breath away, and whisper, "I want you to make that mistake again."

His eyes study mine as if he sees through me. "What mistake is that?"

"The one where you kissed your wife." His fingers weave into the hair at the nape of my neck moments before his mouth crashes into mine.

Goodbye, willpower. *Hello, Warner!*

CHAPTER 15

Warner

SWEET AND SPICY.

The first taste of Delaney is better than the expensive aged bourbon lingering on her lips. I shouldn't have kissed her, even if she did ask, but now that I have, I want to keep doing it all night.

A little moan vibrates in her throat as soon as our mouths merge and our tongues touch. Caramel intermixes with a delicate hint of aged oak, making me want to delve deeper to taste every last drop of this stunner of a woman.

With one useless arm, I feel inept. One strap of her top slides down her arm, exposing the top of her perky breast, but my fingers fumble as I reach for the other strap, so I stop. Instead, I run the fingers of my casted arm gently against the length of her neck.

I pull back enough to see the want in her eyes and the frustration that our lips dared to part. *Still so feisty.* I drag my tongue over my bottom lip, wanting to savor what remains of her flavor. She was right about me. I have no patience, especially with her. Whether she's talking bullshit, leaving a mess around my apartment, or looking like she does, I want her. "Get on the bed."

Her back straightens stiff as an arrow, her tits still begging for attention under her shirt. So damn tempting to tease with my tongue if we don't kill each other first. Settling her hands on my shoulders, she takes a deep breath while her shoulders fall on the exhale. "Should we be doing this?" Her measured, panting breaths jade the words.

"Why shouldn't we? We're married, remember?" Do I feel bad for pretending we're married when I know we're not? I lost touch with that emotion a long time ago in business. Personally, fighting fire with fire is the only way to win, and winning is an aphrodisiac. Even with my dick as hard as it is, it would be irresponsible of me to take what she's giving and not give it back. Something's on the line. I haven't figured it out yet, but only an enemy would go to the lengths she has.

When I smile at her, it's real. I'm beginning to appreciate her company in spite of the spirited streak of hate she holds for me. I can't wait to watch her crumple under me. It will be the best orgasm of her life, and she'll walk away knowing only her rival could make her feel that good. When she seems at a loss for words, I add, "Maybe you have a touch of amnesia as well."

Her eyes follow one of her hands as it glides over my shoulders, dipping with the flow of my muscles, and then her gaze darts back to me. "No amnesia. That's the problem. I remember it all too well."

Her body is soft when I slip my hand under the lace of her short, silky top. The white against her skin makes her look even tanner, and the blue flowers dotting the fabric have me wanting to spend hours connecting each one underneath it. "Maybe the universe is giving us the accident to reconnect."

She grins. "Nice thought, but I'd prefer the universe not try to kill you to bring us back together. Roses. Jewelry. A fancy dinner would have done the trick." Laughter escapes her without her permission, even as she tries to shut it down so fast.

"I can do that."

While her hand keeps her gaze occupied, she asks, "Can do what?"

"I can give you roses. Jewelry. Reservations at the best restaurants in the city. Anything you want." I smirk. "I got us six flavors of gelato delivered instantly."

"Impressive."

"Wait until you see what else I can do."

"I've seen firsthand what you have the power to do. I'm hoping to shine light on the darker parts." She runs her hand over my cheek as if she actually cares. "You can just be Warner with me. No fanfare. No big gestures." Scraping above my ears gently, she rests her hand at the nape of my neck and leans in. "Just you and me." She closes her eyes when her lips press to mine again, and whispers, "You don't have to be the bad guy." Her hand leaves me, ushering in winter without her to keep me warm. Her smile returns, the one that doesn't feel like it reaches her heart. "What flavors of gelato did you get?" Before I respond, she walks into the bathroom, leaving the door open behind her.

It's only a few seconds. Not enough time to decipher the code she's speaking in. Why am I the bad guy? It was said so casually, but left an impact without her realizing. *A tell?* Who does she think I am if not Warner with her? I suspect I'm not as clever as I think I am, at least not with her. I reply, "Pistachio," loud enough for her to hear in the bathroom.

"I love pistachio." She returns with my robe wrapped around her body like it's her property now. If she asked, I'd give it to her. It looks a hell of a lot better on her than on me. "What else?" She takes me by my unbroken arm and tries to pull me to my feet. "What other flavors?"

It's almost maniacal how she transitions from one mood to the next. The serious side is gone. Her upbeat demeanor keeps me on my toes, literally. I walk with her hand firmly attached in mine. Selfishly, I like this side of her. It's almost like we're not trying to fuck each other over. The good in her brings out my better side. "Chocolate with blood orange mixed in."

"Incredible."

Like her.

I'm such a sucker for a pretty face and lips that taste like the finest liquor that money can buy. I'm a fucking fool for this woman's attention. Why does it feel like sunshine on a cloudy day? I eat it up, not realizing how starved I've been to have someone look at me like I hung the moon for them. I'm sure the feeling will fade as fast as it came on, but I'm going to enjoy the moment. How can I not when the gleam in her eyes resuscitates the very organ I didn't think could be saved?

She almost skips to the kitchen, as the anchor weighing her down—me—has finally been released. Her joy is contagious, and all because of gelato. I knew I could convert her over from ice cream, but I'm learning she didn't lie about the sweet tooth. It's definitely a way to this girl's heart. I just wish she craved to finish what was started in the bedroom more. The ache in my belly subsides, but my lingering blue balls have me shifting for a better position on this stool. "Raspberry, stracciatella, lemon, and a lavender basil mix. I went out on a limb with the last one."

"What flavor are we starting with?" I ask as I settle in to watch her maneuver around my kitchen.

With the freezer door open, she peeks back at me. "We only get to try one?"

I would laugh, but she's dead serious. "Let's try them all."

The pint containers are lined up on the counter in front of me before she leaps in excitement and then scurries to the silverware drawer. Looking inside, she says, "Tell me this isn't real silver."

The judgment doesn't bother me. I have expensive taste, but I'm not that extravagant. "It's stainless. I prefer stainless steel to having to maintain silver. Anyway, it's only me here, so I don't need anything fan—" Our eyes lock across the small space, both of us, apparently, realizing the grave error we've made at the same time.

As my wife, she would know the answer.

As her husband, I wouldn't have responded like I did.

But here we are, stuck in a tangled web in the aftermath.

I'm not sure what to say when it actually goes so well. I managed to flip my mood in accordance with hers. Why'd we have to fuck it up? The reality of what we are now is exposed, lying like a death of something good. "I . . ." I release a heavy breath and then look down to stare at the counter like I'll find a plan on how to proceed in the swirls of the stone.

"Big or little?" she asks, holding up two spoons and carrying on like our secrets aren't closing in on us.

Following her lead, this one time, I reply, "Big."

"I'll take the little spoon." She comes over and hands me the spoon without making eye contact. Another tell that I'm positive I'll read too much into. As she takes the lids off the containers, she asks, "Can you eat with your left? You did fine with a burger and fries, but gelato is a different ball game."

We didn't get away with anything, but she's a master sidestepper. "We'll see."

She grasps the bottom of the chocolate blood orange pint. "I'll hold it. Dig in."

I scoop the creamy treat and take the spoon into my mouth, slow to slide it out. Watching her spoon dive in after mine, she doesn't waste time tasting it. "I like that one."

"It's my favorite."

"I can see why. Or taste why." A giggle bubbles up like champagne—the unexpected, quiet burst is something to be savored. I end up smiling for several reasons, but mainly because it's odd how things with her evolve from one minute to the next. I was tasting her not fifteen minutes ago, and now I'm eating gelato like it stands a chance against the sweetness of her lips. The slip with the silverware doesn't seem to matter as much. Knowing that this is probably an act, like everything else she does, doesn't deter me from starting to appreciate her quirks.

Grabbing the base of the next pint, she says, "Try it and guess the flavor."

I already know what it is by the color, but I'll play along. One bite is all it takes to confirm what I knew. "Pistachio."

Sliding the spoon from between her lips, she licks the corner and says, "Salty and sweet. I always did have an affinity for the opposites."

"Opposites attract. Like us?"

A wrinkle of her nose leads to a grin spreading after. "I'll assume you're inferring I'm the sweet one." I tip my head, giving the title without argument though salty might be a better fit. "You're definitely the salty one between us. How many hours a day do you think you're grumpy, Warner? I'm going with eighteen."

"So fucking random," I say, chuckling. "Why eighteen?"

"Figure you typically sleep for six so that leaves you wide awake and wreaking havoc on the rest of us for the remaining hours." She thinks she's funny by how she cackles and digs into the next pint. This time, I'll concur. *She is.*

Raspberry is next, given its deep purple color. I take a bite and wince from the tartness of it. When she does the same, we share a laugh that feels like it's been building up for a while. She says, "Not my favorite, but I do like it."

"I'm thinking you could say the same about me."

"You're not far off, hotshot." Sliding the next pint forward, she adds, "Lemon. Oddly, it's not tart at all. It's really good."

With the gelato on my spoon, I hold it in front of me. "You're growing on me."

Her laughter echoes over the island, the sound weaseling its way into that once beatless organ. "I'd hope so." Waggling that ringed finger, she adds, "Since we're married and all."

"And all is my favorite part." I finally take the lemon dessert into my mouth to savor it. After it melts, I say, "I was starting to think this might have been an arranged marriage. I seem to be the opposite you have an affinity for."

Swirling her spoon around with chocolate on the end, she says, "So you claim, but I'm realizing we're not as opposite as even I once thought." Coming around to my side of the island, she slides onto a barstool next to me. "Tell me, hotshot—"

"Again with the hotshot?"

"If the shoe fits . . ." She licks the back of the spoon,

making my mind go straight to the tightening in my pants. I shift, not making a show of it, but with a knowing smile situated on her face and her eyes brighter with the trouble she's getting me into, I think she's onto me. *God, I wish she was on me.*

By how she licks the spoon again, slower this time, she likes that I see her, that I'm turned on by her. Some of those thoughts I had earlier—imagining her tits bouncing as she rides me with abandon, gripping onto the swell of her hips when I fuck her from behind, having her spread naked across my desk while we fuck with all of New York City outside the windows—return. She's got an incredible hourglass figure that I can't wait to plow into.

It's a game of cat and mouse, but sex is still a factor when there's mutual attraction.

"Earth to Warner." She waves her hand in front of me. When my eyes focus on her face again, she says, "And you had the nerve to complain about me disappearing on you. It's always projection. In other news, back to the gelato. Now that you've tried them—"

"I haven't tried the lavender basil."

"I love the two herbs individually. I don't think they need to be mixed, so I'll spare you the trouble of suffering through it." Taking the spoon out of my hand, she walks back into the kitchen, dumping them into the steel sink and letting them clang around the bottom. I'm busy cringing when she asks, "You were done, right?"

Not sure when I was going to be allowed to reply, but the time has passed to make a difference in the outcome. "All done." After she returns each lid to its pint, she stacks them up and turns to load them back into the freezer. "What should we do now?"

I have ideas that would probably get me slapped if I voiced them. "Movie?"

She kicks the steel door closed with her bare foot, causing me to take a deep breath before I lose my shit. "Sure. What do you want to watch?"

"What about *Mr. and Mrs. Smith*?"

With her hands planted on her hips, she crinkles her face in disapproval. "You want to watch a movie about spies trying to kill each other?"

I move to the sitting area and open a box on the console beneath the big-screen TV hanging on the wall. "Don't forget they're married."

"Oh, I didn't." Delaney's already curling her legs under her. As soon as I sit and dim the lights with one of the remotes, she slides across the middle cushion to lean against me. She's laying it on a bit thick. Call me a fool, but I'm into it. "What about *Entrapment* with Catherine Zeta-Jones?"

"Never heard of it."

"What? How is that possible? You were alive when it came out."

My stare latches onto thin air before turning to her with a cocked brow. "Are you not so subtly saying that you weren't alive when it was released since I'm the old man in the room?" I find the movie and start it. It's dated, but I'm open to seeing if it's any good.

"It released years before I was born." She rests her head on my shoulder, watching the movie studio logo cross the screen. I think she's avoiding eye contact, but what would an old geezer like me know? "My dad loves heist movies."

"So *he* taught you the con," I mumble to myself.

"What?"

"Nothing." I set the remote on the coffee table and wrap my arm around her shoulders. "It's starting."

Forty-five minutes in, I'm fully invested, but Little Miss Priss fell asleep twenty minutes after it started. Her soft snore doesn't bother me, but it does have me considering moving her to the bedroom. Probably not wise to carry her with a broken arm, though. "Delaney?" I don't know why I just kissed her head. It was there, and it happened before I thought twice about it. I gently rock her shoulders. "Delaney?"

Tired eyes that are barely open look at me. "Yeah?" Panic creeps into her voice. "What is it?"

"It's okay." I stroke her hair from the side of her face. "Let's get you to bed." Her breath instantly deepens from the suggestion, her eyes fluttering closed. But as soon as I shift off the couch, bringing her up with me, I add, "Come on. Let's go to bed."

She moves with me, my arm around her back to support her weight as we walk down the hallway together. "I'm so sleepy." Her words are slurred, her mind groggy when she speaks. Her body is limp, but with lackluster effort, she keeps her head upright.

"I know. We'll get you to bed." As soon as I get her to the bed, she crawls in. I start to tuck her in, bringing the blanket to cover her shoulders like I do this all the time. *I don't.* I don't have women over to tuck into my bed after . . . after our activities. Women don't stay the night. This is my domain, and I like it that way.

But something about Delaney . . . is growing on me.

Lying on her side facing me, she opens her eyes once more and smiles when she sees me there. "You're really handsome, you know that? Even with the black eye."

I chuckle quietly. "I like hearing it from you." I lean

down to kiss her head, and whisper, "You're beautiful, Delaney." I don't say it to return the favor. I say it because it felt like something I should admit to her. She reaches up to touch my face, but her lids are too heavy to keep open.

I start to wonder if these newfound feelings are real. They could be. It's been so long since I've cared for someone that I need to sit with the emotion a bit longer. It could just be because the look she had in her eyes was genuine when she said it. She sounded as honest as I was. The truth revealed. With her under the spell of exhaustion, I should leave, but my feet don't go anywhere. Instead, I kneel beside the bed, admiring the plush of her lips and the slope of her nose. She looks so peaceful, like an angel in my bed.

But the devil on my shoulder wins out . . . "Delaney?"

"Hmm?" Her eyes never open as the hum of her response is heard.

"What's your last name?"

The slightest of grins curves the corners of her mouth, and she replies, "Bayetti."

Now that's information I can use. I kiss her on the forehead and whisper, "Good night."

CHAPTER 16

Delaney

"Jesus, Warner!" I try breathing through the terror of waking up to him hovering over me like a murderer. "What are you doing?"

"Seeing if you're still breathing." He falls back to his side of the bed and leans against the headboard—shirtless, I might add, and laughing. *Jerk.*

"Apparently, it's funny to you that my heart just flew out the window."

"Is that where it went?" Since I just woke up, maybe I'm reading too much into his deadpan comment.

With my heart still beating out of my chest, I roll away from him and close my eyes, hoping to regulate my entire body back to what it was before Warner Landers entered my life. *Or did I enter his?* Doesn't matter. We're stuck in each other's lives now. I'm starting to believe it will be for life at this rate.

His big paw of a hand wraps over my arm and rocks me back and forth. "Come on, Delaney. Don't be mad."

"Mad?" I close my eyes, so I don't roll them. "I'm not mad. I'm trying to figure out what I did to deserve this hell." Bet he's smirking. I roll just enough to catch a glimpse of his face. *Yep.* Called it. "You find this so funny, don't you?"

I'm not in the mood for this, at least not yet. It's too early to remember the role I'm supposed to be playing, to have patience for this unreservedly fiend of a man, and morning ruiner to boot.

"Is it wrong if I do?" His slurping coffee injects an extra dose of aggravation into my bad mood. It's like a cherry on top of this affront.

I push up and angle back, resting my weight on my hand. "It is wrong and dangerous if you want to live to see lunch."

"Mornings got you down, sweetheart. You were just a sleepy little angel last night, and now, you wake up as a bear. Shitty sleep?"

"Nightmares all night." I flip the covers from my body and swing my legs out. As soon as I touch down on the floor, I adjust the strap that had fallen off my shoulder, wanting to expose me to him. *Traitor.* "I dreamed there was this guy who thought he was the bee's knees, but really he was just a coffee-slurping creeper who wanted to kill me." I turn on my heel, the hair fallen out of my scrunchie swinging, and march into the bathroom.

Just before I close the door, he says, "I don't want to kill you, Delaney." Why does that not sound like the end of what he wants to say?

Piquing my interest, I hit him with a glare. "What do you want to do with me?" I know better, but setting the trap and watching him get caught is a new favorite pastime of mine. I cross my arms over my chest and tap my foot to add drama as I wait for him to react.

His eyes still hold a warmth when he stares back into mine, and asks, "Have you been initiated into the Mile High Club?" But then he had to open his mouth and ruin it.

I slam the door closed and start the shower. If I weren't already in a bad mood, I might allow myself to realize I came in here like this is *my* bathroom, started the shower like I do it every morning, and walked around this apartment like I didn't barge into his life without his permission. It's not my life or my place. I can only imagine how this would look to the outside world. If my parents knew I was sleeping, as in actual sleep, with the man who is taking over the building and evicting us and the restaurant. I can't let the shame of the act change the means to the end.

They'll thank me one day. Of course, they don't have to know the dirty details, only that the restaurant and our home are safe. I stick my hand inside the glass, and what I assume is marble, to test the water. It's hot. The steam coats the glass as I strip off my top and then my undies, leaving them on the floor as I step under the spray. Closing my eyes, I let the water rain down on my face before I turn around and soak my hair.

The pummel on my shoulders eases the tension that the rude awakening has embedded in my muscles. I take the bottle of soap—a sleek shape with a modern design. I pop the top to inhale the scent that smells like heaven. Earthy yet exotic. I memorize the name to look this brand up so I can buy a bottle for myself at home.

When I lather it on, the silky suds soften my skin as the scent permeates the air. I thought setting traps for Warner to fall into was the best part of being here, but it's the soap for sure.

Instead of rinsing off, I leave the body wash on while I wash my hair, then condition it. Squirting a silver dollar-sized amount of his extravagant face wash like I'm really sticking it to him by wasting it, I scrub my hands over my face. "Ack!" My eyes burn as the soap sneaks into the inner corners. I shove my head under the water, hoping to alleviate the pain when I hear, "Listen, Delaney—"

"Oh my God." I scramble to cover myself, but my eyes still burn, so I can't see where he is or where he's looking. I only manage to flail my hands in front of certain body parts as I screech, "What are you doing in here?"

"I think we should work through our problems."

"Can we do that when I'm dressed and not naked, covered in . . . *water*?" I turn my back to him, giving him quite the show of my ass. "Also, can you not stare at me? Thanks."

"You think highly of yourself. I wasn't even looking, much less staring at you."

"Oh." I duck my head under the water again to clear the remaining soap and then peek through the steamy glass at him. He's standing there with the smuggest grin I ever did see. "You're an asshole."

He walks to the door, holding the edge and looking back. "It's nothing I've not seen before, dear *wife*."

If looks could kill, he'd already be on the floor. But he's won this round, whether I like it or not. "Shut the door on your way out."

Just when I think he's gone, his laughter warns me otherwise. "By the way, nice ass, sweetheart."

"Get out!"

The door closes before the words leave my mouth. He's either lucky or smart enough to know when to get out of the line of fire. I won't give him too much credit, but either way, he's gone. I try to reclaim the tranquility I felt in the shower spa, but everything has changed, and that intolerable man has destroyed any peace I'd gained.

I shut off the water and pull the fluffy towel—because, of course, he has the fluffiest towels known to humankind—and dry off. Chances are good he'll be gone from this room when I open the door. I peek out first, and when I see the coast is clear, I cross the room to the closet where I dumped my suitcase. Bending down, I unscramble the code and pop the lid open. With no idea what's in store for me today, I debate what I should wear. It's Saturday, so he won't be working, and since I don't have a job yet, we'll be spending time together. Maybe I can get him to go to the store to buy real food for the fridge.

The sound of my stomach growling on cue impresses me, and I had absolutely no control over it. I stand and dip into the bedroom again. "Warner?"

"What?" His voice travels the hallway to reach the end of it.

"I don't know what to wear," I yell so he can hear me. "What are we doing today?"

The pause is long enough for me to wonder if he didn't actually hear me. "What do you want to do? And don't say induct me into the Mile High Club."

He appears in the doorway to the bedroom. "That doesn't leave much."

"You're ridiculous." I duck back into the closet.

"I'm also still thinking about your ass."

I still my hands on my head, hating myself for liking that so much. "What are you thinking?" Hatred isn't strong enough to cover the disappointment I have in myself for even daring to play this game with him. He's been an abso-lute jerk this morning, but last night, he was almost dreamy, and he's a really great kisser. I would have gone so much further if we'd kept going. I don't even remember why we stopped now. Though I know it was for the best.

What would today be like if we'd had sex last night?

Much messier than it is already. I'm glad we didn't.

"I like the shape of your body," he replies, sounding unapologetic. His voice is closer as if he's standing right outside the closet. He doesn't peer in or barge in like we're married, giving me the space and privacy I need to get dressed.

I press my hands to my heating cheeks and try my hardest not to love that he likes my body. Getting Warner's approval is the last thing I need, but it sure does make me feel amazing. "Thank you." I keep my volume down, no longer needing to yell. But really, it's because emotion could overcome me if I let the compliment affect me on a deeper level.

It's shallow at best, but he has noticed me. That's on the record for all time.

Dropping both towels to the floor, I grab one of his T-shirts from the pile of disarray cotton and pull it on before slipping on a pair of panties. No use in getting ready if we end up staying here all day.

Entering the room, he's no longer in here, but I catch the slightest whiff of his cologne, inspiring me to take a deeper breath. I walk down the hall to see a huge vase of pink roses on the island. My feet slow, but I still walk toward them, noticing a box on the counter next to them. "What's this?"

"You mentioned roses."

"So you got me roses?"

He comes from the kitchen to greet me when I reach the counter. Taking my hand, he says, "So I got you roses. You mentioned jewelry." Picking up the box, he hands it to me. "So I bought you jewelry."

My hands are shaking so much that I'm afraid to take the dark blue velvet box from him. "I didn't say it to—"

"I know. The timing was right, and I wanted to."

My mind runs through a million ideas, trying to correlate the timing to today, but nothing lands for me. "Why is the timing right?" I manage to take the box like it's not going to bite me. When I pop the lid open, my jaw hits the hardwood floor. My breath catches in my throat as I try to process what I'm looking at here.

I run my fingers over the classic necklace that reminds me of a tennis bracelet I see some of the wealthy clientele wearing at the restaurant. It doesn't matter that it's probably cost him a fortune for this, even with the crystals sparkling like real diamonds. It's a hello and goodbye all in one, since there is no way I can possibly accept this gift. "It's beautiful, Warner, but I can't accept this."

"You can. It will be perfect with the dress you're wearing."

"What dress?" I look around but don't see a dress hanging anywhere, not even draped over the couch. "What are we talking about? What dress could I possibly be wearing that needs a diamond-encrusted necklace as an accessory?"

Sliding his hand around my back, he uses his body to shadow me from the daylight streaming in from outside. With a kiss to my temple, his lips linger only temporarily before he asks, "Have you forgotten about the event tonight? It's been on our calendar for months."

And here I thought I was good. He might be better. "I haven't forgotten."

"Good. The fundraiser for The Met is one of the most

anticipated events of the year. Even an asshole like me enjoys donating for a good cause." He could have let his tone drip in sarcasm, but he didn't. "The car will pick us up at six, so take the time you need today to get ready." He starts back down the hall.

"That's more than seven hours from now." Who needs that much time to get dressed?

"I'm going to shower and get a few hours of work done in the home office."

Looking down at the necklace again, I snap the lid shut. This is too much to keep, but I'm already playing pretend, so what's another event? "Thank you for the gifts."

He stops, looking more like someone I might fall for if I'm not careful. "Can't wait to see you in them. With only the necklace as well."

I laugh, the release freeing what could have been an awkward situation. "Only if you play your cards right, Hotshot."

"I'll be playing them until I win, sweetheart. And I always come out ahead." I shouldn't blush, but under the hunger I spy in his eyes, I never dreamed I'd be going to such a prestigious and lavish event.

I've heard about this fundraiser before and seen photos in the paper the following day. I'm not worried about us attending. No, this will be fun. It's a huge event and easy to blend in. But the best part is that I get to dress up like a princess for the night. Real jewels and all.

I lift on my toes to smell the roses. The sweet fragrance is so pretty, but after this knockout of a necklace, it's the dress he mentioned that has me excited to dress up.

Dashing into the bedroom, I hear the shower running and Warner humming, but the showstopper is the emerald-green dress lying on the chair and the crystal-encrusted heels on the floor in front of it. I should be worried about how I'm going to pull this off with other people around, others who might know Warner isn't married.

It was all fun and games in what could have been a dream come true. But as I take the gorgeous dress in hand, I must get real with myself. *What am I getting myself into?*

CHAPTER 17

Warner

HIDING out in my own apartment from the woman who invaded it is perfectly normal.

That's what I keep telling myself anyway.

There's nothing normal about Delaney's and my relationship, but I'm working within the boundaries of this craziness the best I can. Tonight will break this case wide open. Though I don't put much past her at this stage. She has a way of making a comeback. I'm sure she'll manage to pull something out of thin air to keep this pretense from ending.

Even though she's screwing with my life, is it wrong to be impressed by her tenacity? She gets bothered anytime I mention the missing phone, claiming it couldn't have walked off and broken itself. I don't even know what she means by that. I've learned to let go of some of the wackier things she says.

The phone must be here somewhere, but I've failed to find it. I did a quick search of my home office before hiding out in here to go through some of the emails that have been piling up. If I hadn't been in here early this morning, I wouldn't have gotten the calendar reminder about the event. Good thing I did. It's the perfect occasion to show off my brand-spanking-new wife.

My jacket hangs on a hook on the back of the door as I sit dressed in my suit while she gets ready in the bedroom. I thought she was until she says, "Warner?"

"Coming," I reply, falling into this weird relationship we've formed. Her heels against the hardwood allow me to trace her path from the bedroom to the living room. I finish the email and push send before standing. After stealing the scissors from my desk, I pluck the jacket from the hook and close the door behind me when I leave the room. Analyzing the right sleeve, I rub my thumb over the seam. "I managed to get the shirt over my cast. I'll leave the cuff unbuttoned, but can you help me cut up my jacket?"

I walk to the center of the living room before looking up. My chest tightens from the sight of her. "Delaney?" I don't know what I'm asking. *The concussion is messing with my words*, I lie to myself. It's she who's stolen them from my mouth. The makeup is darker around her eyes but lighter on her lips, bare with only a shine drawing my eyes. The black of her lashes brings out the Mediterranean Sea coloring of her eyes. I could dive in and be content to swim in the calm of her waters.

"Wow." She makes me want to keep her tucked away in this apartment, all to myself.

Pure.

Effortless.

Extraordinary.

Her beauty is highlighted for those who are too blind to see how stunning she is, fresh from the shower. That's not me. I couldn't stop staring, especially when a drop of water had escaped from the threads of the towel and ran along her hairline. I almost reached out to catch it, but she swiped it away as if it hadn't just kissed her skin like I want to do now.

We could skip the event. Who cares if I've donated thousands? Or that I'm expected to be honored during the cocktail hour. Will anyone really care if I don't make an appearance?

I'd have a really good excuse to stay home. *My wife.*

She dares to wobble to the side, her weight balancing on a shyness that's gripped her as if she's not the most beautiful woman I've ever seen. With her gaze falling to the floor, she asks, "Is this not okay?"

"It's more than okay." Tossing my jacket on the island and the scissors on top, I move in to bring her into the safety of my hold. The thin straps and heart-shaped neckline highlight her collarbone and the rounded tops of her breasts. The smallest specks of sunshine cause a sheen across her skin, while the curves of her body command my gaze to travel every square inch to the hem that hits higher on her thigh than I expected. I'm not upset, given the view of her shapely legs. "You're breathtaking." I grin, slipping my arm around her waist along the back of the jewel-toned green fabric and bringing her to me. "Word stealing, in fact." There's not a resistant bone in her body as I kiss above her temple, and then whisper against her skin, "You look beautiful, Delaney."

Her head tucks against my chest. "You sure?"

"More than sure."

She looks up at me. "It's a beautiful dress, Warner. Thank you."

Stepping back, I take her in all over again. She looks so damn beautiful. I feel smug over pulling this off. "It's a good thing I have people with great taste on . . . I would have said speed dial but email in this case. I only pulled this off because you slept in, though."

"I'll start sleeping in more often if I get pretty dresses and expensive jewelry." She steps to the vase, taking one of the stems to bend and smell the flower. "Ow." She pushes the finger to her mouth and then holds it there while her tongue dips out to touch the surface. "A thorn. The prick," she snarks with a half-hearted grin.

I take her finger and hold it in front of me to inspect the damage. I kiss the tiny spot. "I think you're going to lose it."

She laughs. "Hopefully not. But I may not be safe around vicious thorny things." She certainly loves that word.

"I don't know. You seem to do okay with me."

Her smile blooms like the roses next to her—vibrant and pretty in pink. Tapping my chest with the injured finger, she laughs. "That was funny."

With a shrug, I say, "I try." Glancing at the jacket, I realize I still have this to deal with. "The jacket won't go on over my cast, and I didn't have time to have it altered." I pick up the scissors and flip the sleeve to expose the seam. "If we open the seam every other inch, I think I can squeeze the cast through by allowing it to stretch without having the sleeve flap open. And—"

"You're going to cut your suit jacket? That's unconscionable. Look at the fabric." She digs for a tag at the collar, and then her mouth drops open. Turning to gape at me, she says, "This is Tom Ford."

"I know. I had it made for me, but it does me no good if I can't wear it."

"But, but—"

"It will be okay." I chuckle. "If we're careful and keep to the seam, I can have a tailor fix it when I'm healed."

Staring at it, she hugs it to her chest. "I just," she starts, her eyes linking to mine. "It's so incredible. What if I ruin it and you can't get it fixed?"

I rub her upper back, then rest my hand on her shoulder. "Doesn't matter. It's only a jacket."

Sweeping the jacket in front of her, she lays it flat on the island. "Okay. Let's do it." Holding out her hand, she requests, "Scissors."

I hand them to her, and we work together to get the job done—me directing and her opening the seams. At the bottom of the cuff, she says, "Put it on and we'll see how much I need to open up for your hand."

She helps put it on, and though it's a squeeze, we get it all the way to my elbow. Bending down, she stares at the stretched fabric. "We need to release the cuff. Not much but—"

"I trust you. Do what you need to do."

Taking in a deep breath, she exhales. "It's only a jacket." She's so quiet that I think it's her own personal pep talk, but without hesitation, she opens the cuff, sets the scissors down, and yanks the jacket the rest of the way. "There." Her eyes are bright as she looks at me for approval.

"Great job. Thank you." Rolling my neck around the collar, I add, "Now I won't stand out as much."

She steps closer again, but this time, she takes my tie and straightens it. With a pat to my chest, she says, "You look very dapper, Hotshot."

I catch her wrist before she slips away. When she looks back, the determination that keeps her on her toes has been replaced by something softer. A moment of weakness? Or is she coming around to trusting me?

"What is it?" she whispers, her eyes wider from curiosity as she searches mine for an answer.

I take a sobering breath, having lost my own ambition to take her down and send her packing. This feels like a date with someone I care about. I swallow down the emotion trying to swell in my chest. I'm sure it will pass. "You almost forgot your necklace."

Her delicate fingers grace her neck as if she's surprised it's not on. "Did you really buy that for me?"

Opening the jewelry box, the diamonds that wrap around the platinum base sparkle without needing light to make them shine. I slip the necklace from the anchors and undo the clasp. I chuckle lightly, not at her expense but at the thought of gifting something to someone and then expecting it back. "You don't have to give it back at the end of the night." Shit, did that happen to her? I don't think now's the time to bring up the past when we're working so hard to stay present in our fabrications. I bring it around her neck from behind. Sweeping her hair to one side, I fasten it around her neck, making sure it lays flat on her skin.

When I step around, I admire this stunning creature. "You look like a million bucks, Sass."

"Sass?"

"If the shoe fits . . ." I use her response against her.

"And I was just getting used to the sound of disdain when you call me sweetheart, and here you go, changing it up on me." Grabbing the small bag that matches her shoes, she plucks my tie as she passes. "A million bucks says you can't make it one car ride without denigrating into utter irritation."

"We're about to find out, Sass," I reply with a wink, following her toward the door.

"Okay. Okay. Let's not wear it out."

I chuckle as we set out on our first venture, where we'll encounter people from our real lives. *Mine, to be specific.* I'm on the edge of my seat, wanting to see how she handles this.

Something about car rides always seems to quieten her. I wonder if she's using the time to plot or calm. She doesn't appear anxious and has only touched up her lipstick as if she's looking forward to the event. Some small talk is made about the crowd ascending the steps into the museum, but otherwise, we arrive without a hitch or a confession.

Upon entering, I check us in and pin our ribbons onto the front of our clothes. "What does a gold ribbon mean?"

Leaning in, I reply, "It means we donated."

She smiles to herself, but I catch it. "How much?" she whispers, waggling her eyebrows as she digs her nose into my business by lifting on her tiptoes and grinning at me. She's cute, but I'm still not sharing those figures with her.

"Enough."

Lowering back down, she pouts. "Blah. Fine, don't share." She looks around. "Where can we get a drink in this place?" It's amazing how she doesn't seem the least bit worried that she might be busted tonight. I wish I had her confidence. *Oh, wait . . .* yeah, I'm not known to be humble.

"The bar is over here." I place a hand on her back to guide her through the crowd. When it gets too dense, I drop my hand to hold hers. She slips it into mine so naturally that I'm beginning to believe we're a couple. And then I remind myself that snakes slither into your life.

We reach the bar and order drinks. While they pour her a glass of champagne and then reach for the good bourbon behind them, she leans against me, happy, feeling good by how her whole body is pressed against me like I'm not her mark. "I'm glad we came."

"Have you attended before?"

She gently pushes hair from my forehead and off to the side. "Only with you, silly. You don't remember?"

"Guess not."

"I've been thinking about something," she says as we stroll away from the bar with our drinks in hand.

"Oh yeah? What's that?" I sip the liquor as we find a vacant cocktail table near the *La Nuit* bronze sculpture with a view of Central Park at night. I'd rather look at Delaney, who wins my attention over great masterpieces any day.

"Are you really a member of the Mile High Club?" She takes a sip of her champagne and then holds it in front of her with her eyes locked on me.

I start to laugh, which is a good distraction since I really have no intention of getting into my past sex life with her. "Have you ever seen *Washington Crossing the Delaware*? The Met has the original. It's the size of a wall. We really should—"

"It's okay. You don't have to tell me, but just because you mentioned it, I'm not a member."

She peers up at me, waiting to see how I'll react, as if I'd judge her for that. I set my glass down on the table. Brushing my hand over her cheek, I cup it, making sure she's looking into my eyes. "Everyone should see *Washington Crossing the Delaware* at least once in their life—"

I'm whacked on the chest. "You are outright insufferable, you know that, Warner Landers?"

I'm too busy laughing to respond, but I missed a moment I'm already regretting. "I do know, and when I forget for only a second, I have you to remind me." She laughs, but it's light as she looks down at the ring on her finger, catching the slimmest of light in the hall where we're standing. "Hey, Sass?"

When she looks up, I'm forgiven. There's no malice

lingering in her eyes. Thinking back over the past few days, I don't think there ever was. It's the opposite now. The way she's looking at me like I'm the one who can save her inspires me to pick up where we left off yesterday. Lifting under her chin, I lean down to kiss her.

"I was hoping you'd be here, Warner." The familiar voice sounds my alarm before I have a chance to open my eyes. *Incoming. Incoming. Incoming.* As soon as I do, I take a firm hold of Delaney's hand, holding her close to my side. "Mother, I didn't expect to see you."

"Mother?" Delaney whispers under her breath beside me.

Shit.

CHAPTER 18

Delaney

SHOULDERS BACK.

Chin up.

Hands clasped on my clutch in front of me and not on her son. And just when things were getting good, too . . . his mother arrives to complicate our lives. As if they weren't already. I almost giggle, but I hold it in.

He kisses her cheek and returns to stand next to me. "How are you, Mother?"

"Why do you have a black eye, Warner?" No hello. No how are you back. Not even the cliché answer of fine.

"Bar fight."

"What?"

"I'm kidding, Mother. Long story. I'll tell you about it later. It's been a while."

As if nothing prior matters, she says, "Kaley Wrennick has made a disaster of the Upper East Side Social this year, but who am I to complain? The committee put us out to pasture after last year's event when they handed the reins to the 'next generation,' as they called it. All of us were shocked and insulted, to say the least. Darly Scoffield and I started that event. A little respect would have been nice."

I stare at his mother in shock as she takes only one breath during that entire diatribe. Similar blue eyes, a bit darker than his, and her platinum blond hair, though not natural, look nice against her golden skin tone. She's very pretty, but that doesn't surprise me since anyone with eyes and ovaries would be attracted to the man next to me. He's gorgeous and had to get those genes from somewhere. I suspect his father played a role, but I've not seen him to know.

I bet she has a standing reservation at the club to meet the girls for a round of tennis and then drink the next round while picking at overpriced Cobb salads after flirting with the tennis instructor. *Whoa!* That was a lot. I'm sounding like her now. I shake myself out of that because I'm not sure Mother Landers is the woman I want to emulate.

Warner sips his drink and then grins. It's not the smile I get, but it's not condescending. Cordial? A smile he probably wears to exchange pleasantries. So unlike the man I've gotten to know. He says, "Well, I'm sure when it fails, the committee will be begging you to run it again. Otherwise, you're doing well?"

Why does he ask questions like they're casual acquaintances?

"I'm good." The moment I've been dreading arrives. Her gaze lands on me like a ten-ton truck as she looks me over.

Two issues.

One, I'm not her daughter-in-law.

Two, we've never met.

So this is how the plan falls apart. This is where we come to the end of our fake relationship before it has a chance to get to the prize at the finish line. When Warner shows no intentions of introducing us, I go for it. Wrapping my arms around her like we're best friends from the Upper East Side Social club or committee, charity, whatever it is called that she's upset about.

Dammit. I've read her name in Page Six, but it escapes me when I need it most. Her body is stiff and manages to become solid as a rock as fear rounds her eyes when I lean back with my hands still holding her by the arms. "It's so good to see you again, Mother."

I don't need the chuckle from the peanut gallery behind me, so I shoot Warner a look that I hope he receives loud and clear as *zip it, mister.*

His mom asks, "Do we know—"

Warner steps into the fray, detaching my hands from his mom, and says, "Mother, you don't have a drink."

"I—" That's all she manages as her eyes stay glued to mine. "Who is that wo—"

"I need to refill my drink, too," he adds, swooping in by wrapping his arm around hers and pulling her toward the bar. "Let's get drinks." He glances over his shoulder at me. "Feel free to look at the art. That's why we're here tonight."

His mother knocks on his cast. "Did you break your arm?"

"A car hit me. I'll tell you all about it at the bar." That's the last I can hear before they blend into the crowd that's formed near the bar. I don't blame the people. I'd need booze too if I was always stuck going to these stuffy events. I was excited to get dressed up, but when I look around, no one seems to be having any fun. I take my glass of champagne and meander through the statues. I don't stop. Marble and bronze statues aren't typically the art I'm drawn to.

I wander through different exhibits, finding one of their grandest in the Egyptian wing. Continuing, I spend time looking at ancient weapons and jewelry, and paintings from France from the 1800s. I finish another glass of champagne before entering a wing and find another server happy to replace my empty glass with a brand-new one.

More time has passed than I thought I'd be spending with Warner. I don't mind, but I sort of miss the jerk. I finally reach the American wing of the museum. I've seen the painting online and on TV a million times and could describe it by heart. But he talked about it so much that I feel compelled to see it in person. I enter through two open double doors and stop. As I stare ahead, I was expecting a large painting. I wasn't expecting this. It's huge, covering most of the wall space at the far end of the room.

Awe overcomes me as I walk toward it, leaving me speechless.

"It's impressive, no?"

I glance over at Warner. He's standing next to me, his gaze on the painting in front of us. "I didn't expect it to be that big. Or . . ." I start, words still eluding me as the art takes precedence over thought. We stand in silence, both staring at the famous painting. "I've been here so many times over the years. I can't believe I've never seen it before."

"It's a big museum." He says, "It's not the original. But it's an incredible replica. The first was destroyed in a war."

"It's not like I haven't seen this on TV, online, or even in the movies. It's a general in a boat for goodness' sakes. I shouldn't be this emotional."

"There comes a sense of astonishment from the hours it must have taken. We feel like we know it because it's familiar, but it hits different seeing it in real life."

I nod, nothing of value to add to his observation. He

nailed it. I face him, looking around the room to see if I spot his mom. "Where's your mother?"

"Drinking champagne with the lead curator for the glass art that's being introduced tonight. She made a donation to close the gap to make the exhibit possible."

"Quite the philanthropist family."

He sips his drink and leans over. "You're part of that family, remember?"

"I don't think I could forget even if I tried."

Chuckling, he turns to me. "I almost kissed you when I found you in here. You really do have a graceful neck."

Disappointment shouldn't enter my mind, much less my chest, but there it is, weighing me down with the possibility of what could have been. "Why didn't you?"

"Because the last time, I got sucker punched by your bony elbow."

That makes me laugh, easing the heaviness that was creeping in. "You made a wise decision, I suppose. This time."

He looks at the painting once more before looking around as if he's searching for the nearest exit. "As romantic as this painting is," he says with a smirk on his face. "How about we get out of here?"

"The room or the museum?"

"Both." When a server passes with a tray of empty glasses, Warner finishes his drink and adds his glass to the others. "Ready?"

I add my glass to the tray and take Warner's offered hand. "Ready."

Judging by how he weaves us through the halls and straight toward the main lobby entrance, I think he's been here a few times. "Where are we going?"

"Where do you want to go? We're all dressed up and can—"

"Warner Landers."

The lobby fills with applause, trapping us in the dead center of the room, holding hands, like a couple that we're not. I look at him, worried about what will happen next. Exposure? Busted? Getting arrested for impersonating his wife? Frozen in panic, my heart still manages to beat louder than the rousing applause.

The announcer comes over the speaker and says, "We are so grateful for museum gold status saints like you. Without your donation, we wouldn't be able to offer such a robust catalog of exhibits. Another round of applause for Warner Landers."

Gold status? My eyes find the ribbon pinned to the front of his jacket, the same one that's pinned to mine. "What does gold status mean?"

A man comes up to him to shake his hand. He turns to me and replies, "Doesn't matter, Sass."

"I'm just curious." An older woman wearing a museum lanyard around her neck slips in after the man to shake his hand. She's thanking him while I consider pulling out my phone to research. "I'm sure I can find it online." Why is it such a mystery? I know he's rich, but how much could it possibly be? A hundred K or even two? I can't even imagine that kind of money, but that's his world.

He shoots me a look as he shakes one more man's hand and laughs, like we're sharing a secret. Guess we are. We both want to get out of here. Before anyone else cuts in, Warner takes me by the hand and says, "We're leaving."

His hand lands on the small of my back as he guides me through the crowd toward the exit. The heels are works of art themselves, the crystals covering them making them shine under the bright lights of The Met's facade, but for running, not my first choice.

I stop halfway down, needing a quick break from the ache in my feet. He goes four more steps before turning back. He returns, staying a step lower than me. Though to be eye level, he'd need to go down one more, or even two. "My feet hurt."

"I'd carry you if I could." He lifts his broken arm.

"It's okay. I just need a break." He holds out his hand so I can use him to balance. I rest my hand on his and lift each leg like a flamingo, giving it the rest it needs before switching feet. "Why won't you tell me how much you donated? As your wife, don't I have a right to that information?"

A smile splits his cheeks, and he chuckles. "You're relentless." I nod just enough to agree. "Why do you want to know?"

"I want to know how the other half lives." As soon as I say it, I know I've given away a part of my act. It's tempting to hide or try to distract from the mistake, but even three glasses of champagne cause enough trouble for me not to rush to cover it up. That will only make me look guilty, which I am, but he doesn't need to know that.

Warner doesn't blink, not showing any doubt of who I am or that I exposed myself. "Five million dollars." He just says it like it's a buck fifty. To him, it might be. To me, that would be my family's portion of the building. And he just gave it away like it was nothing.

I drop my leg back down so both my feet are planted on the concrete. Pulling my hand from his, my chest tightens as my stomach turns. "I wanted to know, but I wish I hadn't asked." I start down the steps, looking at what feels like a million ahead of me. No fast escape is happening in these shoes.

He walks beside me, his elbow out if I want the help. What I want isn't his damn arm for support. I want my family to have what they love most—their home and restaurant. And they only want those because we are a part of it. The family is what makes both places special and worth fighting for. But it's only me, standing in front of Mt. Everest without a jacket or oxygen, no survival skills, and nothing to help me climb that mountain. I don't stand a chance.

"I didn't want to tell you, but yeah, you can look it up. It's not a secret, but I . . ."

I stop and look at him. "You what, Warner?"

"I didn't want it to come between us." The earnestness of his expression would melt my cold heart if we were at the apartment. It would even add an air of romance if we were still standing together in front of the war painting. But we're not. We're in the middle of Manhattan to celebrate him for handing out millions of dollars like candy.

The wind picks up, and a few strands of my hair escape the spray it had diligently held most of the night. I push it back with my hand so I can see his eyes without interruption. "Listen . . ." I take a breath to calm the choppy waters of my heart. Any other time, I wouldn't think twice about a rich guy donating money to help good causes, and art is a good cause. But this isn't any other time. This is a time when my family is on the brink of ruin. The thing is, I have no right to be mad at him, to tell him how to spend his money, even if it is money earned at the expense of working-class families. My family suffering doesn't mean he owes us anything. I just hoped I could convince him to choose us, to choose good, like he did tonight. *To choose me.*

There is no choice in front of him. In his concussed

head, he already chose me. And he's not running away. He's spoiling me with dresses that I could never afford and shoes that I'm sure cost more than my paycheck. Warner held my hand like I belonged at that event, like I belong with him.

Now I feel bad when he's put in so much effort to make me feel good.

"I'm listening," he says when my head gets in the way of what was a beautiful night. He takes my hand, holding it like he's not giving up on me. Why? Why wouldn't he? I'm a nobody in his world. A pest. A fake. An adversary. "Are you okay?" *His* Sass.

With the resentment that hurried my getaway dissipating under the truth of what's happening, my heart pounds for a different reason. I like him. I care about him. I . . . I look away from the warmth of his eyes that make me feel safe, even protected in a city that can be so cold and gray. Inhaling a breath, I hold it only a moment before releasing it along with my feelings. *I'm falling for Warner Landers.* I've fallen for the enemy. Oh God, what am I doing? More importantly, what have I done?

I just hope it's not too late to turn this back around. I worked much better when I thought he was an asshole and not Prince Charming. Because heaven knows I'm in no position to profess my sins to him.

Apparently, my stomach is, though. It growls, bringing a smile to his face. And that makes me smile because I'm a fool for him. Or maybe this is a mood induced by a lack of food? A girl can only hope. Otherwise, three days in and I've lost at my own game.

"The car's here," he says, glancing down at the curb that has a million steps between me and relief from these painful shoes. He must sense my hesitation even now as I lowered the temperature of my anger. "The shoes?"

"Yeah. I think I'll take them off."

"It's New York." His tone turns firm. "You're not walking on these streets without shoes. I'll carry you." Although I shouldn't find his uptight bossy side so attractive, even that is under the new circumstances of me being mushy-hearted for this man and the whole meatball of emotions that comes with that.

"You can't. I don't want you to injure your arm." Eyeing it, I gently tap the hard cast. "More than it is. I'll just walk. I'll be fine. I'm sure you have a first-aid kit packed with anything I could possibly need to bandage the blisters later."

Standing two steps down from me, he bends before me. "No blisters." Looking up at me, he says, "Come on. It's only a few steps."

"Come on, as in get on your shoul—" I'm swooped over his shoulder before I can finish the question. I laugh from the playful gesture as I dangle over this giant of a man using one hand to make sure my ass isn't exposed to all of Manhattan. This might be the only time I've been grateful to be a smaller package of a person. But do I love being Warner-handled like this? Yes. Will I not give him a hard time anyway? No. I'm definitely giving him a hard time. I slap his ass with my clutch and laugh. "You're the worst, you know that, Hotshot?"

Chuckling, he says, "I know that, Sass."

Warner covers the remaining ten thousand steps with ease and even dashes a bit to show off at the end. Setting me down on the sidewalk beside the waiting black Town Car, he reaches to hold my face, staring into my eyes and stroking my cheek with the pad of his thumb like I'm the most precious thing he's ever seen. He has my head swimming in the feels, and my heart, being the traitor it is, beats just for him.

On the positive, if he has five million to donate to The Met, he has a lot more to splash around the city. So getting him to toss a few mil—five, to be precise—my way might not be such an impossibility. All I need to do is convince him of that.

The negative, I'm head over heels for this man. I'm so screwed. Who knew I'd be the type to fall for the villain of my story? *Not me.* I'm just as surprised as if I were the reader.

He holds the door open as I slip inside. Seems he's already given directions to the driver, and although I love being independent, it's nice to have little things taken care of sometimes. With him, they are. When he gets in and closes the door, he angles toward me. "Hungry?"

"Starving."

Fifteen minutes later, we're leaning against the car and tapping our hot dogs together. "Cheers," I say, and then take a bite. The hot dog never stood a chance against him. He finishes half in one bite. I take another bite, enjoying the clear skies, the bustle of people around us, and the company of one formerly intolerable bachelor. Though bachelor is subjective when it comes to us. I bump up against him, grinning like a girl in love because yeah, it's nice to feel free to be who I am around him. Finally. I ask, "How'd you know I liked hot dogs?"

"We live in the city. I took a wild guess."

"It was a good guess."

He finishes his food and then wraps his arm around my shoulders. "So what do you want to do next?"

"Considering I'm wearing these shoes, curling up on the couch with my big guy, gelato, and a movie sounds like a great way to spend the rest of the night."

"Big guy." He chuckles. "What movie did you have in mind?"

"I haven't seen *Ocean's 11* in years."

"I'm sensing a pattern."

I take another too big of a bite to chew properly because I'm not ready to address that pattern. I don't know what the plan is at this point, much less a pattern. I do know that when I look at Warner, he's not as bad as I thought he was, as I wished he was when I met him. Things just got a whole lot more complicated.

CHAPTER 19

Warner

"CAN I ASK YOU SOMETHING?" she asks, sliding her head up to see my eyes.

With her body nuzzled into the nook of my arm, I try my best to set the bowl that held gelato on the side table using my broken arm. The spoon clatters around the glass dish, but nothing breaks. I would sacrifice the bowl before having her move from this position on the couch. I like holding her. Even if she is about to hit me with something off the wall. I just know it. I can feel it, sense it. I'm getting the hang of how Delaney operates. After two hours of normalcy, she's bound to crack. "Shoot."

Angling out of my hold—*so disappointing*—she blinks a few times as she faces me, bringing her bended leg between us. "Can I have five million dollars?"

I burst out laughing, dropping my head back on the couch. When the echo of only my laughter fills the air, I look back up as my chuckle teeters off into silence. Still grinning like an idiot, I run my hand over my head and down to my neck, where I scratch an itch. "I thought you were going to say something like you're not my wife or you stole my phone. You know," I prod, still wondering if she's responsible for that. "Something like that."

Her expression never changes. "Why would I say that?" Delaney remains staring at me like she was dead-ass serious.

"Ohh, I don't know. Maybe because . . ." Narrowing my eyes at her, I dip my head. "Wait . . ." My brow shoots straight up while my jaw drops. Leaning forward, I click mute on the remote and then sit back again, still trying to figure out if she's pulling my damn leg. "Are you serious about the money?"

"Yeah." She tilts her head, finding humility through drooping shoulders and the corners of her mouth dragging down. The shift in her body language tells me all I need to know. She doodles on her leg with her finger, and her eyes stay focused on the invisible art she's creating. "I *was*. I am."

Hearing nerves I didn't know she possessed causing her voice to shake pulls me to give her whatever she wants, to reassure her that it will all work out. But I can't do that. I'm suddenly reminded of who we are to each other, nothing more than a con job gone wrong.

That doesn't stop me from reaching over to rest my hand on her knee. "That's a lot of money, Sass. Why do you need five million dollars?" *Shit.* I said it myself. We're a con job gone wrong. But maybe it's not gone wrong and has led right to this. This is what it's been about for her? She wants a payday.

"I want to help my family." *Sure you do, sweetheart . . .*

I stand and walk to the sliding glass door. I might need fresh air to help me through this conversation. "You can help more than your family with that amount of money."

When I open the door, I look back at her sitting where I left her. "Is that dollar amount set or it's more of a pie in the sky, shoot your shot number?"

She gets up, crossing the room with sudden energy she didn't exhibit on the couch. "It's set."

Since she's not volunteering much information, my mind wanders the corners of the worst scenarios searching for something to make sense. "You have a gambling problem, or owe someone some money?"

"No, Warner." Her smile is gentle, matching her tone as she touches my chest. "I don't gamble. I owe someone money but not from debts I created."

"Then why do you owe them money?"

She stares at me like the answer is on the tip of her tongue, but she's lost the will to voice it. "It's complicated."

"Money always is." I know firsthand. Walking onto the balcony, I reach the edge and lean my left side against it. The thickly carved balusters support the smooth railing and are reminiscent of the age of the prewar building. I always liked the balance of clean lines with modern conveniences, and then Delaney brought her chaos into my orderly world, fucking it all up.

Leaning against the railing in front of me, she shakes her head as if she has any shame. "I know this is uncomfortable. Imagine how I feel having to ask."

I chuckle, but it's lost to the sounds of the streets so many floors below. It's incredible how even night doesn't bring reprieve from the hustle of the city. Not even in the form of someone I was beginning to trust. Looking into her blue eyes, the skies are gone, replaced by clouds and lies. "You want me to imagine how uncomfortable you are in this situation?"

"I know it's not fun for you."

"Not fun? Uncomfortable?" No humor is heard in my laughter as I walk away from her because I need space to process the absolute absurdity of this conversation.

"I'm sure I'm not the first person to ask you for money, Warner. Look at tonight." She lifts her arm as if some great point is being laid at my feet. "You didn't think twice about donating that same amount to a museum that makes millions each year. I'm asking—"

"Don't."

Her head jerks back. When her arm falls to her side, she asks, "Don't what?"

"Don't assume you know what the fuck I think once or twice about." I turn my back to her, crossing my arms over my chest, and stare down the street that cuts through the buildings. How did I let this get so out of hand? Why did I? I shake my head as regret infiltrates not only my thoughts but also my veins. Scrubbing my hand over my face, I can't stop thinking about how foolish I was to think I could play along, and no one would get hurt. Someone always gets hurt. It's just not typically me.

The feel of her hand on my back has me moving out of her touch. With my back still toward her, I say, "Don't touch me and don't ever ask me for money again." I walk inside, leaving the door open for her.

She can enter or stay on the other side. The choice is hers—physically and metaphorically. Though I have no reason to allow this woman to remain in my life. I'm so fucking stupid for allowing myself to think I could trust her in the first place, but here I am, contemplating whether she'll choose me or the fucking door.

Fuck me.

I walk down the hall and cut through the bedroom to the bathroom. The trash bag to protect my arm from water, and the elastic tie hang over the side of the tub. I never take baths. I was about to turn on the shower, wanting to drown out everything outside the bathroom door, but a bath would be a whole hell of a lot easier to manage on my own.

Turning the faucet, I wait until the water runs warm, then I close the stopper. Sitting on the edge of the porcelain tub, I contemplate life. Not in the grand scheme of things but the day-to-day. I still have no memory of the accident, but I remember how much I worked to avoid the emptiness of the apartment.

Am I really feeling fucking sorry for myself?

I need out of my head and to bury my thoughts, so rogue emotions don't become a regular thing. I need to be working again. Taking a candle from the wooden stool next to the tub, I find a lighter next to the plunger under the sink. I light the wick and then set it on the counter. After squirting soap under the running water, I strip off the sweatpants and tee I had changed into when we got home from the event and step into the water before it's too full, so I don't send water overboard. I fill it up a little more before cutting off the water and resting my cast on the stool, so the plaster doesn't get ruined.

Maybe a shower would have been easier, after all.

Sinking a little more, since that's all I can between my size and the tub's capacity, I lean my head back on the tiled wall and close my eyes. I don't know if Delaney will still be in the apartment when I come out. I have strong doubts about how I left it, but even if she's not physically here, she'll remain in ways I can't use soap to get out or sweep into a dustpan.

I could use a drink, but I'm not getting out to retrieve one. I don't want to run into her if she's still here, and I don't want to be the one to have to tell her to get out. The hints are there and not subtle enough to miss. I also don't want to drip through the apartment, making another mess for me to clean up. She's done a fine job of that on her own.

A knock has me sitting up. "Go away."

"Please, Warner. Can we talk?"

"I'm good. I think enough has been said."

She opens the door like she legitimately lives here. That happened fast. Fast is probably how she's used to operating with her targets. Too much time leads to covers being blown. Peeking in, she says, "I'm sorry."

"Sorry for what exactly?"

"Sorry for asking you for money, for assuming money meant nothing to you, that you spend it without thinking, that you even have that much to spare—,"

"I have it," I say out of spite as if I must prove something to her. That shouldn't have been a trigger, but my ego can't take the hit tonight, not after everything else that's gone on. She's staring at me with nothing more to say. "If that's it, you can go."

Opening the door a little wider, she says, "I could but . . ." She starts taking off the pair of boxers she borrowed from me.

"Don't, Delaney." I hold my hand out as if she needs the visual to back my request. "You need to go."

The boxers drop to the floor and then she starts on the Harvard sweatshirt she stole from me. It's one of many things she's taken without my permission, including my . . . I won't go there. Those emotions aren't real. She's proven me right like everyone else.

"What are you doing?" I ask, my voice lower, quieter in the candlelit space.

She whispers, "We didn't finish the movie."

"You've seen the movie just like I have. There are no happy endings."

"This isn't the end." She drops the sweatshirt to the floor. "Not our ending."

My eyes roam over her skin and the bare parts of her body she's revealed. That I'm hard for her isn't a surprise. She's fucking stunning like I knew she would be. But that doesn't change what happened. It's not something that can be taken back. I inhale and release it on a sigh. "I'm not giving you the money. I'm not a fool who will cave under seduction."

"Seduction?" The word causes her to cringe. "Can we not use that term? It's dated, and it's not what I'm doing."

"Sure looks like it."

I catch a roll of her eyes, but she course corrects quickly. This is the first time it doesn't bother me. I barely noticed since her tits are displayed for me. She says, "Listen—"

"I did listen and then you asked me for five million dollars like I would just hand it over, like I could."

Planting her hands on her hips, she huffs, and then starts twisting her hair on top of her head and secures it. "You're not making this easy, Warner."

"I'm so sorry for foiling your plan."

"That's just it. There is no plan other than me apologizing."

I laugh like an idiot, no humor or authenticity to it. "Come on, tell me the truth." I need to hear her say the words to my face; *we're not married*. I could probably be convinced to give this another try if it weren't under duress. But the lies will destroy anything good, leaving us with only hate for one another otherwise.

"I'm judged for my business dealings. Not because I do anything immoral or illegal. Some people just don't care for those in the business of taking over other businesses. That's fine. They have a right to their opinion. It's never hurt my feelings. I'm not taken for a fool, though."

"I don't think you're a fool. I think you've lost touch with who you really are, though." Standing naked in my bathroom, she hasn't once cowered or grown coy. She's not shy and hasn't covered any part of herself. Her truth is laid bare before me.

There's something remarkable about someone seeing you so clearly that they pinpoint exactly how you've felt for years and kept hidden. And incredibly dangerous that she already knows who I am and seems to care. Maybe this started off as a heist of some kind, but I'm starting to think that it wasn't only my heart stolen. Hers was as well.

I'm an accomplice.

Fuck. I don't know what the right thing to do is in this situation, but it doesn't feel wrong. I hold my hand out for her to take. When she puts her hand on mine, I curl my fingers around hers, trying to find any excuse to keep her around a little longer. "Why did you ask me for money tonight?" I know why, but I need to hear her say it.

She dips her foot into the tub, and as I hold her steady, she slinks under the water and lies down on top of me. With her back pressed to my chest, she leans her head on my shoulder. "Truth?"

"It fucking better be." The heaviness in my chest is vanishing the more our bodies connect. Call me weak to a sexy woman. I don't care. I can have sexy any day of the week. This is about Delaney and how she makes me feel like I'm someone special. Let's just hope I'm not making the biggest mistake of my life. I slide my arm around her, resting my hand on her stomach to keep her right where she belongs.

"I got caught up in the money. God's honest truth. When I finally wrapped my brain around the fact that not only you but so many others there tonight had donated such a huge sum of money like it was nothing—"

"It's not nothing. It's one of my largest donations of the year. I carefully choose where every dollar is going. I want it to matter."

"It's only one of your largest. Jesus." She releases a heavy breath and rolls her head to stare at the window. The shade is down, so I reach up and hit a button near the switch for the jets. As the shade gathers upward, I catch a smile from her profile. It's not showy, but it's real like this moment we're sharing.

She starts to rub my leg. I don't even know if she's doing it on purpose as her gaze stretches into the night sky on the other side of the glass. Or if she finds comfort like I do in the simple act. "I'm sorry for asking for money."

This isn't a conversation that would ever be had with a wife. I can't stop from wondering how this all started and how we ended up where we are—becoming real with each other. The act is getting harder for her to perform, the mask slipping, and exposing who she is underneath the unhinged character she created. This is my favorite version of her. "Money is a necessary evil, but I don't want it coming between us."

"Me either." She scrapes suds from the top of the water and lathers them over her shoulders. "Warner?"

"Yeah?"

"We're in a tub naked together."

I grin. "We sure are. It was bold of you to invite yourself in." I chuckle lightly, not just at my own joke but because it feels good to release the betrayal I felt earlier. I don't have much to go off but my own gut instinct. It's telling me to trust the journey, leaving me to worry about the destination another time.

She slides to the side to look up at me. With her own smile in place, she says, "How's your head?"

"Almost good as new. The arm's still broken, though."

Maneuvering carefully so as not to splash water everywhere, she straddles my lap. When she leans down, she cups my face and gives me a quick kiss before pulling back just enough to look into my eyes again. With her smile reappearing as if I'm the one responsible for putting it there—*I sure the fuck hope I am*—she says, "I can work with that."

CHAPTER 20

Delaney

MY THROAT IS DRY, my mouth hanging open to pull more air into my lungs.

With the warmth of the water and the heat of my connection with Warner, I've stopped caring that strands of hair are stuck to the sides of my face. That my heated cheeks are probably flaming pink and my lips swollen from scraping across the scruff of his jawline.

Reaching up, he gently rubs the pad of his thumb under one of my eyes and the tip of his finger under the other. He slides his hand to the nape of my neck, bringing me in to kiss again.

It didn't take much to open Pandora's box. Now that we have, there's no closing it. This feels too good. He turns me on too much. My head spins along with my heart, and I stop fighting the pull to him. Giving up control, the upper hand, and trying to think five steps ahead vanished after the first kiss. It's fun to feel this free, to feel this me again.

Gripping the sides of the bathtub, I drop my head next to his as I rock against his erection. *Shameless and carefree.* His breathing has deepened, and words are huskier in my ear. I need more—more of everything with this man.

When his fingers tease my clit, I buck, causing the water to splash against the edge of the porcelain. I don't care about making a mess, but I know Warner will. My words are jagged as I drag my eyes to latch onto his again. "We should get out."

"Not until you come." There's such authority to his tone that I find myself drawing a breath as his hand dips under the water and slides between our bodies. A tease of my clit causes me to shift down and harder. His fingers arouse me before one slides further to toy with my entrance. With his eyes still set on mine, he doesn't ask for permission, but I give it by rocking against his hand.

The starting gun ignites, my entire being needing completion as I race toward a finish line I don't want to cross. Why can't I feel this good forever? It's not even a pause, but I find myself already begging, "Don't stop."

"I'm not stopping, Sass." The smile that embeds into my heart has me wanting to stare at him all night. "Not until you come for me."

"I can do that."

"Yeah, you can," he says playfully. I could almost mistake that shine in his eyes for love if I'm not careful. I'm not that foolish to think someone like him would fall so fast for someone like me. We're from different worlds. *Fire and ice.* Even oil and water at times. I prefer cloak and dagger.

I lower my head, focusing on the hunger blooming in my belly instead of the jagged breaths ringing in my ears from a constricting throat. Resituating on his hand, I push onto him, his finger diving into my depths and causing my head to fall back, my mouth to open, and a moan to escape my chest. He pulls back out, but just enough to keep the connection that I'm struggling to hold on to. *Too much all at once.*

"You turn me on so fucking much. I can't wait to fuck you properly." His breathing is just as hard as mine, his tone gravelly and not the one I'm used to. The eyes that would devour me whole if he could, motivate me to drive faster toward relief.

I only close my eyes for a second to find myself at the precipice of what comes next—the descent into darkness and bliss in the light. His fingers never stop the circular teasing that's putting me into a tailspin. I grip the tub to help hold my weight as I rock back and forth, up and down, right side up and left side down. He consumes my every thought, my body conforming to his as I start to lose myself under the weight of what's to come. "God, I want this. So much." I try to focus on him, but it's impossible when they're rolling back in my head. "Feels too good, Warner."

"No such thing." I'm in no position to argue with the man who's about to send me to heaven and back again. I'll just let him work his magic . . . *fingers*. The water splashes around me as I rise and fall, over and again as he pushes me to the edge and pulls me back again. I'm so close I can already imagine the aftermath. The bliss. The calm. The reward of falling asleep in his arms. I want it. I want all of that. So much.

When he's deep inside, his palm presses against my clit. I grind against him, embracing the fall. I don't feel my breath or an ache in my lungs. I'm free from the burdens of pretending and liberated from the past few days. I welcome this feeling and the aftermath.

With the side of my head pressed to his, I whisper, "Why are you so good at that?"

He chuckles, his finger still inside me, which sends another wave of pleasure through me. "Hidden talent."

"I like that it's hidden." I sit up. "Except from me." I lean forward to kiss him. My breathing is still uneven when I pull back. "How about we finish this in bed?"

"Is that an invitation, Sass?"

"To your own bed?" I lift to my feet, but I instantly hate how empty I feel without him. Offering his hand for assistance, I step out of the tub and grab a towel hanging from a hook nearby. "You got the golden ticket, Hotshot."

He stands, careful to step out, and reaches for the other towel. "Our bed."

I stop my hands as my mind races through how to fix the mistake I just made. Nothing believable comes to mind, so I choose confrontation. "Of course it is, silly." I laugh, but let it die off quickly.

Warner is always on top of things, waiting for the slipup to happen so he can study my expression and judge my reaction. It's a lose-lose situation with him. He sees through the obvious, so I now stick to being vague when possible.

He replies, "Yeah, of course," as if I had asked a question. When he's dry, he comes to wrap himself around the back of me and kisses my head. "How are you feeling?"

With the sexual heat between us cooling, I cover his arms with mine, holding him as I lean the back of my head against his chest. Closing my eyes, I savor this moment before everything changes, knowing we're close to the truth coming out. I have no next steps planned. Nothing to trick him into prolonging this charade. I asked for the money against my better judgment and left myself open for the blowback. I don't want to do that again. I don't want to ask him for money. I don't want to need it. I want him to realize the mistake he's making and fix it. And if he doesn't stop or can't end the contract, I need to show him the benefits of spending his money where it matters most. To me, anyway.

That's it. I need to show him.

"Warner?"

"Hmm?" He hums against my neck and then kisses it.

"My family has dinner together every Sunday . . ." I wait for a stiffening of his body behind me or a sigh of discontent. Neither happens. His muscles are strong but pliable around me, his heart not skipping a beat, his breathing stays regulated as if this idea might not be so far-fetched. "As you know." Damn, almost forgot to tack that on. The climax has turned my brain to jelly.

Releasing me, he comes around to the front with a big ole grin on his face like he just won the local bake-off. "Two invitations in one night? I think your orgasm has gone to your heart." *Geez.* Even he's noticed.

I smile like a fool for him. I am, so it comes naturally. "Don't worry. It will wear off soon enough, and then you'll have the crankier version of me back."

"I don't consider you cranky, Delaney." He caresses my cheek and then kisses it. "Stubborn and feisty, absolutely." Tapping my nose, he adds, "Oh, and I accept both. Dinner with your folks, and to finish what we started here out there." He opens the door and walks out, leaving me a bit stunned.

That wasn't a formal invite to dinner. I was kind of just telling him why I would be gone tonight. But now I'm bringing my fake husband to the restaurant. *Lord, help me.* There's no getting out of it without hurting his feelings though, so I guess Warner Landers is about to meet my family.

When I enter the bedroom, he's already in bed with his arms behind his head. A smug smirk shapes his expression, and the covers are already tenting. "Looks like you got started before me."

"No, this is in anticipation of how amazing it's going to feel being inside you."

I drop the towel, but just when I lift my knee to climb onto the bed, I realize that leaving a wet towel on his pristine carpet is going to bother him. That's usually a highlight for me, but we're about to be together for the first time. I don't want him thinking about wet towels on the carpet. I want him to think about me.

After picking up the towel, I go into the bathroom and push it down into the hamper. I return to see him grinning even wider. "Gloating?" I ask.

"Might be." He flips the comforter open for me so I can crawl into the bed and under the covers. I slide up right next to him. I feel so alive being naked with him. The way he looks at me like I'm something to be admired causes goose bumps to erupt over my arms. His eyes drinking me like a man who's dying of thirst is an aphrodisiac.

I don't feel shy with Warner. I don't feel ashamed like I'm doing anything wrong. I kiss him because everything is right when we're like this. Sliding onto him, our lips stay attached as I position myself. It would be easy to have him slip into me, his thickness stretching me to accommodate him and only him. I don't, but he has my walls lowered to the ground, so I wouldn't say no.

Our lips find purchase just as his hand slides around the back of me. He sits up with me straddling him, rubbing myself over his erection. Plucking his lips from mine, he whispers, "The condoms are in the nightstand."

I'm not going to make him struggle with his broken arm, so I fall forward on the bed, catching my weight on my forearms and reaching as far as I can to open the top drawer. But anything inside is out of reach. I drag myself closer and peer inside. Darting my eyes back to him, I ask, "You have a container to organize your condoms?"

He chuckles, still sitting up, but now his weight is on his left arm. "It's a sugar pack holder, like at restaurants. I saw it and realized if you turn it the other way, it fits a condom wrapper perfectly."

"I'm not even sure what to say to that." I laugh. "I'll never look at them the same way." I grab the holder and set it on the top of the nightstand. "It only holds five."

"You got big plans there, Sass?"

Laughing, I turn around. "Not anymore since you only have five."

When I come closer again, he takes my chin and guides me like a missile straight to his lips. "Don't worry," he whispers and then pecks my lips. "I have more when we need them."

I steal a kiss before snatching a packet and ripping it open. I could watch him struggle to do it with one hand, but that only punishes me. I want him now. When I flip back the blanket, my breath catches. "Warner." I don't know why I say it like he's in deep water when I'm the one who is clearly about to be in trouble.

"I'll go slow."

I shoot him a glare. "Let me guess. Don't worry?" I ask, sarcastically. Trying not to worry about what I'm intentionally about to do to myself since there's a major upside, I roll the protection over his length. I can't stop thinking about his finger making me feel full. I'm definitely in trouble.

I stare at him a moment longer when my hand is taken. "Come here," he whispers, giving it a squeeze of reassurance. I look up and then move closer, lying on my side with my head on the pillow to face him. "I can't put weight on my arm yet, but we can take things slow. I'll be gentle. I promise."

I nod and move even closer to kiss him. One kiss leads to another, and then a shift in our bodies. He doesn't pull me on top of him, but I go willingly. I'm intimidated by his size, but my body is already seeking relief as I rub myself against him. "Oh," I moan, the feeling so good even though we've barely started.

Straddling him, I lift myself. His hand rubs along my outer thigh before slipping between us to position himself at my entrance. I'm slow like he advised, engulfing the tip before taking a breath and sliding all the way down. I press my hands to his chest, concentrating on my breathing to get me through the initial burn and stretch.

I close my eyes and take another deep breath, and when I exhale, I whisper, "I need you to move, Warner."

With his hand staking claim to my hip again, his body gyrates underneath mine and then pulls out just a bit to have me on the verge of begging before pushing back in. "Oh my God, you feel so good," comes off my tongue in a hurried exhale. Using my hands on his chest as support, I finally lift and meet his next thrust, and each time it becomes easier, and no burn remains, only the incredible desire for more, more, more.

"I need you," he says, his hand coming to caress my cheek before sliding to the side of my neck while still fucking me.

I won't stop. I can't. My hunger for more, for the bliss, and the push, the thrust, and the climax mingle together, the sensations becoming too much to hold on for long. "God, I need you, too." I do. I find myself stretching my back, embracing his length and taking him whole, owning his gaze, and aiming for his heart. Leaning back, I let my breasts bounce as I release my hair from the knot on my head, allowing it to tumble down.

He makes me feel amazing, so beautiful that the lies we've told don't mean anything in the long run. Living in the here and now is all that matters. I lift and fall, take and squeeze, embrace him, and then fuck him until he starts to fall apart. I feel the effort in his body to fight the surge that will overwhelm him soon. I can see the struggle in his eyes to hold on. I rest my hands on his chest again, fixing my eyes on him and take him thrust for thrust, fuck for fuck, and giving it right back. His arm swoops around me and brings me to the mattress. With our bodies still attached, he angles his weight over me and drives into me with the full intention of pushing me to fall with him. His eyes set on mine, every thrust is punctuated with possession—his arm around me, his lips on my neck, his cock staking claim to every inch of me. "Fuck, I love you." The words come out breathless as he drives into me, seeking his relief and dragging me under with him.

And then I'm falling with him . . .

Unraveling.

Spiraling toward that sensual perfection.

My body tremors for seconds, minutes, even a lifetime as I let the pleasure consume me. I return to this world, into his arms, and collapse on his chest with no energy remaining and no will to move. But when the fog of pleasure lifts, it's the confession that consumes the aftermath.

Being with him has changed me more than I could have understood when creating this mess. This wasn't cat and mouse, me setting a trap for him to fall into. This was us playing house. Lying here, listening to his heart beat strong in his chest out of pure indulgence, I realize I love being his wife.

I thought I was in trouble before. *Oh God, what have I done?* I might be too far gone to save myself.

CHAPTER 21

Warner

BAYETTI.

Delaney's kept me so busy that the only break I've had, I tried to fit some work in. I didn't get far on that either. But I should have done some research. Despite my phone being another limb of mine, I haven't been missing it as much as I thought. It's probably the woman keeping me preoccupied all the time.

Delaney Bayetti.

It's a pretty name. I was growing partial to Landers, though. Which means I need to get my head examined as soon as possible. Side effect of the concussion? Side effect of starting to fall for this woman, I'm afraid.

As we travel the last block before arriving, I realize I'm going in blind. An error in judgment on my part. I'm not nervous, but I don't understand how she plans to pull this off. Has she already involved her family? She mentioned brothers . . . "Who's coming to dinner tonight?"

"The usual."

Not the answer I wanted. But I must give it to her, even after sex, she's still not cracking under pressure. So when we approach the restaurant on the corner, I hold her sweaty little hand a bit tighter. Because whatever happens in *Bayetti's*, we're in this together.

She stops before we cross the street in spite of the sign flashing to proceed. Turning to me, she runs her hands down the front of my shirt. The gesture is sweet when she stops and lifts to kiss me, but I look down to see if there's a trail of perspiration on the cotton. There's not, allowing me to breathe easier. "You look nice. Don't be nervous."

"Am I usually nervous?"

She laughs, adjusting her weight to her left hip. Looking pretty in a red dress, she opted for flat black shoes. I would think short stuff would like a little height, but it's sexy that she doesn't feel the need to compete. With a tilt of her head, she replies, "No. Not usually."

"Are you nervous?"

"I'm . . ." She glances off into the distance as if the answer will be found out there. "Optimistic."

"Optimism is good. So is this dress on you. You look pretty, Sass."

She smiles, lighting my world on fire. "Thank you." When she takes the hand I offer again, I'm beginning to think she needs it more than I do. I can only imagine how she thinks she's going to pull off these shenanigans once her family gets involved. While we wait for the next opportunity to cross, her eyes are set on the restaurant. "We don't have to stay for dessert." Peeking up at me, she says, "We can leave any time you're ready."

"Got it. We've got an out."

"It's not an out. It's an option."

"Okay." The crosswalk sign begins to buzz. We step off

the curb and cross. "We have options." Trying to get some semblance of knowledge before I walk into this lion's den, I ask, "My amnesia has made me bad with names. I need a quick refresher."

Stopping in front of the window, she's still holding my hand when she turns to me. "Pamela is my mom. Anthony, my dad. Joe is my oldest brother, and Lorenzo is every bit the middle child."

"So you're the youngest?" As her "husband," I should know these things. But as the guy who she's now sleeping with, I actually do want to get to know her.

"I'm the youngest." Why does this not surprise me? Placement in the sibling lineup determines everything from personality to how much they get away with. Being the only girl only complicates matters more. Toss in a big Italian family, and I'm screwed. My usual charms won't work on them. Listening more than speaking will be my friend this evening. "Ready?"

"As I'll ever be." *That's not saying much.*

I hold the door for her, the smell of garlic and home cooking escaping through the opening as she walks in with me behind her. She reaches back with her hand, so I take it as she says hi to the hostess and weaves through tables toward the back.

"Delly bean," a woman who mirrors Sass's features— hair color and the same blue eyes—but older, slides out from a large red vinyl booth in the back corner. My hand is released as Delaney hurries into her open arms. I think it's safe to assume this is Pamela.

Her father is easy to pick out from the lineup of other faces. One by one, the three men slide out to wait their turn to greet Delaney. There's a lot of love to share between them. Even her brothers hug her, though I catch the way they both have a straight face when they eye me over her shoulder.

I'm fucked.

Although this is where things should fall apart for her, she turns to me and waves me off like I'm an old hand here. "Warner." *Smooth.*

They're staring at me like they're missing a piece of the puzzle. Me too, Bayetti family. *Me too.*

Her mom captures my face in her hands just to get a good look at me. "So handsome." She pulls me to her and embraces me in a hold that doesn't leave much room to escape.

"Thanks, Pamela."

"Call me Mom." Releasing me like she got burned by the hot potato, she says, "Say hello to the others." She slides back into the booth with Delaney sliding in after her.

"Oh, okay. Yeah, of course."

One of the brothers looks me over and asks, "You look like a money guy. You have a man on the inside?"

"On the inside of what?" *Clearly not Sass's plan.*

He slaps the back of his hand against my chest and laughs. "Business."

Not what I was expecting, but not a topic I'm opposed to. Unless he's trying to sell me something, which I'm getting the distinct impression he is. "I have a few. Are you in finance?"

"Top of my class over at NYU."

"Ah, Stern School of Business. Impressive. I'm a Harvard man myself."

The smile disappears as if I crushed his dreams. "Well, if you need a guy—"

"I know who to call, Joe." Taking a wild guess paid off. He steps aside and then disappears into the back of the restaurant, leaving me to face Lorenzo on my own. I can already tell by the crossed arms and narrowed eyes that I'm about to get a talking-to or maybe a threat. Potentially both.

"Warner, huh?"

I hold out my hand. "Warner Landers."

"Yeah, I know." *Okaaay.* "You're finally showing your face around here."

What the fuck is this guy talking about? He whacks my arm and bursts out laughing. "I had him going. I really had him going."

Delaney says, "He only has one good arm, Lorenzo. Go easy on him."

"Right. Right," he replies, staring at the cast. Cutting off my sleeve isn't pretty, but it got me here looking the best I could on short notice since my tailor isn't open on Sundays. He turns as if he's lost interest and slides in next to his mom.

I turn to her father, who has been extraordinarily patient. I imagine he'd have to be with this rowdy crowd. "My cannoli tells me you were hit by a car?"

I send my gaze from him to Delaney. "Your cannoli?"

"How are you doing?" His concern wrangles his forehead and filters through his deeper tone.

Lifting the cast, I reply, "I lived to tell the tale."

"That's good. I'm sure Delaney's taking good care of you."

"She is, sir."

"Eh." He waves me off as he turns away. "Call me Pops."

Pops? Mom? I don't even call my own mother Mom. Something makes me think that their monikers are well-earned over the years. Mother has always just fit mine.

"Come on, Hotshot." I look at my girl and see her patting the seat next to her.

I slide into the booth until our legs bump together under the table. Her hand finds my thigh and rubs up and down like we do this all the time—eat dinner with her family and touch each other in public. I was never one for PDA, but I'm not opposed to showing the world Delaney's mine. It's barbaric to want to mark her as mine, but damn, the instinct is strong.

Joe returns and slips in next to me. I'm trapped indefinitely. Pamela sets a glass in front of me and pours in wine from a Chianti bottle. She's not shy with her wine. It's filled almost to the top. "Drink. Drink," she says.

Cheap table wine isn't typically my go-to when I eat at Italian restaurants, but I'm their guest, so Chianti it is tonight.

When the others are distracted with conversation, teasing Joe about a buyer at Macy's, Delaney holds a basket in front of me. "Bread?"

"It's okay. I don't want to ruin my appetite."

The chatter stops, and all eyes turn on me, at least at this booth. Delaney hands me a fluffy hot breadstick and whispers only for my ears, "Please eat." With everyone's life seemingly dependent on whether I take a bite, I bite. The volume returns, picking up right where they left off. Delaney says, "So she dumped you for the delivery guy?"

"Yeah, he was flashing a bonus check he'd gotten like it was a fucking bar of gold. Not my loss."

Note to self: Never say no to food when a Bayetti offers. I continue eating the bread because it's really good, but it's also given me a reason not to talk.

Pamela says, "I should think not." Turning to me, she smiles. "Delly bean said you have a concussion as well."

Cannoli *and* Delly bean? The love between them is

evident. My mother and father called me Warner. And it stuck. "I'm healing."

"That's good. Hope you like meatballs."

I don't get the correlation, but I think if I hung around them long enough, I would start understanding a lot more about their transitions and probably end up with a nickname. "I love meatballs."

Joe and Lorenzo hop up and disappear to the back again. I slip my red fabric napkin over my right leg and finish the breadstick. I pick up my wine to wash it down and feel eyes watching my every move. I look at my girl and ask, "What?"

"Nothing." She smiles, but then says, "This is nice."

"It is." I take a drink of wine, regretting that decision before I swallow it down. But she's still looking at me like she's hoping for the best, so I grin. "I'm glad I'm here."

Her shoulders slump in relief. "So am I."

Just as the brothers return with plates of food they're doling out, Anthony says, "You know what I always say."

In unison, they all reply, "What's meant to be yours will be."

He stabs the air with his finger, and adds, "It's true."

Pamela grabs the finger and pulls his hand down. "Eat. Eat, Anthony. We don't have all night. It's a full house tonight."

Lorenzo says, "I'm working with you tonight." He laughs, but then jabs, "Since this one over here isn't."

I glance at Delaney, who's giving her brother the evil eye. I get that what Delaney and I have would fall under the definition of a whirlwind romance. It doesn't make sense, and it doesn't need to for me to be happy. I knew enough, or so I thought. I'm realizing I don't know anything about this woman. What does she do for work? Work here at the restaurant? Where does she live since she sure as daylight doesn't live with me? *Technically.* I'm not kicking her out, though. "You have to work after dinner?" I ask her mom.

She finishes a bite, and replies, "Owning a restaurant means no rest for the weary." Her smile shines like the words don't fit the expression. "We wouldn't have it any other way."

Her father says, "We love this place. It's the sixth member of the family."

Delaney's hand rests on my bicep. "Bayetti's is closed on Mondays, but Sunday dinners are a tradition. On Mondays, we always ate out." The family laughs together. I'm not sure I ever experienced that growing up. Not even as an adult. My parents were married, but they considered themselves divorced. My dad lived in the Financial District so he could walk to work. My mom stayed uptown on the Upper East Side to avoid my dad at all costs. Run-ins only happened when they needed to make an appearance as Mr. and Mrs. Landers. Otherwise, they lived two different lives, with me caught in the middle.

Joe says, "We're ready for something else."

"And not to cook," adds Pamela. "You're not eating, Warner."

I pick up my fork and spoon and start on the pasta first. The sauce is good, reminding me of a home I'd see in the movies, more real than mine. "This is really good, Pamela."

"Mom."

"Mom," I reply, finding it easier to say than I would have predicted. Delaney sets her fork down after finishing a few meatballs and a good portion of her spaghetti, the speed eater that she is, and then leans her head on my shoulder. It's not in the soft smile on her face, but the happiness reflected in her eyes that catches my heart off guard.

She's incredible at my place, but seeing her now, this

side of her that's authentic to who she is on the inside . . . is spectacular. Remembering how she looked when I made her come in the tub and the confidence that glistened on her skin as she sat on top of me, taking what she wanted and what she needed, makes me privileged once again to see her now. Such innocence, in contrast, is truly breathtaking.

"What's it like to have amnesia?" Lorenzo asks just prior to shoveling a bite of food into his mouth. I see why she eats so fast now. *They all do.*

"I've not had it before, and if I have, I don't remember."

Sass bursts out laughing even though no one else does. "Come on, that was funny. He landed an amnesia joke like a pro." She pats my leg. "I like your joke, babe."

Babe?

God, I fucking love this woman. Well, not *love* love but . . . oh shit. Do I *love* love Delaney? My throat feels tight, my chest hot like I need fresh air. I chug more wine to put out the fire, but when the glass is empty, that pesky four-letter word remains.

I love her.

With my elbow propped on the table, I drop my head onto the palm of my hand. What the fuck? Love? Really, Landers? The woman is unhinged, and that's who you decided to fucking fall for?

"Are you okay, Warner?" she asks, rubbing my back.

Lifting my head, I try to take the curiosity off me while I wrestle with the fact that I'm in love with their daughter, their sister, their cannoli, and Delly bean. I reply, "The doctor said amnesia is unpredictable. One minute, everything is gone, erased from your mind. Then bam! It can return in a flood of memories. *Or not.* I'm just hoping for the best."

They all look a bit stunned, other than Delaney, who

leans over and whispers, "You're looking a bit pale. Maybe this was too much with your concussion. We should go."

"Can I get this to go?"

She laughs. "Yes, we can get it to go."

Joe says, "I'll get a to-go box."

"Don't forget the cookies," Pamela adds before he's out of earshot.

I look at my girl, and whisper, "I lasted forty-five minutes. Not so bad."

"Longer than I expected you to last."

Slipping out of the booth, Delaney is hot on my tail and standing before I can turn around. She takes a bag from Joe and gives him a quick hug. Kneeling back into the booth, she hugs her mom and reaches across the table to hold hands with Anthony and bridge the divide. She flicks Lorenzo on the shoulder, and says, "Stay cool, kid."

I say, "Thank you for dinner and for having me be a part of your tradition."

Pamela smiles, and says, "Hopefully, we'll see you again, Warner."

I've got to hand it to Delaney. She didn't prepare them for my arrival. She let it play out naturally. They punched holes in a couple of her stories, but I'm going to let that slide because I have bigger issues to deal with—mainly that I'm in love with her.

CHAPTER 22

Delaney

"WHAT KIND OF COOKIES ARE THESE?" Warner's question travels the length of the hallway and into the bedroom where I'm slipping into something comfy.

"Double chocolate." I rush into the closet after leaving my dress tossed across the arm of the chair. What if my mom only packed a few, and he eats them before I get one? Panic rises, knowing that if he takes one bite, he won't be able to help himself from eating the rest. Grabbing a fandom T-shirt from his closet, I start down the hall, pulling it over my head. "Save me one, okay?"

I run so fast that when I try to slow down on the approach to the island, my socks slide me into home base. Slamming my hands down on the counter, I say, "How many are there?"

"Six." His eyes widen. "They're big."

"As all cookies should be." Taking the one on top, I bite first and talk later. But that first bite . . . I slump against the wall and moan. "Mmm." As soon as I swallow, I say, "So good." Warner's not eating. He's still staring at them like they aren't the most magical, delectable cookies that ever existed. "Have one. You're going to love it."

"The other day, you said you'd only eaten a cookie. Double chocolate, to be exact." I cram more cookie into my mouth, worried and knowing where he's going with this. "From a bakery." He has the courtesy of giving me a brief reprieve before his eyes land on me. "Was it from your mom?"

Now, why did he have to go and ask me flat out like that? Despite all the lying I've had to do with him to this point, I still don't feel good about it. And now I'm supposed to go hard and lie to his face when he's asking point-blank. By how slowly I'm chewing, he must think I lost my ability to speak. I go into the kitchen and pull a glass from the cabinet before I finally swallow it down, along with the will to keep all these secrets from him. I don't have it in me anymore. I pull open the stainless-steel door of the refrigerator to block him from seeing how guilty I am of bad deeds, and reply, "Yes. I went home that day."

When I shut the door, he's right there. "Good lord, Warner." I grab at my shirt over my pounding heart. "If you're trying to scare the crap out of me, you succeeded." He's still staring at me like I wasn't already startled. "What?" I ask, staring back at him. He closes the door before I can get the pitcher. "Hey, I was getting water."

"It can wait."

Rubbing along my throat as if that will throw him off the path he's on, I say, "I don't know, my throat is really dry. Coarse like sandpaper—"

"Do you live with your parents?"

Gulps. "I live with you." *The lies begin again . . .*

"When you're not living with me, do you live with your

family?" There's no detouring this guy. But I've never been known to give up that easily.

"You're my family." I should be more impressed with the skills I've been honing at his expense. *But I'm not.*

"Delaney." His voice is firm, a demand made without uttering one word other than my name.

I raise my chin, offended by this line of questioning. "Yes." Real offended or fake offense? *Hmm.* I'm not sure. I'm teetering on the line.

He touches my cheek before tucking some strands of hair behind my ear. "You moved back home when we separated." Bringing me against his chest, he hugs me to him. I'm lost. Am I busted, or am I still undercover? "I'm sorry I wasn't a better husband to you."

I'm not sure what is happening, but I wrap my arms around him and whisper, "The past doesn't matter. Only the present, and you've already changed so much." Why does the truth sound like a lie? Oh geez.

But this doesn't feel good. It never did. Everything has changed now that he's met my family. *And been inside me.* Without warning my family I was coming, I showed up with this man holding my hand, and they welcomed Warner into the fold with no questions asked. That's who they are as people. That's the family feel Bayetti's strives to give to everyone who dines there. And it was captured just for him.

I'll never ask him for money again, but will he change his mind and cancel the contract after experiencing the restaurant and meeting my family? Maybe, if I'm judging anything by this hug. "Warner?"

When he steps back, his eyes search mine, and a smile appears. Sliding his finger down my nose, he says, "Let's get that water for you." I step back out of his way. Something feels off about this situation. He fills my glass from the pitcher and then continues on his merry way out of the kitchen like nothing happened. This time, he steals a cookie from the box and heads down the hall toward the bedroom.

I ask, "Where are you going?"

"To bed."

What the . . . "With a cookie?"

"Yep." He takes a bite without stopping or looking back.

"You realize they have crumbs, right?"

"I do."

Something is most definitely off. I take my water and grab another cookie before following his same path. As soon as I enter the room, he's climbing into bed. "Crumbs that will burrow into the carpet and on the bed?"

He chuckles. "I know, Sass."

I pad my way across the floor, stepping over the heels I purposely left in his way and noticing the dress is still flung over the chair. "What has gotten into you?"

"Nothing. I just realized that worrying about every little thing is not worth the good times I'm sacrificing."

"What does that even mean?" I set my cookie and glass on the nightstand and climb under the covers. The silky soft cotton feels like the sheets are freshly washed every day. Wait a minute . . . *are they*? Does he come in here and change the sheets when I'm not looking?

"It means I'm focusing on the wrong things."

"Like staying up past nine o'clock? Why are we going to bed so early?" I reach over, pinch off a piece of the cookie, and take a bite.

"I'm not going to bed. I'm getting into bed. With you," he says, leaning over and kissing my shoulder. Now it's becoming clear.

I finish the bit of cookie I broke off as I angle to face him, crisscrossing my legs under the covers. "Did you lure me in here with cookies?"

"I'd like to think you came in to spend time with me, but did I unashamedly use a dessert to get you into bed? I did." With his back against the headboard, he grins like a fool in love. Oh my. Is that what's happening here? My feelings for him have grown exponentially. Have his feelings for me done the same? One thing he said I know for a fact is truthful; he is unashamed to have tricked me into this bed by looking at that gorgeous and not-so-humble grin on his face. "I want you on me," he says, the dulcet tones of his voice just as devilishly enticing as the treat. Maybe more.

I climb over him and kiss those incredible lips of his. *Definitely more.*

With his broken arm at his side, his other hand reaches around, running along the hem of my underwear and then dipping under the thin fabric to caress my ass. Pulling me higher, right where he wants me, and where I wanted him so badly, he kisses me again.

The cookie is forgotten, the mess of clothes I left around the room, the glass of water on the nightstand, and everything else that's not him and me. I lift from the sensations, the pressure between my legs already feeling so good. I'll either fall apart quickly or try to relish this connection to him a little longer. Either way, he knows exactly how to get me to the edge of rapture. Sitting back down on his erection, I can't stop myself from wanting to skip the foreplay and feel him inside me again.

Cupping his face, I lean my forehead against his, gathering the will to leave this position when he feels so incredible. "I need to get—"

"I already got it." His hand disappears from my body,

and the sound of a packet glides out from under his pillow, and he drops it to the mattress. "Lift."

I stand on my knees as he pushes down the boxer briefs on one side. I help with the other, and then they disappear to the bottom of the bed. Eyeing me, he asks, "You want to take that off?"

Nodding, I pull the tee off over my head and toss it to the far side of the bed. He's already working on the side of my panties, so I help him out until they're trapped around my knees. I laugh and get to my feet. I lift one foot at a time as he slides them free from my ankles. Before I drop back down, he says, "Stay there. Let me look at you."

His hand runs along the side of my calf, and then up the back of my thigh. A breath seems to jag when he sucks it in and encourages me forward. "Come closer, Sass." I'm starting to notice that his pattern of commands and requests is direct, with no room for discussion. A discussion is the last thing I want as well, but I find it so sexy the way he's so sure of himself.

Standing with a foot planted on either side of him, I step closer. As his hand slinks up my backside, he cups my ass and pulls me closer. He kisses the lowest part of my belly and then slips his tongue through the slit of my lower lips. My breathing comes hard as I watch him do what no one else has before.

I run my hands through his hair, wanting to share this with him and only him. The emotions blooming in my chest are false flags to distract me, brought on by being intimate with him. Surely . . . but I don't know. They feel real, even with his tongue teasing my clit. "Ah," I release from my lips, though it's barely audible to even my ears.

My knees weaken as he runs the tip of his nose across my skin and then says, "Lie down, Delaney."

I look at him, lightly scraping my nails under his chin, and then reply, "Okay." I turn around and make a show of it. His eyes are on me anyway, and I like the way he looks at me like he can't get enough. I feel powerful in his gaze. *Beautiful.* Equal in his eyes, though he holds so much more stature in society than I do. I face him again before lowering down to my knees.

"All the way. Flat on your back for me." I do as he requests and lie down, staring up at the ceiling and waiting. The mattress shifts, and his weight bears down under my legs as he lifts one over his shoulder and then the other.

My gaze travels from the eyes he has set on mine to his erection—so hard and strong. With both my legs over him, he dips down and kisses my pussy long and sensually, deep when his tongue dives into me and whirls, making my head spin from feeling so overwhelmed by the pleasure. My head falls back, and I close my eyes, taking every lick and nip, scraping his finger over my clit, losing myself to Warner's attentions. *And God, it's so good.*

He slides his tongue up and flattens against me as I push against him, chasing my need and fulfilling my cravings when his finger presses to my entrance. I want him inside me, but I want his cock more. Propping up on my elbows, I watch him savor me like that gelato last night. When he peers up at me, I say, "Don't keep me waiting, Hotshot. Give me all you got."

His smirk just about does me in, but when the foil packet lands on my stomach, I laugh, the levity feeling so good. I'm really beginning to love how we interact. I'm also beginning to love *him*.

CHAPTER 23

Warner

COOKIES CAN'T COMPETE with the delicacy that is Delaney.

Sucking her clit sends her into her release, ecstasy tremoring through her body beneath my mouth. Her legs squeeze around my ears, and I reach my arm around her thigh, realizing this fucking cast hinders my ability to hold her tight.

I steal one last taste of her before grabbing the condom and rolling onto my back. I steady the packet between my teeth and rip it open, pulling the condom from inside it and spitting the packet to the side. I've done this enough in my life. I'm an expert, but having the use of only one hand adds an element of difficulty I could do without. I turn to see Sass lying with one arm wide on her other side, and the other across my chest. "How are you doing over there?"

She rolls her head to face me and smiles. If perfection had a physical definition, she would be it. Glassy eyes make her blues shine brighter, the pink of her lips is richer from kissing, and that smile makes my heart beat faster when she looks at me like that. "There's no word that captures how amazing I feel." She rolls onto her side and kisses my head. "I want you to feel like this."

"I want that, too." I fucking want it so much. I want *her* so badly my dick aches.

Without me having to do a thing, she moves to situate herself on top of me. With one lift, I guide my dick inside her and then slide to hold her hip as she consumes me whole. Her head falls back, the tips of her hair dangling across the tops of my legs. When she starts a slow gyration, I reach up and take hold of her tits, one and then the other, not to leave one out. Pinching the pink peaks, I watch them pebble for me as goose bumps ripple across her arms, and the vibration of a low moan rumbles through my fingertips against her chest.

I sit up, taking a nipple in my mouth, teasing and taunting until her body jolts and she laughs. With her fingers digging into my hair, she leans down to whisper in my ear, "You're such a bad boy when you want to be."

I'd gone easy, let her control the pace and plunder, but not with the words laid out like a dare for me to do. Running my hand up the center of her back and into her hair, I hold her right where she is and turn my mouth to her ear. "You don't know what you've started."

She leans back to catch my gaze and goddamn smirks at me. "Don't I?"

"You're lucky I only have the use of one arm."

"Hasn't stopped you so far." *Challenge accepted.*

I flip her down onto the mattress, her hair flying from the fast action as a squeal rushes from her lungs. I start fucking her like this bad girl wants—hard, fast, deeper than she thought possible. Forcing a breath out with each thrust, I secure my hand to her shoulder and fuck her like I wanted to the first time we butted heads. She's the sexiest woman I've ever fucking met, and that mouth of hers, the snark and comebacks, her stubborn streak have all been foreplay. So I give her what she wants and take what I need.

Digging her nails into my shoulders, she chants my name as if I'm the one she worships. I kiss her neck, licking the base of her jawline, predicting a downfall once the truth comes to light. How will we survive our own lies? I'm not convinced we can.

I bite because she's so goddamn beautiful, and my basest instincts to own every part of her kick in. I start to sink my teeth, but soothe any red I left with a swipe of my tongue. "I want you," I confess on the next breath.

Our bodies slow, the connection still strong between us when she lifts my chin with only her fingertip. "You have me, Warner. I'm yours." She kisses my lips, and then whispers, "I'm right here with you."

I exhale, knowing I'll keep the lies going forever if it means I get to keep her. I pick up my pace, and this time, I slide my hand between her legs. Her body reacts with an arched back and thrust of her pelvis. When I rub her bud, she says, "Don't stop. I'm so close."

As if I could. I'm too damn selfish for that. I thrust into her, so turned on by the tightness and hold she not only has on my body but also on my heart. Her hands grab my ass and urge me forward. I pull back, taking her in before I plunge forward again. She has me staggering on the precipice of the abyss. I don't fight it. I close my eyes and welcome it.

My body moves of its own accord toward the desire to embrace euphoria with her. When I come, the sounds of my girl falling with me fill my space and time, capture and release.

And when I return to the haven of this life with her, I wrap my arm around her and hold her to my chest. Her breathing is ragged while her body recovers, collapsed on top of mine. Sweat slicks over our skin, and a few cookie crumbs stick to her back.

I grin. What a fucking mess we're in, but I wouldn't have it any other way. Not with her. This is heaven. I kiss the top of her head and then remove the condom. "You hungry? I think I'm going to heat up the spaghetti and meatballs."

The rattle of her body against mine, the lift of her cheek on my chest, has me smiling in response. She rests her hand on me and her chin on top of that. "I could eat."

"That's my girl."

"Am I, Warner? Am I your girl?" Her smile is softer, matching our breathing as it regulates back to normal. Her expression is so genuine and not shaped by disbelief, but more by the hope that it might be true.

Sometimes I wonder how this will play out, how the truth eventually finds the light. I'm certain too much damage will be done by that point. But this between us now, that look in her eyes, gives me the same hope she's feeling. "You are, Sass." I kiss her head and then shift to the side. She falls onto the mattress as I slide off. "Mainly," I say with a chuckle, "because no one else would put up with the nonsense." Rolling onto her back, tits up, and a grin so big that you'd think she was trying to win over some pageant judges, she laughs.

I'm already walking into the bathroom, tossing the trash away and mapping out my plan of attack. I'll take a shower and then tackle the cleaning. Vacuuming the carpet to changing the sheets, I'm making a list in my mind when she says, "What you call nonsense others consider treasure. Be careful, Hotshot, or you just might lose me to the competition."

I hadn't thought about her life outside of this apartment until I met her family. That was the extent of it. She could have a boyfriend. Hell, she could be married to someone else for all I know. Neither is reasonable if I have tonight to go by. Her family wasn't in on the grand plan. They would have said something if she had someone special in her life. Right?

Either way, her words, whether she's joking or not, are a punch to the gut. A hit of reality injected into a great night to ruin it. I stop, turning back and filling the doorway. Staring at her, I ask, "*Is* there competition?"

She sits up. "Now, why would you ask me that?" A smile is still on her face, but it's gentler, mingling with the concern in her eyes. "I only left the other day, and then I was back the next. How fast do you think I operate?"

"That's a loaded question."

She gets off the bed and comes to stand in front of me. When I look up, annoyance has replaced the bliss in the aftermath. With her hand on her hip, her eyes stay on the floor, and she shakes her head as disbelief embodies her shoulders. I can sense the shift in her mood. She finally looks up at me, and says, "If you don't trust me, just say it. No use keeping me around if you don't believe I've been true to you."

Before she escapes into the bathroom, I capture her wrist. "True or genuine?"

The question pulls her brows together, and then, with a resolve into indifference, she shrugs. "Does it really matter?" She pulls her wrist away and enters the bathroom behind me.

In the heat of the moment, I convince myself that the lies

don't matter, that the act is over, and she's here for me and not some payout. With the embers remaining and ready to burn out, the truth hurts. I enter the bathroom as she's dipped into the shower to turn on the faucet. "What do you do for a living?"

She drops her head down as if I've exhausted her more from the line of questioning than the sex. Looking up, she sighs. "I get that you have amnesia, but you don't remember anything?"

"Not about you. Nothing. Not one memory that we haven't made in the past few days exists."

"It exists," she says with such conviction she almost convinces me I'm wrong. "You just don't remember."

"Sure. That's it."

She grabs a towel to preload it onto the hook. "What about work? What's the last thing you remember about your job?"

I get my own towels, not ignoring the fact that they're all mine, and hang them on the hook next to hers. "I remember speaking to Jocelyn—"

"Your assistant?" She steps back from the shower and looks at me.

How does she know who she is? Have I mentioned Jocelyn before without remembering saying the name? I take a step back to figure out what the fuck is going on. How would she know that?

That's it. I'm done playing this game. I care about Delaney, but these secrets are becoming too much to ignore. I was hoping she'd tell me the truth, especially when given the perfect opportunity several times over. Yet another test falls off the tip of my tongue, wondering how she'll respond. "Yes, my assistant."

"I almost forgot who she was. Carry on."

"Almost like you're the one with amnesia." I don't know if she's failing or passing since she's got my thoughts all messed up.

She laughs. "Funny." There's no humor heard in it. "So you remember work but not me? I really made an impression, didn't I?" The sound is more restrained, but at least she seems to be laughing to herself this time.

"Yeah, seems so." I reach in to test the temperature of the water. Since it's ready, I'd love to get in, but this damn cast must be covered. "Do you mind helping me?"

She grabs the bag and the elastic and slips both over my arm. There's no irritation in the act or stalled in her muscles, which I expected since I've put her on the defensive. Just kindness, which I appreciate. "You're not about to steal my shower, are you?"

"Nope. Thanks for the help." I step under the spray of the water. "I was already coming in for a shower when you overtook everything." I could say that about a few things. I leave the stall door open as an invitation. I'm sure she'd feel better clean like I will. I'll feel better if I get all this off my chest.

Delaney looks annoyed with her arms crossed over her chest and her little foot tapping in irritation. But that's something she's going to have to work through on her own. I have a bigger mess to clean up—our relationship.

You would have thought she was surrounding a great battle when she enters the shower and closes the door behind her. Somber, the quiet between us gives too much time to stare at one another and ignore what I know we're both thinking. Ignoring doesn't do either one of us any favors, so I ask, "If there was one thing you wish I remembered about you, what would that be?"

She slides against me until she's covered by the spray

instead. I want to laugh, but it's not the time for that. With her eyes closed and head tilted back, the water runs down the length of her hair. She rubs her hands over her face, focusing on her eyes before lifting and opening them. "No matter what happens, I hope you can remember how you felt when you said you loved me." She holds my gaze, not looking away, but searching for something I don't know if I can give her.

The conflict I've felt inside from falling for her to feeling used isn't lessened by her words. They're deepened, though. When did I tell her that? I scroll through the short time we've had together, and when my feelings were heightened. Sex.

Oh shit . . .

My lips were attached to her neck.

Our bodies pushing us closer to coming.

Fuck.

"I love you" is not the same as "I love your body." Though I'm not so sure that I didn't say what I mean, I know it's not how I would have chosen to tell her the first time. I remember what we were doing and how incredible it felt. The emotions attached are more powerful. I might be dabbling in enemy territory and walking a fine line. The wrong words could send this all spiraling, but the right ones sit on the tip of my tongue. I love her and can't lose her.

She pours shampoo into the palm of her hand but doesn't wash her hair. She washes mine, moving behind me and reaching up on her tiptoes to massage my scalp and lather the hair. "I know things aren't perfect, Warner, but they're ours and we're each other's—flaws and all. And that's something I'm okay with. More than okay. Rinse."

I dip my head under the water and rub my fingers through it to get the soap out. Flaws and all. Is that what the lies are? Simple flaws in the biometrics of our relationship? When everything else is so good, can I, *will I*, be able to overlook the issues?

Watching her now as she washes her own hair, still feeling cared for after she washed mine without me even asking, but it's the way she makes me laugh that has been eye-opening. I was stuck in the boredom of my life, but she's shown me another way to live.

I don't want to fight with her, and I don't want her on the defensive when she's with me. "I want us to be together, Sass. How do you feel about that?"

Beaming up at me like I wasn't giving her the third degree not ten minutes ago, she says, "I thought you'd never ask." She might have known where this was going already, but she waited patiently for me to catch up. Now that I'm by her side, and this is my girl, officially, who cares how we got here? We're where we're supposed to be. That's all that matters.

CHAPTER 24

Warner

"You look very handsome, Hotshot," Sass says, running her hands down the front of my freshly starched shirt. I wince, thinking how much can go wrong wearing a white shirt without a jacket. I can't go into a meeting with dirt on my shirt, or food, or residue from the lotion she just put on her hands not five minutes ago.

The Monday morning sun still rests below the tops of the surrounding buildings, leaving the much-needed light for getting ready just beyond reach. I didn't bother turning on the overhead light, trying to be respectful of Delaney's sleep. It's not unusual for me to be awake this early, but I have a feeling she isn't used to it.

But she crawled out of bed and rubbed her eyes as I slid a white button-up over my cast. After pressing her lips to mine, she ambled into the bathroom to be with me. She might be new to my morning routine, but I like her here. Even if she doesn't hustle at this hour the way I do.

I stopped asking questions last night, deciding that daily

life with her would be served on a platter of surprises. Each revelation would have its time to shine. It goes against my nature, how I was raised, and the makeup of my being. It's just what I needed to shake me back into living my life again. The ordinary has become extraordinary because Delaney has steamrolled her way into my life and shaken up my world.

It doesn't bother me so much, not even the mark she left on my shirt. Much. "Since I can't wear a jacket, I think I'll pull on a sweater."

"In May?"

"It's thin, like a spring sweater."

Her gaze glides down the shirt to the spot, and then she looks back up at me. "I have an idea that might look nice and less wintry. Stay right here." She runs back down the hall to the bedroom. She's dressed in a T-shirt from a half-marathon I ran four years ago, and I don't think much else, which allows me a peekaboo view of the lower curve of her ass when the shirt lifts in the back. I stay where I was told.

I check the time on my watch. I always arrive early, and most of the time, I'm flicking the lights on at the office. There's still time to get in before most, but time is ticking by too fast and kicking in some of the unease that's built into me. I like to be early. Not on time. Definitely not late. Early to any event, to work, and anywhere else I need to be. Is this something else I'll need to sacrifice to be with her? If it is, it's going to be a harder habit to break, but I'm sure she'll manage to do it.

"Here," she says, returning with a vest held in her hands. Holding it in front of me, she's hidden behind it. "Thoughts?"

"I think I'm looking at the third piece of a three-piece suit."

She grins up at me. "Warner, it's fine if you don't have the jacket."

"It's two pieces and not even the first two. You can't skip the second piece. That's madness." Trying to reason through this, I explain, "It's like eating lasagna without the noodles. It would be a mess."

Lowering the vest to her side, she angles her head and laughs. "That's ridiculous. The noodles are literally what make it lasagna."

She's not the only one who knows how to trigger someone. I shrug. "I consider the meat sauce to be the heart of lasagna."

Her head jerks unnaturally as her expression scrunches. "What are you talking about? Lasagna doesn't even need meat in the mix to be lasagna. Sure, it's nice, and even a delicious addition, but that's all it is. An addition for variety." *Mission accomplished.* She tosses the vest on the back of the couch. "Fine, don't wear it." I'm not sure why she's suddenly so attached to a vest, but disappointment ruins her smile. I did that, and over an item of clothing. *So not worth it.*

"Fuck it. Who needs rules when we can live in total chaos? I'll wear the vest."

As if she's been given ice cream for breakfast, her smile returns, and it's bigger than ever. "Really?"

"Really."

She grabs it and helps to slip it over my broken arm and then the other. "This will help cover any marks or stains. So you can focus on your bigwig deals instead of that mark I accidentally left on your shirt."

I'm not as slick as I thought I was. Cupping my face, she says, "Have I told you how sexy I think you are with a black eye?"

The confession comes out of left field like so many other of her whims. Chuckling, I ask, "You like that, huh?"

"Makes you look tough." Lifting onto her toes, she kisses me.

Typically, I'd soak in a compliment, but this one stumps me because I'm reminded of how she once said she figured me for a brownie guy because they're soft. "I don't think that's the compliment you think it is."

"You're too sensitive."

"Now *that* is something I've never been told before." I can't keep up with her. Since I haven't had coffee, it's probably best if I don't try. Wrapping my arm around her, I bring her in for another kiss. "I need to go." It's tempting to ask her how she'll spend her day, but something tells me I don't want to know. Or, if she does answer, it won't contain the full story. That will just start the cycle over again. *Let it go, Landers.* I kiss her once more and start moving toward the door with her still attached. By the time we reach the entry, she plucks her lips from mine and steps back. Though two fingers remain hooked around a belt loop even as I reach for the door. "I'll leave you the key."

It's just a nod, but I can see the water gathering in her eyes as if I'm leaving her for good. I return to her, lifting her chin and kissing her once more. I trail kisses toward her ear, and then whisper, "I'll see you later, okay?"

"Later."

This time, I leave without looking back. I open the door and walk toward the elevator with heavy steps. The loud click of it closing behind me doesn't bring me comfort, though all I wanted at the end of last week was freedom from her. The elevator arrives, but my gut suddenly twists. I look back, the fear of never seeing her again washing through me.

Don't be ridiculous.

She'll be here when I return.

I hope.

Since I'm running later than I'm comfortable with, I catch a cab instead of walking.

The ride is quick at this hour with less traffic. When I enter the lobby, I greet the guard behind the desk, "Morning, Jerry."

"Whoa, rough weekend?"

"Rough is an understatement." I grin as I walk toward the elevator. "Hit by a car."

"*Dammmn*, you're lucky to be here."

I chuckle. "I actually am. Have a good one." I punch the button, which opens the elevator. When it stops on the Landers Ventures floor, I step out. There's no one at the desk because it's too early, but I use my card to unlock the door to the offices. An office down in accounting is lit up, and I see the tops of two heads in the cubicle zone. "Good morning," I say, seeing if we have anyone willing to pop their head up.

Both do. Neil, a new dealmaker we recently brought on, and Sharilyn, who runs our online presence. "Good morning," they reply before ducking their heads back down.

Who I don't expect to see at this hour is my assistant. I reach Jocelyn's desk before she sees me, and tease, "Trying to impress the boss?"

When she looks up from her monitor, the gasp can be heard through the large open space. Neil stands to see what the commotion is about before realizing it's only us and sits down again.

Jocelyn's shock causes her to stand. "Warner . . ." She covers her mouth with her hand to hide her gaping. It doesn't work since I know she's still doing it even if it's hidden.

I underestimated the reaction I expected to receive being out in public again, especially from Jocelyn. She's the most even-keeled person I know, after me that is . . . was? Fuck. Delaney has me spiraling on a daily basis now. I waffle my head back and forth. "And here I thought I didn't look so bad."

"You look way worse."

Grinning, I reply, "Thanks."

She lowers her hand, but as her eyes bounce around my face and then to my arm, she adds, "My goodness, Warner."

Coming around the desk, she inspects my arm as sympathy takes hold of her tone by softening it. "I just mean, you made it sound so casual, nothing more than a bump in the road."

I chuckle. "I see what you did there."

"Yes, pun intended." She finally smiles. I prefer that to the concern riddling her face. "I'm glad you have a sense of humor over it." She exhales and starts to calm after the initial alarm begins to dissipate. "Are you okay?"

Raising my arms out to the side, I reply, "I'm going to live, as sad as that might make some feel."

"Stop it," she replies, turning to grab her e-pad and pen. "Let's get you set up in your office."

I flash my key card again, unlocking my door. "You don't have to take care of me. I've been in good hands all weekend."

"And whose hands would those be?" she asks, following me inside. She beats me to the light switch and flips it on.

"An angel I met." I laugh under my breath, fully aware of how foolish I sound, but the truth is what it is. No use pretending otherwise. Too much other stuff under a fake facade to add more to it.

"An angel?"

I try to ignore the disbelief in her voice. I get it. I'm a different person today than I was when she last saw me. I don't believe myself most of the time. "She saved my life, so yeah," I say, sitting down behind my desk. "Guardian angel might be more accurate."

She sits in front of me on the other side of the desk, a worrying ribboning through her forehead. "You really did hit your head."

I'd be reacting the same if I were in her shoes, so I'm not offended. It's hard to explain Delaney. She just is who she is, and I love her for it. As I log onto my computer, I say, "I was surprised I didn't hear from you more often. Taking time off isn't something I've done often."

"Or at all since you became CEO. It's funny you say that, though, because I felt like I was constantly burdening you with emails."

Scoffing, I turn my attention back on her. "Why would you say that? You sent what? One email. Two max. I figured everything was being handled. Was it not?"

"Taking the time to heal was the best thing for you to do, but . . ." Her brow wrinkles as her lips twist to the side as she contemplates with her eyes staring above my head.

"But?"

Setting her e-pad in her lap, she sits back, her shoulders as stiff as her expression. "Warner, I was emailing you every day, multiple times, even over the weekend." She lowers her voice and says, "And you were emailing me back. Do you not remember any of that?"

This news sideswipes my mood, dampening it. I'm not sure what she's talking about. "I didn't have my phone—"

"I know." Leaning forward, she glances at my monitor. "Check your emails."

Dread lodges in the pit of my stomach as I click open my

inbox. Mostly filled with emails that will steal my day to get through, only one was sent from Jocelyn. The one I already read. "Odd."

She's quiet. I'm sure assuming this concussion is taking me out of the game. She'd be wrong. I feel good, great even. Until she holds up the e-pad with her inbox on display and a column of correspondence between the two of us. "I—" I clamp my mouth shut, wondering if the concussion has caused more damage than I thought. How could I have been emailing and not remember doing it? Am I losing my mind? Emailing while passed out? Is that even a thing? I once read that sleepwalking is more common than people realize. Is this a different version of it? Sleep-emailing? Sleep-working? Falling back on something I'm comfortable with, that I excel at, wouldn't be surprising. Holding full conversations is a whole other level of concern.

Delaney...

Apprehensively, I glide my mouse over to the trash folder and click it open. The screen populates with the missing messages. When I open the first one, I catch that *I'm fine, don't worry, I trust you to make the right decision,* and *I'll be offline the rest of the weekend.* The latter is something I've never said in my life. But if someone wanted me all to herself, she might.

Or maybe Delaney thought it best for me to rest. She was looking out for my best interest, which most people never do. Am I kidding myself? I think it's gaslighting at this stage. I want to believe we are real so badly that I'm searching for justifications for her actions instead of demanding answers.

I look at Jocelyn. Trying to act like it was all a misunderstanding, "I found them." Touching my head, I say, "I don't know why I forgot—"

"You have a concussion."

"Yes," I say, laughing to humor her when I'm not the least bit amused. "It's been a weird time."

"I understand. Maybe you need more time to recover?"

"No." I glance at the screen again, scanning the column. "It's fine. I do have a lot of business to take care of, though, so if you'll excuse me."

Standing, she says, "I'll be at my desk if you need me."

As she makes her way to the door, I say, "Thank you for dealing with everything while I was gone."

She stops to look back. "Of course, it's my job, but even if it weren't, I'm always here to help, sir."

"I appreciate that. Will you order me a new phone to be delivered today?"

"Done." When she walks out of the office, she closes the door behind her. The moment I'm alone, I start scrolling through emails. The dread I feel is well-founded and expands into my chest with each one I read.

Every email is another betrayal, another lie piled on a relationship built on them. She didn't bother admitting she was the one in communication. Instead, she inserted herself. How'd she know my password?

Fire runs through my veins, heating my cheeks as I read about deals that should be handled with care. Ones she gave my assistant permission to work through. *Thank fuck I can trust Jocelyn.* She always has my back in business. But some of those decisions she doesn't have the background or inside knowledge to make.

My hands shake as my blood pressure spikes, and I shove away from the desk. Pacing the length of my office, I grab a handful of my hair and tug, finding her gall beyond maddening. My patience wears thin, making me feel desperate to attack.

I keep thinking I can overlook these crushing setbacks to our relationship, sending us two steps back. Nothing is safe with her around, including me. But I also foolishly thought we had more time to work through it, but things are coming to a head. If it weren't for the week's worth of work to catch up on, I would storm back home and demand answers. I'll have to deal with it, *with her*, later.

With access to the world again and information at my fingertips, I type Delaney Bayetti into the search bar. Not much comes up. Part of the Bayetti family, who owns the restaurant, and she is studying elementary education. The tidbit is so casually listed that I'm thrown off guard. She's a teacher, or she's a student? How does her being a teacher even make sense? Why wouldn't she be working? Or does she have the summer off, and manipulating unsuspecting hit-and-run accident victims is her pastime to earn extra funds?

Why does this story—*hers and mine*—keep getting more complicated? For every one truth, five lies are revealed. It's a damn house of cards we're living in. House of mirrors describes it better.

Nothing of value shows up otherwise. She probably scraped the internet using her covert operative skills. Is she CIA, MI6, or part of the KGB? For all I know, my office might be bugged, and she's listening from my apartment, cackling her sexy little ass off.

I smile. Not because I'm funny, which I am, nor because I read about the family ties to the restaurant, since I knew about that. I chuckle because this has gotten so out of hand that I'm not sure it can be reeled back in. And because that little nutball of mine is a sweet little teacher. How bad or conniving can she be if she picked such a generous profession?

Her two personalities, seemingly worlds apart, leave my mind boggled enough not to take that on. It can only be done when I'm face-to-face with her. How can I use this to my advantage? That's my next thought, but I don't want advantages. I want to know her, all of her. I want her truths, even if they're not as pretty as she'd like them to be.

I want to understand what's going on so I can find forgiveness for the havoc she's caused.

It's then, standing in front of the view I've stared at for years, that I see color for the first time. Green treetops dot the sides of the avenue, blue covers the sky as far as I can see, and bright yellow cabs and brown sidewalks. It's not just gray anymore. That's because of Delaney.

This is not about fighting against her tide or giving in to the wave as it crashes down on us. I've been coming at this situation all wrong. It's not about acceptance or denial. It's about compromise and riding the wave into shore. I can do that. For her. Give and take. No more secrets allowed. And I hope she returns the favor.

Two hours later, Jocelyn delivers a phone to my desk. "I updated it with your information and contacts. Photos are organized as they were, and your privacy is protected. Everything has transferred from the cloud and should work the same as your other one."

"Thank you. That's a time-saver."

"Oh," she says, pointing at the screen. "And there's a text from Jimmy that came in as soon as the messages loaded."

"I appreciate it, Jocelyn." I look at my shiny new phone. It's tempting to hug it to my chest, but yeah, that's not going to happen. The reprieve from society was nice for a bit, but I missed having technology at my beck and call.

I tap on the message from Jimmy and read: *Glad we had the bachelor party last month, since you've gone MIA on me. Two weeks until the wedding. I expect to hear from you before then, fucker.*

I chuckle. If he only knew all that I've been through.

I haven't forgotten about his wedding, but it hasn't been on my mind. *Two weeks.* I reply with a zoomed-out sky-view description of the accident, avoiding the details, and let him know I'm back in action if he needs anything. But I find myself grinning like a fool when I let him know I'll also be bringing a plus-one.

CHAPTER 25

Delaney

WITH A DUFFEL BAG of clothes and a few more pairs of shoes, I walk back into the living room to leave.

"Is it serious?"

"You're such a creeper, Lorenzo. Why are you sitting in here in total silence?"

"Creepin'." He chuckles but then holds up his phone. "Checking the emails for the restaurant. I've been running catering for the past month, not that you've noticed or that it's any of your business, sis."

I hold the handles of the bag in front of me with both hands, wishing I had made a clean getaway. In a family this size and an apartment this small, I was bound to run into somebody. My mom would have been a better choice. She doesn't give me a hard time like my brothers do.

He leans back in dad's recliner, kicking one leg over his other knee and sitting there with his fingers steepled. He really thinks he's somebody when he asks, "So is it?"

"What are we talking about?" I look toward the window, as if the shadows of leaves from the trees outside, floating over the wall with the TV, will give me some semblance of the time of day. I lost the morning by going back to bed and woke up in a tear to get things done so I could be back before Warner gets home.

I applied for more jobs and took off to come home for more of my things.

"Have you already forgotten? The guy with the black eye you brought around last night. Ring a bell?"

"You're so annoying. You can say his name. Warner."

"Landers." My stomach clenches as if the name itself causes fear. It doesn't. Only what he represents. And my brothers finding out, which at least one clearly has. He redirects his eyes toward the large bay window. "Same guy trying to close us down." When he looks back at me, he says, "Ballsy move bringing him around to break bread like he's one of us, like he might be a part of the family one day." He stands and walks into the kitchen. "You humiliated Mom and Pops by pulling that stunt. Mom cooked for him."

"It wasn't a stunt." Not for them anyway. I can't tell my brother that it was about showing Warner what could be lost if this deal goes through. "I wouldn't do something like that, and you know that, so stop with the accusations when they're not based in reality."

"If they find out—"

"They won't unless you tell them," I gripe, tightening my fingers around the handles.

He pulls a soda from the fridge and pops the top. My brother is a big guy. Both are, taking after our dad. But they still made sure I earned my Bayetti stripes and learned how to stand up for the family. As the youngest, I was expected to handle a situation with a girl who was mocking the restaurant, calling its food terrible. I handled it. No fists involved, unlike how they would have. So he knows that family will always come first with me, and I'll do anything, anything, to protect us. What he doesn't know is what I'm currently doing, which was a sacrifice in the beginning. Now . . . it might be serious like he can plainly see.

"I'm not going to tell them, but don't do anything stupid, sis." Coming to the edge of the counter, he takes a long pull of soda and then looks at me again as if I'm going to crack under pressure. I haven't with Warner, so there's no way Lorenzo is going to see it happen. "I'm taking it you're serious about this guy. Otherwise, you shouldn't be messing with him. Men like him hold power in this city. You fuck over the wrong guy, and it will come back on us tenfold."

"I'm with Warner because I care about him."

He grins as he returns to the living room. "Good because I actually liked the guy."

The cloud lifts between us, and I loosen my stance. "You did?"

"Yeah. I mean, he's a typical Wall Street guy."

"He doesn't work on Wall Street. He's a venture capitalist."

"If you're thinking that's an upgrade, it's not. But the guy has money, and he wasn't a total asshole to my surprise." He sits in the recliner again. "What's the plan to get him to reverse course on this building buyout?"

"I'm hoping he'll do it out of the kindness of his heart."

My brother chuckles. "Okay. Good luck with that, Delaney." He nods toward the back hall. "We'll keep your bedroom the same, for now. It will make a great gym, though, so keep me posted."

I roll my eyes as I open the door. "Bye, jerk face."

"Bye, ya little rotten egg."

Grinning, I wait until I'm in the hall and the door is closed to cut up. Can't give him the satisfaction of hearing me laugh. After stopping into the restaurant to confirm I wasn't put on the schedule this week, I head a block over to catch the train back to Tribeca.

I stop in a corner grocer and pull a cart around the store behind me. I want to make dinner, but what would Warner like to eat? He can buy any dish and afford the city's nicest and most expensive restaurants. He even ate hot dogs with me.

Why does he have to be so annoyingly perfect?

I can't outcook famous chefs. So I shouldn't try. I'll prepare something he can't get anywhere else. I carry the bag of groceries in one hand and my duffel in the other and walk to his apartment. I can't say I'm mad about staying in this neighborhood. The sidewalks are less crowded and roomier. Those and the streets are definitely cleaner. I bet they pay a private company to sweep their streets on a regular basis.

And I'm getting used to seeing Baker with his big smile welcoming me home to Warner's building. "How are you today?" I ask, sweeping myself inside the lobby when he holds the door open for me.

"Couldn't be dandier." The door closes as he walks behind me. "How about you, Mrs. Landers?"

"Happy as a clam, but what's not to be happy about these days?"

"Ah." He hurries around me. "Let me get the elevator for you since you have your hands full." He punches the button. "Newlywed bliss is a beautiful thing. Hold on to it."

Stopping just shy of where he's standing, I laugh. "Like an anaconda, I'm holding on as tight as I can, squeezing the life right out of it."

His face contorts into uncertainty. "I'm not quite sure— Nope, you know what. None of my business. Have a great day."

With great timing, the elevator opens for me. "You, too."

As soon as I'm in the apartment, I unload the groceries I bought and then dig through the duffel to pull out a few chotskies I brought over to homey up the place, inserting a bit of me into his world. I laugh as I set the little Eiffel Tower dead center on the console under the TV because I inserted myself right into his life as well.

I set a mug I made in elementary school on the counter and drop some mismatched pens I found in my bedroom inside. Going down the hall, I slip into his office and sit at his desk. I've felt bad a few times about the measures I took to convince him we are married, but emailing back and forth with his assistant crossed a line. There's nothing but shame associated with the act. It got me a few days alone with Warner, but at what cost?

Jocelyn seems really nice, too, making me feel doubly bad.

Dropping the duffel bag into the closet to deal with another time, I pull my phone out of my back pocket to check the time. Three thirty. Where'd the day go?

I should be timing everything to be ready when he walks in. The problem is, I don't know when he leaves the office. Is it a standard time? A routine built into the makeup of his being. I wouldn't be surprised. The sun could determine the time of day off Warner's precision and perfection he demands.

Though . . . I smile thinking about him. He's stepped out of his comfort zone for me and played along when he was obviously suspicious. So credit goes to him for being a willing participant in this farce of a fairy tale this long. I really didn't expect to be here on a Monday, preparing for my man to come home. *But here I am.*

My brother's words return to replay in my head. *"You fuck over the wrong guy, and it will come back on us tenfold."* I never intended to fuck anyone over, much less Warner. I did not end up here in malice. I ended up here under duress, worried for his life, and then stuck in this game with him. His other warning comes roaring back, *"Don't do anything stupid, sis."*

Too late for that. All I can do is make the most of a bad situation.

I didn't tell Lorenzo everything, not how much Warner shows his affection for me, or how he'd buy me the world if I asked, as long as it's under five million bucks. And I didn't share that I've fallen for someone who is my opposite in almost every way, from standing in society to our careers, my little messes to his orderly, my ice cream to his gelato. Opposites attract, but they fall hard and fast as well. That's Warner and me.

There's no denying our chemistry. There's only a mountain of untruths to overcome. I have my hiking gear ready whenever he says the word.

Since I know the workaholic isn't coming home before five, I don't have to rush, and I have time for a bath. I grab a giant candle from the coffee table. The ceramic bowl is a mix of blues, golds, and brown. The design is unique and fits the space, but it really needs to be used to be fully appreciated. I take it into the bathroom with me and light it before stripping my clothes off and twisting my hair up.

I made sure to pour myself a glass of Sauvignon Blanc before dipping into the sudsy hot water and submerging myself up to my shoulders in bubbles mounded high like whipped cream on a sundae. The water feels good, and my muscles release the tension from carrying those bags across New York. But as I sink in a little deeper, I miss Warner.

Although it feels good to get the grime of the city washed from my body, it's not as fun as it was when I took a bath with him.

Sipping the wine, I close my eyes and relax, imagining Warner's hand coming around to rest on my belly. The way his breath blew across my neck, causing bumps to pebble across my skin. I take another sip and then a gulp before sliding my hand under the water and between my legs. I'm tender, but it's deliciously sore. He did that. He marked me as his, and I find that so incredibly titillating. I've never been a woman who dreamed of her Prince Charming coming to save her. I can save myself. But something about that man has me ready to tie myself to the railroad tracks and scream for him.

"Hey there." That sultry voice runs through me like an awakening.

I open my eyes to see Warner leaning against the door-frame with a grin on his face. The vest is unbuttoned and flapped open, and his tie is loosened and hanging around his neck all crooked. Even his hair is a mess of brown strands going in all directions. He's basically his usual gorgeous self, while my hair probably looks like I lost a fight against a pigeon today. And the pigeon won and built a nest.

I sit up suddenly, and water splashes over the sides while I try to tame hair that I don't stand a chance of doing. "Hey there. You're home early. I didn't expect you until . . ." I shake my head after giving up the fight with the wild strands of my hair in this knot. "Actually, I didn't know when to expect you home."

"I'm early." He chuckles. "Even Baker was surprised to see me. But I didn't have a reason to rush home before."

If I wasn't already a melty mess from this man for how his mouth did me justice several times last night, I'd be a puddle on the floor after hearing him say that. I start to lift, but he says, "Stay. Enjoy your bath. I'm going to change clothes and watch some baseball."

"I didn't know you liked baseball."

"There's a player I like to watch. Called back to the Major League to play at thirty-five."

I grin. "Does it give you hope?"

"Argh." Covering his chest like he's been shot, he slumps. "That hurt." Thank God he laughs afterward. "I'm not sure I'll ever get enough of your old-man jokes." He disappears into the bedroom.

"Good. I have plenty more where that came from."

"Keep 'em coming, Sass," he calls from a short distance.

Well, guess I don't have to finish what I started when I have an expert in-house to do the job for me. I finish washing up and then get out of the tub. After blowing out the three wicks of the giant candle, I pull on a pair of his boxer briefs and another one of his tees. I hold the green cotton up, and the blue lettering reads *Fuck it. Let's go to Nantucket*. I laugh. My guy is so goofy.

Carrying the ceramic candle back into the living room like Baby carrying a watermelon, I enter the living room and set it in front of him on the coffee table, and say, "I carried a candle."

His eyes dart to the candle. "Huh?"

I lean against the arm of the couch, and reply, "You

know, from *Dirty Dancing*? She carried a watermelon for Johnny."

"I've never seen it." His eyes go to the candle again. "There's a candle in the bathroom. Why'd you burn this one?"

I glance back at the centerpiece, the only thing on the coffee table. "Because you never have, and it's too pretty not to see it lit up."

He stands and goes around the other side of the couch from me and into the kitchen. "I never did because it's not meant to burn. It's art." I turn to watch him open the fridge door, blocking him from my view.

"The bowl is pretty, but it's still a candle, Warner."

The door is shut, and if it didn't have soft closure, it would have slammed. With a bottle of beer in his hand, he twists the top. "It's literally a piece of art, Delaney. I won it at an auction a few years ago before the artist passed away. Now its value has tripled, but you just lit that profit on fire."

Sure the candle was an accident, but I get a sinking feeling that something bigger is going on here. "I'm sorry. I—"

"That's the first time you've apologized for anything you've done." He tips the bottle back and chugs half of it before lowering it back down and wiping the back of his hand across his mouth. *What in the world is going on with him?*

"That's not true. I've apologized when I have needed to."

"Are you calling *me* the liar?"

"The liar? Like if you're not it, I am? Am I catching the gist of what you're saying?" He moves back to the couch when the announcer says Griffin Greene is stepping up to the plate. Standing with his eyes glued to the TV, he appears mesmerized as if we weren't in the middle of something here. "Warner?"

I'm ignored.

"Did you hear me?" I ask. I look at the TV, watching the baseball player step up to the plate. Grabbing the remote, I click it just as the sound of the bat cracking is heard.

He shoots me a glare. "What the fuck are you doing?"

I toss the remote on the couch between us. "You start a fight with me and then ignore me like I don't matter in this equation."

"There is no equation. There's me, my apartment, and the baseball game on TV. Then there's you burning shit down per usual and then acting like it doesn't matter to me."

"I said I'm sorry for lighting the candle." I try to keep myself from reacting to his anger. He has a right to be mad. He doesn't have a right to ignore me. "I'll pay for it. Then you'll have your money back."

He laughs, like infuriatingly loud, and then drinks more beer. "I have a strong feeling that you don't have a hundred K lying around."

I look at it again, making sure we're talking about the same one. "For that?" I ask, pointing at it.

"Forget it." He clicks on the TV again. I see his eyes home in on the tiny Eiffel Tower. I'm regretting leaving it there now. Of course, I didn't know he was going to be upset over a candle, though I should have. "Great. He's already hit, and I missed a homer."

"Don't worry. You've knocked it out of the park of assholery in your very own living room." I walk back to the bedroom without hearing another word from him. I go into the bathroom and grab the glass I left next to the tub and swallow the remainder.

When I walk into the bedroom again, he's standing in

the other doorway. The black eye is already changing from purple and blue to green and yellow, healing more each day. His cast is still pristine like it was just put on today. Last night I was kissing his shoulder, where there is more bruising, but the scratches are almost healed. There's so much broken—from his arm to his skin—but I'm starting to wonder how he's doing on the inside. "How was your day?" I ask, whispering between us.

I see the slightest tilt of his head and the way his shoulders loosen under the question. "It was good to be back at work again. But I had some issues come up with my emails."

My day was better with him in it. *Until now, that is.* I missed him. Not sure how that's even possible to be this lovesick over someone so quickly, but it just hit hard.

"That's good."

"What?"

Moving my eyes to the floor in front of me, I sit on the end of the mattress. "What?"

"You said it was good I had email issues."

"Oh, sorry you had issues. My thoughts had wandered away." And into the ache in my heart that's pulsing for his touch and the comfort has presence brings me.

"Delaney?"

I'm not sure if he meant my name as a question, but it sure sounded like one. I stare at him, feeling confident he'll finish it. Seconds pass, trapping us in an uncomfortable silence. I can't stand it. I'm used to noise, my rowdy brothers, and my parents joining in on the laughter. Even when Joe moved out, he's still there all the time. Silence doesn't sit well with me. It's unsettling like I'm in trouble. "Am I in trouble?"

"Why would you be in trouble, Delaney?"

"Why do you keep saying my name like there's more to what's being said?"

"Oh, I don't know," he says, rolling his head over his shoulders as he comes into the room. "Maybe because I expect you to break my legs when I'm sleeping with all the shit you've been pulling."

The insult sends me to my feet, ready to defend myself. "Are you comparing this past weekend to the plot of *Misery*?"

"If the shoe fits, sweetheart. Didn't you once say that to me?"

Throwing my arms out wide, ready for this fight, I yell, "Everybody freaking says that, Warner." Still staring at him, I add, "You've even said it to me."

"This is what you do, Delaney. You twist the narrative to fit a story that's in your head. You argue with no other goal in mind than to wear me down. It works most times because the hurricane that is you sucks so much energy from the room that it's left devastated after you've gone."

"You missing me when I leave doesn't sound so awful."

He laughs, but there's an edge of frustration to it. "There's a prime example." Taking a deep breath, I can see the change in his body, the ease he's forcing into his posture, and the anger morphing into something else. *Disappointment?* He comes to me, takes my hand, and then leans down eye level with me. "Don't ever mess with my business again."

Jocelyn . . . She snitched on me the first chance she got, bright and early on Monday morning. I can't blame her, though I need to blame someone right now, and she's the lucky candidate. Looking him square in the eyes, which seems to be important to him, I reply, "Understood."

"Good." He leaves the room, and says, "I'm ordering pizza. What toppings do you want?"

I'm still a bit stunned to the spot but manage to reply. "Pepperoni."

"That's all?"

"That's all." Pepperoni pizza beats the cup o'ramen I bought for us. I sit back on the bed again, thinking about what he said. Who have I become? I crossed a line when I emailed pretending to be him. But that's just one of so many more that I've erased completely. I don't recognize myself or the life I'm living anymore. Good or bad, it's of my own doing.

He has every right to be upset. And I need to sit in this reality check for behaving so horribly. Warner is a good man. He stands his ground and protects what's his. He's more than made it clear that I fall into that category. I never intended to hurt him, but I have.

Returning to the living room, I sit next to him on the couch and take his hand between both of mine. When he looks at me, I say, "I'm really sorry. I'm so ashamed of what I've done. I don't expect your forgiveness. I crossed lines that ..." I drop my head forward, staring at the connection of our hands, the size difference, and how his fingers wrap around mine as soon as we touch. "I have so many excuses, but none will justify what I've done. All I can tell you is that I'm genuinely sorry for hurting and upsetting you."

The moment he pulls his hand from mine, the water pooling in the corners of my eyes falls over the dams of my lower lids. His arm comes around my shoulders, and he pulls me in to cuddle against him.

He doesn't say anything else about it, but we both know that there was more to it than just the emails. The truth always comes out, and the floodgates have been opened.

Hours later, I stare at him again while he's sleeping. The shame from earlier still weighs heavily in my chest, but I've also started to feel something else—an emotion I never expected. *Grateful.* I reach over and tuck the sheet under his chin as he quietly slumbers next to me.

I'm so lucky and damn thankful this utterly irredeemable man survived. But more than that, he's letting bygones be bygones when I didn't deserve his forgiveness, or forgetfulness.

Leaning over, I kiss his lips gently, so I don't wake him, and whisper, "I love you, Warner Landers."

CHAPTER 26

Warner

THE DAY OF THE WEDDING...

"Do I think it's cruel and unusual punishment? Yes, I do. Again, I understand why, but that doesn't make it better." This one-handed life still gives me enough problems to swear at least once a day. I lost the right cuff link to that outburst five minutes ago. It's yet to be found in the bedroom, but my girl came to the rescue after she heard the commotion.

I watch as Sass pushes the left cuff link through the hole of my tuxedo shirt, all the while smiling like this isn't a state of emergency. I've never heard a sweeter sound than her laughter, even when it borders on hysteria like it does now and is punctuated with a snort. I ask, "Are you mocking me? It's not funny."

"It is funny. You're being ridiculous, Warner." When the cuff link is secured, she plants a kiss on the underside of my chin. Granted, the little shorty doesn't have her shoes on yet, so that's the highest she can reach without stretching to her tiptoes. That might get her to my lips at most. I'm not opposed to her lips on mine . . . or down there, which is how this all started. Or should I say the lack of her mouth wrapped around my cock? "The anticipation will only make it better," she says, walking toward the closet in nothing more than strings wrapped around those deliciously sexy hips and a strapless bra making me jealous that it has the pleasure of holding her fantastic tits, and I don't. With her hair hanging down in soft curls, the ends sway across her shoulder blades when she walks.

It's quite a view. Almost as good as when she's coming toward me.

That package right there—every bit of it—has brought me to life over the past few weeks, made it easier to wake up each day without an alarm, and helped me fall asleep faster with her next to me. There are still things to work out, but we've become pros at burying our heads in the sand. Maybe the lives we were living and the lies we were telling will eventually fade away when enough time has passed while living in the truth. I see who she is when she doesn't wear a mask of deceit. Seeing Delaney with her family, being protective of me and making sure I felt comfortable—that's who she really is.

This character she plays sometimes is becoming harder for her to portray. She's more her than the unhinged version she pretended to be in the beginning. Though I still think some aspects were pulled from her own well.

The woman loves her heist movies. *Odd.*

She stocks the fridge with apples and carrots only to let them go bad while the box of Cheez-its is emptied and left lying on the counter. Seeing a dead pigeon makes her sad, and she always gives any spare change to someone in need. Her intentions are good, better than mine most days, and her heart is pure. That's why the lies she's told still don't make sense.

I still don't know why her being a teacher is never spoken about, and I haven't pushed the issue since I first asked what she does for a living. The answer was flipped into something else, so I suspect she's picking up shifts at the restaurant while I'm at work. But I haven't verified it yet. She complains about her feet hurting and then tells me she didn't do anything all day.

The smell of garlic perfuming her hair is the giveaway. But if she doesn't want to talk about it, and she's not asking me for millions of dollars, I don't push my nose into her business.

She's been taking care of me when no one else did, even after they found out about the accident. I haven't heard from my mother since I last saw her, and Jimmy's been caught up in his wedding planning. *Who else is there?* The assistant I pay to be in my life? Though I can't fault her too much. She has made sure I had lunch every day and given me ibuprofen when she saw I was in pain before I even acknowledged it.

But my Sass is different. She's here for me. I'm certain at this stage. I mean something more to her than the con I started out as. She's fallen for me like I have her. There's a strong chance of us making it through this storm if we can continue the path we're on—sharing who we are on the inside and exposing our real selves to each other. It may not be a fast process, but I'm willing to give it the chance to grow at the pace we need. Slow and steady. In the meantime, the sand sure is nice and cool to be buried in . . . "Why do you torture me so?"

"We're still talking about a blow job, right?" With her hand on the doorframe, she swings around the corner and disappears. But then her head pops back out. "I think we've crossed into Emmy-winning theatrics at this stage."

I sit in the chair to wait for her to come back out. I'm happy to make myself useful by hanging around and zipping her dress up as needed. "Well, to be fair, if your mouth wasn't so talented, we wouldn't have this issue."

She disappears into the closet again. "The only issue we have is we're going to be late if you keep begging for a blow job like this."

I grin. "So it's working?"

My breath is stolen from my lungs when she walks out in a baby-blue dress showing off her shoulders. Her hair is pushed back, and the necklace I bought her is wrapped around her neck. I'm used to seeing her barefaced most days or the lightest touch of makeup that makes her blue eyes pop, as she calls it. When we go out, she wears more if the occasion calls for it. Tonight, she looks like a movie star.

My heart beats faster with every step she takes, coming for me as if she didn't own my heart already. "You look . . . Wow. So gorgeous."

She giggles, and her cheeks instantly pinken into a deeper shade that drifts down over her chest. The dress is modern in design, more architectural and bolder for her typically more casual style. It cuts in at her waist, showing off her incredible figure. The large yellow flower printed on the side of the fitted skirt reminds me of the sunshine she is in the world.

I stand to lean down and kiss her. It's not a blow job, but kissing her gives that a run for its money. I guess I'm going to live after all.

She twirls and laughs again. "This old thing." Pausing

with her back to me, she glances up over her shoulder. "Do you mind zipping me up?"

"It's why I'm here. Professional zipper upper at your service." I slide the zipper up the length of her back, then kiss the top of her shoulder. Again. And again, sliding my hands around to the front to squeeze her tits. "We could stay, just say the train broke down."

"If he's really your best friend, he would know you never ride the train."

"Fair point." I move in front of her, sliding my fingertips across her shoulders and lower over her arms.

Touching my cheeks, she says, "You look so handsome, Hotshot. Even the black eye disappeared like it knew it needed to be gone by today." She waffles her head back and forth. "Though I kind of miss it already."

Chuckling, I say, "I'll pick a fight in the streets just to get punched for you."

"Let's not. I like the rest of your face too much to take the risk of damage."

My hands land back where I want them. She lets me knead her beauties before she finally rolls her eyes. "You good?"

"No."

With a laugh, she walks out of the room with the back straps of the heels dangling from her fingers. I follow her into the living room and sit on the couch while she does what she needs to do. The mini-Eiffel Tower that suddenly appeared on the console has never been explained. Seems it won't be unless I ask, so I finally do. "Why is there an Eiffel Tower by the TV?"

While packing a few things in the small bag she's taking, she replies, "It's like a vision board but in 3D form."

"So you've never been to Paris?"

She stops and glances at me. "No. Have you?" I can't say she's even trying to dupe anyone these days since I'm certain she knows she's not fooling me.

The question almost stumps me. I run a multimillion-dollar company. My family owns properties all over the world. Sure, we both know we're not married, though it's never been explicitly stated, but shouldn't she know this basic information about me? I'm sure the internet would tell her. "Yes. A few times."

There's not much of a response, though I do hear a heavy sigh. That could also be that she's not happy about something that has nothing to do with me. The ring is still on most days, but when I look over at her, she's twisting it off her finger. Going around to the sink, she washes her hands. Her eyes only meet mine for a quick second before she dries them and returns to her bag. "Ready?" she asks with her back to me, but I can see her slipping the ring back on where it belongs.

Delaney wearing a ring has never bothered me. It has started to feel real in many ways, promising something bigger and that we can overcome the choppy waters of our beginning. *Am I naive to feel hopeful?*

I get up, straightening my pants and tugging at the sleeves of the tux jacket. Having the sleeve widen just enough to cover the bright white cast makes me feel like a scene stealer. I'd rather the bride be the sole center of attention. But there's also something I've been wanting to do. Before we head off for this special event, it seems like a good time to ask. I pull a marker from that terrible art mug she's left on my counter and hold it out to her. "Will you sign my cast, Sass?" Helping her lift her jaw off the floor, I add, "Hell's frozen over."

"I would say so." She takes the marker and then pulls

the sleeve up just a little. "I'm in shock that you're willing to graffiti your cast. Isn't the untidiness going to bother you?"

"Maybe it's good to be bothered sometimes." I shrug, panic-stricken on the inside, but I refuse to stop her. "I'm stepping out of my comfort zone."

"You're going to love it once you get used to it, and then you're in a new comfort zone, which leads to the next discomfort, and so on." The sound of the cap being removed from the marker quickens my pulse. I nod through labored breaths as she leans over. Peering up at me once more, she says, "There's no going back, Hotshot. Once it's there, it's like a tattoo and there for life. Of the cast, of course. So are you sure?"

Don't back out, Landers.

I exhale and then inhale once more. "Who needs comfort zones anyway?"

"Not Warner Landers, that's for sure."

Intentionally moving my arm closer to her, I'll overcome this as soon as it's done. "Sign away."

Studying the options, she asks, "Anywhere?"

"Anywhere you want."

"Anything I want to write?"

This is becoming more stressful by the ticking second. "Anything you want to write."

"Any—"

"Please just do it." I'm starting to sweat. Accepting disorder in my neat and organized world is only a bad habit to overcome. It's not that big of a deal. I have what? Four to six weeks to go. Max. I can survive a mess on my body for that long. My heavy gulp causes her to look up again.

She grins and gets to work. The marker lands on the plaster, and with unadulterated confidence, she starts dragging the black tip across the white surface. "We should bring the marker for your friends to sign at the reception."

"Great idea." *I've created a monster.*

Popping back up, she tucks the marker into the front pocket of my jacket. "All done."

I breathe easier, and reply, "That's good. It's good. Fine." Looking at her, I smile. It's a little forced, but I'll get used to the idea of chaos on my arm.

"Are you going to look or breathe through it?" Holding up her hands in surrender, she adds, "I'm not judging. I'm proud of you for trying something new."

The black ink peeks out from the sleeve, but I need to pull it back to see the full thing. "I love you, Hotshot" with a heart punctuating the I. "Lowercase, bold move," I joke, but there's no lightness to it. My heart is now pounding only for her and the words we've never spoken aloud. Okay, whatever, except that time during sex, but I'm not sure confessing love while climaxing would hold up in court.

"You know me," she replies so casually as she starts toward the door, but I catch her hand and bring her back to me.

"I do know you." Brushing the backs of her fingers, I look into those pretty blues of hers, and whisper, "I love you, Delaney."

Her smile falters, but I can see from the gleam in her eyes that it's not from a lack of happiness. Reaching up, she cups my face and kisses me. This kiss holds promises we've not verbalized, apologizes for misgivings, and a future where we know we can survive anything.

And then she lands back on her heels and licks her lips. "I love you, too, so much."

"Well, now that that's been settled . . ." I prop my cast out for her. "It's time for a wedding." That didn't come out the way I intended. "My friends' wedding. Not ours."

Wrapping her hand around my elbow, she cracks up. "Don't worry. I didn't think you'd rush us off to Vegas for a ceremony at the Little White Chapel, so you can relax."

As we walk to the door, I say, "That's very specific. Is that something you'd do?"

"Only if my family were there." I open the door for her. Just before it slams closed behind us, she adds, "I couldn't imagine getting married without my family present." She looks up at me when we stop at the elevator. "What about you? Don't you want your mother there?"

"I haven't thought about it. There was no need to." A desire suddenly arises as I stare at her and that ring on her finger. *Would it be so bad if it were real?*

CHAPTER 27

Warner

THE MAGIC of the sunset high on a terrace in the New York skyline is captured as the backdrop for the "I dos." While the newly married couple kiss, my gaze gravitates toward the back left of the guests to discover Delaney's eyes already on me.

The guests are clapping, pulling my attention back to the bride and groom as they make their way down the aisle. I follow with the maid of honor on my arm, wishing I were walking this aisle with my girl. I miss the heat between us, the electricity that sparks to life with each touch we share, and the magnetism that draws us together every time we're in the same vicinity.

I lose sight of her as we're shuffled off to the side while the crowd disperses to the bank of elevators that will take them to the reception on the second floor of this grand hotel. After taking too many photos and sharing a solid embrace with my friend on his special day, the wedding party is sent to enjoy the reception while the couple stays behind for a private moment.

The elevator took so long to return to the terrace that I considered taking the stairs down the twenty-five flights to reach Delaney sooner. But I hold it together and pretend to engage in conversation with the others. As soon as I enter the ballroom, I search for the light blue of her dress or any sign of where she might be.

The dim lights create a flattering ambiance, while music pumps through speakers around the room. And even though it's classical jazz, it's too loud to call out for her. Not that I would do that during an event like this, but it's tempting. I search the dance floor and then walk along the longest wall toward one of the bars set up at the back of the room.

I stop to search the dessert bar just beyond the buffet line. That's where she is. I cut through small groups standing in the walkway between tables and weave through the maze, losing sight of her. As soon as I finally make it there, she's gone again.

"Looking for a date?" The sweet sound of her voice has me turning around.

"No thanks. I got one." My ass is smacked in a roar of laughter when I start to walk off. I turn back in a flash and pick her up into my arms before she can escape. Our lips meet in the middle, but before the kiss deepens, because it could so easily, I set her down again. Running my hand over the soft skin of her neck, I say, "I have the most beautiful date in the room."

"Only the room?" Her chest racks with laughter again as she reaches up to wrap her arms around my neck.

"New York City," I reply, chuckling as my gaze wanders through the options I can think of. "The state, the country.

The continent, and the world." Looking into her eyes, I whisper, "You're the most beautiful woman in the universe."

"Is this another play for the blow job? Because this flattery is working."

"Say the word, and we'll ditch this place."

She looks back at the buffet line, which is still growing. "Can we ditch it after we eat? I stole a brownie bite, but I'm starving."

"I can eat," I reply, taking her hand and leading us to join the back of the line.

"Is that an offer for later?"

"You don't have to ask me twice." When we get in line, I lean toward her ear. "You're my favorite dessert, Sass."

"Such a charmer tonight. I should bring you to weddings more often."

Wrapping my arm around her shoulders, I kiss the top of her head. "What can I say? Love is in the air."

We go through the buffet line and then find our two seats at a table in the far corner from the dance floor. I get drinks from the bar. Fortunately, my fingers are getting stronger, even with the cast on, so carrying a champagne stem is not a problem. It's good to feel somewhat normal again. I take a sip of my bourbon just before I'm called up to give the best man's speech.

I try to find Delaney's eyes, but the room has gone dark with an empty spotlight waiting for me to fill on the dance floor. I set the drinks down on the nearest table before pulling my phone from my pocket and recalling memories from Jimmy's and my past, landing a few good-natured jokes about his awful dating life, and sharing a few embarrassing stories to build up to the main event that led us here today. He talked to her on a dare because I knew she was the one for him. Before he did, I added for levity. It was quite the crowd-pleaser. When I wrap it up, I go straight to hug the lucky couple, wishing them luck before I grab the glasses and head back to find Delaney.

When I return to our table, some schmuck has stupidly sat down next to her. My blood doesn't boil because I'm not threatened by his paisley purple tuxedo and slicked-back gelled helmet for hair. But I don't like it when he leans in, forcing her to lean away from him.

And here I thought I'd have to go looking for trouble to get another black eye for my girl's pleasure. Looks like it found me. "Excuse me, you're in my seat." I set the drinks down next to her, getting a strong suspicion I might need my hands free from objects.

The guy glances at me and then returns to speak to Delaney like I didn't say a damn word. Delaney says to the guy, "You need to move. This is his seat."

When he grabs her wrist and says, "Let's dance," my blood fucking boils.

As soon as he stands, Delaney's already ripped her wrist free, but now he'll deal with me. "Don't touch my wife again."

He glances from my hand to hers, catching on quickly that I might be lying. "Wife?" He laughs. "She's not wearing a ring. Only a green stain on her finger, ya cheap bastard. Did you buy her ring out of a candy machine?"

The reflex to send him to his grave has me pulling my arm back, but Delaney's hands land so fast on my chest that I'm pushed back a step. "No, Warner."

"Down boy," the guy says, still laughing, but this time, he begins to back away with his arms up in front of him. "She's got that leash tight around that collar of yours."

I lower my arm. "Get the fuck out of here." There always has to be one asshole in the crowd. He's probably some drunk-ass distant cousin one of their mothers insisted on inviting. From the slightest Midwestern accent I pick up on, he sure as fuck isn't from around here.

"She ain't that hot, man." He's quick to slip through some couples standing near the next table.

The encounter doesn't bother me as much as the confidence I see draining from Delaney. Her expression fell along with her shoulders, which she held back before he came around.

"You know it's bullshit, right?"

"Yeah, sure." Swallowing seems to strain the plastered grin she had for me. "We should eat something," she says, sitting down again.

When I sit next to her, she takes a bite of a roll, but the chicken and the salad are still untouched. She can't seem to will herself to eat despite probably wanting the distraction.

I rub her back and pull her to my side. "He doesn't matter."

"That's what sucks. I know he doesn't, but he still managed to get in my head."

"You know what? Fuck him. Fuck this whole thing. I know a great Italian place on the West Side."

Her smile blooms for me. "Bayetti's?"

"Yeah, you think we can get a reservation on a Saturday night on short notice?"

With her mood lifted, she says, "I can pull a few strings."

I stand, taking her by the hand. When we turn, my mother is there. Her eyes go from me to the hand I'm holding. "Hello, Son." She looks at Delaney without so much as a smile. "I don't remember us being formally introduced last time. I'm Grace Landers. You're Delaney Bayetti. Is that right?"

The sudden shiver in her hand has me wrapping mine

around it and holding it at my side. I'm not sure how my mother knows, but her investigative skills are impressive. Delaney replies, "Yes."

"Bayetti is Italian?"

I hear Delaney gulp just fine over the music, and I'm sure my mother does as well. She exhales and says, "It is. My mom is from Connecticut. My dad is from New York. His family goes back to Italy for a few generations."

When silence falls between them, I say, "We were just leaving."

"That's too bad," my mother says, looking genuinely disappointed. A sympathetic smile lifts the corners of her mouth. "I was hoping to spend some time with your friend to get to know her better." Turning to Delaney, she takes her hand right out of mine and holds it between both of hers. "Warner never introduces me to his friends. Well," she says with an eye roll, "except James."

"I didn't know you were on the guest list, or we would have looked for you."

She leans in conspiratorially and whispers, "I skipped the ceremony. I just stopped by for a glass of champagne and a piece of cake." Shooting her gaze to Sass, she adds, "But then I found out it was carrot cake. Why someone would want a vegetable in their cake is beyond me."

She and Delaney share a laugh while I stand there dumbfounded. My mother isn't a cruel woman. Strict when I was growing up and hands off for the most part, but I was taken care of. I've just never seen this side of her directed at me before, though admittedly, I have when she and my dad hosted parties, and I would eavesdrop. *Turning over a new leaf?*

"Oh dear." My mother's eyes see the green ring around her finger, and the way she's holding it allows me to see it for the first time as well. "Doesn't matter how many times they coat it in gold, the less expensive metal will always wear through. It's best to save and invest in quality pieces. "Although I will admit," she whispers, looking around to make sure no one else is listening, "I have some fabulous pieces I bought myself off the street." You'd never know they weren't the name brand." Unlike how that asshole made her feel, I don't hear any embarrassment in her tone this time. Maybe not the approach I would have taken with her, but I appreciate that my mother didn't make her feel bad about the purchase. I, though, get hit with a glare and crossed brows. "You didn't buy her something to cause this, did you?"

"No," Delaney replies as if she has to come to my defense, though a smile has worked its way across her face as well. She doesn't need to defend me, but I appreciate the sentiment. "It was just a cheap ring I bought myself."

"Don't worry, Mother. I'd only buy Delaney the real thing."

Patting her hand, she says, "She deserves it like that gorgeous neck—"

"Heyyyy," Jimmy's voice booms, and I'm grabbed from behind into one of his bear hugs as he looks at my mother over my shoulder, and says, "Thanks for the check, Mrs. Landers."

"You're welcome, James. Congratulations on the nuptials."

Patting my chest like he's beating a bongo, he says, "This guy, he's the best."

Jimmy isn't for everyone, but he's been a loyal friend and makes me laugh. He's not the one to watch a football game with. His temperature rises with one bad call, and his mood ruins the rest of the game for all of us.

"Careful, my arm's still broken."

He sets me down with his eyes fixed on Delaney. He tilts his head and holds out his hand. "You're Warner's plus-one?"

"Don't be obnoxious, Jimmy," I say, holding Delaney's hand again as she shakes his with her other. "Delaney. Jimmy. Jimmy. Delaney."

His head jerks back as soon as they release their grip. Holding his hand against his cummerbund, he looks at me while pointing at her. "How the fuck did this happen?" Subtle is not his forte. "Last time I saw her, she was yelling at you in the streets of New York. How did you end up dating?"

"What are you talking about?" I stare at him. Nothing of the sort has ever happened. He's never even met her before, and in a city of eight million, I highly doubt he's seen her. He most definitely hasn't seen her yelling at me before. "That never happened."

Delaney's hand slips out of mine, and she clutches her purse in front of her. Her cheeks and those pretty lips have drained of the sweet pink that typically shades them, and her blue eyes shine brighter under the glassy surface.

My mother's exit to visit a friend closes our circle a little tighter. Jimmy is still silently standing here, like I have an answer for him. And then he laughs, boisterous like he is. "You're fucking with me, War." He points at her again, and his gaze follows. "This is the same chick. I was checking her out in the elevator after she made a big stink at the reception of your office." He shakes his head like I'm the one who lost touch with reality. "You remember, right? Tell me I'm not wrong." He faces Delaney again, who has shrunk into herself, her shoulders rolled forward, her mouth sagging down as if she wants to speak but can't find the words. I know the feeling. "You're the same girl, right?"

"*Fuucck.*" He hits my chest with the back of his hand. "That's when you had the accident. You probably don't remember." His grin is normally contagious, but not this time. My chest tightens, and an ache starts to permeate my thoughts. The smile is wiped from his face, and he says, "But I do."

"I think," Delaney says, her voice almost too quiet to be heard, but it's loud in my ears, echoing through the hollows of my chest, "I should go." Her eyes go from me to him as she steps to the side of the chair where she had been sitting. The food on our dinner plates has gone cold, and the drinks are warm. "Congratulations. I wish you much happiness."

She doesn't say anything more to me. She walks away from the table, attempting to slip out of my life without a trace. But we're too far past that point. Her fingerprints cover my body, her kisses linger on my lips, but it's her love that she's ripped away like a bandage.

"She was going off on you, man. I didn't know you were a forgiving man." He looks over at some guy in a pink tie and blue suit, probably someone he works with, and throws his arm in the air. "Coming to see you next, brother."

"So Caroline wants me to introduce you to her cousin. Not attractive. I'm warning you now, but happy wife, happy life, and since you're single again—"

"Fuck off, Jimmy."

"What? You like that girl? She's feisty. Not your type, man."

"You're a real asshole sometimes, you know that?"

"Yeah, but I still got your back." He's not wrong. I don't have the right to shoot the messenger.

Watching Delaney push through some double doors, I pat him on the shoulder. "Congrats, man." I start running.

"Warner? Caroline wants you to catch the garter."

I flip him off as I rush through hordes of guests, seeing plenty of saps who would kill to help him fulfill a stupid superstition. As soon as I push through the same doors, I look both ways and then choose the staircase to the lobby. She's in heels, so I wouldn't think she'd get far, but fuck, the woman can run.

There's no sign of her in the lobby or on the street out front. I look both ways, hoping to catch a glimpse of pale blue, but I'm met with every other color instead. I could run home and probably beat her back, even if she took a cab. I'm not dressed for it, but fuck it, I start running.

Three blocks down, I cross the street and turn a corner, ending up keeled over and gasping for breath. I glance up to get my bearings when I see I'm in front of my office. Water. That would be good. I push through the doors to see Jerry sitting behind the desk. "You work on weekends, too?"

"Every other Saturday. It's good money." He stands and looks me over. "Nice suit. Getting married?"

I chuckle, and then the thought sours in my stomach. "No. I was the best man in a friend's wedding and had to take off."

Shaking his head, he laughs. "Sounds like woman trouble to me. Otherwise, why would you ruin a perfectly good tuxedo like that? Hope it's not a rental. They'll charge you for sweat stains."

"No worries. It's not."

"You always did have good style, Mr. Landers. How's your head and arm? That was a bad accident. I recently saw the footage. You really took a hit." His hand arches through the air. "Like a rag doll."

"Not the image I was going for." He laughs again. I don't care about the mocking. I know he's only teasing, but I do care about this footage. "You said there's footage?"

"Yep. We have security cameras all over the building—inside and out."

Of course, they do. I knew this and never once thought to ask if they caught the accident on video. "I'd like to see it."

"Sure. I have it handy." I'm not going to ask why he has it handy, but I hope he and the other guards are getting a good laugh from it. "Come around here." Tapping a screen, he says, "Watch it here."

It's playing, but it takes a moment for my brain to process what I'm seeing. I lean closer. Jimmy exits and goes one way. Delaney and I exit the building and stop on the sidewalk out front. I can't hear her, but she looks upset, points at me several times, and then balls her fists at her sides.

I'm too calm to be part of a conversation with her, so distraught. Why wouldn't I be helping her? I leave her there and walk to the corner, but she stays. She slowly turns away but takes only a few steps before looking back.

"This is where it gets good," Jerry says. "She says something that makes you turn around and then bam!"

"Oh shit." My heart stops hard in my chest, the vaguest of memories of hearing my name returning. "That was bad."

"Glad you lived."

"Yeah." I laugh, but I can't say I'm at a point to be able to joke about the accident quite yet. "Me too." As I stare at my lifeless body on the screen, I feel sick. My stomach churns as ghost aches cause pain to jump around my upper body in memory.

In my periphery, Delaney draws my full attention back

to her. Her hands cover her mouth, but no step is taken. She's in shock, surely.

"She's cold as ice, leaving you like that."

My eyes are fixed on her . . . silently begging her to run, to help me, to do something other than what she's doing at that moment. When time stretches, I finally look away when anger gets the best of me. With my hands on my head, I pace from the desk just as air strikes deep in my lungs.

She left me to die.

Fuck, was she really?

No. It's too hard to believe. I know her. She cries over fucking dead pigeons. No way would she walk away from an injured person, much less someone she'd been talking to not two minutes prior. "Hey, Jerry? Can you send a copy to my email?"

"Sure, since you're the star. Don't tell the security company. They have procedures and probably don't want the liability."

I'm already heading for the exit to find Delaney. "I won't. Thanks. Have a good one."

"You, too. Hope you catch up to her."

Me too, though I have a feeling we mean it differently. As soon as my feet hit the pavement again, I'm running.

What a fucking idiot I've been.

The setup.

The act.

The lies.

Asking for millions.

The fucking *I love you* she said when I got wise to her con.

She loves fucking heist movies, for crying out loud. I'm so fucking stupid for falling right into her trap. Why, because she has a great ass? I'm so easily distracted, and for what? I should probably check my bank accounts and make sure they haven't been emptied. *Fuck.*

I run too fast for the new guy to reach the door. "Everything all right, Mr. Landers?"

"Great." I push the button to call the elevator when I realize she might not be here. The lies are being exposed. She ran from the reception, knowing the con is over. "Hey, Rob?"

"Yes, sir?"

"Have you seen Mrs. Landers tonight?" The words curdle in my throat, but I can't waste time explaining how I became an accomplice to the con artist as she steals whatever she's after.

His smile brightens. "She got home about fifteen minutes ago."

The elevator doors open, and I jump inside. "Thanks."

No one can ever say she's not fearless. The woman has the audacity of a fighter betting on himself to win a match. That arrogance is always overplayed, just as it has been with her.

I get off the elevator, wondering if she's deadbolted me out of my own damn apartment, but when it opens, I find the minutest relief in the gesture. I close the door and start down the hall. My steps have slowed like each beat of my heart. When I reach the living room, I look right to the kitchen, glance toward the balcony, and then down the hall. I remind myself once again that this is *my* place before calling out, "Hello?" I'm greeted with silence. I reach the bedroom and look inside before entering. "Delaney?"

CHAPTER 28

Delaney

WARNER'S VOICE echoes down the hardwoods of the hall before damping at the entrance to the bedroom. Kneeling next to my suitcase in the closet, I lower the clothes I have in my arms and wait to see what happens next. Will he allow me to collect my belongings and leave in peace, or do the dirty details of what I've done need to be revealed to satisfy his burning curiosity?

Either way, I'm praying I can hold on to a smidgen of the dignity I have left, which is wrapped up in my family, and walk out with my heart intact. I know that's an impossible task, but I have nothing left of myself to sacrifice. I played the hand I was dealt. I've been such a fool for believing that somehow I could win this round—save the restaurant, and my family's home, and get Warner. Why'd I go and fall in love with the jerk?

Squeezing my eyes closed, I drop my head, knowing there's no going back or fixing this. What could I possibly say that could salvage what we had together? I got caught up? The ends justified the means? I didn't expect to fall for you. Those wouldn't be lies like the ones I told before. But would he even believe me anymore?

The worst part is knowing this is how we end. Not by our own admissions since we'd gotten so good at lying to ourselves, but by some sideswipe when we least expected it. That's karma. And we'll pay the price. I just hope I can take the brunt of it since he never deserved any of this.

Warner fills the doorway to the closet, a mass of man and muscle taking up space like he owns the place . . . *Guess he does, technically*. I'm the intruder. From the beginning, I'm the one who broke into his life and stole parts of his identity to selfishly benefit my own and my family. Hell is paved with good intentions for a reason. "Were you not going to answer me?"

"What could I possibly say? Anything I say will sound so off the wall that the truth couldn't win this battle. So my not responding was the answer."

"Just tell me what you wanted from me. You owe me that much."

"I owe you nothing." But that's not entirely true. I wanted something that I should have known he'd never be able to give. "I wanted your heart, but I've been denied twice."

"I don't know what you're talking about, dammit. Make sense, Delaney." My gaze already left his, but I can still feel the heat of his stare. "You're leaving? Just like that? No courtesy of an argument, or giving me the option to hear your side of the story? You're going to slink out of Tribeca like you did the reception? Like . . . Like a thief in the night, which probably isn't far from the truth. How mature of you."

"Maturity wasn't something I was concerned with. I had my reasons." I didn't know those reasons would hurt him when I was only trying to protect my family. But I should have. I tempted fate by messing with his emotions. I can't feign innocence over that aspect. *But where did it all go so wrong?* My life has been spiraling out of control ever since I got into that ambulance.

"You owe me the truth, Delaney." He stabs his chest with a plea that causes my stomach to twist in knots.

"Do you know how many times I've tried to tell you? But the truth wasn't what you wanted. You wanted a wife, and I was here giving you just that." My words come out softer than I intended, my spirit not able to rouse to the fight. I don't want to hurt him, even now when I'm under the spotlight to be interrogated.

"And in return, what was in it for you?"

I take a breath and look down at the mess of clothes I've shoved in the suitcase. The answer isn't going to be found inside because there isn't just one thing. There's more than this suitcase can hold. I finally look up at him again. "You deserve answers. I just don't think they're going to be what you want to hear."

We've crossed canyons to be together, so as we stare at each other, the divide feels greater than it ever has. I'm not a weak person, but the will to attack him or even defend myself feels fruitless when it comes to Warner. He'll throw out facts that will counteract my truth, no matter how valid it is.

He turns his back to me and scrubs his hand over his face, walking away. I watch as the jacket slides off his shoulders, and he tosses it on the bed. He doesn't move or say anything. He doesn't even look at me as if the sight is as problematic as the secrets we keep. "We'll never know with you evading the answers." He turns to shoot his gaze at me. "But I deserve to hear the truth after the nonsense you've put me through. This speaks volumes about what you really think about me as a person."

"How I think of you as a person is why I'm not bothering. Not because I think you're bad or evil. I know you're not. I also know that nothing I say will make a difference to you." I grab a shirt and squash it into the suitcase before reaching for another and repeating the process.

"How about this?" He sounds so reasonable that I'm worried about being hit with what he says next. "I'll do the talking, and you can chime in if I get something wrong in this story of yours." One glance out the window, and he takes a breath before facing me again. "Jimmy was right. Fuck." Shaking his head, he's not amused, though his tone leans toward it for a split second. "That's not something I can say very often."

He looks down as if disappointment has taken over. When his eyes strike mine, the pain he's carrying is drawn through the lines of his face. "You could have been the one to tell me that you were at my office and we knew each other before the accident, but you didn't. You made up this fable in your head that we were married. Do you know how horrible and confused that made me feel when I was dealing with my injuries?"

"I'm sorry."

"That's not fucking good enough anymore, Delaney!" he shouts. "Your sorry doesn't fix the damage you've done. It doesn't turn the lies you've told into the truth. You're nothing more than a liar and an opportunist. Get your shit and get out of my penthouse."

He rips the bow tie from around his neck and throws it on the floor before he storms out of the bedroom. "That's bullshit, Warner, and you know it." I get to my feet and follow his footsteps into the living room. He can call me a liar. That's the truth. I've lied so much that I've let it overtake my entire personality for him. "Don't call me an opportunist when you know it's not true."

"Oh yeah? How do I know that? You asked me for five fucking million dollars like I would hand it over and not even miss it."

"You wouldn't miss it!" I shout right back, matching him in volume and upset. I slap my hands onto the island countertop, leaning over like my words won't reach him on the other side if I don't. "That's just it. Money is meaningless to you because you have so much of it. That's why you're wretched at work and miserable at home. You have more than you could ever need, and sadly, it's all you have to keep you warm at night."

"So let me get this straight." I hate the condescension in his tone, but it's the lack of emotion in his eyes that hurts the most. "In your teeny-tiny worldview, I deserve to be fucked over because I have money? Got it!"

I have to take a breath after hearing that. My teeny-tiny worldview? He thinks so little of me. He's upset. I am too. We're bound to say things that cross a line or two. The art of fighting isn't determined by the winner but by what is said that leaves the most damage. I've never operated by those rules, but I can't say the same for the both of us. He wants the win more than I do. "No. You deserve to be happy. You just won't allow yourself to be."

"I did. I was overlooking your lies and gaslighting myself into loving you."

I hope the first stab hurts the worst because I have a feeling there are more where that came from. "Lies. Lies. Lies. God," I reply, throwing my arms up from my sides. "That's all you've got on me—"

"Well, there's a lot to unpack on that topic." His brow is

cocked, and the arrogance I saw oozing from his pores the first time we met sits on his smug jerk face. "If the shoe fits—"

"Screw you." I turn around and storm back to the closet to get "my shit," as he calls it, but stop and turn back once more. "Once I'm gone, your money can get you off instead."

"I knew it was an act," he says as if he has nothing to lose. "You never fucking cared—"

"I cared!" I come racing back, pointing right at him. "I cared about you when no one else did." My breathing is as harsh as my words. I hate myself for putting those out into the universe, and for saying the words I never should have, no matter how much I was pushed. The momentum I carried deflates, making me feel empty inside. "I cared, Warner. You're getting what you want, though. You can finally be miserable without me." I walk toward the bedroom, the rush in my veins losing speed with every step I take away from him.

Dropping to the floor, I just grab a pile of clothes in my shaky hands, shove them inside the case, and try to close it. It won't. I sniffle, desperately trying to leave before the tears in my eyes fall, so I switch my attention to the shoes and load them into the duffel bag. Why is he like this? Why can we not talk like we usually do? Why did he turn on me so quickly?

He has valid reasons, but what's my excuse? I fell for him and lost sight of my purpose for being here in the first place.

"I always knew the truth would come out," he says, back in the doorway with his sleeve rolled up on his forearm and the top two buttons of his shirt loosened from the holes. His hair falls over his forehead like it's been overworked in frustration. Those blue eyes still hold so much warmth when he looks at me despite the chill of his words. I shouldn't notice such things under the circumstances, but even when he challenges or assumes the worst about me, he's still attractive. It's his insides that need work.

"I didn't know how bad it had gotten until this point. And it's so much worse than I imagined." He shakes his head to scold me silently, and his anger begins to grow again as if it's been watered. "You lied to get my money. When I didn't fall for your act, you came out and asked for it."

I'm too tired to go in the circles he wants to travel, too hurt to think clearly enough for a good comeback. I finally look up at him and say, "You missed a detail. When I was falling for you, I stopped caring about the one thing that brought me into your life."

"Which was?"

"My family." My chin quivering in his presence taps a source of embarrassment that makes me regret engaging. *Get your stuff, Delaney, and get out, like the man wants.*

"I didn't even know your family existed before I met you—"

"That's the problem." Why does he have to make this so difficult? I grab another shirt and lower it to my lap. Pushed too far this time, I finally snap, losing any inhibition I had been restraining. "You think you're better than me. You always did. Living in this high tower, only to leave each morning to go work in another, reeks of "let them eat cake." But the people who live beneath you, the ones too busy working, barely have time to look up before you crush them under your expensive designer shoes. Guess what, Warner? I'm one of them. My family will suffer at your hand, and you'll never be forgiven."

He rolls his head back, then levels me with a glare. "Forgiveness?" His laugh holds nothing of the man I thought he was. He's become unrecognizable, worse than the man I met in the elevator of Landers Ventures. "Business is business, sweetheart," he says with less venom than before.

I thought I hated myself for causing this, for being pushed into a corner and saying things I knew I'd regret. I hate him more. "I wasn't your business. I was your—"

"What were you, Sass? My girlfriend? My wife?"

"The label doesn't matter. I should have been safe with you."

"Nothing is safe in this city. Not if I have a say." The severe lines tracking across his brow collapse as he pauses, seemingly losing his footing in the anger.

I thought I would be immune to attack if he loved me enough. He doesn't, not like I love . . . *loved* him. His words cut like a knife. There is no coming back from this, so I let the wound bleed out. "Not even me."

The intensity of his glare has me looking back at the suitcase. I don't care enough about these clothes to continue this fight. I start to close it, but he reaches down with his eyes set on the case. "My heart wasn't enough. You want my shirt as well?" He yanks a maroon tee from the stash, sending something hard flying out with it to land at his feet.

As if things weren't bad enough already . . . I feel sicker than I already did watching him bend down and pick up the broken phone. Fuel to his already blazing fire, he looks from the phone to me and grits his teeth. "Is this what I think it is?"

I'm not going to be able to negotiate a smooth release by pleading momentary insanity. I cringe, thinking about all the things I've done to keep a charade going that should never have been a thing in the first place.

He says, "You're awfully quiet for someone who claims to be innocent in all this."

"I never claimed to be innocent or virtuous. I was doing what I thought was best."

"Fucking me over? That's a great fucking plan there." His eyes ice over, the chill causing me to shiver in front of him.

My tears finally fall, unable to wager against a tyrant. "There's no point in talking to you. You don't want the truth like you claim. You want another apology and a yes-man. I'm not your guy for that."

"You weren't anything to me except a stranger who wanted me dead." He shrugs unapologetically. "Guess what? I lived, sweetheart."

I close the case, this time locking it, and grab the duffel bag. Despite my push to honor his wishes, he stands in my way while I stare at his chest. I have a stubborn streak, and sometimes that involves having the last word, even when it would benefit me more to keep my mouth shut. Looking him straight in the eyes, ignoring that my heart is shattered in my chest, I raise my chin and say, "And here I thought the accident made you a better person."

"Guess it didn't stick." He moves aside.

I keep my eyes locked on his when I pass by. "You're an asshole. You know that, Warner?"

"I'm okay being an asshole because what you see is what you get, but not with you." He follows me down the hall just to get his licks in. "You're so deep in your lies that you don't even know who you are anymore, Delaney. If that's even your real name."

I stop and turn back, shocked by how low he's willing to go. "You know good and well that's my name." I snub him by raising my nose in the air. "I wear it with pride."

Just as I turn back, he says, "Sure as fuck could have fooled me, considering how you jumped at the opportunity to be a Landers the moment you saw an opening. You tossed it around with my doorman, worked over my mother to get on her good side, and anyone else you could force to listen while you name-dropped around the city."

Setting the bags down, I slow clap for him. "There he is. I knew the real you was still in there somewhere. Bravo for holding back for so long."

"Speaking of high-dollar performances, kudos to you for going the extra mile in bed." He winks like we're in on this together. "It really paid off."

Anger creeps over my chest like fog, reaching my head and causing my blood to boil over. *He has some freaking nerve!* "How did it pay off exactly?" I ask, crossing my arms over my chest to restrain my hands from breaking his other arm.

He walks around me and replies, "I'm not one to kiss and tell."

"No. You're just one to add insult to injury any chance you get."

"You would know," he says, leaning against the island. "You know the old saying, if the shoe fits."

"Stop saying that—"

"Where's the lie?"

I start toward him but stop myself from falling down this hole with him. Going tit for tat was never what I wanted. I get my bags and start again for the door. "I hope you feel better."

"So much better." He smirks, but it's neither sexy nor cute. It's too arrogant for that. Seems that, and money, is all he needs.

Relinquishing any power I won in that round, I reply, "You think you're protecting yourself, that cutting me out of your life will give you back the life you once had, but you weren't happy. You never will be until you realize that losing me won't make you whole. Sure, me and all the lies we built our relationship on will be out of sight, but they'll never be out of mind because I reached the one thing you didn't even know you had. A heart. And what becomes of that when there's no one left to tend to it?" I can be indignant all I want, but on the other side of that coin lies what hurts *me* most—*losing him*.

So I walk toward that door, trying so desperately to hold myself together until I can break down in private, well aware that losing him was never about losing access to his world despite what he thinks or insinuates. I never needed expensive dresses or invites to balls or events at The Met, or to attend weddings at the Plaza, for that matter. I was content with hot dogs on the street, Sunday dinners with my family, and falling asleep in his arms like I was his and he was mine, in spite of knowing it would only last a short time.

While he lets his heart disappear, I walk away from him, knowing mine will no longer be intact either. How could it be when the beats I felt were his all along?

"You gave up on me when I was still holding out hope. All I wanted was the person I was given a glimpse of the night at dinner with your family. That was the real you that the lies couldn't disguise. Where did she go?"

With my toes facing the final door of this obstacle, I look back over my shoulder. "You never really let me in. So you win, Warner. You have this penthouse all to yourself again."

He opens the door for me, though I'm certain it's not from chivalry. As soon as I step into the hall, he slams it closed. The latching of the bolts is the final blow. I'm no longer welcome here.

I no longer have Warner.

He's right because he lost me, but I also lost myself along the way.

Cutting through the lobby, Keith stands when he sees me. His eyes dart to the bags I'm carrying, and then he asks, "Going on a trip, Mrs. Landers?"

"Going home." He holds the door open for me, and when I walk out into the June night air, I say, "Keith, it's Bayetti. My name is Delaney Bayetti."

The empathy in his smile makes my heart clench, like he saw through me the whole time. "That's a pretty name, Ms. Bayetti." I'd tell him to call me Delaney, but we know we won't be seeing each other again.

"Thank you. Take care, okay?"

He tips his hat before I turn and head for the nearest train station. Despite the fight I had upstairs, I can still appreciate how nice this neighborhood is. It has a charm about it, but maybe it's too pristine for someone like me, someone who needs to feel the pulse of the city. Two blocks down, I can just make out his building, but the penthouse is too far above me to see.

This is it.

The tension in my body begins to alleviate, breathing coming easier as if I'd been holding it since the moment we met. But as soon as I hop on the train, those tears I held back at his apartment fall carelessly from the corners of my eyes. The emotion of the day is finally hitting a tipping point that I can no longer balance. I need to finally admit the truth. It's not the emotion. It's the loss of Warner that hits hardest.

Trying my best to swipe the running mascara from under my eyes, I stop outside the restaurant, catching sight of my mom through the window. She's bustling through tables with plates in her hands and a big smile on her face while my dad laughs with a group of men seated in the corner booth. He glides to the next, sharing his joy, like he always did with us kids, ensuring everyone who dines at the restaurant feels at home.

I carry on, tugging open the door and going upstairs to enter the apartment. As soon as I enter the room, I kick the door closed and drop the bags in the middle of the floor before falling onto the bed and crying some more.

CHAPTER 29

Warner

THE DARKNESS of night lifts from the Eiffel Tower she left on my console. What little light morning dares to bring allows my eyes to focus on the trinket when I wish she had taken it, like she removed herself from my life.

Did I tell her to go? I had no other choice when she wouldn't even fight for the little that was real in our relationship. I would have. I can handle yelling. It's the silence that killed the possibility. We could have fought through it to get to the truth and built a new foundation from there. But she packed her bags so fast that we weren't given the option.

My phone lights up with another message. I always check just in case it's Delaney. It's not this time, just like the past four weren't. All are from Jimmy. I finally reach for it on the coffee table and flip it open, only reading the last one: *You better reply or I'm going to assume you were in another accident.*

To be fair, it *was* a hit-and-run. Describing the driver to the police would be easy: Shorter, about chest high, long brown hair that's probably twisted up on her head, most likely wearing a stolen Harvard T-shirt, these incredible blue eyes that look at me like I hung the stars and moon when she's not mad at me, which is quite a bit of the time, and considers cookies in bed an aphrodisiac.

I text: *I'm alive.* I don't mention barely, though I feel my life slipping away from me again. *Stop making your bride jealous by bugging me and enjoy the honeymoon.*

When the screen brightens with another text, I feel my heart kick in again. But it's not from her. Jimmy replies: *Glad you're alive. Beers when I get back from Aruba.*

I stare at the screen for so long that I only see spots when I look away. I toss my phone to the other side of the couch and drop my head into my hand. I know I shouldn't, but I already miss Delaney so fucking much.

She's a habit. That's all. A bad one at that. I've broken bad habits before. Twenty-one days. That's all it will take to get her out of my system. *Focus on that, Landers.*

Lying down, I rest my head on the couch cushion with my broken arm anchored by my bicep. Seeing how the black ink bled into the fibers of the cast makes me realize nothing, no matter the intention, is only perfect for a short time. The lowercase "i" with a heart dotted was a distinctly Delaney choice when she could have chosen capitalization. I not only lost her and her spirit filling the vacancies in this place, but now I'm stuck staring at a blobby heart until this cast comes off.

Getting upset after the fact won't do me any good. I close my eyes, wishing the amnesia I had also involved the time I spent with her. The short time we were together caused more damage than the accident, but being trapped in these memories hurts more than any injuries I sustained.

My eyes grow heavy in the early morning hours . . .

A long-overdue contract finally hits my inbox first thing on Monday. I open it and start reading through the details. My supposed "closer," Carl, failed the company on this deal. We should have been signing papers, not sending them through both legal teams for a fourth round of negotiations. It's time for me to step in. If he can't get this deal closed, I will.

I messaged Jocelyn to order lunch for both of us so we can go over every page of this contract. Four hours, a storm brewing outside, two Italian subs, and more cups of coffee than I remember later, we sit back in the chairs of the conference room and look at each other, shocked by the findings.

Jocelyn doesn't jump in, so I finally say, "Mystery solved. Now I know why she asked me for five million dollars."

"Did you give it to her?" There's no judgment in her tone. I think she'd like to hear that I did. Unfortunately, that's not how things turned out.

I release a breath that's needed to get off my chest for a long time. "I didn't. But if I had known the circumstances for why she needed the money, I might have considered it."

"It wouldn't have been a wise investment, but I wouldn't blame you if you did. Must have been difficult to say no even without the facts."

I stare out the window where rain has been threatening the city all day. "This changes everything."

Taking the long way home meant catching a cab to the West Side and standing across the street from Bayetti's restaurant like a creeper. I only catch a glimpse of her here and there as she leads guests to their tables. The few times I've stopped by to spy on her were in the evening, so I'm not sure if she's a teacher by trade during the day, but she spends the evenings working the hostess stand for her family.

It gives me a good view of her when she's weaving through the tables and satisfies some innate urge I have to still connect with her despite making no contact.

The sky finally decides to open up and pour down. I duck under an awning that doesn't give much cover. I should get out of here despite already being soaked. But I stay a minute longer, needing it to soak her in as well.

Her eyes meet mine, sending me back into the shadows, but there's no hiding. She's seen me, so I raise my hand just the slightest as I hide my cast under my jacket and leave like I'm not going to be back here before the end of the week again.

Six weeks later ...

"THE LAST X-RAY LOOKED GOOD. You healed nicely." The doctor taps on the cast like he expects it to crumble. "I bet you're ready to get this cast off."

Staring at the colorful get-well messages from some of my coworkers, Jocelyn's purple calligraphy signature, and Jimmy's artistic interpretation of eating a hot dog that suits more the toilet humor of his college frat days than a CEO in New York, I feel sentimental that they'll be gone. I'd gotten used to letting go of things being a specific way and started to go with the flow on others. Seeing the scribbles didn't kill me and brought me much-needed smiles when no one else was around. It's strange how I finally put myself out there only to still end up alone anyway. "Yeah, but can you do me a favor?"

"Sure," he says, with a giant pair of scissor-looking tools in hand.

"Save this one for me."

He tilts his head and reads, "I love you, Hotshot." I should be embarrassed letting a professional read something that probably seems so silly to him, but to me, it's been a lifeline. That and the elastic hairband she left for me to use to protect my cast in the shower. I guess I won't need that anymore. He chuckles. "Girlfriend?"

"Wife." The word slips from my tongue before I can stop myself.

The first cut is made, jerking my arm to the side. "I didn't realize you were married."

"I, um . . . it's complicated." I steady my arm against my leg as he slices down the center.

"Isn't it always?" He sets the tool next to me and says, "My wife lives in Aspen year-round."

The cracking open of the cast reveals my pale and skinny forearm and hand. *Oh, how I've missed you.* "And you live here in the city?"

"It's complicated." He chuckles.

"Sounds like it."

He cuts around the section I requested for him to save and hands it to me. "How does your arm feel?"

I open and close my fist a couple of times. "Good."

"That's good. You can wash your arm up at the sink and then go to the nurses' station for instructions on care." He heads to the door, but before he leaves, he adds, "Good luck with the complication."

"Thanks." I'm not sure why I reply like Delaney is still in my life when she's not. "You, too."

I leave the office and head four blocks uptown to meet my mother for dinner since I'm in the area. She's made a conscious effort to stay in touch, and we've been meeting for a meal every other week. I think that's more than we did when I was a child.

I find her sitting at a table in the front corner. She waved, though the hostess was already expecting me. I suspect my mom showed her a photo of me. She's been more interested in my dating life since she met Delaney and now knows I'm single again. When I think about it, she's been more invested in my life in general since Jimmy's reception.

After showing off my healed arm, we order drinks and the nightly special at Johnathon's Bistro. Over a bourbon for me, and a glass of white wine for her, she tells me how she secured the committee chair position for the Upper East Side Social for next year and is quite pleased with herself. I hold my glass up. "Where there's a will."

"There's a way," she says, tapping her glass to mine.

It reminds me of something I've been meaning to talk to her about. "My father always said nothing is safe in this city—"

"Yes," she says with her eyes on the task of cutting into the pork chop. Her face sours. "Not if I have a say. I always disliked that saying."

"I said it recently."

She pauses with her fork in one hand and the knife in the other, both aimed in my direction. Looking at me, she asks, "Why?"

"I don't know. It just came out."

"Well, why are you mentioning it, then?"

"I don't know." I don't know how to answer her question, though I search the restaurant to see if the answer is hidden in the decor or on a server's face. No luck. I look back at her and add, "The words rolled off my tongue as if they were my own. The strange part is that I thought I'd feel better repeating his mantra. I felt worse. I still do."

Her hair is pulled back and held tight, so there's no hiding her feelings. It's written in the expression on her face. Lowering her fork and knife, she taps the cloth napkin to the corners of her mouth. "There's more to this story. Do you care to elaborate?"

"I said it to Delaney." The admission tightens in my chest, and a lump forms in my throat. I don't speak her name to anyone and only give myself the occasional permission to even think about her. "I said it as if it pertained to her."

It's the subtle things—the soft sigh, the corners of her eyes that lower, the thoughtful pause—that tell me what I already know. I fucked up. "That's not a very nice thing to say to someone you care about."

It's the disappointment heard in her tone that hurts. "No. It's not."

Peering up at me, she asks, "Is that why you're no longer together?"

"It's one of many things. It's complicated." I repeat what I told the doctor as if that somehow justifies it. "She eats cookies for dinner and spaghetti and meatballs for dessert, wears leggings around like they're regular pants, has klepto-maniacal tendencies when it comes to my T-shirts, and leaves knickknacks around the penthouse. How does that even make sense to anyone else?"

She takes a sip of wine, but I have a feeling it's to cover her laughing. I wasn't allowed to walk into certain rooms if they were freshly vacuumed, so I assume she would side with me. When she lowers her glass, she says, "What a wonderfully unique young woman." *I assumed wrong.* It's hard to be upset when she's siding with Sass, though.

"You don't understand. She's walking chaos in human form, a tornado that comes through, leaving dirty dishes and Cheez-it boxes in her wake. She lit my Radafo art piece like it was a candle from Bath and Body Works. The artist has died. It's irreplaceable."

"I never liked that piece, but it's wax, Warner. When it's burned through, you can have it refilled. Problem solved."

"It was an investment piece, Mother."

"Art should be about evoking emotion, not hoping it gains in value."

I release the heaviest of sighs. "Well, it evoked an emotion, alright."

"Listen, son, not one thing you've said about sweet Delaney would make me dislike her. If anything, I like her more for her carefree spirit." She leans in and whispers, "She changed you in ways that you're oblivious to, but I give her credit. The changes are good. You smile more, well, more lately. I know it was tough in the beginning. You had people sign your cast, and you didn't give them strict instructions or require the same color. I've not reversed a meal order like she has, but maybe that's something we can try next time we meet for dinner."

"Dessert first?"

"I love a good apple pie à la mode and New York-style cheesecake. What's your favorite dessert, Warner?"

Delaney. Not something I can say to my mother. "Double chocolate cookies."

She starts back on her pork chop and says, "I love chocolate. Where do you get those?"

"I know a place. Maybe I can take you some time."

"I'd like that." She takes a bite. I do, too, but when she finishes, she adds, "What are the chances of you and Delaney mending fences?"

Making peace? I can't say I thought it was a possibility. She went her way, and I went mine. Neither of us made the effort to contact the other again, although I have passed by more recently. I haven't seen her the past two times I walked by Bayetti's, which makes me wonder where she is, though I have no right to ask. "I don't think she wants peace because of how it ended. She wouldn't even fight with me."

"My dear Warner. Have you ever thought that she didn't argue as a way of sparing you more pain?" No, that hadn't crossed my mind because it didn't seem like an issue prior, but I'm in a different place these days with the distance between me and the pain that haunted me.

"It's not like that. She wouldn't even answer my questions. I was left to fill in the blanks after she left, and that didn't do me any favors."

Reaching over, she covers my hand with hers on the table. "It makes me wonder what the answers involve. She was smitten with you. You didn't see it, but everyone else did. So playing devil's advocate, maybe she was trying to protect you."

"From what?"

"Yourself. If there's one thing I know for certain, it's that you are looking for reasons to close yourself off from the world." Resting her hand on her chest, she says, "That's my fault. It's your father's. You always had to deal with things yourself, so you learned that if the walls were strong enough and taller than anyone else, no one could scale them or hurt you inside. I'm sorry I wasn't a better mother. I don't have an excuse, but I will tell you that you are my greatest joy in life."

I never expected to bond with my mom on a deeper level. But we have simply by spending more time together. I regret that we didn't start doing this sooner. I look at her, the face that smiles every time she sees me, and smile right back. "I love you."

"I love you, too, Warner."

We eat some of our dinner before she adds, "You have a brilliant mind for business, but making more money won't make you happier."

I swallow the bite and ask, "What will?"

"You already know the answer."

I do. She's been the answer all along. I just refused to ask the question before now. "What if it's too late and I've lost her for good?"

"It's funny you knew exactly who I was speaking of." She's tricky, this one. I grin. "It's never too late for true love. But you need to show her that she'll always be safe with you. Love and security. The rest comes naturally."

Loving Delaney is the easy part. Proving I deserve a second chance is more difficult. Words—lies and mistruths, bad mantras thrown out like they were meant when they weren't—got us here. It's going to take more than words to win her back. "Oh shit. What if Delaney is seeing someone else?"

"She's not," she says, raising her glass to take another sip. "Your old mom did the research her son should have done more than a month ago."

It's good to know she has my back.

I take the train home from dinner, wanting the detour into the city I never visit anymore. It gives me time to think about all that was said at dinner, and what's happened since

Delaney left. It's not been good without her, but so much has improved because she was once a part of my life.

She's not seeing anyone, according to my mom.

Maybe it's a miracle or the sign I've been waiting for to spur me into action. Perhaps it's learning that Delaney Bayetti hasn't moved on. *Like me.*

CHAPTER 30

Delaney

IT's criminal to have teachers working in August without air-conditioning. Walking to the window to open it, I pluck at the front of my dress to cool off. A breeze sneaks in through the crack as soon as the window is lifted, giving quick relief and helping to clear the musty scent in the room after being closed up all summer.

Three-quarter sleeves were a mistake, but I wanted to wear something nice on the first day of my new job. I add fans to my never-ending list of supplies I need to buy to outfit the room before school starts in two weeks.

"Knock. Knock." I look up to see an unfamiliar face. "Hi, I'm Art, but the kids call me Mr. Johnson. I teach in the science lab down the hall. Wanted to stop by and introduce myself."

"Hi, come on in." I stand to shake his hand. He's older, older than Warner, which seems to be my baseline for comparison with men these days. "Delaney Bayetti."

"Bayetti?" He walks to the window to look out, like he's

comparing my views to the ones from his room. "Like the restaurant? Great food. Have you ever been?"

"A lot." I rest my hands on the back of the chair. "I was practically born in that kitchen. It's my family's restaurant."

He looks back at me over his shoulder. "Whoa, we got a real-live celebrity working at Astor Elementary."

"I wouldn't go that far." Waffling my head, I laugh. "Okay, go ahead."

Laughing, he scopes out the outside area again. "Nice view."

Working at this elementary school was at the top of my list of schools when looking for a job. It's tucked into a pocket of the city with a great neighborhood vibe, trees lining the street, and less traffic. "I like the trees."

"I face the air-conditioning units. They're loud, but I know how to project." Coming back, he says, "You shouldn't wear a necklace like that. It's a safe neighborhood, but it could stir trouble."

Clutching the necklace Warner gave me, I smile half-heartedly. "Nothing to worry about. It's just crystals or fake stones."

"Those aren't crystals. Trust me, Geology was a minor. But I can prove it to you."

Not crystals? Of course, they are. That would be ridiculous to give someone you barely know an expensive diamond necklace. "Okay, how?"

"I'll be right back."

When he leaves, a memory returns of his mother scolding Warner when she thought he'd bought my knockoff ring. I spoke too soon for him to address that issue, but now I'm confident he would have reassured her. The velvet box, the weight of the metal, and the heft of the clear stones. *No way.* This has at least thirty diamonds, probably more like fifty, wrapped around it.

When Art rushes back in, he holds up a handheld device. "This is a diamond tester. The kids love it when we find real 'diamonds' on the playground." He laughs. "It's not an expensive machine, but it works most of the time. It often confuses moissanite for diamonds, so I place tiny chips around the playground for the kids to find for us to test."

"That's cute."

"Its accuracy is iffy, but it's right at least fifty percent of the time."

"The odds don't sound good, Art."

He holds it to my necklace and says, "It's all we got."

The machine buzzes, so he moves it to another stone and presses the button again. By the time he's done, the machine sets off five times. "So what do we think?"

"I think you shouldn't be wearing that necklace to school, is what I think."

My jaw drops. "It's real?" I don't know how to feel about this information. I've loved it since he gave it to me, and figured he paid good money for a solid knockoff, but what kind of money did he pay exactly?

"It's real, alright." He stands on the side of the desk and says, "Typically, we find fakes when the person thought it was real. Here you are with the opposite issue." He heads for the door while I stand there in shock. "Welcome to the Astor Elementary family. I'll see you around."

"Yeah, see you." I pull a mirror from my purse and hold it up to find a good angle on the necklace. My compact is so small that I can see it—stunning as always—but I can't get a good look. I tuck the mirror away, wondering if I should hide the necklace in my purse somewhere. *Great.* Now I feel like I need to protect it or myself. It's frustrating that I wore it with confidence before without concern. Do I need to fear for my life with this around my neck?

Don't be silly, Delaney. I can wear it as I have been, just not to school anymore. Sitting at my desk, a different emotion sneaks in. I had no issue taking it with me when I thought it was fake. It's been my favorite piece to wear day-to-day and was perfect for the two dressier events I attended with Warner. But I don't think I can accept this gift knowing it's real. *What to do...*

Arriving at the building fifteen minutes before five, I open the door and head for the elevators. I've only been here once before, and that didn't turn out so well. I'm hoping this time goes better. It should. I'm only dropping off the necklace, and then I'm gone. I can even leave it at reception. No, I probably shouldn't do that. Well, there *is* the infamous Jocelyn. I can leave it with her.

I ride the elevator, wondering if she's as pretty as her name. I'm sure she is. Warner's probably surrounded by beautiful women. Wonder if stunning and statuesque are requirements on the application, with a photo attached to submit. He probably prefers blondes as well. The opposite of me. *Ugh.*

The doors open, and I step into the lobby, only to be greeted by Jimmy, who stands when he sees me. "Delaney?"

"Oh," I say, surprised to see him again. I stop just off the elevator and reply, "Jimmy. How are you?"

He shoves one hand in his pocket, rocking back on his heels, and wiggles the fingers on the other. "Good. Great. Married."

"Yeah." I smile. "I remember."

Snapping his fingers as if he just recalled a memory that had slipped his mind, he says, "Of course. What are you doing here?"

"I need to drop off something for Warner."

The receptionist stands and says, "Mr. Lange, you can go on back."

He nods toward the door and asks, "Why don't you come with me?"

I should hesitate and think twice about walking through that door to surprise Warner like this. Instead, I reply, "I'll be quick. I'm leaving it with his assistant."

We start toward the entrance, and when he opens the door, he waits for me to pass in front of him. "I'm sure Warner would like to see you."

Although I appreciate the suggestion, the thought has my tummy doing flips. "I'm not as sure about that. Me showing up in the middle of his workday—"

"End of day. I came by to drag him out for a beer." We reach a corner of the walkway, and he stops to look at me. It feels like a protective barrier by how he shields me from whatever lies ahead, making me regret it every time I silently curse his name for pinpointing me from that day. "You two should talk."

"I'm not sure what's left to say, Jimmy. He was pretty clear about how he felt."

"Clear, but went in the wrong direction."

"I don't know what that means."

He glances at a guy walking, keeping his mouth clamped closed until he passes. In a hushed voice, he says, "Warner is his own worst enemy sometimes. He might have said one thing, but he misses you."

His persistence is persuasive, causing my heart to ache for a man who broke it, but I can't fall into that trap. Warner and I had so many opportunities to fix what was built on quicksand, but we didn't. It was always easier to ignore than go back and revisit what we had done wrong. Ever since I left his penthouse, he's been passing by the restaurant like he has business in the area when it's obvious he's just spying. I've had to reckon with that in my own way. He's not crossed any boundaries, but his presence, even in the vicinity, makes it hard to put him behind me when he keeps popping up.

The real rub is hearing how he misses me because the way I've been missing him has been devastating. I'm shattered after I see him, reopening wounds that are never given time to heal properly. "I'll think about—"

"Jimmy?" The warmth of that voice coats my insides, calming the gymnastics class currently being taught in my stomach. I would have expected the opposite.

When Jimmy shifts, I'm exposed, coming face-to-face with the man I thought I could walk away from and leave in the past. That hasn't happened. I think about him more than I should, considering how things ended.

Warner stands outside an open office, staring at me, and reminding me of how he would stare at me when I first came home with him. I'm sure the shock of seeing me now matches the same feeling he had back then.

I didn't expect to see him, but I knew the potential was out there. Why does he look more handsome than I remember, especially when I thought he was already perfect? His hair is a little longer—not by much but enough to be unruly, which is so damn sexy and has me wishing I could run my fingers through it. Like he is now. It's the vest he's wearing with no jacket that I can't get over the most. It's almost like he sensed me coming by and pulled out all the stops. He says, "My arm's not broken."

He was never one for small talk. "Looks good."

"It's skinny compared to my other one, but I was once told I'm a little doughy." A lopsided grin lifts his cheek.

"You were never doughy. Whoever said that lied to you."

"Mmm." He nods, pressing his lips together. "I suspected as much, but good to hear."

"So," Jimmy says with a thunderous clap, "I'm here to drag you out for a beer, but I can meet you down there."

Warner chuckles. "Last time you came to the office like this, I never made it to the bar."

"I'll come looking if that happens. Or better yet, Delaney can make sure you arrive safe and sound." He glances at me. "Does that work for you?"

It's a terrible idea, like me standing here. Too late to turn around now, and it doesn't seem like I have much choice but to babysit the CEO. Since I'm not looking to make a scene at Warner's office, I reply, "I'll take care of him." The words come so naturally. As odd as it feels to admit, I've missed caring for him. Since he's healed from the concussion and the broken arm, I'm not sure I'd have a place in his life anymore.

Jimmy nods, looking from Warner to me and then back at him again. "I'll see you at the bar."

I'm curious if it's the same bar where he once took me, or if he's had the nerve to go back for a burger. I don't know whether to laugh or cry at my behavior. I was pushing hard to trigger him every chance I got. Looking back, that plan didn't even make logical sense, but I sure was committed to it.

When Jimmy walks away, I'm left standing there on my own. I pull the velvet box from my bag and take a few steps closer, holding it out in front of me. "I can't keep this."

His gaze dips to the box. When his stunning blue eyes land back on me, he asks, "Why not?"

"Because it's real."

He blinks twice, but I see the connection isn't made. "I'm going to need more, *Sas*—Delaney. What else would it be?"

"Not real. Even if you did believe I was your wife when you gave it to me, you didn't remember who I was. So why would you buy a stranger something so expensive?"

"We were going to an event, and I wanted you to have something to wear."

I'd been so busy staring at him that I missed the set of eyes on us from a nearby desk until I glanced out of my periphery. Swallowing becomes harder as my throat thickens from having an audience. I hold it out to him again, coming closer in hopes he'll take it, and whisper, "I appreciate the gift, but I hope you kept the receipt."

"I didn't, so I guess you're stuck with it."

"Warner . . ." I don't know what I'm even saying. I feel as disconnected from him as he was to the idea of my returning the necklace. I thought I hated him when I walked out of his apartment, but I hate this distance between us more.

He angles closer. "Can we talk in my office?" he whispers.

I hesitate. This isn't how the return of the necklace played out in my head. I wasn't prepared for a conversation with valid points or comebacks. The details of how we came together and why we broke up have become hazier with each week that passes, other than one thing that led to another and lies were told.

I also hadn't given him due credit for how tall he is, how broad his shoulders are, and the way I always felt safe in his arms. Not just physically but also emotionally. That was destroyed when I realized no one is safe in his presence. He said it himself. I need the reminder to keep myself from traveling down Memory Lane.

Unsure what's right to do, I need time and space out of his personal orbit to think clearly. I need to address the third wheel of our conversation. So instead of focusing on him, I look at the woman who's got kinder eyes than I expected, some gray streaking through the middle part, and has discovered the perfect shade of red lipstick. I smile to return the sincerity of the one she's offering me. "Hello," I say, nervous about whether she hates me for what I did to her boss and what appears to be a good friendship, or if she understands the taste of desperation. How I was standing on the brink when I decided to impersonate Warner in the email exchange.

She smiles, providing me with some relief that she's hopefully not holding my bad deeds against me. "I'm Jocelyn. It's nice to finally meet you, Delaney. I've heard so many nice things about you." Giving me grace is more than I could have expected, but I appreciate it.

My gaze shifts to Warner. I can't imagine he'd have that many nice things to say about me, or any for that matter. I reply, "He speaks very highly of you." I turn to Warner, who doesn't appear to be breathing. Is he waiting with a hope and a prayer that I'll stay or leave? I won't make him suffer, especially not in front of others, including Jocelyn.

"I only have a few minutes." I won't go into the reasons why I still work a few shifts at the restaurant, though he's a smart guy and can probably figure it out. When I close the space between us, images of running into his arms, wrapping myself around his body, and kissing him again flash through my mind. I fight those strong instincts and maneuver around him to enter his office, though his scent elicits memories of showering with him and that soap that smells incredible.

I hear the door close behind me as I walk straight to the

window to look out. I said horrible things about him in his towers. As I stared out through the glass, I wasn't far off, but I still shouldn't have said it. Glancing back, he returns to his chair behind the desk and settles into it.

Feeling like I've been called into the principal's office, I sit down quietly in front of him and cross my legs with the velvet box resting on my lap. I'm unsure if I should start or if he needs to discuss something specific, but I'm glad he speaks first and asks, "How are you doing?"

"I'm great." I dismiss the ache in my chest, hoping it will disappear if I don't give it life. "How are you?" Small talk at its worst, and the ache is still there.

"Truthfully?"

I laugh. "It's probably best knowing our history."

"Probably." He chuckles, though there's no weight to it, given the uneasiness between us. His smile remains, and he says, "I'm actually doing really well."

That his response feels so much like a betrayal tells me I should have moved on a long time ago. "That's good," I muster, fidgeting with the box. "I'm glad." My voice has all but vanished as the corners of my eyes begin to flood with tears.

He glances out the window and takes a breath. When he looks back at me, he says, "I'm doing better because you were in my life. You opened my eyes to so much that I was missing. I don't know, it's strange, but I'm not mad anymore." His chuckle would say otherwise. "That's a lie. I'm still working through things."

It's wrong to be attracted to him like I am. Hearing Warner express feelings he'd buried and find happiness without me stings, but it doesn't burn. I want him to feel the joy he was missing. I still can't help but wish I could be a part of this transition, to see the changes firsthand instead of hearing about them. "Like what?"

"With you, frustration led to fun. Your chaos became a comfort because I believed you cared about me. But that was something I was trying to convince myself of and not truly experiencing. Not because you didn't. I know you did. But so much of it was spun through the distortion of the lens I was viewing my life through back then."

"You say back then like it was years ago instead of months." This is all so confusing. He's had some great life epiphanies while I've been silently suffering.

"It feels like years have passed since you left."

"I was thrown out, for the record."

Leaning back in his chair, he keeps his eyes on mine. Seeing him in this setting has me imagining he gets his way all the time. Is that what this is about? He feels I left him, so he's jockeying for a chance to get me back so *he* can dump *me* instead? To put a proper bookend on our relationship, at least in his head.

"I still miss you, Delaney. I still—"

"You know what I miss? That damn soap of yours. I went in to buy it, but when I saw the price, I couldn't do it. I don't have money to throw away, even after finally finding a job, and I regret not taking your bottle with me." I toss my arms out as if I'm too much of a lost cause to waste any more time on. "You called me an opportunist, and I am when it comes to you and that soap, but I failed it so miserably and lost access to both. So don't make confessions of the heart when I made it clear that you had me, but then you threw me out because I couldn't fight on the timeline you had in mind." What am I even doing here? I stand and slip around to the back of the chair.

"What does that mean?"

"It means I was packing because I knew I would never survive hearing you telling me to get out. But guess what? I did survive, and I'm trying to move on. So you coming around to see me at the restaurant doesn't heal my pain. It only helps you. But that's all that matters, right, Warner? You have this revelation about being a better person, disregarding how you're still affecting my life."

"I didn't say I was better. I said I was happier."

"Well, guess what? I'm not. I was happier before you started taking over my world to destroy it. Honestly, I was happier than I am now before I ever met you, but you want to know when I was happiest?" His expression tells me this is not how he saw this going, but he's wise enough to keep his mouth shut. Neither did I, but since we're here, I might as well get it all off my chest and out in the open. "I was the happiest I'd ever been when I was your Sass and you were my Hotshot." I thought I'd feel better getting it out there. I feel worse. "How pathetic is that?" I toss the box on his desk and turn to leave. The walk seems so far with him staring at my back, but it goes too quickly. I know when I walk out of here, that's it. That's it forever, and the thought alone makes my feet feel like they're stuck in concrete. With my hand on the doorknob, I look back. "You had every opportunity to do the right thing, and you blew it."

"I was accepting the lies to be with you."

"I'm not talking about that."

He stands but stays protected behind that large desk of his. "You're talking about the building." He angles his head and says, "The deal is already done."

"Who's the opportunist now?" I walk out, trying to avoid his assistant, who probably heard everything. Pushing through the exit, I hurry to punch the button for the elevator, hoping I can escape with fewer wounds this time. When

I reach street level, I look both ways and then back into the lobby. The tiniest part of me wishes he would come running after me. The fairy-tale ending is always just out of reach, it seems.

I'M GREETED by a brown bag with striped ribbon handles sitting on the kitchen counter when I arrive home. I open the tag to discover my name written in calligraphy. I have no idea what this is, but I'm a sucker for a surprise.

With the bag in hand, I retreat to my bedroom. Dropping off my schoolbag, I sit at my desk to open the gift. I pull the tissue and peek inside, grinning the moment I see it, though I should probably temper any excitement. Warner and I let things lie between us, so I find it a bit odd for him to send me a gift, though I'm grateful for the thoughtfulness. He was listening while I was busy condemning him for being happier without me.

"Did you hear?"

"Jesus," I screech, slamming my hand to my chest. "Stop doing that, Lorenzo."

"Did you hear?" He's laughing as he flops onto my bed. He knows I can't stand him being on my bed, but he's got my attention on the other matter at hand.

"Hear what?" I hate being out of the loop.

"The building was sold—"

"Yeah. I already knew that." Why in the good Lord's heaven is he so excited about that? *Yay, we're losing our home and family restaurant*, I deadpan to myself. "Why are you so happy?"

"What do you mean? I thought you heard?"

"I did." *Straight from the traitor's mouth . . .*

He sits up. "What's not to be happy about the tenants being allowed to stay?"

I pull the bottle of soap out of the bag with the receipt floating to rest on my desk, but then stop. "Wait, what? What do you mean?"

Getting up like he has somewhere more important to be, he heads for the door. "It means the buyer didn't evict us. We get to stay."

"Who's the buyer?"

He's already in the hall when he replies, "Your guy on the inside. Landers Ventures."

"Warner." Why wouldn't he tell me? I look at the soap again—obviously a gift from him—and then at the paper that fell out with it. I unfold it, realizing it's not a receipt. It's an invitation.

CHAPTER 31

Warner

"Yes?" When the door opens, I glance away from the monitor to see Jocelyn peeking in before I return to the email that I'm crafting.

She says, "There's a Mrs. Bayetti here to see you." My fingers freeze on the keyboard. My heart might have stopped in my chest as well. I know my breathing has. She smiles and says, "*Mrs.* Bayetti."

"Mrs.?"

She nods, her smile too big to show any restraint. "Should I send her in?" She lowers her voice. "She brought cookies."

"In that case, send her in." I'm only half joking since I've tasted those cookies before. They're incredible, like her daughter, but that's not something I can allow my mind or heart to delve into. I stand when I see her enter my office. "I wasn't expecting you, Pamela."

"Mom, remember?"

I grin. "I thought that option left with your daughter."

Not really funny, but if I don't keep it light, I'll descend into a place I'd rather steer clear of. It took a lot of time alone to realize that the best is ahead and not to dwell on what could have been in the past.

She shoos away the very thought while making a beeline for me with a plastic container held in front of her. "I brought these for you."

"Double chocolate?" *Please say double chocolate.*

"The one and only." She sits in front of my desk, plopping her leather bag in her lap as Jocelyn closes the door to give us privacy. Pamela glances out the windows and says, "Nice office, kid."

I laugh, setting the container on the desk and sitting in my chair. With my arms resting on a small stack of files, I slide forward. "Thanks. So," I reply, "what brings you by?"

"You do. My daughter does." Sitting back, she has no issue taking on the task that is apparently on her agenda today: me. "What's going on with you two?"

"I'm not sure what you mean."

Lowering her chin, she looks up as if she sees right through my act. "Listen, Warner, you care about her. I knew that the moment we met. Anyone could see that, but what I know doesn't matter. *She* doesn't know you care about her. So why are you stirring up trouble where there is none?"

"I'm not stirring up trouble," I reply, my tone is defensive like trouble is exactly what I'm stirring up.

"Sure you are. You and Delaney together are making a big mess of something that seems straightforward."

"Seems is not the same as is straightforward. It's not as simple as you make it—"

"BS." She shakes her head as if she's had it with me. *Damn, she's tough.* "It isn't as complicated as you make it. You like her, although I'd call it love. She loves you. Be together. Start a family. Live life together instead of apart. Simple."

It's a struggle to keep my eyes in my head and my jaw from hanging like a fish caught on a hook, but she's got it all figured out, so there doesn't seem like much left for me to do here. I slow blink twice to bring myself back to reality. "There are things we need to discuss—"

"Talk is for the birds. You're not birds, Warner. You're in love. Just admit it."

She's good. I'll give her that. My feelings for Sass have only grown, not dissipated. Time hasn't done its job if I was meant to move on. "I'm not denying how I feel about Delaney." The words coming from my mouth stun me. Sure, I felt strongly about her. I was making small strides in hopes of us working through the problems. Even hoping we could move into starting over again. *But love?* I love her so much that the ache has outgrown me and spread to exist in every facet of my day. I swallow hard around my feelings and say, "I asked her to meet me."

The response doesn't seem to be one she expected, as she sits back and appears to process the new information. "What did she say?"

"I didn't want her to feel pressured. I'll be there whether she shows up or not, but I'm hoping she does."

"She didn't tell me." She takes a breath that appears to settle the excitement she embodied when she walked in, then smiles. "I can't tell you what she'll do, but if I were betting in Atlantic City, my money is on you, Warner."

I like her. Not only because she supports me and the relationship with her daughter—because approval matters —but she's also not afraid to pull some levers at her disposal to make things happen. Delaney inherited that trait. I'm pretty sure that's how we ended up married in the first place. *Not married.* Whatever we were, a lever or two was pulled.

She stands and wraps the strap of her handbag over her shoulder. "I need to get back to the restaurant. I wanted to bring you cookies as a thank-you for not changing the terms with the residents of the building. I know that wasn't your original plan, but it saved lives. Thank you."

I stand next to her. "It was also your daughter. Delaney made me look at things in a new light. It wasn't a hard decision to make once I knew the details."

Opening her arms, she hugs me. And I slowly and awkwardly embrace her as well.

Slipping away, she walks to the door and says, "Don't tell Delaney I was here. She'll kill me."

"Your secret is safe." Before she leaves, I say, "Thanks for coming by."

She opens the door with a smile on her face. "Don't forget dinner on Sunday."

"I think you're more confident than I am."

"I believe in love, Warner." She looks back again. "Hope you're taking care of that heart of yours."

"I'm surviving."

She grins like the cat who ate the canary. "I meant Delaney's. She left it with you." She doesn't wait for a reply. The door closes, and I'm left thinking about Delaney's heart being in my hands the whole time we've been apart. It causes mine to beat harder. Though under closer examination, my chest has been ringing hollow ever since she left. Was it only an echo of what used to exist?

Pamela has said some things that make a lot more sense than they did before. It wasn't my heart I was feeling. *It was Delaney's.*

Shit, I can't let this opportunity pass me by. I open the

door and run after her, catching her in the lobby just before she gets in the elevator. "Mom?" I feel silly, but I also don't, so fuck it.

With her hand holding the doors open, she looks back. "What is it?"

"Can you help me with something?"

Without hesitation, she says, "Whatever you need."

CHAPTER 32

Delaney

"Slow down, Mom. The park doesn't close until ten tonight. It's not even seven." She's been hustling from one train to another to the Boardwalk and now to Luna Park. "What's gotten into you? I thought you hated this place."

"I don't hate this place. I just thought it would be fun for us to come to Coney Island." Her grip tightens on my wrist as she drags me forward.

The thing is, I know what she's doing. I don't know how she found the invitation to meet Warner, but she's putting on quite the performance to get me here. She didn't have to. I was already planning to show up. I'm just wondering how my entire family got involved. "Shouldn't we wait for the others?" I glance back to see Lorenzo and Joe encouraging my dad to keep up like he's running a marathon.

With a good thirty yards to go, I'm pulled to a sudden halt for her to start fussing over me. "You look so pretty, Delly bean."

"Thanks." She holds my hands out to get a good look at

me and then embraces me like she's never going to see me again. The outfit was laid out for me on my bed when I came home from work. The lipstick was pulled from my makeup, sunglasses retrieved from my dresser, and she insisted on straightening my hair before adding soft waves around my face and the ends. Asking questions didn't get me any answers, so I went along with the plan and recreated my graduation look, complete with my shirt tied around my ribs, showing off my midriff.

I figured I was being sent out the door because she liked the way I looked the first time I wore it. Now, with the family in tow, and what I hope is Warner waiting for me, I get butterflies in my stomach.

My dad comes huffing, with my brothers patting him on the back. "You did it, Pops," Lorenzo says. "Keep your eye on the prize. Not far left to go."

Joe laughs and starts pulling him toward the entrance.

Lorenzo looks at me and says, "You're growing up, Sis."

I can't help but laugh. With a shrug, I say, "Thanks."

Clocking the time on her watch, my mom says, "We should go."

"Come on." We've come this far. I don't want to miss him —more than I already do.

While Lorenzo jogs to catch up with the guys, my mom and I start walking again. Our pace is a bit slower, as if we both know where this ends. She glances at me and then takes hold of my hand. When I wrap my hand around hers, her eyes get glassy. She laughs as she wipes under her eyes with the back of her index finger. "I don't know why I'm getting all choked up."

I was tempering myself, but the excitement was getting the better of me. Her tears and that earlier hug are making me nervous. I wrap my arm around her shoulders and side hug her while walking. "It's okay. Everything is going to be alright." It's such a cliché thing to say, but despite the sudden nerves for not knowing what's ahead, I believe what I said. It's going to be alright. *I am.*

Looking ahead, I don't see him, so I steal one last opportunity. "You sure I look alright?"

"Beautiful."

We approach the entrance to the carnival, and the guys who have been hanging around waiting like we were the slow pokes. I don't see Warner. I check over my shoulder and then into the distance in the other direction, getting more nervous by the second. I check my mom's watch. "He said seven."

A song begins playing, a familiar one from an old movie. I remember dreaming about the ending of *Sixteen Candles* after first seeing the movie with my mom one Sunday afternoon on TV when I was fourteen. Hearing it brings back that swoony feeling, but then I side-eye Lorenzo, who's holding his phone in the air, blasting it.

He grins and steps to the side. Joe and my dad shift to the other side, revealing Warner standing behind them. I gasp, covering my mouth. As tears flood my eyes, I raise my chin, hoping to keep them from falling, but I know it's a losing mission.

Warner pulls a small bouquet from behind his back and comes toward me. My mom is still wiping her eyes when she joins my family as they close in behind him. His shirt-sleeves are rolled up, showing off that arm that's made a fine recovery. The vest is fastened, but he left the top buttons of his collar open. I have a feeling I might get my wish to run my fingers through that sexy hair of his. Nothing beats that smile that moved right into those blue eyes. Those damn crinkles that make him even sexier are on full display. He hands me the flowers and then says, "Hi."

With my emotions blooming in my chest, I won't be able to hold them in for much longer. "Hi."

"I'm glad you came."

I glance at my family, who are busy talking among themselves, giving us the little privacy Coney Island will afford us. "Me too." I nod toward the others. "You got some help from your friends."

He chuckles, running the pad of his thumb over his bottom lip as he steals a glimpse of my family before turning back to me. "I didn't really have a choice."

I hold my nose to the flowers that are wild instead of picture-perfect roses. I like these better. Tilting my head, I look up at this tall drink of a man and say, "I was already planning on coming. You didn't need backup. You were enough, Warner. You were always enough for me."

Closing what little gap still exists between us, he caresses my cheek. "When a Bayetti is set on a plan, they go all in. Reminds me of someone else I know."

I laugh. It's light, but it feels as if a heavy cloud has lifted, leaving us nothing but blue skies ahead. "No lies detected."

He leans down and brushes his lips against mine. "Let's keep it that way." Not leaving me any room to argue, which I wouldn't have anyway, he kisses me.

My arms come around his neck as his arms reach around my body, landing on my lower back and holding me to him. When our lips part and I open my eyes, I shoot Lorenzo a look again. He says, "It's like a real-life soundtrack."

"I think we're good."

I release Warner and ask, "Now that you got me here all

dressed up in my graduation outfit, what are you going to do with me?"

Swinging his arm over my shoulders, he begins to lead me to the entrance. "First. We're getting the photo you should have gotten the first time without asking." Placing me beneath the Luna Park sign, he kisses my forehead and says, "Stay here." But then he comes back, running his hand along my exposed neck and says, "You look beautiful, Sass."

I've never felt more beautiful than how he makes me feel when he looks at me just like that. He steals a quick kiss, takes the flowers when I hand them to him, and backs up ten feet or so. Holding his phone in front of his stupidly handsome face, he says, "Say Warner."

Putting my hand behind my head and posing for him, I say, "Hotshot."

He lowers the phone and signals to my family. They rush in, surrounding me. My dad wraps his arm around me and says, "Love you, Cannoli."

"Love you."

My mom hops in next to me with her arm around my waist. Lorenzo is on her other side, while Joe stretches his arm around my dad's shoulders. My heart is so full that I struggle to hold back the tears that threatened to fall earlier. Just as one slips down, Warner says, "Say cheese."

"Parmigiano Reggiano," we say in unison, then crack up laughing.

My mom says, "One more." They disperse as she walks to Warner, taking his phone. She holds it up. The slow-motion walk of my man coming to me sends my heart racing. Fine, that was all in my imagination, but Warner has a damn good walk. He wraps himself around me from behind, kisses the top of my head, and then says, "I do."

I glance up at him and laugh. "I do? She said, 'Say cheese.'"

Coming around, he drops to one knee in front of me. My mouth falls open. "Warner?" I don't know what I mean because words are lost under the shock of what's happening.

Holding my hand, he says, "I don't want to fight you."

"Not the romantic start I imagined for my proposal."

He chuckles. "Felt like a good preface for the rest."

"I'll allow it." It doesn't matter what he says, my heart was already his from the moment we met. Okay, maybe not the *moment* we met, but a few days after, I was all his, and he was mine.

"I think we both know the lies we got caught up in. They served a purpose, and then when they didn't, we fell apart. That's not going to happen this time. I want to start over with you."

"I want that too. Clean slate. No past. Just moving forward from here."

He nods as if I stole the words out of his mouth. Oh no, maybe I did. I need to let him do this proposal how he wants. I don't need to control this. I'll let him work his magic. Because that's what he is to me—the dream I never thought could come true.

He says, "The one thing I will carry with us from the past is how you showed me how to live. I have loved every off-the-wall and unhinged moment we've had and don't regret a thing. But what I love more is the way your heart is always at the center of it. I've never known anyone as selfless as you, putting your family first, and then a total stranger that you hated. You helped me when you didn't have to." His head bobbles. "After you left me for dead, that is."

"I didn't leave you for dead. I debated, sure, but you were

an asshole back then." I cup his cheek. "I have no regrets saving you," I smirk and give him a little wink.

"Glad to hear it." He chuckles again. "Whatever happened then led us here. I don't want to miss another day of your gelato-hating, cookie-in-bed eating ways."

"If it makes a difference, I prefer gelato these days."

"I knew I'd convert you."

Bending down, I kiss his cheek and whisper, "You converted me, alright. I'm a full-on fool in love with you, Warner Landers."

"You're lucky you're so hot since you're stealing all my good lines."

I stand back up. "Well, skip to the good part, then."

"I love you so much, Delaney Bayetti. Will you be my wife?"

When he stands, I reply, "I will." I lift on my toes, and he leans down to meet me in the middle. "I do from this day forward, Hotshot."

We kiss. Just as it deepens, the rest of the world disappears, and that song starts playing again, making us laugh. He digs in his pocket and says, I got you something. He lifts the hinged lid on the blue velvet box, leaving me gasping. "Warner."

"It's real this time," a woman calls, getting our attention. We turn to see his mother standing next to mine. Two families becoming one for us makes my heart clench.

I turn back to Warner, slipping the diamond ring on my finger. Holding it up, I wiggle my finger, admiring it. The diamond is one I would have chosen for myself. Not too big and showy. The band is gorgeous, with diamonds on the sides of the centerpiece. Just enough to make it look like a million bucks. Wait, he wouldn't spend that, right?

It's too pretty to worry about. They have insurance for

that kind of thing. "I love it." Wrapping my arms around him once more, I say, "I love you more than I knew was possible."

"Same."

I roll my eyes. "Same? That's all I get?"

"How about this? I have all these people showing up in my life now, people who stepped in when I thought I needed them most. I didn't. I only need you, Sass."

He leans down to kiss me, but just before he does, I say, "So much better."

We join our families and make the rounds of hugs. My mom says, "I'm so happy for you."

I overhear her tell Warner, "Welcome to the family."

When Grace and I embrace, she leans back and says, "He's waited his whole life for you. I'm so happy he has you, and I get to call you daughter."

I hug her tight, probably more than she's used to, but we're family now. "Thank you. Seems destiny had a plan for us all along." I don't bother bringing up that if he weren't trying to usurp the little guy, we wouldn't have met. He did us one better when he saved the building and the tenants, my family's restaurant, and gave me the memory I always hoped for today. And he did it all for me. If that isn't a love story, I don't know what is.

Falling back into his strong arms, I lose myself in his incredible scent and the warmth in his eyes, the way he licks his bottom lip, and later that night, into that heavenly bed of his again. We leave the past in the past. And when I roll over breathless and happier than I've ever been, I turn to look at him next to me. Warner's eyes are closed, but a smile lies on his face. It's the only kind of lies we're going to allow in our lives moving forward.

Cuddling up to his side, I kiss his chest, remembering

that very first time we met. I ask him the same question he asked me that day, "What do you need?"

His eyes find mine as he rubs my back. With that smile still owning his expression, he replies, "I have everything I ever wanted. Your heart."

It was a wild ride to get here, but as I lie in pure bliss and contentment, I wouldn't change a thing. *All's fair in love and Warner.*

EPILOGUE

Warner

WE MOVED out of the tower, as she called it. I liked the penthouse, but it was never the same after she left. Her moving in didn't feel like the way for us to start a new chapter. That chapter includes renovating a brownstone to suit us as a family. Living on the West Side has been a good change. It's close to her school, and it's only two blocks from her family.

It makes Sass happy, so I'm happy, even if they do tend to let themselves in at the most inopportune times, like when I had her pinned to the shower wall fucking her last week. I don't think her brother Joe will ever come over again.

But seeing her now, I don't mind if they stay away. My Sass, dressed in white, her diamond necklace back where it belongs, along with a matching wedding band, does something to me—a growl rumbles through my chest as I claim my wife for the first time. It's only a piece of paper, but knowing we're bonded in every way possible is all the foreplay I need.

The sugar dish of condoms is beside the bed, but when I lift from her to reach for one, she says, "How do you feel about trying to make a baby?"

I open the nightstand drawer and slide the sugar dish inside, slamming it shut before returning to kiss my wife. "Thought you'd never ask." I chuckle, then dip to kiss her neck.

An hour later and fresh from the shower, she walks across the room and into the closet we're sharing until our individual spaces are built. With one towel wrapped around her torso and the other around her hair, she disappears inside. "Warner, what is that?"

"What?" I ask, still lying in bed after a quick recovery nap.

She comes out holding the plaster. "This." I'm certain she knows what it is since it's her writing on it.

I'll humor her, though. "Part of my cast."

"Why do you have it?" I'm struggling to figure out from her tone if she's happy or bothered by it.

My shrug loses effect since I'm lying down. "I wanted to keep it."

Her gaze falls to the souvenir again, and she smiles. She moves to the dresser and sets it on top, standing back and admiring it like it's a source of pride. "This is so unlike you."

"I've changed, baby."

"You have. I'm impressed. You're spontaneous, and the other day, you left a spoon in the sink."

"I was running late."

"Still. I call that progress."

"I consider it a failure, but of course it's a good thing in your book." I laugh.

She flips the towel off her head and crawls back on the bed. Resting her head on my chest, she says, "You are miles out of your comfort zone. Lifting her head to catch sight of my eyes, she adds, "But you'll always have me right there with you."

She never had to say the words, but hearing her confirm what I already felt feels good.

The only regret I ever had was repeating my father's mantra. I'll spend the rest of my days making sure a word of it never touches her life. If there's one thing worth protecting, it's Delaney. *I love her so fucking much.*

Even more, if that's possible, when she made me watch the video to the end. She was right. She didn't leave me for dead, but she sure thought about it. I don't blame her. I was an asshole back then. Thank God, she came along to save me.

LOOKING for something entertaining to read next? I have just the book for you! Never Got Over You is the perfect binge-worthy book. *Turn the page for a sneak peek!*

Never Got Over You

New York Times Bestselling Author

S.L. SCOTT

Cover Photographer: Regina Wamba of ReginaWamba.com

Cover Models: Claire + Noah Villalobos

Cover Designer: RBA Designs

Editing:

Marion Archer, Making Manuscripts

Jenny Sims, Editing4Indies

Proofreading: Kristen Johnson

Beta Reading: Andrea Johnston

1

Natalie St. James

I'M the first to admit I have no business taking another shot.

Especially after the past two.

But what's a girl to do when a room full of strangers is chanting my name and a particularly wild best friend places the shot hat on my head along with a small glass of liquor in my hand?

I drink.

In a little hole-in-the-wall hidden from the main street in Avalon on Catalina Island, I down the liquid like a champ, then promptly proceed to fall from grace, also known as the barstool.

My eyes close, bracing for impact, except . . . someone catches me just before landing. With my breath caught in my throat, I hang in the balance of arms made of steel and open my eyes.

Laughter fades away with any drunken shame that threatened as I stare into the soulful eyes of a stranger.

"Hi," whispers the future hero of my dirty dreams . . . *oh, wait.*

Maybe I'm unconscious? Maybe I was knocked out cold, and I'm dreaming. I blink. Why are my eyes open? Letting my lids fall, I keep them closed long enough to pray, "Please let him be real. If he's not, I'm begging you to leave me in this dream a little longer." My lids drift back open to find him still staring at me.

"Are you okay?"

"Perfect," I reply. *I think.* I'm not sure if I actually voice the response or not. I feel pretty damn perfect in his arms, though, the response still fitting in any circumstance that involves me, him, and those arms wrapped around my body.

Naked would be nice, but I'll save that for our second date.

His brow furrows, but a smile curls the corners of his lips.

The fog of alcohol clouds my mind, creating a heavy blanket on my brain. Regardless, I try to calculate the odds of a ridiculously sexy stranger—the exact man I'd craft if Create-a-Hottie was an actual thing—being in the right place at the right time to catch me if I fell.

It's impossible, so the only logical answer to this conundrum is that either he is the best college graduation gift ever or I'm dreaming. "How are you so hot?" I ask, worried he'll disappear in a puff of smoke and mirrors. Clamping my eyes closed again, I whisper, "Dear Lord, please don't let him be a mirage."

"I'm real." *Yes!*

Does that mean my friend set up this encounter for me? She's always been a great gift giver. It is our job, after all. I squint one eye open, biting my bottom lip. "*Mm*, so real," I purr. *Too perfect to be real, though. I must be dreaming.*

His grin creates dimples that could compete with the Grand Canyon. *How did I know I liked dimples enough to add them into this delirium?* I don't know, but score one for me.

"I think you're going to be okay," my dream man says, his voice as delectable as his face.

Wait, what? No. "As for me being okay, not so fast, buddy. No need to rush toward the waking hours. Anyway . . ." I drape my hand across my forehead. "Dream or real, I'm going to need mouth-to-mouth resuscitation."

His dimples dig deeper. "Is that so?"

"*So* right," I pant.

"Do you think I should call a paramedic?"

"That's a little kinky for me, but if you're into it . . ." I press my lips into a pretty little pout to seriously consider this twist. "Nah. Changed my mind. I only want you. Just the two of us resuscitating each other."

"You want me?" he asks, surprise tingeing his tone as he cocks an eyebrow. He readjusts me in his strong, manly arms. "Circling back to the real part, you do realize you're not dreaming, right?"

I reach up and wrap my arms around his neck, wanting to melt in his arms again. Totally obsessed with how I fit so perfectly, I pull him closer and hold tight. "You do realize you're stupidly attractive, right?"

He chuckles, his grin lifting higher on one side.

That smirk would totally get me into bed, given what it's doing to me while dreaming. I close my eyes again. "I'm ready."

"For what?" His deep, dulcet tones vibrate through my body.

"Resuscitation. I'm ready. Resuscitate away."

When nothing happens, I peek one eye open. He's still

staring at me with the smirk I'm ready to kiss off his sexy face, and whispers, "I don't think you need me—"

"Trust me." Opening both eyes, I also run my fingers through his shiny, chestnut-hued hair, taking in the feel of the soft strands. "I really, *really* need you."

When he leans down, I prepare my lips with a quick lick before meeting his . . . or at least, that's the direction I hope this dream is going.

"I was thinking—"

"Yes?" My gaze floats from his mouth to his eyes again.

"We've been at this a while. Maybe we should get you off the floor?" His head tilts to the side, and the industrial lights above him shine bright in my eyes, almost like a place of business, a restaurant, or a bar would hang. My senses begin to return, starting with the stench of old beer scenting the air.

"Yuck." Next comes a wave of cedar-y cologne and salty air. That's a scent I approve of, but that's when something else hits me. *What if I'm not dreaming?*

"Up you go," he says, shadowing me again as he tries to lift me to my feet.

I don't budge. "Dream or not, I quite enjoy being horizontal with you."

"Are you always this, *should we say*, flirtatious?" he asks, laughter punctuating his question.

"Not when I'm awake, no."

As if he couldn't be more gorgeous, little lines whisker from the outer corners of his eyes, enticing me to drag my fingertip along each one. I don't, but I want to. "Are your eyes hazel or brown? It's hard to tell in this light."

"Brown."

"Brown does them a disservice. A kaleidoscope of colors

is trapped inside them. I'm going to need a closer look in the sunshine."

"The sun will be setting soon."

"Then we should hurry."

A restrained chuckle wriggles his lips. "You can stare into my eyes, but I have to warn you, once you do, you'll fall madly in love with me. And I'm leaving tomorrow, so if we're falling in love, you better get to the loving part since you've already fallen."

"Good point."

"Get up, Natalie," my best friend says, rudely barging into my fantasy and peering at me from beside his shoulder. "The floor is filthy! Now you're going to have to wash your hair."

My eyes shift her way. "Please go away and let me have this one little dream, Tatum."

Snapping her fingers twice in front of my face has me jerking my head back. "You're wide awake and making a fool of yourself."

Noise from the crowded bar filters into my consciousness. Instead of looking around to confirm, I stare into Dreamy's eyes a moment longer and then exhale as embarrassment becomes reality, returning me to the present. "You're real, aren't you?"

A slow nod accompanies a smug expression.

The heat of my cheeks has me pressing my hands to them in hopes of cooling my skin down. "Do you mind helping me up?"

"I need to know something first."

"What?" I ask, knowing I should leave before I'm sober enough to realize how absurd I've been behaving.

Still holding me in his arms as if I'm light as a feather, he leans closer with his eyes on my mouth. When his gaze rises to meet mine, he asks, "Did you fall in love?"

My heart rate spikes, and the sound of it beating whooshes in my ears. Maybe I did hit my head because I swear at that moment, the one with my dream man so close I can kiss him or even lick him if I want, I can answer honestly.

Despite all the physical signs of me feeling otherwise, I reply, "You know. I think it's time for me to go." *Before the last few minutes really sink in.*

My feet are set on solid flooring while his hands remain on the underside of my forearms to steady me. Like the perfect gentleman. "I wish—"

"Nat," Tatum says under her breath. She moves in and grabs my hand.

"What?"

Her hair catches the light when she flips it over her shoulder, an exhausted sigh following right after. Every blonde needs a brunette bestie, and Tatum Devreux was destined to be mine since our mothers exchanged silver spoons from Tiffany's as baby shower gifts. I'm not exactly the calm to her wild ways, but she can out party me any day.

"A party on a yacht down in the harbor. We have to go now, though."

Panic rises in my chest. I know I should want to hightail it out of here to save myself from further mortification, but I don't want to go. I'm perfectly content right here.

I'm not shy about it. I look straight at him, but I'm smacked with a dose of candor I wasn't ready for, my ego crushed under his expression that mirrors pity. Now I regret not making a quick getaway when I had the chance.

My stomach plummets to the floor I was just hovering above. "Yeah, it's time to go," I tell Tatum, my hand pressing to my belly in an attempt to keep myself together. My hand is grabbed, and I'm tugged after her as she calls, "Ciao, darlings."

I turn back to catch Mr ... *Dreamy, Smug, Sexy, Pity-er of Drunk Girls* watching me. I'm left with two options to make an escape without further incident. I *could* blame the craziness on a head injury, or I *could* just leave. "So ... thanks," I say awkwardly as I back toward the door. *Yes. Choosing the latter.*

"Are you sure you're okay?" His voice carries over the lively crowd.

I dust the dirt off my ass. "I'm fine. Guess I'm not a tequila girl."

"You drank rum," he replies with a lopsided smile that could sweep me off my feet again if I'm not careful.

"Rum. Tequila. Same difference." I wave off the idea because it doesn't really matter. "I'm not good with liquor." That should settle it, but I make the mistake of daring to look into his eyes again. The five feet between us virtually disappears, and mentally, I'm back in his arms again, reading the prose that makes up his features. It would take me days to interpret, capturing not only his thoughts but a history that's worn in the light lines. He makes it hard to look away.

Stepping forward, he raises his hand and then lowers it to his side again as conflict invades his expression. "You sure you're okay? You might have a concussion."

I can't say I'm not touched by his concern. Grinning, I ask, "Does a concussion involve my heart?"

"What's happening with your heart?"

"It's beating like crazy."

Smiles are exchanged. "I think you're experiencing something else, but if you'd like me to call an ambulance—"

"Nope," Tatum cuts in, yanking me toward the door again, and laughs. "He's cute, but we don't want to miss the yacht." She whips the straw hat off me and tosses it to him.

I twist to look back. "Thanks for the lift. *Literally*."

"Anytime," he says with his eyes set on mine. When he shoves his hands in his pockets, he looks like he's posing for a Ralph Lauren ad. Tan. Rugged good looks. Tall. Those dreamy eyes and a grin that call me back to him. But life isn't a dream. It's time to return to reality.

Goodbye, dream man. It was nice hanging with . . . onto you.

2

Nick Christiansen

Two DAYS without the worries of late-night study groups, working my ass off interning at a law firm, and the constant micromanagement of my dad. At twenty-five, I've been ready to break out from under his thumb for a long time now.

He just hasn't received the memo that I'm not a kid anymore.

A last-minute invitation for a quick getaway before graduation from Stanford Law School and the pressures of my family brought me here. That's all this was supposed to be. A night of hanging with my best friend, a day of kicking back around the resort pool, and then barhopping to celebrate my final year of school behind me, today should have been much the same.

So, what just happened?

I know. Grinning as I recall how one minute, I was finishing my beer to the sound of spinning keys around my best friend's finger, and the next, chanting was filling my ears. *"Shot. Shot. Shot."*

I saw *him* first, an asshole ready to take advantage of an opportunity. The opportunity—a certain blonde in a loose white shirt, wide open between the top two buttons. Cutoffs reveal a lot of leg—shapely tan thighs—and a brown leather belt hangs around her waist more for decoration than for a purpose. Her sandals, only noticeable if you're looking for them, don't add any height. Bracelets of silver and gold with touches of turquoise covered her wrists, and the bar's raggedy shot hat had just been placed on her head. Clearly, I spent more than a few seconds taking her in without regret.

She was a vision in any state—from New York to California, drunk or sober—but it wasn't her outfit that had me acting on instinct and running into others to get to her. It was the asshole bragging about fucking her before she realized what hit her. Sure, I could have snapped back that no one would even know he was fucking her since he has a minuscule dick. But the hard lines of his face and the anger found in his dark eyes had me believing he meant what he said, not in jest or as a threat, but as a mission he intended to complete.

I should have punched him in the fucking face, but I didn't have time. I dashed the second my attention was grabbed by the sound of a squeal, the sight of arms in the air, and the pretty woman flying toward the floor.

Because I'm good with my hands, I've caught everything from the attention of college football scouts to a swordfish on vacation. I've also been called a golden boy my whole life growing up in the Golden State. But catching this girl right before she hit the floor might be my best catch yet.

She weighed nothing but made quite the impression. I

flexed my fingers under her back to rid myself of some weird energy burning through me. *God, I sound like my mom.*

I swore I'd never believe in that New Age stuff. She did her best to preach it, but logic has to play a part in our outcomes. But there's no logical answer as to why I'm still thinking about the woman I held for so long as if more was at play than two people colliding into each other's lives without their permission.

The back of Harrison's hand lands on my chest. "Nice save, but why'd you let her get away?"

"She's free to do as she pleases."

"What?" he asks, his brow careening between his eyes. "No, I mean, why didn't you get her number? She was hot, and the way you held on to her was like you had no intention of letting her go. It was becoming awkward watching the two of you cling—"

"We weren't clinging to each other. I was—"

Shaking his head, he says, "Save it, Nick. I don't need to hear about you falling for some chick."

"Technically, *she* was the one who fell."

"Let's not make this weird." He nods toward the door. "Taylor put us on the list. We've got to go before the yacht leaves the dock."

I follow him toward the door, but not without stopping by the asshole on my way out. "Today's your lucky fucking day because if we ever cross paths or you go within thirty feet of that woman again, you'll be flat on the ground before you know what hit you. Got it, fucker?"

He stands up but quickly realizes he has to look up to meet my eyes and sits back down. "Fuck off," he grumbles through a wiry beard.

My arm is caught before I have a chance to land a hit. "He's not worth it," Harrison says.

He's right.

This fucker also isn't worth a night in jail.

As the asshole cowers on the barstool with his head lowered, flinching from a hit that won't come, I lower my arm. "Lucky fucking day."

The conversation slowly resumes as Harrison and I head for the exit. My friend laughs under his breath just outside the entrance. "What gives, Christiansen? We haven't been in a fight in a long time." Cracking his knuckles, he adds, "Don't get me wrong. I'm up for it, but why are we fighting some guy twice our age in Catalina?"

"He needs a lesson in . . ." *Blonde. Tan. Blue-eyed beauty.*

"In what?" Harrison asks as he whacks me in the arm.

Ripping my gaze away from the blue-eyed beauty kneeling beside a scooter, I glance at Harrison. "Huh?"

When I return my attention to her again, I hear him grumble. "Ah. It's all so clear now."

I seize the moment. "This is a coincidence. Hi, again," I say, raising a hand while my voice pitches like a thirteen-year-old hitting puberty. *What the fuck?* Clearing my throat, I mentally berate myself for sounding like an idiot.

Harrison and both of the women turn to look at me. The blonde stands up with a reassuring grin on her face and shoves her hands into her back pockets. "Hi again, yourself."

I'm not the only one seizing the day. Harrison saunters up and asks her friend, "What seems to be the trouble?"

"Trouble with a capital T. Hi, I'm Tatum," she says.

Harrison takes her hand. "Pleasure to meet you. I'm Harrison."

Although she appears to blush, she pulls her hand and then points at the tire. "We have a party to get to, but we have a flat, and the rental company won't be here for an hour."

"That's quite the dilemma. Maybe we can help," Harrison says.

It's funny how he was in such a hurry not three minutes prior. He moves in to take a closer look. Harrison Decker was born with two trust funds and a gaggle of nannies. He didn't exactly grow up knowing his way around mechanics. I can't judge him too harshly since my background is similar, but I can still laugh at him because at least I know how to change a tire.

He leans back, glancing up at the brunette. She's pretty but doesn't hold a candle to the beauty beside me. Speaking of . . . I walk around the Vespa and lean down. Squeezing the tire, I listen. My eyes meet Harrison's, who's stepped off to the side with his new friend. His lack of loyalty isn't a surprise when there's a pretty woman around.

Her friend called her Natalie, but since we haven't been introduced, I just say, "You have a slow leak."

"Announce it to the world, why don't ya." She can't keep a straight face and cracks up. "Sorry, I had to."

I chuckle because of how much she makes herself laugh. She still waves it off. "Sorry, as you were saying." Another giggle escapes, though.

"The company shouldn't have put you on this scooter without checking it properly."

I look to my side to find those blue eyes staring into mine. "So we're stuck?" She grabs the tire, pumps it a few times like that might bring it back to life, and then drags her hand over a few treads. Leaning awkwardly on it, she adds, "Together?"

Is she flirting? It's not the approach I'd take, but it's curiously entertaining. "Afraid so." We both stand back up.

"You don't have to be afraid. I won't bite."

Something tells me she might by how her gaze darts down my body and back up again.

"I didn't mean I was actually afraid."

"I know. I was just teasing." If I didn't know she was drunk, I'd assume she was odd. She definitely has a quirky sense of humor. Maybe I do too because when she rubs her temple, she smears black grime along the side of her face, and I have to stop myself from laughing.

I reach forward, determined to help her out, but a spark fires in her eyes, and she says, "I knew we should have rented the golf cart. Tatum insisted on the Vespa, but I don't trust anything with less than four wheels."

"Wise." That response brings her earlier smile to the surface. "I heard your friend call you—"

"The party," her friend cuts in, wearing an expression scrunched with concern. "We're not going to make the party if we don't leave now."

"We can stay—"

"That's it!" Harrison snaps his fingers. "You can stay and help with the tire, and I can give Tatum a ride. Problem solved."

"A ride? Yes, that's great," Tatum says without missing a beat, already heading for the scooter with him in tow. He pats my shoulder on the way, the message already received loud and clear. *Guess I'm staying.*

"You don't mind, right?" Tatum asks as she slips on a helmet and swings her leg over the back of the Vespa. I'm about to answer, but the beauty next to me replies instead. "What about our girls' trip?"

"It's going swimmingly, don't you think?" Tatum points at Harrison and silently mouths, "He's so hot." For Harrison's ears, she adds, "We're turning lemons into lemonade."

The beauty next to me exhales and then frowns, her eyes

reflecting her change in mood from the fun-loving girl I met inside. The sun shines in her eyes just before she rolls them. "Swell. All we need is vodka."

"Thought you didn't know much about alcohol?"

Rocking her hand back and forth, she laughs. "I'm no expert, but I've had a few lemon drops in my life." Looking right at me, she asks, "Have you had one before?"

"No."

"You should." It's as if she's forgotten about her friend altogether. "They're really good."

"Maybe we can get one together."

"Maybe." Her grin is sure and quite stunning. But that grease . . . I should really tell her about the smudge on her face, but it's sort of cute how unsuspecting she is of the mess.

Harrison backs out of the parking space and stops in front of me. "I'll see you back in the room."

"Yeah. Sure." I'm not bothered he's taking off with a chick. That's how we've always operated, not giving each other a hard time over a hookup.

Just as he pulls to the edge of the parking lot, Tatum motions to her friend's temple area, but then says, "I promise to make it up to you back in the city."

When they blend into traffic and travel around the corner, we're left in their dust. I'm more interested in the blonde next to me. She stares down the street with her hand as a sun visor and then shifts to the curb, sitting down on it. She laughs at some inside joke, then turns to me. "Guess you're stuck with me."

I sit down next to her. "There are worse people to be stuck with, I suppose," I reply, gently nudging her like we're old friends.

"You sure about that?" Her smile breaks through the

disappointed façade she briefly tried on for size, the other one never quite fitting her natural disposition. Nor her drunk one. "For all you know, I could be a nightmare to deal with."

"I'm fairly certain I'll be okay. You're not a serial killer, are you?"

Offense colors her expression but is whisked away just as quickly. "*Me?*" Her fingers swirl near my nose. "I'm not the one with that boy-next-door face."

Capturing one of her fingers, I hold it hostage and grin at her. "You say that as if it's a bad thing."

"Handsome guys are always so cocky, too."

"All I heard was handsome."

I'm granted another front-row seat to an eye roll, this one more dramatic and aimed at me. "Of course, you did." Her eyes lock on something lower. "That Omega watch was probably stolen from a victim. If it's real . . ."

"Let me get this straight. Your serial killer radar is going off because I'm wearing a *real* Omega watch? I'm no expert in detection, but I'm pretty sure that's not a reliable method." I reluctantly release her finger, but I hold onto the fact that she never once tried to pull away.

"Money is always a dead giveaway for lady killers."

"I thought we were talking about serial killers."

"Lady-killers. *Serial killers.* Tomato. *Tamahto.*" She nods. "It's all the same thing."

I chuckle. "I'm still curious about money being a giveaway. Care to expound on that train of thought?"

"Money makes people mean."

"Do you know this firsthand or something you've surmised?"

"A little of both. Anyway, what other method would you suggest I figure out who the bad guys are? I can't ask because what serial killer would ever admit they're a serial killer?" The way she angles her head to the side as if I'm going to give her a meaningful response to this insanity causes me to sweat under the collar. Just a little. *I'd hate to disappoint her.*

"Serial killer conversation aside," I start, holding my hand out. "I forgot to introduce myself. I'm Nick."

She slips her hand against mine, and our fingers wrap around each other. Ah, there's the gorgeous smile from before. "Hi, Nick. I'm Natalie."

CONTINUING READING IN KINDLE UNLIMITED, download from Amazon, or listen to the audiobook on Audible or Amazon.

YOU MIGHT ALSO ENJOY

Recommendations - These are books you'll enjoy reading after *Love and Warner*. These books will have you falling in love along with the characters.

Read in Kindle Unlimited and Listen in Audio

Never Got Over You - Third times a charm. The banter, the wit, the antics, the friends to forever will have you falling you head over heels in love and smiling along with these characters. This New York City love story has the best meet cute and is Free in Kindle Unlimited.

Read in Kindle Unlimited and Listen in Audio

Head Over Feels - Friends to lovers at its finest. The banter, the wit, the teasing, the sneaking around is so fun in this New York City love story where Bachelor of the Year is brought to his knees over the girl next door friend he's crushed on since college. Free in Kindle Unlimited.

Read in Kindle Unlimited and Listen in Audio

Long Time Coming (if you haven't read book 1 in the Peachtree Pass series) - You met Tagger and Christine in Small Town Frenzy. Now read the captivating and joyous journey as they find their way in this small town, big ranch, single dad love story. Free in Kindle Unlimited. *Turn the page to start reading*

ACKNOWLEDGMENTS

Thank you so much to this incredible team:

Kenna Rey, Content Editor
Jenny Sims, Copy Editing, Editing4Indies
Kristen Johnson, Proofreader
Andrea Johnston, Beta Reading
Cover Design: RBA Designs
Photographer: Ren Saliba
Back Image: Depositphotos
Audio Producer: Erin Spencer, One Night Stand Studios.
Narrators: Aiden Snow & Callie Dalton

Thank you Super Stars and my awesome Facebook group members. And sweet thanks to my amazing friends!

My husband, sons, and little dog, Ollie, are my entire world. I love you more than the universe! Thank you for your beautiful support and love. Love you always. XOXOX

ABOUT THE AUTHOR

Suzie loves a great view of the ocean, spicy margaritas, and spending her free time with her family and sweet dog, Ollie.

New York Times and *USA Today* Bestselling Author, S.L. Scott, writes character driven, heart-racing, and swoony romances that will leave you glued to the page. With stories ranging from witty beach reads to heart wrenching and heart healing, her stories are highly regarded as emotional, relatable, and captivating.

Her books are more than escapes for the voracious readers of today. They are journeys of the heart that always come with a happily ever after reward at the end.

Find her at: www.slscottauthor.com